EPHRAIM'S HURT ROOM

AMARIE AVANT

ISBN: 9781697880243

✺ Created with Vellum

BLURB

Where hurt people go...

Ephraim Levine had it all, except Maliah Porter.

She isn't the one who got away, *she is the one who walked away.*

He has adored Maliah Porter since they were children. She has epitomized beauty, innocence.

Everything about her captivated him. As they've matured and their love grew, he worshipped her body and soul.

And then, without reason, Maliah Porter left Ephraim Levine, and shattered their unbreakable love. *He was suddenly held captive by her memory.*

His obsession with her ruined him... But it also shaped the attractive, brilliant Ephraim into a calculating man.

One who would stop at nothing to take what he wanted. Maliah.

He will set the perfect scene— build the perfect cage to entrap the Queen.

And finally free himself of the restless need to dominate the one who stole his heart.

1

<hr>

"I saw that ass last night, sweetheart . . ."

At the sound of the cocky voice, Maliah thought she'd been daydreaming. No, it was a nightmare. She was a fraction away from the white picket fence to her home. But that voice had come from behind. For her sanity, she concentrated on all the years her rage brewed for *him*. Hate would make it easier to stare into the eyes of Ephraim Levine, Esquire. Just his eyes. Not that those damnable dark orbs weren't incredibly attractive.

This was the worst morning of her life, and the devil knew exactly when to arrive. "I'm so very disappointed in you, LeeLee," he said.

She spun around to cuss him out, but all the air in her lungs evaporated. A few seconds ago, when locking her one-story home, she'd been deep in contemplation about the Hurt Room. Dread had filled her at the thought of having to return. She hadn't noticed the bastard sitting a fraction away. Not the slightest chance in hell to prepare for him either.

Now, Maliah needed to stop staring. Shoulders squared, she gritted out, "You don't have the slightest right to call me Lee—"

"That fuck-off runs *the Hurt Room*. A thousand a night, right?" He pulled out a roll of hundred-dollar bills. "You know good and damn well that I can do much better than a thousand. So much better. What do you prefer? A check? The money to be wired?"

While other people could throw theirs away, she needed essentials. Tears pricked in her eyes. "You never could buy me, Eph."

"I didn't buy you. *I had you.*" His fist knocked across his chest. "I had you, LeeLee."

Maliah's fingers tightened around the iPhone in her hand. She lunged it at him, yelling, "We were kids! That was almost a decade ago, you idiot."

One leisurely hand held up, he caught the damn thing. He sat back in the chair, so comfortable that Maliah vowed to set it on fire the second he left. Heartbeat bursting in her ears, she took a few steps back, ready to flee the front of her own home, to save herself from the intensity of his presence. Instead of running away, she bumped into the white picket fence, which symbolized status in America.

"I've stayed away, LeeLee—Maliah," he corrected the use of her old nickname. The first nice thing he'd done for her in years. "But you've been out with—" His teeth raked over his bottom lip, anger held at bay. He had no rights to anger. "I've been told you were out. So, you're calling some man *Sir*, now? Little Miss Maliah, answering to a man."

"You don't have the slightest right to question me." She clasped her arms around her waist, holding herself tight. The warm sun beamed down on her, yet it wasn't a match for Ephraim.

"I had my people look into *him*. The bastard runs some sort of school? You have a master's degree, Maliah. Far as I can tell, *he* is not assisting with a second, nor is he helping you obtain a doctorate. What the fuck do you need with an instructor? C'mon, Maliah, speak up." His deep voice became tantalizing. "You've always known how to do such pretty things with that mouth of yours. Tell everything to the man who loves every part of you. Let me in."

She stood tall, regardless that he sat and had made her porch his throne room. Maliah looked past his gaze like her trainer had taught her.

Her teacher had given her instructions when taking off her coat for the first time to expose her naked body. First rule: a submissive does not meet another man's gaze. The Dom/sub crap wasn't something she'd planned to do. The thought of it sent more dread in the form of ice water shooting through her veins. But she had a nonprofit learning center in the inner city of New Haven, CT, that needed to survive. She had bills, a mortgage, and perhaps a chance to stop neglecting herself.

"Tell me, LeeLee!" Ephraim's voice grew so strong that she felt it against her chest.

Instead of meeting his eyes, Maliah murmured, "I am not cleared to speak with you, Ephraim." *Ha, I'm not some little sub who can be walked all over. I don't want to talk to you,* she thought with a grin. *But seeing your gaze when you think I'm some little fuck toy, well, I enjoy that.*

"I remember the day I met your grandparents, LeeLee. We were kids, but I had to take care of you." Ephraim stood up from the chair. He still had the money in his hands, and she knew that it would lead to more. All she had to do was ask. They had been best friends, so he'd give freely without expectation. No, that was the naivety in Maliah. She assumed he offered his love, without expectation. He was insatiable.

"No, thank you." She stepped back. He was still at the top of the steps, but that wasn't nearly far enough away from here. Though she edged toward the gate again, Maliah asked, "Will you leave now?"

He stood rooted to the front of her home, ironically so close to the welcome mat. Like the devil offering her wildest dreams, he held out her phone. Even in the dead of traffic before work, there wasn't a person Maliah knew who wouldn't return home to grab their phone. "I'm your friend. I'm offering you money. Save face for your parents. Don't have Granny turning over in her grave. That life you're looking for is not for sweet, little girls like you." With that, Ephraim tossed her phone.

Breath caught, she clasped the phone. Suddenly, Maliah was aware of all her movements and her need for oxygen. She'd done the unthinkable and took a good look at him. Some businessmen wore suits, tailored specifically for their measurements. Ephraim had impeccable measurements. Wide plains of shoulders. The tease of wanting to unbutton and caress his abdominals almost controlled her.

His words sent a flood of saliva in her mouth. *"You've always known how to do such pretty things with that mouth of yours..."*

Maliah cleared her throat. "I'm heading into the office. I don't intend to see your face again, Mr. Levine."

This time, she turned curtly on her stilettos and opened the quaint fence. All the things Americans score for the illusion of happiness were at the tips of her fingers. The house. A BMW. Maliah rubbed her hands together, focusing on her brittle fingernails. While she didn't care much for fake nails or paint, spa days were a necessity of life. The Hurt Room would help with that. Her teacher was not only assisting her out of insurmountable debt. But he was also helping her become stronger, helping her not look back . . .

2

Ephraim shoved the tightly rolled hundreds back into his pants pocket and watched Maliah strut toward the gate, her crinkly hair billowing out. Such a fierce, little lioness. The tight skirt she wore clung to more curves than he remembered. All the photos he'd received over the years had focused on her soft cheeks and plush lips. What would he look like requesting specifics from his informant? The thought was enough to boil his blood.

At the sight of her ass, the left side of his mouth tipped. In high school, he'd hold her books, be her slave, with one goal: watch that ass. She'd wear that little private-school printed skirt. Her ass swished left to right, and he'd follow her anywhere. Up to heaven, down to hell. She'd belonged to him, and there wasn't anything in this world he wouldn't do for her.

He'd caught the last bit of her conversation as she'd locked the door. Her shoulders were tight, mouth pulled pensively. Yolanda had been a mutual friend in college. Cute, smart, and team "LeeLee & Eph."

Pulling out his phone, he watched as she glared at him

through the window, the lioness in her rising by the second. She'd been shocked to see him at first. Now, her glare warned him to still be in the front of her house by the time she left We Rise Learning Center.

The Porters were black royalty in Connecticut—leave it to Maliah Porter to not follow suit. Her father, Rick, wasn't impressed when she'd worked at a Montessori school serving the upper-middle class. Her mother, Annaleigh, never understood the need for Maliah to work at all. She'd one-upped her dissatisfied parents by opening a nonprofit learning center in a crime-riddled area. But her long commute to the inner cities wouldn't be occurring today. She'd lied to him.

Ephraim grabbed his cell phone from his pocket and dialed for his driver. Less than three minutes later, a custom SUV pulled up where Maliah had driven away. Ephraim got into the car and closed the door.

"Where to now, boss?"

"The Hurt Room."

"Maliah, say this to yourself ten times please," her friend cut into the radio speaker. She drove past the elite homes in Greenwich, where rich kids had ample space before running into their neighbors' lots. Old Rolls-Royces and new, shiny toys dotted lofty driveways.

"Yolanda, don't. I'm not feeling up to a mantra."

"Sure. Well, I feel sorry for pedestrians walking by."

"What?"

"They have to view the Hunchback of Notre Dame when you drive back. You're tense, all the way down to your sphincter."

"Honey, comments like that will get you hung up on, blocked on all social media," she began, chuckling with each word. "Yolanda, no you didn't? Sphincter? I could've gone my entire life and never used the term."

"Yes, I did. These are my efforts to prepare you for the Hurt . . . Sheesh, I can't. I won't say it. I'd rather say that you and Ephraim were friends your entire lives. Let him be your friend—from a distance."

"Yolanda!" Maliah hissed.

"Well, are you slouching?"

This time, Maliah laughed hard—good, down and in her bones laughter. It was all the response her best friend needed. She stopped at a stop sign, where a trio of house-wives jogged by. Each woman wore full-blown makeup. The sweat dribbling down into their sports bras probably came from Fiji Water. Maliah stopped herself from continuing to hate on them. Either one had the flirty manipulative ways to make a better submissive than her anyway.

She cleared her throat and said, "You're supposed to be my best friend."

"I'm not your best, *best* friend, sweetheart. The two of you have a lot more history."

"You said you weren't going to say these things. You're team LeeLee." Her airy tone weakened a bit. "We made a pact in junior year, right after your hardest Cognitive Psychology exam and my . . .'"

"Much easier English Curriculum course, yes, Maliah, I recall. Nevertheless, the *us* hating him part is all you. I'm Christian, so I can't do it. I also can't do this . . ."

"Hurt Room stuff." Maliah turned into the area of Greenwich that with each climb the houses become grander. "Six whole weeks of this—actually, five left. Then I can start paying myself again."

"Yes, paying yourself to own a business. I like that concept, Maliah."

"I'm getting ready to pull into my teacher's home; I've got to go."

She hung up at the sound of Yolanda's scoff. The last time Maliah had mentioned that the Dom was instructing her, Yolanda had been terse. Her friend made a flippant remark that they both had more education in their pinkie toes. For the most part, her best friend had been supportive of her plans. She could still recall the moment she'd showed Yolanda the email. Yolanda tugged a hand through her dreads and offered her a loan.

The loan that people give when they love you and don't anticipate receiving a single dollar back. Maliah might have been down on her luck, but she had inherited some of her parents' qualities. They paid back every penny lent to them.

She picked up the purse in her passenger seat, the faux leather reminding her of how her mom cringed and mentioned being allergic the last time she came by. Her childhood home was two miles down the hill. A seven-bedroom, with some luxury. Ephraim's family home was one mile above. The socio-economic difference made the air smell even more sweet up here. She stopped outside of the wrought iron gate and pressed the button to roll down her window.

"Mal . . . Miss Honey." Maliah cleared her voice, refer-ring to the name she'd given herself. Her eyes shut tight for a second. The day she'd completed a video message for the Hurt Room, she'd recorded the damn thing a thousand times. Her first mistake was not wearing a mask. She'd rushed to Walmart in a hoodie and sunglasses, bought a mask—a bright red, Mardi Gras one that covered half her face. Lips painted the same vibrant color, Maliah had completed another fifty takes. It had taken forever to cut the tremble of anxiety in her tone.

After traveling along a curvy trail, Maliah stopped her car in front of a stone estate. Black shutters were open on the first level of the home. With one look inside the windows, she thought the home might belong to a filthy-rich senator. Marble floors, chandeliers, and all the gilded trappings of success positioned to perfection. The shutters upstairs were closed, also, reminding her of a senator with secrets.

Her legs shook as she got out of the car. The second she did, Maliah climbed right back inside and closed the door. "The agenda," she mumbled to herself.

She opened her purse, clicked onto the Gmail application, and scrolled to a stream of messages. The first email congratulated her on being one of the select few. It boasted that this was such a rare opportunity. The Hurt Room was vying to win a contest of prestige in the BDSM world. They were campaigning against other prominent schools in the States. Maliah had skimmed over the dynamics. What intrigued her was the money. That and the fact that they needed new submissives, none with previous ties to the community.

The contest vetted and ensured each submissive candidate had no prior experience. Maliah had no idea how that process could occur. The per-hour payment from the Hurt Room hooked her. Also, a $50,000 check to any of the subs who completed a six-week curriculum at the school. A litigator from a firm in competition with Levine & Levine checked it out for her. Maliah learned that the flier had been legit. That was all the homework she planned on doing. She'd say, "yes, Sir." Using that idiotic reference made her cringe. But Maliah determined that it was required of her on Saturday mornings, *only*, after which she'd continue with life as normal.

Except, today was Monday morning. She'd canceled last minute for this past Saturday, but by late evening, Maliah had changed her tune. Not junk mail, but scary bills, had coaxed her to leave an email. An email filled with excuses and begging to reschedule for today.

She clicked on the email link for 'Week Two" and scanned over the day's requirements.

"The Trust Factor," she mumbled to herself. Of course, it meant absolutely nothing. Who trusts a person after such a short time? Though her instructor seemed knowledgeable, there was no way in hell he'd have control over her body. In one week, she'd learned mumbo jumbo. A submissive's desire was to please his or her Dom. Whatever.

At the front door, her hand was poised to knock when the door opened.

A tiny maid, with pale skin and almond eyes, spoke. She had captured a tone that Maliah had never quite been able to master while on her submission video. "Hello, Miss Honey," the maid purred. "Please follow me."

The maid's hand movements were seductive and deliberate. Maliah arched an eyebrow as the woman's palm smoothed over her stiff black-and-white uniform. Was she accentuating her tits?

Well, besides using you people to save my learning center, and the life I have as I know it, I could use a lesson on seduction. Maliah smiled to herself. *You'd have to have a man, LeeLee.* Still, the thought shocked her. The makings of BDSM were for sexual gratification. To think, she hadn't considered the uses presented to her. Maliah Porter was out of her element. She hadn't worked a stiff cock in ages.

Gulping down unease, Maliah allowed herself to be

escorted across the room. She towered over the maid, although she stood at five foot five. Shoving her hands into the pockets of her blazer, she followed past a massive sitting area and a dining room. She wondered if her trainer dined with a wife and kids in that room.

"Why aren't I being led upstairs?" Maliah asked. Though one instance didn't quite set a routine, she clung to consistency.

"The order was for you to dress in here, ma'am," the maid replied. She continued a few more feet, then opened the door to a bedroom. "Take all the time you need. I'll wait here for further instructions."

Chewing her lip, Maliah paused a moment. Seeing Ephraim for the first time in so long, hearing the sound of his voice—a voice she'd never get out of her mind—had all been too much. Her lips moved the slightest bit at the edges as a token of her appreciation, and then she entered the bedroom. While it wasn't as large as the one she'd been to upstairs, the beige coloring and four-poster bed didn't seem BDSM. She didn't believe her teacher planned to enter. On the center of the bed was a royal blue, glossy gift box. She plucked at the note.

"Hello, Pet," she murmured the words. "Today, you will begin to learn about subspace." Her thumb rubbed over his name. *Nori.*

"Let's see, shall we," she murmured, picking up her phone to complete a common internet search. Her gaze scoured over words such as "emotional" and "psychological." Maliah huffed. "I should make Yolanda do my research."

One article, in particular, stated that similar to an orgasm, subspace differed for each person. A line from a

"Hello Flo" article seemed to pop off the screen: *a trance-like euphoria of intense emotions.*

———

MALIAH FOUND herself seated on a silk-printed couch across from the bed. The words intensity, dizziness, and incoherence still rang in her head. How long had she sat here? She chewed on her bottom lip, iPhone clutched in both hands. She worked the phone in her palms, turning it and turning it. "This is easy. A few ass slaps, no penetration. No control is taken away."

She tried ruminating over how she was a light submissive, and how she'd only be on the bottom for a short amount of time. All the workings in her mind clashed. Ephraim had done this, she considered. He'd gotten into her head.

Somehow the thought that she'd lose control hurt more than giving up her body. A wry chuckle raked through her. "Yeah, idiot, that's because you haven't *done it* in ages. Done it? You sound like one of the kids at school before they care about what proceeds out of their mouths."

Okay, now you're talking to yourself in long monologues, Maliah mentally condemned herself. She tried to push her thoughts to butterflies and roses. It didn't work.

She stood up, grabbed the gift, and went into the bathroom. No amount of pep talk kept her at the moment. During her entire shower, all her thoughts went to Ephraim Levine.

———

"WHY ARE YOU HERE, EPH?" Nori asked. He wore black

slacks and a black button-up that was opened at his milk-colored chest. He began to go off in Japanese, grabbed a tuft of jet-black hair. The ammunition in each word lessened as he slowly tapered his frustrations. "We need time to work."

Ephraim played with a cufflink as they stood at the top of the hall. "You have no right to touch her."

"That's impossible."

"You know just what the fuck I mean when I say don't touch her."

His dark gaze narrowed. "I follow every line in *your* contract, *tomodachi*—friend. The beauty belongs to you. I've given my word to everyone involved."

"That's right." Ephraim bit his knuckle in thought. He shouldn't have seen her yet. Should've followed the rules until the right time. "But you scared her off last time. You couldn't even convince her to come back after round one!"

"You are mistaken." Nori pressed a stiff hand into the palm of his other hand. "I said, she rushed off, a little. Obviously, she's here now."

"Yeah, I got her here." *You tell Maliah not to do something and she does it*, Ephraim told himself. "Start the training for today. I don't give a damn if she's not supposed to meet her Dom until week three, Nori. I got this. Get her started, and I'll give you the signal when I'm taking over."

"Yes." He gestured down the hall, ready for Ephraim to disappear in *his own home*. "That is my intention. Although, Ms. Porter is not easily trainable."

Ephraim had no desire for her to be trainable, to obey another man, namely a world-renowned Dom. But they were in this together. Nori had never met a woman he couldn't train. And Ephraim, while he could have anything his eyes landed on, he'd lost sight of her.

The entire dynamic of Maliah coming to the Hurt Room

had been his idea. There wasn't a competition to win. Nori had a harem of subs in Tokyo; the maid who'd escorted Maliah into the house a few minutes ago was one of them. The rest of his subs expected him to return within six weeks, hence the reason Nori was a safe bet for her training. He'd soften Maliah for Ephraim. No touching—just assist her with becoming more agreeable.

But had this been a bad idea? The proposal reminded him of that old movie *True Lies*. Arnold Schwarzenegger meets his wife in a hotel room, has her do all the beautiful seductive things her body was made for.

Maliah Porter had forgotten why she was made.

Maliah was sculpted to be adorned by trinkets—trinkets and his cock. But she'd smell him a mile away. There was no way in hell they could start at that point in time. Them falling back in love. So, this was where they had to begin. Nori did not have rights to Maliah. He'd soften her for him, and him alone.

3

NORI YAMAZAKI STOOD EYE LEVEL WITH MALIAH. SHE HADN'T expected him to come down to her room, but then again, one meeting hadn't constituted a routine. The air was wet from her shower. Her skin felt alive beneath his touch, and extra lush from the expensive hydrating soaps.

His bone-straight raven hair came down to his shoulders. In another life, Maliah didn't have the time nor the day for a man who had long hair. The style worked for Vikings in ancient history or bikers in the current era. But Nori's chiseled features and the way he held himself oozed confidence. Sex appeal radiated from his skin with one look. Rarely were words necessary to get his point across. His fingers wove between hers.

"Sorry," she mumbled. She stopped fidgeting and moved her hands away from the apex of her sex. The thin barrier of a silk teddy that fit like a second glove burned against her skin. The material had felt like butter after her shower, warm to the touch. Now, it was the means of exposing her. Also, they were in the guest bedroom where she'd changed.

Those beige walls were a constant reminder that this was definitely not the Hurt Room.

"Do you want to be here, Pet?" He read her mind.

I am too friggin' smart to be called pet. Please stop. "Yes." She held her head high. Although, her version of "here" needed to be conducted in the room with coal-colored walls. There was something about Nori's lair upstairs that promised secrets would be kept.

He didn't make a move toward the guest bedroom door. He shoved a hand through his ultra-straight hair and said, "There's a difference between a slave and a sub, Pet. What is that difference?"

Black people don't like BDSM. Maliah stopped being condescending in her head. She cleaved to her black roots. It was safer to say that not a lot of her people ventured out for different things. For reference, certain forms of sushi that still had a heartbeat. And sure, BDSM seemed like a world away, but she did need to be courteous. Her instructor had never disrespected her. At least she could respect that the BDSM world started with rules. Maliah Porter loved rules. That meant assholes like Ephraim stayed in their lane. She stopped pondering.

He'd done it again.

Stolen all her thoughts.

She licked at the red paint on her lips and sighed as she sifted past the best memories of her life with Ephraim. Why were such strong memories so easy to remember? The good and the bad with Ephraim had overshadowed last Saturday's training.

For a second, she thought about her father's people. The Porter lineage could trace their family back to slavery. Even after, her great-great-grandmommy had had to fend off her

employer while housekeeping. But BDSM was totally different. Only, she was preconditioned that titles like "Master"
churned her stomach. Maliah reiterated the words Nori had
said during their first training. "Okay, so the difference
between a slave and a sub? One completes a task by *force*.
The other fulfills the desires of another based on a previous
agreement. Hence, the BDSM contract, which should be
initiated first. A Ma-master—" She stopped and gritted her
teeth. *C'mon, LeeLee, humble yourself for an hour.* "A Master
wants the best for his sub, and the sub in a sense receives
extreme pleasure from her Master."

He chuckled softly. "Extreme pleasure. I like that
update. And yet you didn't take pleasure in my teaching
you about subspace. You took the liberty to teach
yourself."

"Well, this place is called the Hurt Room. I'm here for
the spankings," she said curtly, then laughed and shook her
head. "I'm sorry . . . I . . ."

"I'm sorry that we have gotten nowhere in our training,
Miss Honey. There are so many things that you've yet to
learn about yourself."

She sighed. "And I'd like to learn. Thank you, Sir."

Their eyes connected. His hand skimmed over her bare
shoulder, and then he clasped her arm. Not tight, however;
the strength in his touch, the closeness of his body sent her
heart rate soaring. His mouth stopped a fraction away from
her earlobe.

"My responsibility is to expand your horizons, almost to
the brink, Miss Honey." He pulled an arm around her from
behind and slammed her body flush against his front. Maliah's eyes bugged out as she stared at him through a gilded
mirror.

"Just enough, Miss Honey, where you are almost

broken." His voice rumbled on low against her ear again. "Just enough for you to learn that you can't be broken."

Her breathing stilled. *This is BS.* The self-defense mechanism in her brain detonated like fireworks. And yet, she couldn't pull away from Nori. Couldn't bring herself to say the safe word. The safe word she never expected to use. Maliah Porter was strong enough to pull through anything.

"Are you ready?"

"Yes, Sir," she murmured.

Silence ensued as his mouth met the most vulnerable part of her neck. His lips trailed across her spine. His spicy smell infused in her nostrils. Nori stroked the length of her curves, his hand weaving over her hips, sending her senses into a tailspin. Her brown skin contrasted against his. Ephraim was white, but Nori's skin was a few shades paler. Her breath almost hitched at the thought of how easy the man she abhorred entered her mind. His mouth went to her neck again, and he sucked until the pleasure lit on fire.

Nori came around her, and his mouth crashed against hers. She moaned at the taste of him. While his fingers caressed the back of her neck, undoing her top, Maliah tensed.

Of all the marks she'd checked to get into the Hurt Room, she'd left off even more. No dick penetration—nice and simply put. She agreed to dildos and other sex toys. No anal. Why hadn't she added no breasts?

He was studying her as the top of her teddy fell, displaying her golden-brown breasts. She never liked the size of her areolas. There wasn't a storybook cliché euphemism for them. They sure weren't Hershey's Kisses.

"Let us walk, Pet." He took her hand. Maliah felt almost infantile as he guided her out of the room. "We lost time last week when you ran out."

"I apologize, Sir."

"Therefore, we don't have much time to increase the trust you have in me, Miss Honey." His hand steered the small of her back. "Normally, we work our way up to such activities, but you're a strong one."

Maliah tuned him out as they ascended the marble steps. Instead, she concentrated on the faces of children who were years behind in school. It might sound ridiculous, but all the success stories of students who had the world stacked against them would be her reason to comply.

As he walked her along the corridor upstairs, Maliah's pace faltered again. She smelled something, a familiar, pleasing scent.

He finished off with, "Don't you agree, Pet?"

"I'm sorry, I thought I . . ." She closed her mouth and followed after Nori. In seconds, she set aside the notion that this handsome stranger had seen her breasts. They entered the room that took her breath away. Along the edge of the room was a crystal hearth that spanned the length of the room.

Candles of every size were aglow. Their flickering brought her orbs to the center of the room, where a chain hung from the tall ceiling. There was a vast, intricate picture frame along one wall. It was long and wide. With there not being a single candle near it, Maliah could only make out that the painting was a bunch of splashes.

Maliah bit down on her tongue, warning herself to see things through until she had to say the safe word. *Maybe the chain would hold . . . gummy bears? Like they could be wedged into the slots.* She rolled her eyes. *LeeLee, you have lost every brain cell that you have!*

Nori removed a small electronic device from his pocket. Calm music streamed from some sort of invisible speakers.

"This is a lengthy process, Pet." Nori's fingers moved down the buttons of his shirt. Her eyes were hypnotized as he made quick work of removing it, one arm after the other. Every second of the act entranced her. She watched the silk button-up shimmy down to the padded floors. Her eyes landed on his abdomen. An eight-pack of muscles sent her pussy walls quivering. She glanced quickly away, and then her gaze fell on his body again. The stacks extended all the way to his pants.

Nori stepped forward, pressed his palm between her breasts. "Our breathing needs to be in sync. Slow yours down, Pet."

Fire flushed beneath the skin of her cheeks. She'd forgotten to internally take offense to the word "pet." He'd sounded so endearing as he spoke to her.

Nori nodded, and as fluid as if she were a real sub, Maliah went to her knees. The slightest smile worked at his lips. She noted that the floor was softer, with some sort of rubbery material that took a lot of the force from her knees.

Nori walked around her, his slight eyes keen as he viewed her. He crouched down in front of her and gripped the sides of her teddy, pulling up softly. Her body trembled. The material between her legs tantalized her clit before he reached behind her. Maliah gaped at the sound of the material tearing. He smirked and held up a pocketknife before putting it away.

She had the words in her mind to tell him she'd never worn anything so nice as the teddy. It had been made specifically to the measurements she sent with her video. She stopped herself from speaking.

Nori stood up and left the room.

"Really?" She scoffed to herself. Maliah rubbed a hand over her face, warning herself not to run. *Don't talk back,*

LeeLee. But can I get a friggin' itinerary? That "we're going to learn" to trust crap didn't work for Maliah Porter. Had she been the Domme, she'd have sent the submissive home with a book on subspace. Reading freed the mind.

———————

EPHRAIM STOOD, staring through the two-way mirror. This house had taken almost a year to be reworked, for this precise second. He had an entire view of her. In the Hurt Room, there was a large frame along the room that was about twenty feet in width and length. On that side, a rendition of some famous painting. On his side, all opportunity.

His cock strained against his pants. He'd been seated in the only chair in this room for the length it took for Nori to bring her to *him*. When Nori had left to retrieve Maliah, Ephraim sent a message to his assistant. There were no cameras downstairs. A man like Ephraim Levine didn't get to where he was based on trust. He'd need to have more cameras installed to ensure Nori stayed in his place.

Ephraim had seen the beauty of bondage, but Nori was reluctant to start here with Maliah.

"I'll start with the breast tie," Nori said upon entering the room.

"Yes, just to start, Nori. I'm paying you enough to . . ." Ephraim stopped staring through the window at the only woman to deny him. He couldn't flaunt his money at Nori Yamazaki. The Dom had a good amount. As long as the guise continued to work in Nori's favor that he had a challenge, then he'd do as told. "Test her limits, Nori."

"Ultimately, she's in charge, Eph. You've had a few subs in the past. You know the rules."

A submissive had more power than a Dominant. A submissive had all the rights, being that she could say no at any time, ceasing every ounce of pleasure he held. Yeah, he knew. But the real issue Ephraim had? Maliah Porter had all the power and his fucking heart too.

4

HER HEART CONTINUED TO BOOM INSIDE OF HER CHEST. No amount of disarray in her mind could help. She continued to tell herself that she was innately motivated to help her students. She continued to believe the motto that as long as she was humble, she'd leave this place. She'd put this part of her life behind her before she fell in love and married.

Maliah continued to lie to herself while Nori entered the room. He had strips of corded material in his arms. A horde of cuss words went off in her head, but she stayed in her spot, kneeled on the ground.

"Breathe with me now." Nori placed down all the strips except for one. She matched the movement of his lips, out and in. The strip in his hand leveled around her back, where her bra would attach. He pulled the soft material around her. Her gaze kept to his lips, her breathing trembling yet working to match his.

Once her breath tapered, Maliah glanced down to see the intricate confinement of her breasts, lifted by the weaving of the strips. This was what perky tits looked like. High, mighty. Pure beauty.

"What is your color?" he asked.

"Green," she muttered. Although, she almost went to yellow as he'd stopped modeling the breathing technique for her. Nori's hands went to her legs, his palms pressing against the insides, pushing her knees wide. A small gush of wetness emitted from her pussy. Since she was still on her knees, Maliah doubted Nori had a view of it. He could see everything except her treasure. Still, the thought of becoming wet scared her. Maliah closed her eyes, warmth traveling over her skin again. Her eyes opened instantly.

His dark orbs twinkled, and he modeled the right way to breathe. "That's right, Pet. You are doing well."

Nori was patient every second while applying the intricate ties. He even subtly joked that they'd still work their way up to the use of chains while Maliah sat on the floor. A plethora of pillows rested behind her.

Maliah's arms were bound behind her back. Her legs were jutted up to the sides of her chest so as not to take away from her breasts—breasts that she couldn't help but begin to feel fond for. Nori had done this for her. Made her enjoy the sight of her tits.

Now, her labia had been set free. The coolness of the air-conditioning teased at the slick coat of wetness against her sex.

"Close your eyes and focus on how the rope is restraining you, Pet." Nori sat before her.

She started to close her eyes, but that brought on an extreme loss of control.

"What are you feeling?"

Maliah chewed her lips. She'd expected another threat, another question about if she would prefer to be here. Her eyes blinked close, though opened a moment later. "I love how my breasts look," she blurted.

He smiled at her.

"Never thought of them as beautiful." She sighed. "I'm—there's no reason for me to tell you this."

He seemed to be ready to ask for more. Maliah almost got the feeling that she could open up to him. Her legs were wide open, pussy on display, but she *could* open up.

Nori slipped his phone from his pocket. He glanced at it and put it away. When Nori looked at her again, she caught a slight bit of hesitation. He pulled a black handkerchief from his back pocket. "May I?"

"Yes, Sir," she murmured.

Blood pressure rising, Maliah could hear the sound of it rushing in her ears. He placed the material over her eyes and tied it in a single knot. Each time she exhaled, the restraints around her body seemed all the more profound. *I am not a slave. I am pretending to be a sub, only pretending.* She hoped the mantra would bring down her blood pressure.

"You have moved a lot swifter than I expected, Miss Honey. Are you ready to meet your new Master, whom we're training you for?"

This is all pretend, I have no Master . . . "Yes." The word echoed in her ears. She had to say yes. The Dom she was training for also had the same rules as Nori: no penetration whatsoever.

Over the sound of the jazz music, Maliah heard the door creak open. Her ears perked, focusing on the sound of new footsteps. A touch so soft pressed against her collarbone, delicate enough to drive her crazy. Maliah instantly went to pluck at her blindfold, but the confines stopped her. She peered through the darkness, saw that her Dom's outline was more filled in than her trainer's.

"Who are you?" she asked, wild thoughts blazing

through her mind. She knew her new Dom was touching her, but all her instincts flew to one thing: Ephraim.

Ephraim knew about the Hurt Room. Did he know the guy viewing every inch of her body? Was it Ephraim? That thought shot to hell. The attorney who'd created her contract with the Hurt Room was from a different law firm. She'd told herself that a thousand times. If anything, Ephraim knew, and it *hurt* him. She wanted so very badly to hurt him.

A feather brushed across the outline of her hip. A moan coursed through her lips. The dainty touch seemed so vanilla, but what she breathed in melted her inside. A scent so intoxicatingly dark that her pussy ached. Satisfaction attempted to bloat out years full of memories—with the wrong man.

The only touch she wanted in the world belonged to a man she hated. The feather skimmed across her breast. A gush of wetness seeped along her outer folds. The deep groan of her Dom had her attention. His eyes had to be zeroing in on her hardened nipples. But Ephraim Levine still had her heart. The feather descended and tickled across her belly button. The feeling scared and enticed her. Was the feather going toward her—

The damn feather danced back up and traced back up to her other nipple. Maliah's senses heightened. Her labia throbbed with the thought of being touched by a feather, and Maliah gasped. This torture was enough to make her go insane, as the feather traced over the silk of her brown skin.

She'd forgotten to breathe when the feather floated across her sex. The plume sopped up all the juices her Dom had made in mere seconds and the little Nori had left coating her body.

When the feather left her pearl, Maliah whimpered.

Laughter shot out of her as the feather skimmed along her lips. The plume coated her lips as it was dragged across. The perfume scent of her sex twirled with the darkness of his cologne. Yet for all her Dom had done to her, even with her unable to see him, one man still stole her every inhibition.

"Please kiss me, Sir," she begged. *Erase every thought of Ephraim from my mind . . .*

5

Had he heard her words, right? Ephraim had been using the feather to caress the outline of her full lips when she made the statement. The white ostrich feather had begun to drag, weighed down by the sopping wetness of her cunt. A slight shine marred her mouth. Made it perfect.

He sent the feather back along her jaw, down her breast, and straight to her mound. All the while he reminded himself to move slowly; Ephraim wanted to commit every second of this to memory.

Hand in a fist, he pushed the tie away from his Adam's apple. He pressed himself down onto his belly so that he was eye level with her pussy. The delicate folds were as plump as he remembered. Outer and inner folds, plump, untarnished by anyone else. Shit, he should've brought a magnifying glass, but from the naked eye, she looked untouched by another.

He had all the power in the world to know any man who looked her way in the past. To stop anyone from having his possession. And he had. Now, he had to stop the psychotic obsession he had for her. His love for Maliah Porter had always been enough. The mania hadn't come until later.

"Kiss me, please . . ."

"Kiss you?" he groaned, voice lower than normal. A whole lot lower. Forget a magnifying glass—he had to invest in some sort of contraption to speak with her. His words whispered across her aching, wet lips. The feather flicked over the clit of her as he looked up again.

She'd asked him to kiss her lips. His mouth pressed to the plump valley of her cunt. He kissed with enough affection that had it been her mouth, she'd need to come up for breath. Ephraim French kissed her little clit, his jaw becoming wet by the passion he bestowed on her mound.

Maliah gasped. "I-I me-meant my lips."

"These are your lips," he whispered. *Fuck, what if she knows your voice, idiot.*

As if in agreement, her lower back arched to him. Well, as much as she could after how Nori had *pretzeled* her body. Ephraim glanced over at the painting on the wall. It had been the only anchor he had to her beautiful body a mere moment ago. Now, the scent of her intoxicating, sweet pussy was funneling in through his nostrils.

"Please . . ." She arched even more, submitting that heaven of hers on a pedestal for him.

His lips shaped into a frown. He wanted her and he wanted her to know that it was *him.* In the entire year it had taken him to scheme and cook up this plan, to toss money every fucking way he could to get it executed, he'd forgotten the beauty in her gaze when she looked at him. Not looking at him in derision, but love.

He wouldn't kiss her. Not her mouth. Those lips had snarled and lied. But the heady scent of her sex did compel him enough to slide his tongue out. He took a leisurely lap across the thick folds that had belonged to him from day one. Ecstasy moaned from her mouth. That sheer sound was enough to stop him from lying to himself, and he did kiss her, again and again. His mouth went over her hot mound. Ephraim gripped her restraints. Every inch of Maliah was exposed to him in the creation that Nori had made. Her voluptuous thighs pressed against the sides of her chest, her sexy tits, big and heavy. And even heavier? The juicy folds of her cunt as they quivered for him. He wanted those fat folds to try and milk his mouth like she'd once did with his cock while fucking her. His tongue probed her G-spot, teasing her arousal.

"Oh, yes," she screamed.

Ephraim explored the tight depth of her, signed his tongue on every inch of her honey walls. A declaration that he'd never get over her and he'd never let her get over him. His tongue continued to pound inside of her slit, his biceps bulging while he pulled at the constraints around her hips and legs. Maliah's orgasm came hard on his face, his square jaw, the tip of his nose.

Then Ephraim sat on his haunches, looked at her sex. She'd said no penetration. It burned the skin from his body to know that she'd given in. He licked his lips, the taste of her coating him perfectly. His fingers dragged through her kinky hair, curling into a fist. Anger started to brew in his heart that she'd agreed to a kiss. That she'd agreed to this.

"Please stay," she moaned as he arose. "Thank you, Sir . . ."

Her words echoed after him as he left the room.

IN THE FRONT of her home, Maliah leaned her forehead

against the steering wheel and let out a shrill cry. Every second that had transpired in Nori's company was against her religion. Every second with the stranger who'd loved her body until she'd grown delirious went against the fiber of her being.

She started to pray, until the words scrambled in her brain, not forming at her lips. She got out of the car, her pussy lips jolting and jumping, still playing traitor to her morals.

In the house, Maliah turned on the news on a tiny television in the living room. She'd traded the flat-screen her parents gave her. Apparently, they were running out of gift ideas when buying the huge flat-screen. Books were her escape from life—not the sweet ones with heroes abound, but nonfiction. Up until the moment, the stranger in the Hurt Room had shattered all her thoughts, Maliah believed her brain was a vessel. She'd helped transport other youth out of the inner cities, because they hadn't been born with her snobby parents. Now, she sought capital to keep this dream a reality.

With the news on in the background, Maliah went to the kitchen. The quartz countertops were bare. Who knew pawnshops needed expensive cappuccino makers—a thirtieth birthday gift. Dad had even made a flippant remark that her new caffeine machine could put her in the big leagues, expand her horizons to more thoughtful jobs. He sought more for his daughter than her desire to help children. He continued to remind her of his connections, an interim professor position at the University of Maryland.

She opened the refrigerator, closed it and then worked her magic. Fingers wriggling around, Maliah spoke a spell of incoherent words. With a chuckle, Maliah opened it again.

"Guess it doesn't matter that I can't afford wine," she snorted. The way the stranger ate her out had made her body nice and giddy. She pulled out a half carton of milk from a mostly empty rack and then she took the Honey Nut Cheerios from atop the cheap, old, yet new to her refrigerator. It didn't fit in the state-of-the-art kitchen like everything else. Her stainless, smart refrigerator had been hawked for a pretty penny. At least with this one, she could see over the top a lot better.

Her cell phone began to ring the instant Maliah headed toward the cupboard for a bowl. Her pathetic existence dragged back through the living room and to the phone.

"LeeLee? It's . . ."

"Tonya, what's wrong," she encouraged.

"I know you said I'd be kicked out of We Rise if I continued to skip days. I'm stuck and I need your help."

"Where are you?"

"Well . . ."

A few months back, Maliah had taken a four-hour drive to pick Tonya up from a dump of a motel outside of North Adam, MA. At the hotel, there had been men sitting at the table playing cards, condoms scattered across the room.

"Where are you, Tonya?" Maliah asked more assertively. The kid was a high school dropout, who let her family dynamic dictate her future. "I'll come get you from anywhere."

"Miami," she mumbled.

"Miami," Maliah shouted.

"LeeLee," the girl screeched.

Hand on her hip, she stopped herself from telling Tonya that the use of her nickname had been revoked the second she went so far.

"I'm going to . . ." Maliah forced herself to inhale. A case of anxiety took over her. Tonya had refused to go to the nearest police station in the past. What would make her go now? "We'll figure out a way to get you. Text me an address."

After connecting with a few social worker friends, Maliah learned the art of resources. Maybe one of her employees had family in the area who could meet her half-way. Just as she was working the dynamics in her head, her phone pinged again.

6

"WE NEED TO TALK, MALIAH. WILL YOU COME WITH ME TO dinner?" He waited with bated breath for the cursing of his life. The taste of her had made him do this. Alter their plan. She'd get used to him as Dom and forgive him. He was a man—it seemed so simple. Yet the notion that he was altering shit was enough to unsettle him.

She murmured, "Okay, tonight."

"Tonight?" Ephraim arched an eyebrow. Did she know who had given her multiple orgasms a few hours ago?

"Yes. I'd like to eat in Miami. If you're unable to help— um, fulfill that dream of mine—then tonight won't—"

He perked up. "Don't ask me if I can't make something happen, Maliah."

"Ha! I hate this overly confident Ephraim Levine, but I'm ready now if you are."

EPHRAIM HAD WORKED the scenarios in his head. Dinner in Miami? That was a place he'd wined and dined a harem of women since they'd parted ways. In less than an hour, his driver brought Maliah to a private runway.

Dark blue slacks and a V-neck adorned Ephraim's muscular frame. He stood up from his seat as she entered the jet. Maliah hadn't changed from the jeans she'd worn this morning. The neckline of her blouse plunged between her breasts. The second she'd confided in Nori about her breasts, he knew that he had to get his hands on her.

Maliah's eyes roamed over spacious seats, stopping at a silver bucket of champagne. She glared at him.

"I'm using you, Eph." She didn't sneer, though the hurt in her gaze was enough. "You were, what, ten? You didn't want to play with someone beneath you, who had a means to use you. Well, I'm using you."

Ephraim had learned not to listen to half the shit exiting her mouth, a while back. He chuckled from low in his throat.

They shared the same pain and hurt; although hers was misguided, and Ephraim hid his a whole lot better. As she continued to linger near the entryway, a slightly cool breeze brought her alluring scent to his nose. Too many years had passed for her to cave so easily. Well, if she knew his status as her Dominant, that would present another can of worms. Later.

So he asked why she was using him. Though he doubted it, he said, "For a nice dinner?"

"No."

"I thought so." He cocked his head toward a chair. "We're going to pick up a wayward kid who holds your heart, right?"

"Don't be pretentious."

"I'm assuming, which is something I rarely do." Ephraim told himself to smile, to soften his tone. Her caring heart made it past the point of impossible to fall out of love with her. But if she had to stare at him with derision, he had to taper his real feelings, the dormant sensations of anger.

She plopped down in a seat. He went to the champagne and poured two glasses. Handing one over, he said, "The only person in the whole world who I don't mind using me is you, LeeLee. If at any point during our trip you want to hop on my cock and really fucking use me, I'll take that too."

———

"You know what, Eph?" She hated the sound of her voice, the echo in her ear for the words she did not have to say. Speaking made her sound bitter but stopping wasn't something she had strength enough to do. "You are such a whore."

The door to the cockpit was open, and the pilot's cheeks were ablaze, denoting that he'd heard her choice word. His mouth was slack, as if he'd been prepared to make an inquiry.

"We're ready," Ephraim said.

He claimed the seat across from her. Even as he'd poured the drink, she was under the heat of his gaze. Maliah crossed her leg as a warning to her pussy not to become traitor. Nerves shot, she paused from placing the bubbly to her lips. She had no desire to show how defective her body became around him. She pushed the glass onto the glossy ledge. Had he noticed the slight tremor in her? While he had enough self-control to look at her coolly, Maliah had drunk him in the second she'd entered. His chest massive, the V-neck begged for her reverent fingertips to stroke. And she'd played herself a fool, looked at his huge Jewish package.

"Tell me about myself." Ephraim claimed her thoughts. "Whore. What else?"

"You're the user." Again, words echoed in her ears. She assessed each one; this last bit sounded juvenile, like some kid who had been pushed down and had a nasty boo-boo. "You used me. And now, you're sowing your wild oats. Shouldn't you be preparing to settle down—no. Probably not. You can't trust any woman with your money . . ." *With your family . . .*

He gestured for her to continue.

"Money doesn't make a person happy." She spat the cliché.

"Nah, you have it wrong, my little LeeLee." Ephraim was up again.

Eyes wider than a deer in oncoming traffic, she watched as he squatted before her. *What-what-what are you doing?* Maliah's thoughts were a delightful chaos. There was no trusting herself to ask the words aloud.

"Allow me to lock you in, sweetheart."

He took her hands from her lap, his fingertips skimming the sensitive base of her wrist. When he lifted them to his mouth, his breath tickled the soft spot before she snatched them away. Again his restrained laughter sent goosebumps racing across her skin, her hands covering her heart as Ephraim locked her in.

"We were talking money, right?" Ephraim's eyebrow cocked as he stood.

She said nothing. Cheeks flushed, supple brown skin already calling to him, there was no need to speak.

Ephraim locked himself in the seat. "Money sends families on vacations, right? Coming together to enjoy new experiences. Happy memories create content people. Remember when we delighted in new ventures together?"

She shrugged, all the thoughts in her brain competing for the spotlight. They had so many good moments. The pain of him taking her virginity became the pleasure of sharing their love. He'd taught her how to drive, and they'd almost died when she mistook the gas pedal for the brake. All the moments warped in her mind while her body was tugged back against the seat, the jet racing across the tarmac.

Ephraim's eyes never left hers. Was he experiencing those moments too?

"I miss you, Maliah Ann Porter."

"I . . ." She couldn't finish the sentence, couldn't utter her hatred of him anymore. "Can we not talk for the rest of the ride, please?"

7

"YOU SHOULD STAY IN THE CAR, EPH." MALIAH CONNECTED gazes with him. So far, he'd complied to all of her wishes. They'd sat in intense silence for the duration of the plane ride. He rented a sedan that seemed light-years away from the Ephraim Levine she knew. Well, the one she knew by way of social-media stalking.

"Not on your life, LeeLee," he said.

Getting out of the car, Maliah took a deep breath of the putrid air. She was somewhat relieved that her ex-best friend and lover didn't agree. Latin music clashed with rap. Maliah placed a hand over her mouth and nose. She prayed the cheap-skunk-like smoke didn't get her high. Her gaze searched the dark outline of an apartment building with rickety stairs on each side of it.

Ephraim came to her side.

"This isn't the place for your kind." She almost felt herself smile.

He dragged his hand over his hair. "You thought I was a little mixed when we were kids."

"Yeah, your Jewish Afro was . . ." She stopped short of

bumping him with her hip. Nostalgia had wrapped itself around her and it was warm, welcoming. Through the darkness, she saw his hungry gaze, and her eyes flitted away.

"Let's go save your friend from another mistake, LeeLee." He held out his hand, but she placed hers inside her pocket.

THE SUN WAS BEGINNING to ascend. Ephraim had scooped up Tonya, and she was in his arms as Maliah opened the front door of her home. A stench emitted from the kid's soiled body. Her grim jeans stuck to her like a second skin, but still he held her.

Why are you doing this to yourself, LeeLee? Maliah silently begged herself not to look at him through those old lenses, the ones that shaded all the bad shit and clung to everything good about Ephraim.

As she led him to a guest bedroom, she took fleeting glances behind her. Most of her wanted to see the disdain on his face at how empty her home appeared. The death grip she had on her house and the mortgage she could no longer afford was evident by the lack of furniture. Heck, one of the bedrooms was now empty of name-brand furniture. The claw-foot tub in her bathroom had been created by her mom's favorite designer. The world they lived in, so rich that a person could have a custom-made tub, had baffled Maliah all her life. Although she'd been born somewhat in that world, she'd been blessed enough to see reality too.

"Lay her there, please." Maliah planted herself at the door. With no strength to enter a bedroom with her ex, she leaned back against the doorframe.

He placed Tonya down, the young woman groaning and moaning.

"You have water, aspirin?" Ephraim asked.

"Yeah." She walked into the bathroom. When he continued down the hall, curiosity overtook her. He had started into the kitchen, his hands riding over the seam of his V-neck. Was he undressing? She scurried around him at the instant Ephraim had started to pull the shirt from one arm. His bronze chest caught her eyes.

"What are you doing, Eph?"

"The kid is coming down from a high." He continued to shove one arm out of the shirt.

"St-stop, please." Her hands flew over his, and a nanosecond later, she let go as if his skin were scalding hot.

"I smell really bad, LeeLee." One arm after the next, he tugged out of the shirt. Her gaze flew away from his biceps, though he didn't seem to notice, while heading to the refrigerator. His head tilted. "That's small."

"Wasn't it you who told me it's not the size that counts?"

He held up an index finger, and then he began to chuckle. They'd been fourteen when she'd seen his cock. Might as well have been a foreign object. Ephraim must have assumed when he mentioned "size" because he hadn't been tiny at all. The trepidation came from seeing a penis— in the flesh. She still remembered opening for him, stretching and molding for him. The walls of her pussy began to contract at that thought. By the time they were in college, his cock was large and veiny.

Suddenly, Ephraim's hands were at her ass. An electric tingle ran straight from her bulbous buttocks to her sex. Gripping tight at her flesh, he pulled her onto the counter. His thick frame wedged between her thighs. "LeeLee," he growled.

Heat spiraled through her as kisses planted against her neck, traveling up to her earlobe. Her fingers had a mind of their own and began to run through his soft, dark hair.

"Let me back in, baby. I don't know what I did. Let me in."

His hand clasped the back of her neck, thumb drawing across her vulnerable pulse. "I never let you go, Maliah Porter. We made a promise that I wouldn't."

"We were kids, Eph." She groaned. His lips flew to her mouth, stopping any more arguments that went against his goal. He took siege of her lips, kisses deep, tongue exploring and halting all her thoughts.

"Yeah, we were young, doing grown-up shit. I tasted you and you were mine." His kisses trailed across her skin. Her pussy went off like fireworks, responding in a static of contractions. "And you tasted me, beautiful. You let these thick lips gloss all up for me, remember?"

He stole her hand, placing it between them, his other hand skillfully pulling down his pants. She skimmed her palm down his abdomen, into his boxers. Maliah's soul cried for his domination. If he were the Dom Nori had brought to her, and if they could get back what they used to have . . . The deliberate movement of her hand along his slick hardness obstructed all her thoughts. Her thumb pressed over the tip of him, so hard a bit of stickiness milked onto her hand. A flush spread across her body. In her greed to search every curve of his shaft, Maliah reached down, massaging his balls in her hands.

"This is so bad, Eph," she moaned against him. "This is bad."

He stroked her cheek with tenderness. Cupping her breast through her bra, Ephraim grazed it over with his teeth. Soft kisses were planted around her areola, and he breathed across her skin. He glanced up at her, pawing the round melon with his palm. Ephraim smiled. "Let me back in, Maliah."

His smile did her in. She nodded.

"That's right, LeeLee, baby, you're my woman." His hand clasped her hair, and he brought her down off the counter. In one fluid motion, Maliah was on her knees before him.

With her mouth a fraction away from his cock and her throat filled with saliva, Ephraim held her away. He fisted her hair and brought her eye level with him.

"You've tortured me for a long time, LeeLee." He squeezed, her hair follicles sparking while the walls of her sex jolted. "Take me in your mouth, sweetheart, inch by inch. You do it too fast and you're in fucking trouble."

She opened her mouth to agree to anything he said.

He squeezed her hair tighter. "No talking. That mouth is focused on one thing right now, Maliah. I bet that mouth of yours is as wet as that pussy, am I right?"

He tugged softly at her hair this time.

She nodded.

"I'm going to torture you, LeeLee. You're going to drink my cum so many times that you beg me to fuck you. You want that, don't you?"

Tears pricked her eyes. Memory served her with the delight of his cream. With his hand clamped around her hair, Maliah could only dream about gulping his seed.

"There you go."

Her lips flew around him. Though her gag reflex wasn't ready, Maliah brought his cock all the way back to her tonsils. The hard bump of his crown against her throat hurt delightfully. He yanked her back out.

"You didn't listen, LeeLee." Disappointment wove into his tone.

Maliah licked her lips. "I'm sorry, Si—Ephraim. I'm sorry."

Darkness blazed in his eyes. Her gaze cast down, away from his anger and to his glorious shaft. Body trembling, she waited for another taste. This time, she would do what he said. She'd be the submissive she never thought she could be.

The familiarity of taking Ephraim into her mouth made Maliah smile. She sucked his cock-head, careful only to take in a single inch. The sheer length of him proved to be an extensive job. Two inches in, and with so many more to go, the pool of saliva in her mouth dripped down her chin. Three inches in, Maliah reminded herself of patience, that she'd soon have all of him stuffed in her mouth. Relaxing her mouth, Maliah was able to enjoy the thickness of his cock better.

He fit deep down in her throat. Her tonsils vibrated against him in a heavenly moan. Ephraim let go of her hair and sighed. His hips arched, and she sucked with fervor. The control he had over her intensified as he placed two hands on her cheeks, guiding her in and out. His shaft thrusted hard, disappearing into her mouth, knocking at the back of her throat.

"That's right, keep pumping my cock in your mouth."

Maliah's mouth gradually opened wider. Resistance fled. She stole more of him than she thought possible. Her lips tickled his balls. He ravaged her mouth with each push. Those satisfied groans he made spurred her addiction to taste his cum. When his entire body tensed, desire radiated from her being. Her body was desperate for his orgasm. Sensations sparked, taste being the primary craving. A ribbon of a sigh flushed through Maliah as his semen coated her tongue and her entire mouth. She kneeled there, sucking down every drop he had to offer.

Chest pumping with abandonment, she knew she could stay here forever. Satisfaction enveloped her.

Ephraim reached down, his thumb strumming along her lips. "Better than I remember."

She took his awaiting hand and stood up. A giddy feeling overcame her as she licked her lips. His cum settled in her stomach like a good meal.

"Eph, this is . . ." *Perfect.*

A loud, throat-wrenching sound came from the guest room. Maliah closed her eyes and took a deep breath. "Things went haywire before I even thought of putting a trash can in the room," she mumbled to herself.

"To your left," Ephraim said. He hadn't heard her, probably wouldn't understand as Tonya launched herself out of the bedroom.

They both repeated, "To your left." Vomit propelled across the hallway as Tonya skidded on her socks to her left and into the bathroom. The door slammed shut.

Ephraim pulled up his slacks, did up his belt, and then opened the refrigerator. "You don't have food."

"You've got to go, Eph."

"Really, you want to handle that by yourself?" He held up his hands. "Not that I know how to use a—a—" He made a movement with his hand, gesturing like life was a game.

"Mop," she scoffed. "Thanks, Ephraim."

"For what, the dick or the jet ride?"

"No, the very nice—" she began but cringed at another loud heave. Placing a finger beneath and parallel to her nose, Maliah turned back to Ephraim. "We made a mistake. Albeit a nice one, but a mistake all the same." She grabbed his arm and guided him toward the front door.

"Mistake?"

"Yes. One that we can blame on a lack of sleep." Pressing back on her heels, she tugged him along.

"We should get her into rehab."

"Hello, she hated the county one. Remember the last words she said before falling asleep on the ride?" Maliah gritted out, pushing him farther. "Can you help me and move your ass?"

Ephraim moved away from her grasp. "LeeLee, you don't know the slightest thing about taking care of someone on meth."

"What do you know?"

"I know good rehabilitation centers, that's what the fuck I know, sweetheart. Can I get her into one?"

"Oh, you know good rehab locations. Why?" She folded her arms, ready to play judge, like the million online users who had commented on his disappearances in the past.

Ephraim scoffed. "You left me, Maliah. That's a good reason to need hard-core services."

She shook her head. "Are you serious?"

"Yeah, and I can tell you coke never had a hold on me like you did. But you quit me!"

"Get the fuck out, Eph."

8

So far, Ephraim prided himself on not matching Mariah's snideness. She took him there a few times, but to throw a dig while the kid needed help had been the last thing on his mind.

The door slammed in his face. Out of all the places he'd ventured into in the world, *that* was the greatest place he'd been tossed out of. His fingers curled under, balling into hard fists. She was right there, so close, almost his again. Sunshine warmed his back. He left the shirt. He rubbed the back of his head and turned around.

From his position, Ephraim noticed that the driver had leaned back in the seat. He sauntered down the stairs, contemplating the first time he'd met Maliah.

He'd met associates the same way. One of his oldest best friends, Daniel, he'd also met the same way. But her, well, she had been different . . .

"Damnum absque injuria?" Ephraim's father, Abner, asked while he climbed out of the back seat of his Volvo.

Ten-year-old Ephraim never paused before responding in memory. His family was filled with litigators, and the law firm was at the tip of his fingers. They were tight-fisted people, and Levine & Levine was his legacy. Grandpa Ian always said that he'd rather take his last breath than put someone else's name beside his own. It wasn't that the partners in the firm weren't up to par. Some deserved it.

"Ephraim, my boy, what is . . ."

Abner followed where his son was staring.

Puffy pigtails bounced. Laughter rang out while Ephraim glanced at the girl in the front yard. Two other white kids were working double ropes that he'd one day learn was called double Dutch.

"We're doing it?" one of the kids asked.

"Yes, see. You've got it." Maliah's pigtails continued to bounce off her warm brown skin. "You want to try."

"Uh, I'll watch you," the other giggled. The two kids turning the rope had to be sisters, and their wrists moved with deliberation. They hadn't grown accustomed to double Dutch.

"That is a peculiar game. Maybe Maliah will teach you. Get over there." Abner placed his hands onto Ephraim's shoulders to guide his son.

Maliah . . . So, they were here for her family.

Abner gasped, "Why aren't you moving?"

Their routine ended the second Ephraim found out his father's client had children around. He could start a conversation with anyone, make them laugh.

But Maliah was already laughing with her friends, and the sight was the most beautiful thing he'd ever seen. He considered moving closer to hear her laughter, but his legs refused to move.

Abner patted down the thick curls on top of his head. "You like this one, eh? Make sure she's Jewish."

He stood rooted to the ground. "She's not likely, Dad. I'm going to listen in to your meeting, if you don't mind."

"I had a feeling Maliah wasn't Jewish, Ephraim. What

happened to you being the king of jokes?" Abner chortled. "Now, what's this business about listening in? That's been a dream of mine for years. You once listened by force when Grandpa Ian felt you needed more time studying."

"If I couldn't answer your question. And I-I didn't answer it," he stuttered. *The definition of "amnum absque injuria" was somewhere at the back of his brilliant mind. He began to ramble, staring up at his dad. "Then I must listen. Grandpa Ian has a way of asking if I'm . . ."*

"Excuse me?" The most angelic voice made his shoulders jolt. She was too close. The sisters who had helped her jump were chatting loudly as they passed by and toward a grand home. How had he not noticed any of this?

When had she come over? Ephraim's ears burned. He listened as she held the same level of articulation that he was accustomed to. When Maliah waved his dad inside the gate, she turned to Ephraim. No amount of speech therapy or his genuine charisma could help because he'd fallen in love.

When Ephraim blinked, the driver was standing on the curb. The driver had short blond hair, thick lips, a wide nose, and pale skin. Yesiv's Russian accent was heavier with consideration. "You okay, boss?"

"Yes. Home now. I'm staying in town for a while. Get some rest, and I'll need you back at my place by 1:00 p.m."

"Good news," Yasiv murmured in Russian. He arched an eyebrow, though he nodded. He was compensated for working overtime and had done so all night. And now, Ephraim was staying in town for a while.

Ephraim typed a quick text message as he got into the car. He needed his assistant, who was like a unicorn— someone who worked without seeing him. She'd have to wake up the pilot and get to Chicago. Ephraim had some

groveling to do, and Miss Anna Mae's food set the foundation for success.

———————

MALIAH HAD TAKEN A DRIVE-THROUGH SHOWER, making
quick work of her hot spots. The taste of Ephraim's cum was
enough to sustain her belly for the day. And here she
thought Monday would be awful. The day had started with
anxiety clutching at her heart. Now, Tuesday descended,
and she hardly noticed hunger pains while working. She'd
left a note for Tonya to stay put and apologized about the
food choice, which consisted of cereal and frozen vegeta-
bles. She was headed to work.

The corridors of We Rise Learning Center were tagged
in graffiti and other urban art. Some of the students had
helped spruce the place up when she'd opened the doors a
few years ago. She'd supervised the site, helped volunteer
interns, and greeted all the staff. During the summer, life
was rough. Truth be told, she could've employed all tutors
and let go of the staff. But she'd stretched the grants in order
to have a place for youth to visit. There weren't grand
summer camps with amusement parks on the roster
anywhere near here. Her center, which assisted with
tutoring during the school year, kept its doors opened. The
arts, and of course tutoring, were still available to keep
young minds pliable. And at the very least, the kids had a
cool place to go.

Now, she let her body fall into the peeling-leather chair
in her office. The wheels, which never worked, slid back and
her pathetic existence croaked. Maliah pulled herself up
onto the chair with a huff.

It was too late to ask God "why me?" She'd done very bad, bad things this morning. Things she'd vowed never to do again.

So Maliah glanced at a framed self-affirmation across from her, the one that stumped her most of the time.

"I am worthy . . ."

Last year, one of the kids had painted the phrase on a tiny canvas. She'd gotten a stock of the canvases for a miracle price from the dollar store.

"Must've been psychic?" she murmured to herself. The youth had given her the painting and took home a few more. Maliah didn't have the heart to tell the child that everyone got one canvas. She then received the one she needed most. The scrawled yellow-painted "worthy" popped off the white background and leaped out toward her.

With a glance at the wall clock, Maliah realized her best friend was en route to home. She placed her cell phone on speaker.

"Hey, LeeLee?" Yolanda said. In the background, an upbeat ABC song blared. "Marcus, turn that thing down please."

"Oh, my baby Marcus," Maliah sighed. "How was school?"

"Good!" the kindergartener replied.

"Turn it down or—" Yolanda cut herself off.

"I'm a mandated reporter, you know." Maliah smiled. Her friend's only fault when it came to Marcus included an insanely expensive kinder class, one that Maliah's father had encouraged her to apply at upon abandoning her nonprofit.

"Humph. You and me both."

"I need help, Yolanda," Maliah whimpered.

A hitch came through the phone. "Where are you? Did that trainer lock you in a dungeon?" A battery of questions came from the protective mom.

I want to be a mom too. Maliah gulped back that thought. The Ephraim she once loved would've made a good father. The man who'd cared for Tonya had the same paternal instinct. Too many magazines and the Entertainment News channel had painted him as a bad-boy attorney. But this was the world they lived in. Celebrities and professionalism had collided.

She stopped prattling on in thought to reply, "Worse."

"Where are you? You're still sharing your location with me? Tell me where you are, LeeLee." Yolanda sounded like a Lifetime mother who'd do anything to save her child. They had this sort of relationship.

"I'm at work."

"Sheesh, you have my heart beating! I recall you mentioning running out of the damn place last Saturday and rescheduling it."

"We talked yesterday morning, Yolanda," Maliah sighed.

"So what, this is my life! I can't remember five minutes ago," she snapped. "I'm on the freeway, merging over to the darn suicide lane, ready to flag a cop over."

"Well, that might be a good idea. I did some *stuff* with Eph."

Yolanda groaned. "I'm sorry, I can't have Marcus listening to this. Though, I'm sure the tales you have would slow me down enough to not only recall what day of the week it is and—"

"Tuesday, and strictly why I said *stuff*."

"Humph, that's what I mean. Sound more intelligible.

He takes in everything. Say something like we had relations. Or spell out words. Actually, words with five letters or more."

"What's relations, Mommy?"

Maliah tuned her out while Yolanda gave an adult explanation. She rolled her eyes, remembering Yolanda chewing the head off her husband, Grant, for baby talk.

"What did you do?" Yolanda asked.

"Well, five letters or more! This isn't *Jeopardy!*" Maliah murmured. Oral, suck dick, and head were out. *Is blow job one or two words?* "I took him to that restaurant—you know, BJs?"

Maliah heard a hunk, then a slight chuckle before Yolanda spoke into the receiver. "Hmmm, did you like the meal?"

"Yolanda!"

"Oh, Mommy, I would like to go to BJs . . ."

"Sorry, Maliah, I have another call that I must take."

Click.

EPHRAIM LAY ON A COUCH, the material thick and sturdy. He scooted over to get a hard toy wedged from beneath him. He turned the action figure in his hands, then handed it to the black man, who wore leather flip-flops.

"I would apologize for my son's toys," Grant quipped, "but you have this habit of thinking my wife is your shrink."

"We have history, bro. She is."

Grant shook his head with a chuckle. "Oh, they're home now. I'm going to pretend like I had a productive afternoon."

He sat back down on a burnt-orange sofa across from Ephraim. There was a MacBook on the coffee table, a steaming mug next to it. Grant picked up a stack of papers and plucked the red pen from behind his ear. Everything about him read old-school.

The front door opened. "Food!" Marcus squealed, running down the hall.

Grant went after him as Yolanda stopped at the entrance to the living room, hand on her hip. "What services do I owe you for the peach cobbler?"

Ephraim banged his head back onto the soft pillow. "Miss Anna Mae's was all out of peach—"

"Then our deal is out the window."

"Yolanda, I need your help." He plucked up a throw pillow and held it to his chest. "LeeLee let me in. For the briefest of moments, I was in."

With a sigh, Yolanda dragged a hand through her dreadlocks. She sank down onto the couch across from him. "I practically hung up the phone on her when I noticed your driver dozing in front of the house."

"So, what did she say?"

"What happened to..." She paused to glance toward the hallway. "The Hurt Room idea?"

"It's on."

Yolanda's dark brown eyes twinkled, enough to tell him she already had the details. "How's it going for you, buddy?"

"I detect a hint of 'I told you so.'"

"From me? No, that would be overkill. I distinctly recall saying as much for the last year and a half while you texted me the grand houses you planned to buy to fulfill this twisted, dark dream of yours. I uttered those words again when you shared the construction that would be done. The vetting." She glanced out of the room again. Grant hadn't liked the idea at all. She had mentioned not being too keen on it, but also mentioned that white people were a different breed. "That Nori is a looker."

"C'mon, Yolie, you're not being a good friend." He placed a hand at his bulky chest; flirting came too easy.

"*Au contraire*, I'm team LeeLee. Rings better than team Eph. Nevertheless, I've supported your less-than-stellar ideas. Even the dysfunctional ones. Like your quest to mend your sexual relationship with Maliah in lieu of . . . oh, more important facets in a relationship."

"Why is my wife and college friend chatting about sex?" Grant glanced between the two before shaking his head. He shoved his hands into the pockets of his khaki shorts and groaned. "Eph, you're aware of how many cheesy romances I edit." He held up a manuscript for emphasis. "All that coke, buddy. What happened to the brilliant, calculating Ephraim Levine, Esquire?"

"*I want her back*," Ephraim growled. In the beginning, the notion of a sex room blew his mind. A million-dollar decision, if he had to say so. Well, it cost more to execute. Ephraim craved Maliah, even if that meant one single part of the woman he loved.

"Said every so-called alpha who goes after a buxom blond." Grant chuckled. He flipped to a page and held it for Ephraim to see. His friend knocked the pages away.

"Yolanda, you know better." Grant settled down beside her, slapping and then gripping her hip.

"You're right," she murmured, kissing him.

Ephraim looked away. He'd been there before Grant. Heard the berating Yolanda gave him while Maliah chatted about how "sprung" he was. Yeah, Ephraim recalled those old slang words they'd used. Now, looking at their love had the opposite effect. He couldn't be happy for his friends, not when money couldn't buy back his love.

"What the fuck did I do wrong?" he mumbled again, rubbing his face.

"Eph," Yolanda spoke with tender care. "You treated her like the queen every woman should be. I haven't the slightest idea. Maybe the answer is in her."

9

SATURDAY MORNING

Since the crashing of her ex back into Maliah's life, her thoughts took a detour to him. He'd been an obsession of hers before they'd laid eyes on each other.

A friend of hers, Daniel, took the same piano classes as her as a child. He'd mentioned Ephraim. Not Ephraim Levine, Esquire, but Ephraim Levine, the Funny Guy. Since her parents had an image to uphold, and Daniel was about the most down-to-earth billion-dollar baby she'd met, his words had intrigued her.

The day her dad's business grew large enough—with white-collar illegality—her dad got to sweat bullets. He got to cuss up a storm while swearing that the Levines better be worth their weight in gold. Maliah, on the other hand, prepared to meet the Funny Guy.

The moment her mom, Annaleigh, finished poking at her, Maliah changed from the Southern belle outfit. The silk taffeta itched her skin. Nothing would make her be the debutante her Southern mama—who refused to go by mama, by the way—desired.

Annaleigh had a pair of scrutinizing light blue eyes, inherited from her mom. Annaleigh's mother was white, and Rick was black; Maliah hadn't taken an ounce of her mother's lighter skin tone. Their hair once had some similarities, though Annaleigh's was blonde, and her parents had had the kinks processed as soon as she could sit still in a chair. Annaleigh always swore she did not know how to do "black hair" when dropping Maliah off at a different beauty salon than she attended. That was after Annaleigh had burned a chunk of her hair while flat ironing it. Maliah always thought her mom had fried her hair on purpose. Granny, Rick's mother, refused to let Annaleigh relax it. Maliah's voice had been tiny when she wrinkled her nose and mentioned a burning smell. Her mom had patted her shoulder and continued to sizzle the same spot. Maliah could still see her mom, minutes later, running with a chunk of her long hair. She'd started working on her tears before entering Rick's office, shouting, "I simply ruined it! There are easier ways to straighten those cotton balls!"

Aside from the thick hair that Annaleigh refused to embrace, Maliah had inherited some of her mother's vindictiveness. Once her mom left, she changed into the hidden garments that her grandparents had bought—overalls. She mussed up her press and curl, placing it into two ponytails. Her parents' need for her to fit into "the life" wasn't going to tarnish her first encounter with the Funny Guy.

Only he never said a single word to her.

"Well, that was a sign," she told herself, pulling up at Nori's home.

Three months later, the dark cloud over Rick Porter's construction company had lifted. She still hadn't heard a single joke, let alone the sound of his voice. She had spent Friday nights preparing for Saturday mornings, when Abner would arrive. Her silk scarf stayed on for goodness' sake.

"Then you had to go and threaten him," she mumbled,

letting her head fall back against the seat. "I forced him to like me ..."

She shrugged. A million theories had controlled her. This one seemed the most plausible. Ephraim Levine had ducked and dodged her during their parents' discussion of Rick's case. But with others, he was all charisma, all sex appeal. *Okay, he grew into sex once he lost the fro*, she thought.

"Why won't you talk to me." She had combusted with infuriation one day. "You scared of black girls?"

Today, it sounded so bad for her to say as much. But growing up with her mom, who was half-black and embraced her whiteness, she knew some people were afraid of black folk. Maliah shoved the embarrassing thought from her head and replaced it with her trainer, Nori. As a kid, she'd spent every Saturday for three entire months training for Ephraim's arrival. She'd sucked it up and worn the dresses too, switching from nonchalance to a debutant all because Daniel's stories had intrigued her. Now, her Saturday mornings were to be filled with Nori having all control. The email scheduled to her for today included role play.

"I can't act for shit," she groaned, climbing out of the car.

At the front door, it opened without prompt. The same tiny Japanese maid, with perfect, oleander white skin, allowed her to enter.

Maliah studied her movements. Graceful, poised . . . submissive. She blurted the question. "Why are we starting upstairs?"

The maid still hadn't addressed her.

Nori's attractive accent floated down the stairs. "Miss Honey, my little one has taken a vow of silence."

"Why—may I ask why?" Maliah controlled her urge not to be seen in the same light as the maid. Rick had taught her to seize the moment. Her mom had *attempted* to teach Maliah to play upon her prowess. Until this moment, it all meant the same thing.

Don't question a man. She stopped the sardonic look on her face from reigning. Questioning a man, woman, whomever had answers was in her blood.

Nori smiled at her. Maybe he hadn't said *don't question a Dom.* A question didn't imply distrust, right?

"I was in the midst of my morning meditation." He descended the steps, his presence captivating every single one of her senses. Nori looked good, smelled even better, and his alluring slanted eyes were only for her.

Move over, Maid Sub, she thought.

"What were you concerned about?" she asked, each question strummed along with interest. He had to be thinking of her. No conceit necessary. His eyes were drinking her in, and so he had to have been meditating about her.

"I'm not permitted to view the time you have with your Dom, Maliah. He won't allow it."

Heat flushed across her cheeks. "I can agree with that." Her voice was strangled. Maliah hadn't thought that anyone could view them, unless they were in the same room. She'd prayed that God had looked away.

"Don't worry, Pet. I came up with an alternative." Nori winked. "Atsun will."

"Will what?"

"You stipulated no man in your contract." His fingers skimmed across her chin, sending her sensations into tiny tingling endpoints. And her chin rose a bit. Nori smiled. Damn, did he have a way of making her body follow his command, without a word. "We must follow the contract,

Miss Honey. BDSM is set on a foundation of trust, and that begins with your agreement."

A gilded chandelier gleamed overhead, the grandeur of it adding to how small she felt in this moment as they stood in the foyer. She found her voice long enough to inquire, "How will Atsun help?"

"Just her mouth, Miss Honey. Her hands, her *mouth* will help us."

Maliah's gaze slid back and forth between the two. "I'll have to pass."

He stepped closer to her. "All right, let me know how you'll return the funds rendered for this month—prorated of course. The accountant will provide you with an actual amount."

EPHRAIM SAT rigid in a plush leather chair in the viewing room. He stared at the horde of cameras linked to the house. He noticed it, the instant Maliah's brown skin flushed. What had Nori said?

Only the rooms were equipped with speakers. With a construction team on call, the downstairs guest room had a security camera installed. He hadn't liked the thought of not being in control last time. Atsun had brought Maliah to Nori the first time. And this past Monday, Nori had retrieved her himself. What had he done in the process of bringing her upstairs? Ephraim didn't like having unanswered questions. Now, he wondered what Nori had said to her.

"We'll have this fixed too," he growled. Ephraim felt around in his suit pocket, prepared to text the construction services. He'd need audible access to every room downstairs, even the hallways. After the quick text, he looked up.

On the screen, Maliah started to back away. His heart lurched. Had this been a mistake?

Allowing Nori to take her out last week was done to set the guise that she was being followed. Of course, he had her followed. Always had. But his people wouldn't know about Nori—about the two men's plans. And Nori had a specific set of rules, the most fundamental being don't touch her. Second, Nori wasn't to take her from the house. Not after their one encounter out had led to Ephraim's "knowledge" that she was seeing someone. When Ephraim mentioned seeing her ass out with a man the first time he'd spoken to her in ages, Maliah had been livid. In her emotions, she wasn't able to see through him.

But he had to keep tweaking the rules. No touching. No outings. No bringing her up from the guest room—well, he had cameras there now. But while Maliah had her list of no's, he had his too. The most important one.

No. Fucking. Touching.

Thoughts continued to swarm in his mind. And when he tuned in again, Maliah was in the changing room. Instead of opening the gift he'd left for her, with Nori's writing and signature, she had her phone out.

His vibrated in his pants. He stared at the screen, pressed the Mute button on the panel, and answered. "LeeLee?"

"Eph, hey . . ."

"Talk to me."

"I'm so sorry."

His hand went to the stricken look on her face. It took sheer will not to go straight to her; she was closer than she'd been in so long.

"I've been awful to you, Eph. I forced you to take me to get Tonya. Then we . . . Then I . . ."

"LeeLee, baby, talk to me. What do you need? What can I do for you?" His eyes were glued to the screen, then the next as she turned away. Every inch of the room was covered.

"What can I do for you, Maliah?" His voice hardened. Maybe Yolanda was right. Little LeeLee walked all over him. When she was old enough, he'd bought her expensive diamond stilettos. Ephraim didn't mind the woman he loved walking all over him. Though he preferred it to the arguments they couldn't stop having as of recent, he gritted out, "Maliah, whatever you're doing, don't do it. Let me see you tonight. We can go out. Anywhere you want. Any continent. *Sweets*, talk to me."

"Mmmm, sounds like a dream, Eph." She chewed on her bottom lip. His thumb caressed the screen's outline of her shape. "Dinner, tonight. Since I manipulated you into the Tonya thing. We can talk. Promise me it will be talking? Nothing else."

"Yeah," he lied easily. She didn't know the asshole he had become. Not to the full extent. Saying anything and meaning nothing came without thought to him. "Dinner, talking, that works. Go home, Maliah. Get ready for me."

"I can't. See you soon."

She'd hung up. He didn't know what he hated worse: her sleeping with him, not being aware, or the fact that part of him craved this.

———

AN HOUR LATER, Ephraim watched Maliah be escorted to another bedroom transformed for his viewing. This room was encased with weathered silver walls, diamond trinkets abound, and she adorned the room beautifully. A silk red robe cinched at the waist embellished her curves, sending his cock on the rise. He lazed into the seat, like a vulture, his prey unaware of her true vulnerability.

She kept taking subtle glances at Atsun, which unsettled him. On day one, she'd practically ridden the maid's heels on fear. The maid had become an unspoken ally. What the hell had happened?

He stopped fidgeting with his palms the instant Nori entered the silver room. He looked for any social cues that the trainer had scared his woman in any way.

Atsun began to strip herself. Ephraim cast a glance at the sub for a moment. He studied Maliah's face, captivated by the love of his life. In their room, he was capable of listening in, though the music was the only sound.

Atsun brandished a whip.

"Pet," Nori began, "it's imperative that we don't stretch your limit too far. Even in your eagerness to satisfy . . ."

Ephraim's eyelid twitched. Who? Was Nori about to say satisfy *him*? After a deep breath, the jealousy mellowed.

" . . . your Dom. He will know how well you do."

"You'll tell him?" Maliah said.

"Of course."

She pressed her fingers to her lips.

"Do not ruin your lipstick, Pet," Nori ordered.

Her hands went to her sides. Ephraim loved seeing her thick lips smeared with lipstick after he fucked her mouth. From the camera's angle, Atsun appeared to be reapplying Maliah's lipstick, the sub's thumb following the contour of Maliah's bottom lip, and he gulped.

"Hands and knees, Pet," Atsun snipped, her nonexistent hips cocked.

Maliah's chest compressed for a moment before she did what she was told. Ephraim watched the shape of her form

—the perfect arch, ass out. Gaze glued to his everything, he undid his belt. With precise movements, he was inside his pants and fisting his cock.

"Miss Honey, what are the rules?"

"Uh, green good. Yellow, you'll sl-slow down, or red—"

"Red, you *pussied* out." Atsun's seductive voice primed each word with a swat to her palm. "It's okay if you can't handle it."

Nori reached down, summarizing his sub's words with more sincerity. "Every experience is meant to gauge your limit. Say you can only take ten hits—"

"Ten!" Maliah almost flinched.

Atsun slammed the whip into her palm again, disappointed.

Nori smiled. "Say you take ten today, we will work our way up, Pet." He brought his hand behind Atsun, their tongues twining. The sucking and moaning turned Ephraim off.

Nori nodded to his sub. "Atsun is topping today, Pet. Topping describes a submissive controlling a scene, while still claiming her sub role. Her qualities and ability to attune with the body are my gift to you."

"The fuck she will," Ephraim murmured to himself. *No touching.* He noticed the same derision in Maliah's eyes as she continued to hold the position, with her ass jutted in the air.

He anticipated her first hit. Craved it with all of his being. No matter what delusions were going through Maliah's mind, Ephraim had never hurt her. Willingly or otherwise.

TEARS PRICKED HER EYES. The female Matrix had stolen her attention. Or rather, the thought of recalling the classic movies, after laying eyes on Atsun's getup. Black leather covered the sub's thin body, and it was silly. The whole Dom/sub thing had been silly to her. Until Atsun lit a match on her left ass cheek with a single swat of a leather paddle. Three would leave her sucking her thumb; seven would be the end of her life. But ten?

"What is your color, Pet?"

"Green." *Money green.* She thought about how Nori seemed nice.

Smack. Her ass jiggled. The second swat took away the desire to care for herself. She no longer needed money for food, shelter, or any of the other necessities of life. It was hard enough to make her want to find a street corner and a cardboard box. This was insufferable. She tried to focus on how many hits might satisfy Nori, without him threatening to pull the plug on her check.

"Your color, Pet?" Atsun shouted like her words had echoed a thousand times already.

Purple. Hurts so bad my skin has to be purple! "Grrr-greee-green."

"I appreciate your confidence, Pet. But I'm not so sure." Atsun's lips were pillow soft where Maliah's skin burned. The touch, though delightful, caused a tennis ball to lodge in Maliah's throat.

A woman was kissing her ass!

Every muscle in Maliah's body tensed. Atsun kissed the perimeter of Maliah's red mark. She whispered in her ear, "Ask me to enter you. Ask my tongue to go anywhere you'd like, and we can call it quits. Would you like my tongue to hide inside of that virgin asshole? The puckering of it is calling me."

Maliah stopped herself from shaking her head. She didn't want Atsun to look in her direction let alone offer her extra towels later. She lied, "Please don't stop, Mistress."

She met the woman's gaze. It had been hard, seasoned with insult, when Maliah denied her earlier, only to soften just now.

"Later please, Mistress," she asked, voice shaking. *Shit, that no-man-will-enter-me crap has come back to bite me in the ass!* "Please enter me later. I-I love this spanking."

No amount of beatings would help work Maliah way up to Atsun having a taste.

"Where is my Master?" Maliah screeched. Of all the times, she never expected to cling to the thought of having an owner. Yet, when she screamed for him, her heart didn't lurch. Hundreds of years of hatred for what her father's side of her family had gone through didn't line her belly. Her body sagged. The sinew holding her thigh and arm muscles together had deteriorated. Throat raw, she knew she couldn't succumb to more pain.

Maliah.

Needed.

Her.

Master.

"Twelve lashings," Nori said. "You were green all the way, Pet."

"Let me make you feel . . ." Atsun's glistening white skin, from the exertion of her spanking, was submerged in darkness.

The lights had gone out.

Maliah's pupils dilated as they went to the bedroom door. But her Dom had entered before she could see more than the width of his left shoulder. It was huge and extended into a muscular arm.

She'd asked for him, gone to a world belonging only to herself and Ephraim. Then she'd asked for *him*—a stranger to bail her out. She hadn't even known he was here, but he'd come right on time.

As her Dom neared, Maliah's body became malleable. The pain, still tangible, beckoned her. Maybe this was all a mind-fuck.

He had rights to her body that Nori and Atsun did not. Though his rights didn't include penetration, she'd rather fall to her knees for his pain than theirs.

He came to her, a dark figure, the outline of him perfect. She made out his other shoulder, the entire width of it. The sharpness of his jaw.

"Hey," she croaked.

He scooped her into his arms.

The door opened.

A morsel of light became her trainer and her maid's offering for the slightest of seconds. They left the room. But Maliah couldn't look up from her place nestled in her Dom's arms to see his face. She didn't have the strength.

"I'm thirsty."

He began to unzip his pants.

"I'm so thirsty," she groaned again, only to realize he was offering her more than she needed. Sustenance, as well as a drink. She started to suck on his cock. His hand, warm and callused, rubbed over her pain. Funny—though Atsun had palms softer than heaven, his felt a thousand times better. She sucked him, eager for nourishment. The girth of him ached at her jaw, but she focused on how her Master would fulfill her thirst. The thick veins in his cock made her want to pause, slither her tongue down over his princely dick. Cherish the powerful length and curve of him. But she had to survive. His cum would be the reason.

This hadn't been part of her contract. Maliah had learned that pleasing her Master, in turn, fulfilled her.

He came quick, nice, thick seed that spurted for ages. Quick for her because it counted, but perfect where it counted as her throat became glossed and soothed by his seed.

"Thank you," Maliah said, delighting in how he hadn't stopped rubbing her ass. She turned her body in his lap so that he continued to be her source of comfort. Her head in his lap, her hip on the padding.

"Will you talk to me?" she asked. "Please, Sir."

EVERY FIBER in his being hurt. He'd never cheated on Maliah. Never saw a girl—or a woman, when the time came —comparable to her.

But she'd taken comfort in a stranger.

He pressed the button to a control, hooked up to the lapel of his suit. The voice scrambler had been purchased by his assistant this afternoon. All those slight tweaks and adjustments and he hadn't thought of talking to her.

"Did you like the pain?" He let his fingers rove through her kinky strands, brushing it over the backs of his fingers.

Her body stiffened. She couldn't have recognized him, not with the hard automation of his tone.

Maliah's voice was lush like a cool breeze. "I was waiting for you."

His hand became a fist in her hair. And then he stopped. *You started this shit, Eph*, he reminded himself. The warmth of her body made it easy not to be ridiculously jealous of . . . himself.

"I have to hurt you now." His finger stroked down her

spine, to her ass cheeks, and he gripped one in his palm. The flesh was hot, and her sudden inhale warned that she was still in pain. "You'll love the hurt, Pet."

"How do you plan to hurt me?" Her tone was quiet, delectable, as if she were contemplating the deliciousness of it.

"I'll spank you if you ask." He hoped she could sense the underlying joke.

She did. She laughed softly. "Please spank me. Also, can I ask something of you, Sir?"

"Ask away, Pet."

"Do something to me that nobody has ever done."

HAD SHE HEARD HERSELF CORRECTLY? *Do something to me that nobody has ever done . . . Maliah, you are so stupid! He will hurt you.*

He had to be the same size as Ephraim. But she didn't know him. How the familiarity of him made all her fantasies come easily.

"Can I see you?" She had an urge to look into his eyes.

"No. You cannot." He moved her from his lap. A sudden pang of sadness overtook her. She'd expected pain from him. Physical hurt, yes. Emotional pain, no. Then Maliah recalled a scientific journal that she'd read. The gist of it was that women were intricately connected to the men they bedded. Men had it easy. Island hopping and bed-hopping were similar indulgences for males. For women, sex made them create connections where there weren't any. In Maliah's quest to save her learning center, she hadn't thought about connecting. The stranger pleased her.

He removed something from his pocket before allowing her to lie back into his lap.

"Can you sit on your ass?"

"Yes." It would hurt. She moved around, until the back of her head was in his lap instead of the side. Her ass cheeks began to scream.

"You're in pain, still." He rubbed his palm down the center of her breast. "Let's channel that hurt somewhere else, shall we?"

Thank goodness he couldn't see her smile. Maliah had the feeling that she'd commit to self-deprecation later. Now, she waited in anticipation.

His hands stroked across her breast, palms brushing over her hard nipples. And then she hitched. As promised, the hurt had redirected to her right nipple. Then the clamp bit down on her left nipple. Material from the clamp swayed over and nestled down her abdomen.

"Five-carat diamond tassels each. Now, they belong to you."

"Th-Thank you." That was very generous. She'd hawked off a lot to survive these days. As quick as the thought entered in her mind, he consumed her once more.

"Now, concentrate on this pain. We'll go back and apply it to your ass in a few minutes."

"Mmmm," she groaned. The thought of him applying the hurt back to her ass frayed her nerves.

"Stay with me, Pet." He applied his teeth around her side cleavage. The warmth of his breath jolted the lips of her pussy. How? She had no idea.

Nori had promised that she didn't know her body.

And her Dom had diminished her doubt.

He sucked and bit at the sides of her breast, then pulled at a chain.

"Ohhhh," she moaned. His hand went to her throat, clasped it tightly as he kissed the shout from her lips.

"Shhhh . . ." He encouraged. "This doesn't hurt; you love this pain."

He pulled at the other clamp. Maliah whimpered, biting her tongue against the need to holler.

"Tell your Master you love this pain," he ordered.

"I—I love this pain, Sir."

"Hands and knees," he gritted out. The automation of his voice was unearthly, steely.

She whimpered as he removed her from his lap. Maliah's body sagged.

"You were in perfect position earlier—for them. Not your Master?" He clucked his tongue.

I have no Master. Be glad that you please me! Body shaky, she pushed up. The Dom reached down, rubbed at the inside of her thigh.

"Please fuck me," she begged.

"You. Did. Not"—he stressed each word—"call me Master."

Grrr . . . okay, shit! "Fuck me, Master," she groaned, the craving consuming her resolve.

Ephraim's lips pulled into a smile. She hadn't been calling him "Master." Sir at times, but not Master. Now she desired a fuck? His hand wove its way up her thigh. "I'll fuck you after you love this new hurt I have planned."

His fingers moved along farther, caressing her glistening pussy. His thumb tapped softly at her puckered hole.

"You have so many fucking rules. There are so many beautiful delights of BDSM you denied yourself when creating your contract." He stopped himself from saying her name. "Now you want penetration."

"Yes," she begged.

"Yes, *what*?" His hand slammed down on the same target Atsun had earlier.

"Master," she screeched, and his hand slammed down again.

"We won't be playing those games. Those colors games. Everything I offer you is green, pleasant, good pain, little one."

"Yes, Master."

"I know your body, your limits," her Dom gritted out. This was against BDSM policy. But she was his.

He lubricated the butt plug while providing an order. "Place your head on the pillow. Keep your ass up. Keep all these pretty cheeks," he said while massaging the pain, "in my face, little one."

She complied, lifting her anus for his easy viewing. His mouth covered up her tiny hole, and he slithered his tongue around it.

———

A GASP TORE THROUGH HER, and Maliah lost position for a fraction of a second.

His hand slammed down, but she kept her ass up for his access this time.

"Better, little one." He groaned against the thickness of her rounded cheeks. Then something cool, hard met the tip of her sphincter. It couldn't be his mouth. That mouth of his had done glorious things to her.

Her ass resisted the lubricated butt plug. He rubbed a

hand over the small of her back, curbing her pain with his touch. The plug slowly worked its way inside of her.

Maliah breathed, fingers digging into the fur rug, her soul welcoming what her body worked at getting used to. Her anus clamped around the plug. Her Dom's tongue jutted between her labia. Pleasure and pain mingled into heady bliss, robbing her of oxygen, bringing her close to the edge. Damn, she was close to the brink all too soon. His mouth continued to slither inside her pussy, while he pressed the anal plug into her.

"Thank you for allowing me to have this first," he murmured, kissing one ass cheek after the other.

"You're welcome." Bliss blossomed across her body. Her Dom turned her over. He could tell that she was searching hard to detect his features.

"I'll only enter you on one condition, little one."

"Please, Master," she groaned, her pussy pulsating and begging for his cock.

"That I take you, with the plug still in your ass," he said, pulling on a clamp. Gone was the hurt. "You'll love the pain, *Sweets*."

Tormenting moments passed while he waited for Maliah to free her entire body to him. He thought to eat her pussy out, cajole her to it. But she spoke first.

"Please, Master," she said.

Ephraim's erection plunged into a tight, soaking wet vessel. Her pussy was so tight with the plug in her ass that it strangled his cock like their very first time. His thrusts came harder.

"You're so wet. Cum all over my cock . . ." *My sweet Maliah.*

Her cunt became his pleasure, sopping wet with each stroke. He forced the length of him inside her. His balls slamming against the anus plug. She clung to him, her erotic groaning transforming into a cry as she did as told. Her cum slicked his hard cock.

He was relentless, diving into her pussy. Each thrust sent his balls clapping against her clit. His lower abdomen slammed against the pearl ass plug. Her screams became pants, voice even more hoarse than it had been after Atsun's spankings. Ephraim picked up the pace, and her body arched for him, the access becoming better as the small of her back dipped. He plundered her magnificent pussy. The fleshy part of her ass jiggled when he gave it a good smack.

"Master," she growled low, her walls clamping down on him again. His hand grasped all over her buttocks. A pressure started low in his balls.

And then his cock pulsated inside of her. Maliah's body shook violently beneath him. Damn, but she was coming for a third time. This one matched the intensity of his ejaculation. As Ephraim came, he continued to plow his entire cock into her cunt, extending the length of his release. That first release in her mouth had built up to this—this never-ending eruption. He grunted, his weight dead on top of hers. He expected to pull himself up after his eruption ended, but she panted, "Please stay this time, Master."

10

Sweets. The Dom had called her *Sweets.* That endearing word belonged to none other than Ephraim Levine. Maliah knew every angle, every vein in his thick cock. When she'd sucked him dry to clear her throat earlier, she hadn't expected that huge cock had belonged to Ephraim! And it all added up.

The psychotic control he had over her even years later.

And *Sweets.*

Maliah told herself to be patient, to bait him. While she and her Dom were in the midst of foreplay, Maliah concentrated on one thought. If the Dom hadn't called her *Sweets,* there'd still be no dick penetration. The second he said the nickname, all the jumble of nerves in her body deflated. She knew her ex had created such a scandalous affair.

Dammit, Eph, you have always been my weakness! She drove home from the mansion that she had assumed belonged to Nori. It was Ephraim's place for fuck's sake. Her mind was consumed with the devious attorney.

He had people watch her. Still did after all those years.

But he'd played her when saying he'd seen her ass out one night. His people were smart enough to learn about Nori, without it having to include the convenience of being their first and only outing.

On her long ride home, their session roamed through her mind. She'd been lying when she said she wanted to be fucked. Of course, by Ephraim. This was guilt-free sex. No emotional ties. No wondering about him later . . .

Sweets had been the word to transition her from nipple clamps to continuing to appeal to his every whim.

They were sixteen and horny when Maliah had said they needed a better term for her sex. He had a vulgarity about him even then. Maybe it was a telltale sign to the whore of a man he'd eventually become. But she'd stopped him from referring to her lady bits with the "p-word."

"Then what should I call your pussy?" he'd asked, pushing a tendril of hair from her face.

"Sweets." She straddled him on top of her huge, comfy bed. There were unicorns and fluffy bears on the wall, but the girl in the bed, not so innocent. "Call me Sweets when you want it, Eph."

He gripped her hips, the palms of his hands not so callused then, more so tender as he caressed her skin. "Sweets," he had said.

"Yes. Call me that when you want to fuck, Ephraim. Even when my father is around. Doesn't matter. Call me Sweets."

He shook his head. He'd never understood that his last name meant more to Rick than Maliah ever would. Her dad had this obsession with image. And she had this obsession with the boy she'd grown up with.

Couldn't live without him.

Ephraim had glanced at the cracked door. He started to nudge her over, but she tightened her legs around him. "Would you like Sweets now, Eph?"

He groaned. His eyes flitted from the door, roamed over her body. Her fingers were over the buttons of her jean blouse, already plucking the fastenings apart. Ephraim reached up, cupped her breast, kissed her heart. "Sweets, I like that."

The moment the Dom called her that, she determined that giving in to him would mean the world to her.

"I guess I don't mind being a sub," she murmured, turning onto her street. The desire to please a Dom— Ephraim—encouraged her to do anything. That thought might sound contrary to her entire character, but he'd presented them with the perfect scenario. No ties. Just sex. Filthy, dirty sex that she was beginning to derive pleasure from.

Maliah's eyebrows knitted together. A Civic was parallel in front of her yard. Her neighbors weren't the Saturday-night party type. She pulled up behind. A second before she could kill the engine, Ephraim's cell phone number lit up on the radio screen.

Clearing her throat, she spoke nonchalantly. "Hello, Eph."

"I'll have Yesiv by within the hour."

"Rain check?"

"No."

We just left each other, you freaky fuck. "I probably sounded crazy earlier when I called. Thank you for the . . ." *Sex.* "Willingness to be there for me, Ephraim. We are—we can be good friends in the future. I see that now."

"A car will be there around seven. There will be a gift for you. You can choose to wear said gift. That is your only choice."

"Thanks for reminding me that you're an asshole." She chortled. "I've changed my mind, Ephraim. Let's say I was all caught up in something a little while ago. Almost killed me, in a good way, Eph. So no worries—I'm not going crazy now. Don't need any friendly chats either."

"See you soon."

She stared at the radio. The call had cut. An old SWV track was on low now.

MALIAH WENT INTO THE HOUSE. At the sound of voices, she simpered. Tonya hadn't left, which she didn't have a problem with. Extending the olive branch made the world go around. Though, if she were going to help the young woman, this wasn't it. Ephraim made her irritable. He stole the humbleness right out of her. She wasn't a good model for Tonya at this moment, not after Ephraim tried to switch up the rules. Fucking at the Hurt Room had been a brilliant idea? Why didn't the horny bastard get enough of her earlier? Dinner meant connections! They were past crap like that.

An elderly woman exited the bedroom, wearing jeans, a shirt, and ultra-padded sandals.

"I'm Lettie." She held out her hand.

Maliah shook it. "Maliah Porter."

"Hey, LeeLee. You look shocked." Tonya's head tilted as she walked out of the guest bedroom after Lettie. "This is Lettie. Ephraim has her helping me."

"Since when?"

"Well, after tossing my cookies Monday and Tuesday, I tried the rehabilitation center he suggested, while you were out on Wednesday."

"Oh," Maliah mused. "And here I thought you were home all alone this week. How? I brought you a few GED study packets on Wednesday."

"Yeah, because I walked in, saw a lifestyle that would make my eyes green, and walked my ass right back out. Then he got her for me. I thought . . . I'm so sorry. I know you said no people at your home, but—"

"Oh, that was very thoughtful of Ephraim. You saw him today?" She shoved a hand through her hair. The old friend of hers called jealousy wanted to work its way back into her life.

"No. Text. I haven't seen him since um, we came home from Miami. He's sent a few texts. Encouraging stuff. Oh, and he said to get you out of the house tonight." She stared at Maliah with a triumphant smile. "I'm not built for that life, but if you guys have leftovers, I wouldn't mind a shrimp."

Maliah rubbed a hand over her face.

"Oh, he's rich-boy kinky, huh? Too much?"

"I'll wait in the room." Lettie's cheeks reddened as she headed toward the extra bedroom.

"Tonya," Maliah gritted out.

She held up her hands. "I'm going to get back to my wellness coach. Your version of grown-folk business is too much for me."

Maliah pulled out her phone and texted him. '*You hired a wellness coach without my consent?*'

ALMOST AN HOUR LATER, Maliah had showered. Even while drying off, she'd glanced at her phone for a response. Now, the bastard was being deliberative. If he could command her Saturday mornings and he expected to have her again Saturday night, then . . . Maliah walked out of the misted bathroom and into her bedroom. She scampered back and picked up the cell phone from the quartz counter, just in case. In her room, she rummaged around for pajamas. After putting on a cotton pajama set, Maliah glanced at her cell phone screen for the umpteenth time. Nothing.

She and Tonya sat with bowls of Honey Nut Cheerios—the catalyst for "Miss Honey"—when there was a knock at the door.

"Hold that thought," she told Tonya.

"Oh, it's okay," Tonya replied as she started toward the front door. "We can talk GED math later."

"Now works for me." Maliah opened the door. She folded her arms in front of her, though she always wore a bra to sleep. She hadn't been gifted with perky tits and needed those suckers to stay up one way or another.

The driver she'd met before, who was about as thick as the door, gave a nod. "Miss Porter, ma'am . . . do you need time to get ready." Yesiv started to back away. "I can wait."

"No, don't wait."

"Eh, I actually have to." Though his size still intimidated her, he had a humble aura.

"I understand the pressure." She smiled. "I'll let him know that you can go."

"*Nyet*, um, please," he said to the sound of the door closing.

Maliah reclaimed her seat, lifting one foot under her thigh as she sat. She reached over and plucked up the GED booklet on math.

"Can we chat about that, LeeLee?" Tonya gestured.

"No."

"Or about you checking your phone every other second?"

"Not even." Maliah skimmed over the pages. "We've

talked fractions before, Tonya. What is the number one rule when needing both base numbers to match?"

The phone lit up. Tonya arched an eyebrow.

"Thanks," she murmured, picking it up. She read his message.

EPHRAIM: My driver is still at your place.

LEELEE: Not coming. Why don't you consult me before making moves?

EPHRAIM: Be there soon.

She started to type: *don't* but stood up.

"Sorry," she mouthed to Tonya, then sauntered toward her bedroom door. Maliah pressed the call button for Ephraim's contact. She bit her tongue from saying they'd seen each other today. When they were young, days and nights could pass away with her in his arms. "Why the life coach?"

"Why not?"

"Because—because you don't need to do things for me, Eph."

"My apologies. The life coach wasn't for you. You need one?"

"Don't get smart. You do one thing for me and expect a lewd act in return."

"And again, I'll imply that the life coach wasn't for you, Maliah."

"All right. But if I come to dinner, it's just dinner? No expectations?" She preferred him slapping her ass, claiming her breasts, hurting her. No opportunities for the future. At least this new agreement hadn't co-signed her to become the pure definition of insanity. She had him all right. Maliah might not be done meeting Ephraim Levine in the Hurt Room, but she'd had her fill for now. She just needed to keep a tight rein on her control.

"Just dinner," he lied to her.

"See you soon," she lied back. Her return of power meant that he'd be waiting a while . . .

11

THREE HOURS LATER, MALIAH STRUTTED ACROSS THE outdoor balcony of a rooftop hotel. Yes, that sounded bad enough, meeting Ephraim at a hotel when the Hurt Room was the only place she'd compromise her morals for her lust.

Twisted Tapas was a Spanish restaurant. The name had been tossed around by Maliah's rich friends and associates. She expected crowds of people, waiting to get in. The six-month reservation list had also been tossed around, like that was a good thing.

Maliah continued to walk. Instead of the slinky black number Ephraim had dropped off for her, she wore her favorite black dress. The one she'd worn fewer times than she had fingers on her hand. The one she'd worn to the token funeral of her father's older associates. Despite the reminder that there was no reviving their relationship, the dress received more than its share of compliments.

She did, however, pair it with the shoes. The bastard knew an esteemed, shiny stiletto. It was so quiet that Maliah could hear the sound of her heels clip-clopping off the ground. The entrance to Twisted Tapas was beyond a pool. The edge of the turquoise water was encased in glass that spilled off the side of the building. For a Saturday night, she'd expected elite hotel guests to be lounging around. This was a party hotel for the wealthy youngsters, twenty-year-old millionaires who wrote code and owned the tech world. They never slept.

At the wide entryway, she stopped, noticing the back of Ephraim. He was dressed in another famous suit. The sight of him did something to her heart.

He turned around and caught her with his gaze. Then his stride made it past impossible for her to flee.

"Thought I'd have to go get you myself."

"You made enough threats, Eph."

"You made enough promises," he gritted out.

Hips swaying, she stormed past him. The restaurant had an indoor/outdoor had blue lights twinkled down a high ceiling. It appeared like streams of water in a tropical oasis. The seats were turquoise leather with chrome studs. Acrylic paintings of white sands and Spanish shores were on the walls.

No people.

"Where is everyone?" She turned to glare.

"Rescheduled the entire night and meal comps."

"Why?"

"Because—" Ephraim cut himself off. Growling, he mussed with his thick, dark hair. For the slightest of seconds, he looked as shaken as her insides felt. "I required time alone with you, Maliah!"

There was so much more to that statement than what he'd said. Her eyelashes brushed across her cheeks for a moment. Damn him, he was putting her in the position to need to guard herself. She murmured, "You could've paid for drinking water for children in—"

"Give me a list of philanthropic endeavors later, Maliah. I can guarantee they'll all be handled."

"Aw, so you're like Daniel now?" She arched an eyebrow, praying her words had gotten under his skin. Mentioning their mutual childhood friend wasn't like bringing up another man in general. But the dynamic of it. Loving him had taken years away from her life, years best devoted to another man.

"Fuck no. Not like Daniel at all. He builds shit for people. Houses and stuff. I have better shit to do. I can toss my money at it though."

"You can't toss at me." She dared him with her gaze. Dared him to come clean about his devious antics with Nori.

Ephraim's fingers wove through hers, and he led her to a table in the center of the room. With many alcoves around the place, Maliah wondered what compelled the horny toad to sit in the center. Until she looked up.

The ceiling had been pulled back. Crystals rained from the sky. What could be the largest chandelier she'd ever seen in her life glittered above her. It was anchored down to mounts at various corners of the room. Above that were stars, a lot more than she'd seen in a while.

The clearing of the popular restaurant and his willingness to hijack the entire pool section stole her breath. Ephraim was doing it again, planting her at the center of his universe. She knew what lightning caught in a jar felt like—the epitome of luck.

"We don't get along anymore, Eph."

Ephraim circled her, standing too close. His soft breath tickled the hair at the back of her neck, his fingertips thrumming up her spine. "Are you done?" he asked, helping her into the seat.

"Done with what?" Maliah asked as the waiter came by with two bottles of clear liquid in his hands. He offered sparkling or spring water.

"Spring," she replied.

The waiter began to mention wine, spouting off about different vintages.

"Bring food," Ephraim ordered.

"Done with what, Eph?" she reiterated as the poor, unappreciated waiter started toward an open kitchen.

"Done accusing me of whatever conspiracies you have, Maliah?"

"So, I'm crazy?"

The wide planes of his shoulders lifted into a shrug.

"I'm not crazy. I know what I know."

"Cryptic." He shook his head with a soft chuckle. "Lee-Lee, that was cryptic as fuck."

The waiter had returned and announced their first course. Tiny bits of colorful art sat in the center of square saucers. The same situation played out for dish two. Maliah couldn't figure out why for the love of all things holy the place wasted so many dishes. Sure, the plump shrimp lying on a bed of caviar had made her moan while various flavors sparked in her mouth. But the awkward silence strained across her chest.

The third course was held in one hand. Maliah watched the waiter like a hawk as he moved across the room, his huge ears flushed, his face reading like their interaction was making his skin crawl too.

"Skirt steak with . . ." The waiter droned on about the famous chimichurri. The background music and the meat sizzling on a rectangular cast-iron skillet drowned out the silence.

Ephraim ate, and she glared at him. Finally, she spoke. "You have this way about you. Women love you at the simplest hello."

He scoffed. "You did cop an attitude when I was nice."

"Too nice," she blurted. *Dammit, LeeLee, you sound insecure. And that's not the real issue.*

Ephraim stuck a fork into his steak, then pointed at her. "You're about the most unforgiving woman I've ever met in my life."

"You're in denial. We don't make good friends let alone lovers. We argue."

"I remember the arguing." He slammed a hand down on the table. "But guess what, Maliah, I'll take that fucking mouth of yours over any woman. Any day!"

"You'd rather us together miserable."

"This is the dysfunction you brought me to, *Sweets*."

"You want Sweets!"

Ephraim's hand swiped across the table. Her body flushed hot at the sound of dishes crashing to her right.

Her Dom wanted sweets . . . Okay, so maybe they were improvising. The Hurt Room didn't have to be the spark for all their fun. Just as long as sex was the "period" to their relationship.

ANGER ROSE in him in waves. He'd gotten snarky with her a little. With other women, it was blunt to the point of burning. Such as, "I'm fucking tonight, baby." All the shit he said had a clause to it; no bang sessions would lead to anything more. Rarely did they even lead to round two. But Maliah had the pulse in his neck ticking the seconds he'd waited for her to arrive.

As the dishes went crashing to the ground, he caught the eye of the waiter. The death glare kept the idiot at bay.

"Show me my sweets," he ordered.

"Eph . . ." She glanced around. If she spotted the waiter, he'd kill the guy. "This place is wide open."

His eyes latched onto hers. Would she deny him now after consenting earlier? Consenting to a "stranger"?

"On the fucking table, Maliah. Do the splits." He reached across his arm around her waist. Again, this was where he didn't play BDSM rules. She was his. She had no limits; he had the say-so.

With his arm around Maliah's waist, Ephraim yanked her onto the glass table. His thumb grazed over her cheek, and he touched his lips to hers, slowing down for a slight second. "Can you still do the splits?"

"Of course!" she snapped. Everything offended her.

That was the magnitude to them going slow tonight. Chaos returned. On the glass table, Maliah started into position, her curvy limbs extending outward. He yanked the stretchy material of her dress up to her hips, leaving her fat ass on display behind her. Her hips were his to hold. He sat forward at the glass table. "Don't think I forgot you were to wear what I had brought to you, Maliah. Splits now!"

She moved into position, thick legs at her sides. He reached over, grabbed a steak knife from the ground, and tore the sides of her thong. Then he placed the part that covered her cunt into his mouth. Like a dog with a bone, he spoke. "Fuck the table, Maliah." Ephraim pushed his chair back and slid down onto the slick marble beneath the table.

"Good God," he murmured to himself. From his position, he watched her pussy pressed against the glass above.

So close, yet so unattainable. The sultry sight did something to his mind. Made him even more of a dirty man. "Get the table wet, Maliah. Get it good and dirty. I paid a shitload of money. Give these people something to clean."

"You're all about money," she shot back, though her hips started rocking. Her pussy pressed against the glass. He reached up and gave the glass a little lick, delirious about how good she tasted earlier. Ephraim chuckled, put his arms behind his head, and lay back. Soon she'd cum all over the table, while he had a first-row seat. Not just to her body, but to the workings of that tight little cunt. Her thick folds glistened along the glass, wetting it. But maybe he wouldn't have the waiter clean it off. The thought of that made him jealous.

THE COOL GLASS against her labia lessened the ache of wanting him—wanting him to take her so hard that walking would be an issue later. She worked her hips, legs fully split in half. Maliah concentrated on her pussy. How did it look with Ephraim watching her twerk below the table? Juices continued to flow. What did he think of that?

She slid back and forth, and the coolness of the glass disappeared, leaving her hot for him again.

"That's right, Maliah. Keep working that cunt on this glass table. You're getting it so wet. Get it dirty. Give me a reason to tip the motherfucker, Sweets!"

She grunted and groaned. Screwing the table made her feel weightless like the whole world had faded away.

"Flick your clit."

The thought hadn't crossed her mind. The only consideration she had was pleasing him. Her view was of the turquoise waters of the pool yards away, and the darkness as it descended over Greenwich. Damn, she was doing filthy things in her hometown. While she glanced across the way, Maliah pressed to fingers against her pearl and stroked.

"Ephraim, fuck, I'm-I'm-I'm coming on the table." Her statement sounded outrageous in her ears. But the truth was gliding all over the table. The entire restaurant was immaculate, except for the glass and food scattered to the side of her. She moaned, watching below her as Ephraim's hand slipped into his pants. Biting her lip, she let her fingers guide down between her coils, inside of her.

"I said flick, Sweets. Not fuck!"

She couldn't stop masturbating. She screamed, leaving a trail of sticky cream on the glass.

Ephraim came up from beneath the table. He rubbed the side of his hand across his mouth, spit out her thong. "You didn't listen."

"I'm sorry, Eph."

"You can make it up to me." He pulled her off the table and in front of him. Maliah's tiny fingers found their way between them. She pulled down his zipper titillatingly slow.

"I'll make it up . . ."

"Not that way." He stopped her from falling to her knees. "There's shards of glass down there, LeeLee. Clean this table for me."

"Clean it," she murmured, determining how to do his bidding.

"Yeah, I'm too jealous to let the waiter do it." His eyes roved over her face, searching for any sign of her denying him. One thing was true. He was envious as fuck. Of the waiter. Of *himself*—while at the Hurt Room. All those orgasms he'd given her. Finally, he had the pride of knowing that she *knew that he did this*! "Clean it with your mouth. Clean it with your mouth while I enter you."

His nasty words caused warmth to blossom in her stomach and rise across her chest. "Yes," she groaned. "I can do that for you."

Maliah placed her hands at the edge of the table, legs wide. Her ass jutted out, becoming more than accessible for him. Ephraim aligned his cock with the apex of her sex.

Maliah purred as his cock slithered against her throbbing lips. His hand wove around the back of her neck, gripping tight. He issued the order: "Lick all the sex off that table, Maliah."

Her tongue swiped over her juices at the same instant he plunged inside her pussy.

"Ephraim," she screeched, globs of cum all over her mouth.

Ephraim gripped her hips, arched his own to go deeper. He placed a hand around her waist, pulling her up. His cock still thrust against her core. He licked the fuck from her lips.

"Yeah, tastes so good." His tongue swiped over her bottom lip. In their position, his heartbeat slammed against her back, his cock so deep her pussy massaged it with tiny pulsing orgasmic waves.

After she came, Ephraim pulled out, letting the head of his cock nestle between her slit.

She mewed, unable to speak. Ass pressed back, she encouraged his desire. He claimed her slow this time, with her pussy eating his cock inch by inch.

"You've always been mine." His whisper glided over the back of her neck. Ephraim pressed his hand firmly against her lower back. The sweet scent of her cunt infused into her nostrils as Maliah was splayed across the table again. This time, her nipples became taut against the cool glass. He took her, in and out in a delectable rhythm. When her walls contracted one torturous last time, Ephraim came inside of her harder than he'd ever done before. They stayed frozen for a while. She didn't have a thought in the world, no desire to keep up scruples, not even a morsel of self-torment for allowing herself to be placed back under Ephraim's thumb.

His entire body was atop her as she dangled across the table. He kissed her shoulder. And as they stood up, close enough for him to keep control over her, his mouth descended on hers again.

12

THE INTENSITY OF EPHRAIM'S KISSES HAD LEFT HER FROZEN. Most men kissed a woman breathless as a means to get into their panties. Maliah, on the other hand, had come down from the high of being fucked by him. The passionate way his lips caressed hers, and then his tongue surged into her mouth, stole the air from her lungs. Had to be a crazy notion for her to concentrate on a silly kiss after all the crazy moves they'd made. But she lay beneath the softest sheets in the world, her mind becoming her worst, best enemy, her thoughts weighing out the good, the bad, the ugly.

All the years she'd spent in contemplation of them, and this one kiss left her stumped. She looked up at him as he slept. His dark hair, in the thickest of waves, short-cropped. His Jewish nose—she couldn't mind it, because those lips of his matched the intensity of it.

"If you're waking me up," he spoke in a grave, low voice.

Maliah jolted, fire burning her cheeks, though he chose not to open his eyes while he continued, "You could at least do it the right way."

Boisterous laughter flew through her lips. "The right

way? Oh, you mean sex. I gave you enough of that yester—last night, you freak."

The long, dark lashes against his cream-colored skin fluttered open. That kiss stole all her inhibitions again. Maliah craved it. They'd gone on to suck faces through the restaurant. She'd stopped touching him to argue about his pretentiousness for having a room key. His coffee orbs shined over her. "Last I recall, you were the freak."

"I have never been a freak."

He pointed a hand at her. "You stole my virginity, Maliah."

"That was a mutually beneficial moment. We stole from each other at the same time. You got better."

"You got wetter," Ephraim shot back.

The cheesy grin on her face faltered. As long as their banter stayed the same, without transforming into an argument, they'd survive.

"Sweets so wet and tight." He pawed at her hip and brought her close enough to skim her forehead. "I'm considering keeping you all weekend."

"It's Sunday, Eph. I can consent to that."

His eyes shed for a second. "Shit, it is. All week. Till the end of the month. Or will you give me forever, again? Second time's a charm?"

With a hard gasp, Maliah pushed away from him. Her forearms were between their bodies. He grabbed them, rolled on top of her. "What the fuck, LeeLee?"

"We were *married*, Eph."

He thumped his index finger against her chest.

"Ouch!" she screeched, pressing against him, but he controlled her harder.

"Oh, so we were married?" Ephraim gritted out. "You

forced us to get it annulled. Maliah Levine, I haven't the slightest idea why!"

"It's Porter."

"I guess. Most women keep your last name, with half your shit. I didn't require a prenup. If anything, I should've constructed a 'You belong to me, forever' clause. Seeing that Elvis wasn't good enough for our vows!"

"Let me go, Eph."

"No. I'm done listening to you. The greatest mistake I made was signing an annulment half a week later. Like we were some shit-brained celebrities who got lust mistaken with love."

"We're not having this conversation."

"How about this? My entire family is attorneys. Who constructed the document, Sweets?"

"Don't call me Sweets!" She wanted to scream the truth. Blaming someone other than them—other than *herself*—for their demise felt right.

"I can and I will, *Sweets*. You turned me into a sex fiend." He reached down to kiss her. Maliah's head twisted around. His fist caught a handful of her hair, and his teeth chewed into her bottom lip.

"Shhiiii . . ." she began. Ephraim's tongue darted into her mouth.

THE SLIGHT ZING of copper went into his mouth as his tongue swirled around hers. The grip on her hair tightened. Though he wanted to drag the truth out of her, Maliah became responsive. At the burst of her heart against his chest, Ephraim pushed all his weight onto his forearms and legs. Her soft breath tickled at his face.

"How long will you give me to show you that we can't live without each other, Maliah?"

She stared him straight in the eye. "Till next Saturday morning."

"So, do I need you to sign something that I have you this whole week? Seeing as your words hardly count anymore?" he snapped.

She reached over and picked up a notepad and pen, each with the hotel emblem. She scrawled over the paper and flicked it over to him. He caught it.

"Eph owns LeeLee, for an ENTIRE WEEK" was written at the top, her unintelligible signature below.

"Appreciate it. I'll keep this in my safe," he retorted.

Ephraim made a vow. If Maliah chose to return to the Hurt Room after the time they had together, she'd scream louder for him than she ever had. *Fuck twelve swats*, he told himself. *She'll get the punishment of her life.*

13

LATER THAT DAY, MALIAH WORE A NEW OUTFIT. EPHRAIM'S assistant, Rosa, had come by while she was in the shower. The women didn't have a chance to see each other, but Rosa knew her size of clothes all the way, down to the panties— well, except for her skirt size. Although, Maliah had a feeling Ephraim had something to do what that. She wore a vintage Biggie Smalls shirt. Her fuck-me skirt looked a lot like the plaid monstrosity that she'd always had to keep down in high school. Leather boots finished off a kick-ass look.

Maliah stood at the front of valet, waterfall pillars coasting down on either side of them. She folded her arms, gasped, and then pushed down the skirt.

"It's a good look for a speed demon like you, Maliah."

"Yeah right. I could max-out a speedometer in a hoodie." She hid a smile, although a chuckle was ready to let loose. "Are we robbing a bank? Wait, I'm the only one dressed like a punk rocker. Am *I* robbing a bank?"

She eyed him up and down. Though he wasn't in one of those suits that made women do a double take, his jeans and signature V-neck were enough to make her sigh. And he had on nice boots too.

"No. But you like fast rides—that outfit screams fast ride." He turned away from her, growling at how long the valet was taking.

A second later, a matte-black Lykan Hypersport floated toward them. The engine's purr sent her pussy lips in a tizzy of desire. Maliah gulped down the desire and cocked an eyebrow. "You honest to God have your harem of cars here? This was strategic—you want me to fuck you in this car!"

"*Supercars*, baby. You had the 'midlife, new sports car fetish' when we went to get our licenses, remember. I bought this for you."

She chuckled. They'd made their appointments at the same time. Ephraim had whispered in her ear about not having a "fat" foot on the gas pedal while they'd entered the DMV, one she'd vetted and selected as a bit more lenient than in their neighborhood.

"So, why do you have your cars here?" She popped his hip, since he was griping about valet not moving fast enough. "You don't have a home here . . ." *Come clean about the Hurt Room, dirty man.*

He smiled at her. "You threatened to burn a house down if I bought one in Greenwich, Maliah."

She sighed. "Yeah, I said all kinds of shit to get you to sign those annulment papers. But we made a promise not to talk about that a little less than an hour ago."

"So, then let's not talk about it." He gripped at her ass, kissed her forehead. "You hear the sound of that?"

Maliah murmured against Ephraim's lips. Their eyes connected while the Lykan Hypersport glided to a stop in front of them. Her gaze wrenched away to eye the black beauty.

"Nope. Keep your eyes on me, Sweets. Now, I remember why you liked road trips instead of Italy and South Africa."

"And Paris, and . . ." She delighted in the taste of his mouth. Then she squealed, "You're going to give me head while I drive, right?"

He tasted her mouth, whispering, "Long as I don't die."

"Did you ever?" Maliah pushed at his chest, grin wider than the sunshine. She strutted toward the valet as he got out of the car.

Ephraim walked around with her and gestured for the man to give her the keys. She took them and Ephraim's hand as he helped her lower into the car.

"Answer me, Eph."

"Almost. I almost died."

She looked up at him, brown gaze sparkling. "We've broken a lot of promises."

"You, not me," he corrected.

"Shhh. This one I plan to keep. I won't murder you with vehicular homicide, Ephraim. But you have to promise good head while I drive."

They clasped hands. He shook his head with a laugh, made sure her body was safe and closed the door.

The valet stood there, his ears burning red. He'd heard the entire exchange and mumbled, "I like her . . ."

"You and me both." Ephraim took a wad of money out of his pants pocket and handed it to him.

The passenger door closed a second before Maliah revved the engine. The ass of the supercar jolted into the sky; the front wheels skidding, sending smoke all around the ritzy hotel entrance. Ephraim locked eyes with Maliah. This was what he loved—the drug she became when she let him in.

"You're not going to tell me to stop scaring the rich folk?" she asked, continuing to rev the engine.

"The longer you go, the harder my tongue fucks your sweets."

She slowly nodded. "Eph, for the first time in my life, my whole heart agrees with you."

An attendant started toward them, no doubt prepared to ask her to stop adding tire marks to the marbled cement. Maliah kicked the shift into gear with her hand. The car zipped with precision along the curves of the hotel exit, taking each one to the limit.

"We get a ticket, you got it, right?"

He laughed. "The last ticket you got was with me—how did it get handled?"

She clicked her tongue. "Stop being a creeper, Eph. It's like telling me you've kept tabs on me is a show of how big your balls are."

"Or the truth is comparable to a reminder that the last time you saw me was also the last time you took a good, deep . . ."

"Don't say dick," she retorted, pulling onto the freeway in record time.

" . . . breath of air. You haven't breathed without me. You haven't lived."

She chortled. He hadn't taken his eyes off her as she commanded the big beast. Maliah's hand glided over the silver finishes of the gear shift's perfect phallic shape. She stroked the sensual beauty of it. Then she choked it, toggling it. There was a slight tension in her mouth before weaving around cars. The honks. The disarray. He must have experienced oodles of this disarray with sexy women in other countries. Although, he never allowed anyone to drive his babies. She had to believe he was just that anal-retentive that he didn't let anyone but her drive. She imagined convertibles filled with women, eager to please, daring as fuck. They didn't match her. They didn't match the intensity of Maliah Porter—his gaze told her that.

The chair hugged the sides of her body when she shifted and zipped by people. Working the gears, Maliah ordered, "Stop staring, Eph. I might clip someone's ride."

He sat back in the plush leather seat and asked, "Where are we going?"

"Not Vegas," she replied.

An hour into the ride, Maliah had dropped the top on this baby and tapped out the odometer. After the first cop car stopped them, Ephraim had gotten out.

They'd passed more cop cars, but none had stopped them. He'd done this before—showed her that the Funny Guy, who everyone loved, had power.

In upstate New York, they stopped for gas, and more importantly, gas station souvenirs. After the first year in dorms, Ephraim and Maliah had shared a townhome. Their refrigerator had had a magnet for every station they'd stopped at, the first being when they were sixteen. A license and a father who loved the ground the Levines walked on meant infinite freedom.

"I forgot the art of going slow," Maliah said while sliding the sleek, sexy ride into traffic. "I hate slow."

The tires screamed and smoked at each instance she had the chance to cut someone off.

"Let me remind you why slow is better."

She groaned. He said shit that would otherwise sound cheesy, except the lips of her pussy had started to sing. The frenzy in Maliah settled. She glared at a redhead in a mommy car, who was also glaring at her. Envious daggers were shot Maliah's way while Ephraim undid his seat belt and went down on her.

His nose nudged her clit. She slipped up her skirt, still staring at the mom with a smirk on her face.

"Eph, fuck me with your tongue," she begged. Her senses heightened as he took a leisure lap of her walls.

Maliah went twenty miles an hour—no complaints with him digging her pussy out with his tongue.

The warm rays of a setting sun on her face, she moaned and groaned loud enough for anyone with their window down to hear. Being with him did this to her. Put her into a trance. Made her forget inhibitions. Made her transform into an addicted slut.

She gripped the passenger headrest, screaming to the heavens. Ephraim's tongue stroked her core with all his worth.

"Eph—" Her throat caught in a loud screech. Maliah bathed his tongue with her sopping wet orgasm. Her hand rubbed at his short, thick hair. She grind her pussy down, giving her all to him. Half of her hoped he didn't suffocate down there; the other was indeed in slut mode. She rode bliss. Ephraim and a Lykan Hypersport were the perfect makings of euphoria. And then she was honked at again. This time didn't have to do with her cutting anyone off.

He sat up in his seat, orbs darkened as he dragged the back of his hand over his wet mouth. Ephraim growled, "Wherever the fuck are you taking us, Sweets?"

"Please wait," she asked. Before, while in the throne room of her favorite car, she'd toss a "just be patient." After the claiming he'd given her, Maliah felt like being nice. "It's a long drive, but you'll like it. Promise."

"Add a detour. I need you now." He placed his hand into his pants, fisting himself. "Find somewhere before I fucking explode, LeeLee."

Maliah's eyes flitted along the slow lane, though every lane had parking lot status. She placed on the hazards.

"Now, Maliah!" he barked.

THE SUN WAS STILL TOUCHING down on the horizon when Maliah slammed on the brakes. There were golden fields of sweet corn on either side of them. They'd moved into the thicket and away from the road, a short ways from Albany, New York. In 2.2 seconds, she had straddled Ephraim in the passenger seat, her juiced-up walls sliding the thick length of his cock. His hands gripped her hips, sending her farther down on him.

"No coming, Sweets," he growled in her ear. "I'll tell you the precise second you can cum."

The sound of his voice, the fire in his eyes were all the tantalizing she needed to give off a falsetto. A static of tiny orgasms spread through her.

Ephraim yanked her up. The crown of him lodged at her slit. "I said no coming!"

She pressed her mouth against his neck, sucking and licking. "I'm not strong enough, Eph . . ."

"Oh, but you are." His biceps braced, and he entered her one inch and then out.

"Ephraim, please," she groveled, her mouth muffled by the delicious taste of his neck. She breathed in testosterone and fine cologne. "I'm not strong enough."

With his arms hard as boulders, Ephraim gave her two torturous inches of his dick before lifting her off. Maliah gaped. He bit her breast through her blouse, and the pain made her howl and center her self-control. The submissive training came to the brunt of her thoughts. Her Dom had a requirement, and she had to fulfill it.

"No coming," he growled again. "You had your turn. I'll let you know when we can climax together."

With that, Ephraim tested her. He slammed his cock all the way to the hilt, the girth of him widening her. The length hurt and the width molded her. And he held her there for a moment.

Pink elephants, pink ele . . . Maliah thought. He pulled her up in the nick of time.

In appreciation, Ephraim pressed his lips against hers. He murmured against her mouth, "Good."

Again and again, Ephraim rammed her cunt down onto his cock. Each thrust sent a symphony of gush and wetness. Each languid thrust sent her in a tizzy as she attempted to remember pink elephants.

When he'd seemed satisfied that she wasn't going to cum all over his cock, without consent, Ephraim rested. He placed his hands back against the headrest and shifted the seat until he was in a semi-lying position. "Jump on my cock, Sweets." He leaned forward, clasped her throat, and squeezed it. "No coming."

Pink elephants hadn't made for a good enough motto. Maliah alternated to pink-and-yellow polka-dotted elephants while pumping his dick. It helped a little.

It may sound crazy, but Nori's words came back to her. "A submissive has one desire in the entire world: Please their Dom. Self-sacrifice, Pet. When all is said and done, the sub learns that her Dom has done more for her than she thought possible. All that sacrifice comes to fruition. Uncharted territories . . ."

Nori's speech continued at the back of her mind, each word a seed of encouragement.

Staving off the orgasm torpedoing through Maliah commanded every ounce of self-control. She'd had therapy for this shit at the age of seventeen. Exploding was all she wanted to do. *No, scratch that. Pleasing Eph is all I want to do.*

Her ass bucked and she stroked his cock with her pussy. Mist coated her skin as she worked him.

Ephraim leaned forward. His lips pulled into a naughty grin. The devil was playing *her.*

His mouth became pure bliss against her chest. He nipped and nibbled.

Purple . . . uh, pink. Pink and yellow . . . Maliah, you are stronger than this. The will to please her Dominant became her focus as his tongue slithered around her nipples.

"I hate you," she gritted out, bucking harder with the craving for him to cum. He'd let her cum, right?

His breath tickled her rock-hard nipples while he chuckled low in his abdominals.

"I hate you like, so much." She focused on that while riding him. "So much."

Ephraim's teeth clamped down on her nipple. Little did he know that the pain stalled the building climax. Or maybe he was a master manipulator at sex.

"Hate. Hate. Hate." She popped her ass with each word.

"Love. Love. Love." He nipped one breast, then the next —painfully hard.

His cock pounced against her cervix, and she took each thrust. Biting her lip, ass bucking, Maliah screamed. "Come, Eph, please cum."

Ephraim pulled the bulbous dome of his cock against her slit again. Then his hands gripped down on her hips. Ephraim buried his dick all the way inside of her.

"Come. Hard." His order unleashed tendrils of thrill in Maliah's body, like the first real exhale after a shitty day. Her muscles worked his hard cock, fingernails digging into his shoulders. Maliah ventured to heaven as he released into her body, their sexes coupling, loving each other.

The beauty of the male anatomy. His cock, which had been a piston, so powerful inside of her, slipped from her pussy. She wanted to lick his dick. Taste them. Coax the power back into it with her tongue. Though her thigh muscles screamed, and she had no desire to move. This had been work.

Ephraim and Maliah's heartbeats thundered against each other. She started to pull away, didn't need the reminder of how they didn't work.

"Don't." He groaned against her slick skin.

Her body melded farther into his. Maliah closed her eyes and prayed that she could go back to the start. All the counseling in the world couldn't fix how she'd ruined them. And she'd tried. Spent a good portion of her dad's fortune to fix *herself.*

Ephraim had never been the problem.

Maliah held that title. The Shitty Person In An Ended Relationship. She was the bad in them. Her and her alone.

14

EPHRAIM GOT OUT OF THE CAR. BRIGHT LIGHTS FLOODED THE dark sky, illuminating the parking lot. Fog puffed up and out of his lips as he sighed. They were too late.

They'd stopped for dinner a little after having sex in the rural area of New York. Then he'd forced her to get some rest having figured out where they were headed.

A magnet from Niagara Falls never graced their college fridge. The one time they'd prepared to go, Maliah's grand-parents had been in an accident. A train derailed, and her grandfather had died on the operating table. Granny followed with a crushed lung and a broken heart.

He knew what this meant to her, but they'd missed the midnight tour by a long shot. Three cars were in the lot: theirs, an old Mercury with a "security" emblem on the door and a sleeping guard in the driver's side, and one other late-model sedan. There was a continuous stream of rushing water in the background. Ephraim glanced back at Maliah; she hadn't moved. He headed toward the single-story building.

Before he could press the bar along the door, the door

swung open. A young woman with groggy eyes perked up at the side of him. And not like most other women did. She looked over him wearily, and then her blue gaze went to the security guard, her mouth set in a smirk.

"Get lost."

"I'll pay you for a tour—"

"No, thank you."

As his hand went to his pocket for cash, hers went to her pocket. He determined that creeping out the sole tour guide around was a bad idea. Maliah had asked for the tour tonight. She'd been half-asleep while murmuring about it. Waiting until tomorrow night would work. But Ephraim had only ever caved to her desires.

He held his palms out and proceeded to compel to the stranger's sense of humanity. "My wife and I are on our honeymoon. The flight was delayed, and we don't have a hotel yet. Would you please . . ."

"Oh please," she snorted. "Sports cars cost more than my entire lineage has spent in a lifetime. Flight delayed, my ass. No ring. That woman in your car is probably a prostitute. You all want to get your kicks at the top of the falls. Seen it before."

"No. She's not a prostitute." He growled at the barely twentysomething—if that. "We aren't married anymore. I love her more than anything in this world, kid." Ephraim followed the tour guide toward her car, keeping a distance.

"You're still in love with your ex-wife—pathetic." She stopped the chuckle. "So, you're busting moves to get her back."

"Every one of 'em. We were supposed to come here on her eighteenth birthday. We were freshmen in college—"

"I'm bored already." She took her keys from a ratty, beaded purse, the kind that should've met its demise in the

'80s. She pushed one of the keys into the keyhole, ancient tactics allowing him a few more seconds to grovel.

"We were an hour away," he said, cutting off the part that they'd stopped to bone. "Her grandparents died."

The door creaked open. "Pretty good sob story."

"True story. We had a refrigerator covered with magnets too. I can show you the exact spot that the Niagara Falls magnet would have been." He had her attention, but not fully. He opened his phone and scrolled to the photo application.

Heavy lights blared in their direction. "You okay, Beverly?"

"Thanks for giving the rich freak my name, Wendell," she shot back.

"But are you okay?" His voice carried over the sound of water.

"Yes!" Beverly chuckled and addressed Ephraim. "As if he was going to hop his ass out of the car. Show me the photo."

He had pictures of them uploaded to every iPhone he'd gotten in the past. Ephraim showed her the picture of their old refrigerator. It wasn't as if he'd deliberately taken a photo of it. Maliah had been making Granny's famous banana pudding during sophomore year. Her cotton pajama pants stopped where her ass cupped to perfection.

"Oh, I'm seeing lots. Actually, TMI, but since this can't be unseen, show me." Beverly chortled. "Where?"

"Right there." He pointed to a space on the stainless-steel door. For someone who had claimed to be so sleepy, Beverly was nosier than anything.

"Okay, how much?"

He grabbed the entire roll from his wallet and handed it over.

"I'm really not about the money," the teen said, pocketing the wad. "So, all this will get ya the grand tour, and it's too late to ask for change."

"I don't need it."

"What are you waiting for? Go get wifey."

―――――――

Maliah was cajoled out of comforting bliss. Her eyes fluttered open. She groaned as Ephraim kissed her.

"Your tour awaits, LeeLee." A rapid-fire of kisses blossomed across her face. Felt so good, but she groaned. She thought she'd been speaking, telling him that tomorrow would have to do, but he didn't stop kissing her.

"LeeLee, get up, baby."

"I won't make it," she moaned. Her tone was a lot more coherent as she added, "Need a few more hours. Just a few."

He wrapped an arm beneath her knees and behind her back, scooping her into his arms. The misted chill of the night sent the tiny hairs rising on her arms. The constant fall of water also helped pull her into the present as he carried her somewhere.

With her gaze shaded, Maliah was content to stay in his arms.

"Hello, wifey," a sarcastic yet upbeat tone called out.

Maliah glanced around. Her gaze adjusted to the streetlamps.

"I am Beverly Hills—don't get any bright ideas. I may be the rookie at this here comp'ny, but I promise my comebacks are better than anyone else I've ever met or ever will." The woman had to be nineteen tops. She removed her hands from her cardigan and started pointing around. Hands poised like a flight attendant, she explained different things. Her demeanor made Maliah smile. "First, let's get the heck out of this parking lot, shall we."

After a walk through the lot and behind the building, Maliah caressed a hand over Ephraim's jaw. "I can get down, now."

He was reluctant as he placed her down onto her own two feet.

"I had a feeling you could walk, wifey."

Maliah leaned into Ephraim as they followed. "Should you tell her that little bit of slang went out of style already?"

"I can hear you, wifey." The guide spun on her heels, held up a hand. "Maybe wifey isn't slang; it might be a metaphor."

"For what?" She arched an eyebrow.

The narrowing of Beverly's eyes read crystal clear as she said, "For wife."

Maliah shot a glower at Ephraim. He squeezed her hands subtly.

This time when Beverly whirled around to lead them up some steps, Maliah whispered in an even lower voice, "Can I have the keys?"

He cocked an eyebrow but complied.

Maliah tossed the keys up and caught them in her hand. "She tries to kill us, I'm pushing you in her direction and taking off running."

———

THE NIGHT never ended for them. It segued into Monday morning, with Maliah in Ephraim's arms. Beverly had left after an hour. She'd come back though, obnoxious when sharing her presence as they canoodled and kissed. The odd tour guide had handed Maliah a refrigerator magnet and given them a blanket, then left.

Resting her head back against Ephraim, Maliah glanced down at the rush of water. Their bodies were wedged into an alcove, in a blanket. They'd gotten used to the cement ledge, which was a few feet away from the plunging water.

"What's on your mind, Sweets."

"Oh hell no." She grinned. "No calling me Sweets. Not right now. LeeLee works; Maliah is also an adequate choice."

"LeeLee is for when you remind me of the girl I fell in love with. Can't call her Sweets. She had pigtails and was playing in her front yard."

She expected him to press a massive boner against her. He held her tighter. It was enough for Maliah to know Ephraim would pay a penny for her thoughts.

"I'm supposed to be fighting traffic, headed in on a Monday morning."

"You promised me a week. Till Sunday morning." He patted his pocket, where the piece of paper would stay.

"Saturday constitutes the end of the week, Eph," she murmured. If she stayed with him through Sunday, her Saturday morning training at the Hurt Room would have to be . . . postponed, terminated—she did not have the slightest idea.

Ephraim saved her from a whole lot of unnecessary self-contemplation. He asked, "Tell me about the kids at We Rise."

"Three of last year's participants are at UCLA." She spouted off various colleges. "We have a published poet in our roster now. Oh, and one of the girls was admitted to—"

"MIT."

"How do you know, Eph?" She lay on her hip. Even with the thick blanket, the cement crushed at her bones a little.

"When you said girls, I figured." He kissed her. "Your website photo sucks."

She pressed away from him with a laugh. Neither of her parents had commented on her website. She'd worn a blouse, pearl buttons to the throat, a three-strand pearl and earring set. Neither of her parents knew how well the youth were once they left We Rise Learning Center. Ephraim hadn't guessed—he'd read about their super-success stories.

She kissed him so hard her brain became dizzy for lack of oxygen. "Ephraim," she groaned against his mouth.

"Yes?"

"Find somewhere for us to stay. I need you now."

"Now, Sweets? You need me now?" He started to fist her hair. The mere action was the facilitator for his domination of her body.

"Not so fast." Maliah rolled away from him. It was time to go because against better judgment, her body craved his.

15

JASPER, CANADA

GIVEN THE NEED TO USE A SINGLE WORD TO DESCRIBE Ephraim Levine as it pertained to Maliah Porter, she'd use "insatiable." Being the center of his universe had never been far from the back of her mind. The man bottled the essence of love and handed it to her. Every single day of their life together, he'd handed it to her. Well, after she'd learned that he was too shy to speak. Yes, from that point forward, love blossomed for them. It was unfathomable how she'd had his love for years and let it go. The list of his qualities had always been stilted in her favor. And she'd done the unthinkable. Let another person in her head—toy with their love. Then that person had screwed the life they'd come to know. Bleed the love right out of them.

But Maliah knew that outside forces weren't an object when she had a solid foundation. She'd make it up to him starting now. Maliah's fingertips grazed across the taut skin of Ephraim's chest and twirled across the dash of dark hair. His hum vibrated deep in his bones across the vast bedroom of their bungalow. The place had all the makings of home, with milk glass vases and woven tapestries on the wall. With all the bedroom's rustic comforts, Ephraim lay like a king.

Where the amenities lacked, they'd declared to make it all back up by loving each other. No television, phones. They only allowed the outside world in when they needed to take a deep breath.

Her pillow-soft lips pressed kisses on his erection, standing proud like a tower before her gaze.

"Maliah," he groaned. "Suck me."

Up and down his cock again, Maliah continued to bestow tiny kisses. At his balls, she gave the perineum some love before widening her mouth enough to suck each one. When she reached the head of him, she tasted the tip. Coated along her tongue were a few little drops that promised so much more once she finished him. Wishing his cock slammed into her pussy instead of her throat, Maliah flicked her tongue against his dick. She brought him to the back of her throat, got him good and slobbery. Then she flicked at his cock with her tongue again, relishing how time meant nothing here.

Ephraim grabbed her hair and pulled her off. He leaned up, his lips savage against hers. "You enjoying yourself?"

"Hell yes."

"Then do what I said, Maliah." He nestled back. Beautiful muscles claimed his pillows, her pillows, the whole damn bed. An aura of royalty surrounded him.

She got back to her knees and sucked him into her mouth like a vacuum. His massive limbs stiffened beneath her.

"My balls, Maliah. Love them," he demanded. "No fucking teeth either."

Completing his commands sent a super-wet stamp of approval between Maliah's legs. Her tongue glided over one fat ball, and she slowly enveloped the monstrosity with her mouth, then the other. She flicked each sac, then returned her attention to the king. His cock, from which all her pleasure derived. The shape was perfect in length, the girth enough to test her skills as she took the tip of him in. Maliah determined that the underside of his cock needed attention. Her tongue skidded up and down.

"That's right, suck my cock, Sweets," he growled. "Get sloppy."

The sounds of her sucking and stroking got louder, messy, wet. The resistance at the back of her throat gave less slack as she sucked.

"Put that ass in my face, Maliah. But don't you dare remove your lips from my dick."

She'd been so busy with a desire to please him that Maliah had begun to neglect herself. The command did something to her body, her walls shuddering tight, desire building within her thick folds. With her insides on fire for him, she continued to work his thick cock in her mouth while moving around on the bed. She concentrated on moving into 69 position, without skimming his shaft. Every movement she made scared her. Fear heightened at how he'd react, Maliah moved slowly, her mouth full and her pussy gushing, ready for action too. Once her knee was near Ephraim's ear, he gripped her about the waist and planted her straight onto his face. She straddled him. With her mouth full of cock and his mouth pressed against her mound, she ceased. Her dirty, moist mouth came up, a full-blown grin creasing her cheeks.

Then her labia was abandoned. Ephraim's growl teased against her throbbing clit as he threatened, "You stop, I stop."

"Sorry," she moaned, taking a mouthful of his thick

cock. Hips twirling on his tongue, and her tongue hard at work, Maliah caught a stride, her thick lips gliding up and down. She came hard and fast on his beautiful face. Ephraim's hands clamped around her hips, forcing her to gyrate on his face faster.

"Fu-fuck," she screeched.

"No stopping." His tongue ceased its assault on her pussy.

"S-sorry." She latched onto him, sucking for dear life. Could feel his abdominals vibrate into a laugh before his warm mouth took her once more.

Ephraim's sensuous mouth worked magic. Maliah pumped her hips down onto his face and wrapped her whole mouth around his cock. Her lips were a tight O halfway down his cock, when Ephraim sat up. The movement sent her face down, ass in the air—and not in doggy style. Her entire body was upside down, thighs hooked over his shoulders. Blood rushed to her head, and she gobbled at his cock.

EPHRAIM HELD HER IN POSITION, with her still straddling his face as he sat up in bed. He gripped at her hips, pumping her down harder onto his member with one bicep. He needed her to go deeper. She wasn't going deep enough. The craving for her hurt so bad that he commanded all control. The change in position had startled Maliah enough to send his cock bruising the back of her throat. And that had felt like heaven. He needed more of it. She'd grazed him with her teeth once, and she'd pay. When she'd least expected it, she'd pay.

"Perfect, baby. Keep face fucking my cock, Maliah. And

I'll keep face fucking your cunt." He growled before diving back inside her slit. Maliah's pussy grabbed at his tongue; she was milking him every time he made a command. He knew she loved being his bad girl. She started sucking the contents of his balls through his cock.

Ephraim was amazed by her clit, and he sucked on it, flicked at it. The beautiful little nub made wetness rain down on his face. He got some good eats. He pressed his mouth over her outer folds, licked all the sweets from them. Ephraim repeated the same meticulous process with her inner folds. His tongue coaxed her orgasm, but her cunt continued to rain down more sweets. Ephraim used his arm around her waist, pumping her mouth up and down his cock. Her body was glorious, and he was a professional at pleasing her while she pleased him. Their moaning and groaning filled the room, sounding as good to his ears as when she'd been slobbering all over his dick head earlier. Her walls contracted on his tongue as she came. The greedy way she continued sucking on him made Ephraim's chest flair with pride. He cleaned every corner of her cunt.

Now it was time for payback.

She'd bit him a little with her teeth.

He'd bite her a lot.

Ephraim's teeth went vampire crazy on her ass cheek, and he bucked and slammed his cock at the back of her throat. While his teeth continued to sink into Maliah's buttock, his sticky cum sprayed all over her tonsils.

MALIAH FELT his teeth sinking into her flesh. Being that she was upside down, she held on to the scream that ripped through her body. The pain radiated across her flesh. She knew he'd bitten down hard enough to leave a brand. But the power of his cum squirting into her mouth sent her into another climax. Her pussy walls were sopped up as Ephraim laid her down. Her body ended at the foot of the bed, her face a lot closer to his beautiful cock than anything else. She couldn't help but love how he never truly went flaccid. His meat was always pretty, so she chewed her lip and stared at it. Her slick body was quenched and too exhausted to bring his semi-hard shaft back to attention.

Ephraim twined his fingers into her hair, fisted through her kinks, and then massaged at her scalp. The tender touch reminded Maliah of her plans of recompense for all the years she'd hurt him. All the years she'd pushed him away. She climbed off the bed.

"Damn." His voice was deep, low, and sexy.

"What?"

"You're supposed to be tired."

On key, her body arched, and she sighed. Maliah felt his eyes glued to every inch of her frame. The small of her waist, the apple of her ass as she curved into a yawn. "See, tired."

"Then what are you doing, now?" He cupped a pillow to his body. Hers again.

"Eph, you literally know I had a move planned before I even made it. Maybe I had to use the restroom." She winked and went across the room toward a tweed eggshell-colored sofa. She shoveled through a few bags from a Canadian store that reminded her of a Target supercenter. The refrigerator had been stocked, and they'd bought a few garments and toiletries. Maliah seized a travel-sized bottle of lotion that she'd grabbed last minute at checkout. The scent was generic, far from erotic lotions and lace, but a back massage was a good place to start.

At the foot of the bed, Maliah twirled her finger. He arched an eyebrow.

"You scared, Eph?" She grinned, not showing the contents in her hand.

"If that's lubricant, you'll regret it," he shot back, turning over.

The sight of his back muscles and his ass sent a heavenly sigh rolling through Maliah. She moved on her hands and knees, then straddled his back. Next, she reached over the side of his shoulder and showed him the tiny bottle of lotion.

"Not the sexiest lotion there is," she murmured, "but do I have the okay?"

"Yes, you may," he replied.

"Thank you—" Maliah cut herself off. Was it too soon to call him Sir?

She applied the cool lavender scent to her palm, then rubbed her fingers together. Friction warmed them up some before Maliah placed her hands against the center of his back. His firm physique molded beneath her fingertips as she worked her palms into him. A deep sigh of satisfaction groaned through Ephraim. She worked her way up to his trapezius and kneaded at his shoulders. For a while, Maliah became lost in touching him. The guilt of causing him hurt for so long wormed its way to the recesses of her mind. *I love you so much, Ephraim. Always have*, she thought. Maliah applied more of the lotion to her palms, and her hands worked their magic.

"What are you doing to me?" He groaned, turning over.

"I'm topping," she said, without consideration. Per Nori, it meant that a submissive seized the moment during a scene. Her fingers pressed against his chest, and she continued to manipulate his tan skin.

Ephraim placed his hands over hers, stopping the soft strokes. Even with her straddling him, he was able to push up into a seated position. "How do you know about that term, Maliah?"

"Don't play me for a fool, Eph. You've gotten your kicks in reminding me of your ultimate power. How you've had access to me for years." *My mistake for bringing it up, but you know good and damn well my knowledge of BDSM.*

She paused, met his gaze, and then waited for him to come clean.

"I'm keeping you until Sunday." Ephraim climbed out of the bed and onto the plush-pile carpet. "Say something, and I'll let you go on the day after forever."

She watched his retreat into the luxury bathroom. While the place needed updating, the bath had a massive shower with marble tile. The kitchen was the next eye-catcher, and the master suite had a balcony to a spectacular view.

At the sound of the rainfall shower-head turning on in the bathroom, Maliah simpered. He was avoiding her.

She returned to the bags on the sofa. She'd tossed the Niagara Falls magnet inside and thought she'd seen it while digging for the lotion. A faux-silk robe met her fingers. She placed it on, then continued her search.

Maliah plucked up the magnet and started onto the balcony. It was early morning, and she burrowed tighter into the robe, wishing she'd gone for comfort instead of sexy. But the beauty outside was enough to suffer. The area spanned across the entire bungalow. It had been the selling point for her. They could've stayed at a five-star hotel somewhere else in Canada, but she needed Ephraim. Needed him alone so that she'd have time to make amends. Now, to think, the first time she'd step outside on the balcony was on her own.

The sight was enough to take her breath away. Nature

abounded, trees jutting into the sides of the mountains. Through the branches, she saw steam fizzling up from natural hot springs about a half-mile away. Maliah took a deep breath of fresh air as she waited for Ephraim. He had to realize that the Hurt Room and Nori were equations that he alone added to their lives. Though she had no right to be angry with him. So, she sat and looked at the magnet, remembering her reason for the obsession. Ephraim had fed into those needs before. He'd given her the world.

16

"You know, son." Rick patted his hand over a fourteen-year-old Ephraim's shoulder. He glanced across the table filled with every staple for Sunday dinner. Fried chicken, roast, macaroni and cheese, black-eyed peas—the list went on. Dishes were piled along Maliah's granny's yellow, weathering lace line. "This might not be up to par for you, but we can promise you good eats."

Maliah rolled her eyes. Every time her dad talked down about something they had to lift up Ephraim, he'd start with "You know, son." And he'd only had one daughter. Since she was seated on the opposite side of Ephraim and closer to Granny, Maliah held his hand under the table. She engaged in a sidebar conversation with Granny before her dad said anything else. And he had lots to say to Ephraim.

After an hour of "well, you know, son," with Rick dominating the conversation, Ephraim followed her into the kitchen.

"I'll help wash," he said, shoving a hand through his thick hair. "Is your dad following me?"

"Good call, Eph." Maliah chuckled and shook her head no. She'd been embarrassed at first but now was a little sorry for

Ephraim. If her father treated a wealthy lawyer's son with such adulation, how would he treat true royalty?

He stopped inside of the kitchen, his eyes glued to an ancient refrigerator. Magnets covered every inch of the teal blue surface. He mumbled, "Wow! What's with all the magnets?"

Granny sidled up to his side, entering with an empty charger. "Proof that I lived, and I ain't done living yet," she said to him. Her weathered hand took hold of his, and she guided him around to the side of the refrigerator and then the other. "I love my country, so I started with the States first. Also, I needed a little more change in the bank to go to some of these other places."

"That's a lot of places," he said.

"Each one tied to a good memory," Granny assured him. She started toward the soapy suds in the sink.

Ephraim continued to look at the magnets. He took Maliah's hand in his. "We'll have our time, Maliah."

She stared at him, chewed her lip.

"All my best memories are with you. What about you, LeeLee?"

She gulped, her eyes trailing over to Granny, who had started humming. Maliah could see the side of Granny's profile had formed into a bright smile. Shyness crept up her cheeks. While she wanted to shout yes, she whispered, "Yes, Eph, all my best times are with you."

Granny chortled. "Maliah, you aren't shy at all. So go ahead and make your promises. Don't worry 'bout me."

MALIAH STOPPED TWIRLING the magnet around in her hand and looked up at her reason to smile. Although she didn't want to, the edges of her lips crept up at the sides. Water dripped down Ephraim's muscular body as he stood on the balcony. His breath puffed out in the cold air.

"Eph, you're going to catch a cold," she reprimanded.

He squatted down in front of her, his cock almost touching the cherrywood floor. His hand skimmed the side of her face. "LeeLee, is my time running out with you?"

Her gaze cast across the forest, her senses heightened. Birds chirped, the wind bristled across the branches. And the man she never stopped loving had an impossible question for her to answer.

"I have that slip of paper. Your new promise to give me a week," he said, his thumb pressing across her lips. "But you saw me crazy before. You know what type of person I turned into after you left."

Maliah groaned. She was a fly with its wings pinched.

"I've missed everything about you. Even with you here right now, I miss all the time we can't get back," he growled. She silently prayed that he'd stop talking, kiss her. Kiss away any inquiries that he had. Fuck away any expectations. But his words were tender and heavy with emotion. "I knew the day you graduated with your master's. Attended the commencement."

"You did?"

"In a crowd full of people, Maliah. I knew the second you opened We Rise Learning Center."

She smiled. "Your mom came for almost a month to volunteer read. Brought pastries. She still comes ever so often during the school year."

"Damn, I only had my people watch you and tried to figure out how to help fund your nonprofit. But you wouldn't take anything from me or my family."

"I broke up with you all." She glanced down to the ground.

"You don't have to tell me why we didn't work, at least not today, Maliah. All I need you to know is that I've only ever seen you as mine." His thump tipped at her chin. "You went on six dates since—since I signed your fucking annulment papers. Three of them ended a few minutes into the date. One of which I allowed to be completed because"—he shrugged—"the motherfucker wasn't your type. The investigator cornered the other two in the men's bathroom."

She gasped, smiling wide. "Oh, so that's why I was stood up in the middle of the date. One of those dates, I got left with the bill, Eph. The waitress felt sorry for me and let me slide—wait . . . Damn, that was all you're doing?"

"Yeah, you're welcome. I paid for you and some shit-face's dinner. That's what happens when you deny me, Maliah. Stop denying me because after this week, if I can't have you, there won't be any half dates. No nothing. You'll know my misery."

"Your misery." She almost chuckled at that, but his sincerity toiled her guilt.

"I've known everything except for what's going on in here." Ephraim pressed his reverent lips to her forehead. "When you're ready, tell me what's going on here. Tell me so that we can work through it."

Silence slipped between them. Although he was face-to-face with her, Maliah chewed her lip. She noted a flash of hurt in his eyes. Ephraim had shared so much with her, and she clammed up. He saved her from this moment by cocking his head. She stood a head beneath him. Ephraim placed her hands into his, gestured toward the magnet. "How about you and I make more memories?"

"Thank you," she murmured, following his lead. They had later for truths. A whole lot later.

17

STAYING AT THE AIRBNB MIGHT AS WELL HAVE BEEN A KEY TO an alternate dimension. By Wednesday, their uncanny twilight zone included "no bickering."

They'd hit their stride by cooking breakfast together. Long walks toward the Canadian Rockies and conversation took precedence. The hot springs offered another setting for the plentiful sex that they refused to get enough of. Maliah laughed so hard at what he'd said one morning during a walk. A flock of birds took flight in the trees above. Everything she missed about him came flooding back into her life —like the fact she hadn't laughed like that since the last time he'd made her laugh.

She awoke a little earlier than their usual cooking time to check her emails and have a quick chat with Tonya. Maliah sat at the couch. Though the thing wasn't eye-catching and hadn't made it into the owner's B&B photos, the lumpy seats were a lot cozier than she anticipated.

Her eyebrows furrowed as she read over an email from the site supervisor at We Rise. She dialed the number. "Hey, Rina, what's going on?"

"There was a shoot-out a few blocks down. We had to close the building today."

"What? Oh my God," she murmured. "Did anyone get hurt?"

"No. Just our people reminding the world to perceive us *all* in the same negative light."

"Rina, I-I can come back."

"Hell no, Maliah, excuse my French. Summers are the hardest. We don't get grants. If we were working at a school, I'd be doing Lyft today." She chuckled. "I'd have all my degrees sitting in the windowsill, hoping it compelled people to pay me my *worth*. You keep the doors open and still pay us."

Maliah recalled the last time there was a shooting in the neighborhood. Her heart clenched at the thought of some of the students' responses. There were those with flat affects, in which the scenario had already become the norm to them. The other children were so shaken up it hurt to breathe. Maliah didn't know which was worse. "But are the kids—"

"Boss, enjoy your vacation. Tomorrow is the last day for us. We go dark next week. Let the kids and their families prepare for the new school year anyway."

That word, *worth*, echoed into Maliah's ears. The youth We Rise Learning Center helped were worth so much more than the actions surrounding them. She looked up to see Ephraim at the bottom of the stairs, in a pair of navy blue sweats.

Rina spoke into the receiver. "Hello, Maliah?"

Maliah took a pensive bite of her lip, offering Ephraim a half-smile. "I'm still here, Rina. I can be there . . ."

"No, no, no. We're preparing an automated broadcast to

send to the entire phone list. We have tomorrow. Friday is the last day for black and brown folk to act like our ancestors worked hard for better."

"Okay, thanks." She gave a weak grin while hanging up. "Sorry."

"What happened? Do we need to go?" He seemed more sincere and willing to do her bidding now than he did about letting her go on Saturday morning.

What am I going to do about the Hurt Room? Maliah knew the answer to that. She spoke up. "There was a shooting. Some gang mistook early-morning hump day for your typical Friday night."

He settled onto the couch beside her, pulled her legs into his lap. "Maliah, we can catch the next plane there. Let me know."

"Nobody died." Her eyebrows furrowed. "Wow, that caveat kind of normalizes things. *If nobody dies*, that makes it okay."

His hands worked at the arches of her foot.

Maliah sniggered. "Why aren't you asking me the old tried-and-true questions?"

As he thoughtfully rubbed, Ephraim shrugged. "What questions?"

"Such as 'why do you work in *that type* of neighborhood?' or 'shouldn't you be using your elite education elsewhere?'"

"Those were your father's words, Maliah." Ephraim started on her other foot, his knuckles drawing into her arches, the magic almost squashing her curiosity. "You need to argue?"

"No." She sighed heavily, shoving a hand into her kink of hair.

"Because I can insert myself into your business by forcing bulletproof windows on you. I can employ security guards around the learning center. Metal detectors? Though I'm not sure if that will scare the students. I can have my assistant schedule a trainer to come give a module to the educators on your roster. See the trend?"

"Yes."

"You had a dream to work in a certain place. And God— I'm not one to bring His name up, since going to a certain Baptist church." He lifted her foot, planting a kiss on her sole. "God saw fit for you to open your business in New Haven."

Maliah was quiet for a moment. Ephraim grew up in a synagogue. She reminisced on the first time he went to church with her. The preacher had enthusiastically "threatened" the seated folks during worship time. Even folks with crutches had to get up. She started to thank him, but his cell phone was going off in his pocket.

"We both should've kept them off," she grumbled as he took his phone out.

"Daniel left calls and texts. Let me know what I can do about your school—your safety is important to me." He moved her legs to the side and reached into his sweats to grab the phone.

"Oh, how is your friend?" Though she was genuinely concerned, a combination of sadness and pettiness controlled her.

"Speak of the devil." Ephraim placed the call on speaker.

"Eph, where the fuck are you? No, I retract that statement. I don't want to hear about snorting cocaine from bleach-blonde ass cracks in Hawaii or cute little geisha's licking coke off the tip of your dick."

She pressed the Mute button. "This is even worse than Google. I need to clean my ears with a Brillo pad, you freak."

Ephraim unmuted him. "I'm a reformed man."

"What rehab center have you been holed up at?" Daniel snorted. "If you can go a month without snorting one line, I'm sending the place a ridiculous, fat check."

"Damn, Daniel," Maliah chuckled. "Is this *the* Daniel Rutledge? You were the definition of quiet and broody before *Twilight* was invented. You're a betting man, now?"

"Oh hell no," he blared through the speaker. "The fuck is going on here, Eph? Is that Maliah? A sound-alike Maliah—are you in some type of cult shit?"

Seconds later, Ephraim's cell phone flashed. He pressed the disregard button for Daniel's FaceTime invitation.

Daniel growled, "Put me on FaceTime, I have to see this shit!"

"Goodbye, Goldie Locks." Ephraim hung up on Daniel.

Maliah held up her phone. He was calling her too. She burrowed her face into Ephraim's shoulder and laughed. "We blew our childhood friend's mind, Eph. *This is too much!*"

Daniel called him back, and he put his friend on speaker. "Eph, put me on FaceTime."

"We aren't dressed," Ephraim warned.

"Listen." Daniel lowered his voice. "The wife is riding my balls right now, not in a good way. I'm supposed to be seeing why you didn't respond to our baby shower invite. It's coed—not that I expect you to take the plunge, but don't agree to coed. And if that is *our* Maliah, I've seen enough of her. Tits bouncing in your dorm room, Eph. FaceTime, now."

Ephraim shrugged. "Sometimes we did forget to lock the door."

Maliah chortled. "Please accept that man's FaceTime. He never goes postal."

He pressed the button. Daniel's face popped up on the screen. Ocean for as far as the eye could see came up on the screen. Along with it were blue eyes, blond hair, and the straightest, whitest teeth that Maliah swore he'd bought. Daniel had become a whoremonger with Ephraim, though she always thought Daniel had the kindest heart. When they were very young, she'd attended the funeral after his mother's suicide, then couldn't believe she had to repeat the process so soon for his father's freak car crash. They only became the three amigos after Daniel swore he'd met the "funniest guy on earth."

"Maliah motherfucking Porter, in the flesh." He grinned at her.

"Wentworth Daniel Rutledge the Motherfucking Third. Bro, *how are you*?" She smiled back at him.

"I'm . . ." He paused, pulling a tuft of blond hair. "I'm soon to be a father."

"So, did you knock her up, or are you married?"

"Ooooo, that's sand slung in my face, Maliah." He gave one of those barely-there smiles that she remembered when they'd been little. Daniel had spent most of his time under his grandfather's thumb. So, when she'd learned that he'd made friends with Ephraim, in a sense she'd made friends with him at the age of twelve, after all those years of witnessing the Rutledges' powers and tragedies. Someone had said, for every ten billion the Rutledges claimed, their family size shrunk.

"I'm kidding, kidding, Daniel. I know you're married. Google's my closest confidant."

"Hey, you got Yolanda in the divorce, I got fucking Eph."

She could feel Ephraim stiffen after Daniel's joke. Their

"divorce" had blindsided him. They'd never gotten the chance to tell their friends about the annulment. And what happened in Vegas stayed in the dark. So, Daniel's joke hit too close to home.

After a few beats, Ephraim chimed in with the best comeback. "Sounded like a good deal to me."

She bumped his shoulder, thankful that the dumbest mistake of her life wasn't up for discussion right now. "Daniel, I also saw some pictures of your wife," Maliah mentioned. "Is it me or does your white girl have a super tan? Like Meagan Good tan, lips, ass, everything?"

"You know what, she'd take that as a compliment. But not for the next few months." He groaned. "Desire is pregnant."

Ephraim said, "Pregnant women are supposed to be freaks. Don't pussy out, Wentworth."

Daniel lowered his head for a moment, and when he looked back up, Maliah's pussy lips jolted. There was a bright smile on his face.

"Bro, talk to me," Ephraim groaned in interest. "I take it she's six months? So she doesn't even have a big belly yet. Wow, when she gets that big ol' belly, you are gonna be in for a treat."

Maliah shoved him. "How do you know?"

He held a hand to her face. "Pregnant chick porn, LeeLee. Stay out of grown-men business."

"Well, there you have it." She shrugged. They did have a porn fetish that began in junior year of high school, so she couldn't complain.

"All right, I'm not telling the two of you anything." Daniel sighed. "We sent the RSVP to your Maldives address."

"Yeah, I said I'd be there for the next year after you had me in Texas fighting off Crackhead Becky."

"Who?" Maliah looked at her man. "Crackhead Be . . . oh, shit, Rebecca? Your cousin, Daniel. Oh, no, what did she do?"

"Tried to stick him for his papers. Titan Aerospace, his legacy."

"For real?" Maliah breathed.

"Yeah, and you were nice enough to continue giving her scraps. I had that bitch in my palm, bro. Fuck a monthly allowance—she doesn't deserve a few thousand dollars a month off your family."

Daniel's jaw set. "We don't need to talk about my cousin. She's back on the pole. I'm texting you a screenshot of the invitation. Remember what it looks like. Desire is pop quizzing every single person. These hormones."

"Can he plus one?" Maliah asked.

"Sweetheart, bring everybody you know. I miss you, Maliah."

Ephraim growled, "No calling my woman '*sweetheart*.'"

"Goodbye, sweetheart." Daniel glared at Ephraim. "Bro."

The call disconnected.

"Your woman?" Maliah arched a brow.

He pressed his mouth to hers. "No matter what you do, you'll always be mine."

His cell phone pinged in his hand.

"Is that the invitation, Eph?"

"Yes."

"When?"

"This Saturday. You don't have plans."

"Ephraim . . ." She groaned, leaning back on the couch.

He rubbed the side of his neck. "Maliah, the party is in a few weeks."

Her eyes closed momentarily. The date didn't conflict with the Hurt Room. Something in her craved more rounds with Ephraim Levine at the kinky place he'd created just for them . . .

18

He'd been in heaven for an entire week. Met bliss between her ebony thighs. Drank everlasting water. Fucked with her head in so many ways, which reminded him of how captivated he was by Maliah's wit. Now, hell welcomed him back into the fold. This was a hell of his own creation.

The Hurt Room.

Ephraim heard the soft sound of the front door closing. He turned over in the ultra-soft sheets at his Greenwich hotel suite. Her scent was all over the place. Embedded in his memory. But instincts warned that she'd left him. Left him for *him*.

Ephraim thought back for a moment. Midday Friday, Maliah begged for calzones they'd dug into after weed sessions in high school. They headed back toward home, had sex while driving. For all intents and purposes, everything was perfect. They'd done all the good shit. By nightfall, they were parked at an old, hole-in-the-wall pizza joint. With a box of piping-hot pizza, they'd returned to his hotel. And not only did they screw, they talked, and they connected.

Ephraim clutched at the sheets, tore them away from his limbs. He'd been all tangled up in them. Had the door closed any softer, the dreams playing in his mind would've continued to scroll. Paradise crashed and burned before his eyes, as he breathed in her fading scent. Almost ten years ago, Maliah had blindsided him.

Ephraim was twenty-one years old, the world at his fingertips. All the facets that made up Maliah Porter reminded him of the formation of a diamond. She'd been created, no flaws. Stubborn enough to speak her mind. Utterly captivating. His.

He'd plucked his precious jewel at a young age and thanked God he'd never deal with some of the shit he'd seen or heard about. Controlling, lying, manipulative, vindictive . . . he'd dodged every bullet.

They'd returned from Vegas less than twenty-four hours ago. While she went to the gym, he'd gotten a thought into his head: create a grand party to announce their marriage. He'd tell the universe about them.

By the afternoon, a Michelin-star chef exploded their townhome with delicious aromas. Soon as Maliah returned home, they'd try it. A master of calligraphy sat with him in the living room. His assistant had calculated the time frame for this evening —last-minute planning at its finest. With messengers dressed in penguin suits, each invitation would be sent in the nick of time.

Ephraim had texted Maliah about an hour ago that they were having a party. He was wrapping up the final touches with the calligrapher when he noticed Maliah's car outside the window.

"Keep working on that," he told the calligrapher while arising from the couch. "My wife might want to change some of the verbiages, so I'm going to stall her until you're done. We're on a tight schedule for the night."

. . .

EVEN THOUGH THEY'D been blinded by the lights in Vegas, he'd planned to show off his new wife to their world. Tell everyone who meant something that she finally belonged to him. Maliah had ruined those plans.

THE NEXT TWO hours went by with white noise playing in his ear. Yesiv, who'd had the week off, dropped him off at the mansion he now loathed. His informant sent various text confirmations that Maliah had returned to her home, then one about how she sat at the table with a cup of coffee with Tonya. Then she was on her way.

She's not even coming for me, fuck! She's coming for another man! A stranger. Ephraim swiped a hand across the fireplace mantel. The fortune that was spent on staging this place sounded good to his ears as figurines crashed.

Atsun kept her gaze to the floor as she kneeled on the marble floor across from him. He stopped himself from reminding Nori's submissive that she was, indeed, playing a maid. And that she needed to clean this shit up.

A real maid, with puffy white hair and in the same black-and-white outfit, came from out of nowhere. *Damn, I forgot I actually hired a maid*, he considered. She moved like a robot, sweeping all the broken crystal and milk glass bits into a dustpan.

Nori was prattling in his ear. Ephraim didn't give a rat's ass how much education the renowned teacher had in bondage and the likes. Nori served one purpose and had so many more that were denied to him. Like touching for instance. Nori and his Atsun were not to touch Ephraim's Maliah.

"Today, ice is our medium, Ephraim. I sent Maliah the

email already." Ephraim groaned. Nori pulled at his button-up, fanning himself. "Last week, role play, including a psychological aspect to her training, was on the agenda."

"Then why the fuck didn't you do role play?" he snapped, knowing that he was the reason.

"We did bondages at your request. My name is tied to this training, Ephraim. Even if Maliah is still utilizing Miss Honey as her alias, she knows me as *Noritaka Yamazaki*. Besides, I didn't bring any one of my pets, Ephraim. Atsun is the best."

"Ice and flogging," he gritted out.

"You have a gorgeous woman—let's broaden her horizons. May I show Maliah that this world is a lot more than most people get to see? They know about ties and whips. They aren't privy to every facet, such as the psychological aspect, the bonding between two or more people! The beauty of BDSM!"

The glare he issued to Nori was enough to shut the man up. Had Maliah not been claimed, Ephraim knew in his gut that the trainer would've wanted her. As a lawyer, he spotted loopholes in contracts a mile away. Nori had an intrinsic interest in training an untrainable. Jealousy rode over the sinew in Ephraim's taut muscles. Were he not careful, the trainer would try to claim Maliah. He breathed deep and snarled, "Then play with fucking popsicles. Bring out the whip, flogs, paddles." *Screw ice, she will be punished!*

Ephraim stared at him head-on; he then glared at Atsun. For all the meek vibes she gave off, he'd seen the bitch in action with Maliah. Envy had transformed into lust when she'd done it, but still. Ephraim's glower snapped back toward Nori, waiting for the trainer to bitch about what he'd ordered.

Something flashed in Nori's gaze. He backed away, stopped, then returned. "You're angry with her."

Fuck, yeah, I'm angry. I gave her the fucking time of her life all night long, and she leaves. Leaves!

"Mr. Levine, If I hear red, I'm stopping you myself. Pull the plug off this entire operation."

"Then she will be ordered to whisper." Ephraim smiled. "You and Atsun played that little game last week. What did you whisper into my woman's ear, sweetheart?"

Atsun continued with her head lowered, on her knees next to her Master.

"Make her answer, Nori."

The teacher stroked the top of his pet's head.

She never looked up. In a demure tone, she spoke. "I asked if she'd like me to taste her yet, Sir."

Though every fiber in his body burned with the notion that he'd brought this on himself, Ephraim chuckled. "You like her?"

Atsun's face rose, a smile crossing her lips. She looked past him and said, "Very much, Sir."

"Only Nori and I were in this initial contract, but I must respectfully warn you." He flashed her Master a tense smile. "You try something with her, sweetheart, you'll regret that."

"Atsun is a professional," Nori assured him.

Ephraim placed his hand on her chin; since she'd touched what belonged to him, he'd touch what belonged to Nori. "Keep your eyes down when you see Maliah next time too."

"All right." Nori stepped before her kneeling frame like a trainer unsure of his pup's safety. "We have made a few stipulations in our contract. My pet won't eye your woman. You won't hurt your woman to the point where you ignore *red* today."

Ephraim glanced out the picturesque window. "She's here," he growled. He preferred to lie through his teeth during opening remarks, all the lofty words that made grand juries think. Maliah could say "red" until her lungs were raw—he was going to spank the bad out of her.

19

"I'm a sex addict . . ." THE WORDS ECHOED IN MALIAH'S EARS. She sat in her car in the front of what she now knew was Ephraim, and not Nori's, mansion.

From the outside looking in, the man she loved hard had this ability to be the bad guy. He certainly had funny guy down. Women caved to his smiles. Their need to touch him while laughing at a joke painted him as a potential culprit. His money, attractive face, toned body—it all gave him the motive to be the bad thing in them.

Maliah was the silent bad in them. From a tender age, she had an image to uphold with her parents. That image shone more severely based on how each of her parents sought different things from her. She had a mom who'd molded her to be a beauty—no brains required. Her dad had craved a marriage between herself and Ephraim the day he noticed her compulsion with what outfit would make the damn boy speak to her! He'd consented to her Ivy League education, with rich friends like Daniel, under a few grounds. One, she became Ephraim's trophy and joined their family legacy. Rick never saw two young kids falling in love; his eyes were full of greed. Or he'd agree if she built her own legacy. As a last resort, he paid for her education so that she'd join his legacy—in his scheming construction business. We Rise served the wrong clientele to be considered anything at all besides charity work. Legacies were measured by profit.

In her parents' chaos, Maliah had this thing with feeling worthy while growing up. Ephraim had done everything in his power to make her feel it. But only in the throes of sex did she have a hold on worthy. And someone played into that worthiness. Someone ruined them.

"I'm a sex addict," sixteen-year-old Maliah repeated.

Maliah had her hands across her chest as she lay on a paisley chaise. She looked over at her therapist.

The redhead's face tilted, and she removed the glasses from her eyes. "Maliah, you are not a sex addict. You're in love with your boyfriend. You're seeing him, and him alone. You have a healthy sex life for a teenager."

"I am."

"By all means—" Dr. Hart waved a hand. "—tell me why you believe you're a sex addict."

With a huff, Maliah prattled on. "What kind of father lets his daughter sleep at her boyfriend's house at age thirteen! He let us go into my bedroom—shut the door before then too."

Dr. Hart nodded, pausing for a beat. "I understand that you have some anger with your father for his parenting choices—"

"Dad places Ephraim on a pedestal," Maliah took over. "We were twelve when I put my hand in Ephraim's pants. I don't think—I know for a fact that he wasn't ready." She stopped to chuckle.

"Care to elaborate on what you're laughing about?"

"I tried for a few years to have sex with him. Not that he isn't attracted to me." She snapped her fingers. "It took until I was

fourteen for it to dawn on me that he'd been shy about how he thought I was cute when we first met too. Ephraim could've given in to me a long time ago, but he didn't."

Tears began to prick her eyes. She sniffled them back, and her voice shook. "I wanted to spite my father, fuck Eph, and—I guess that's it. And fuck Eph, but he waited, made it perfect, last year."

"I'm gathering that you and Ephraim have had a solid foundation for a while now, Maliah."

Her body shook with tears. While other girls thought losing their virginity at prom was the holy grail, she'd been a rich, spiteful kid. "I'm on the honor roll at school, and yet, I would have Eph in my room. I'd sit on the edge of my desk, no panties, wanting to moan so loud that my parents heard."

"What I'm hearing is you wanted to get a rise out of your mother and father. See how they'd handle things."

"Yes! All for the sake of missing a great experience." She huffed. "While half my family doesn't play, my uncle would beat my niece's ass if she knew she had sex. My cousin's parents pray for her safety at school and that she grows up and marries a God-fearing man. You know, black people stuff?"

Dr. Hart blinked. "Well, yes, I understand."

Maliah rolled her eyes. Her therapist was probably an atheist. Daniel's grandparents went to the same church as her. Ephraim was Jewish. She knew in a lot of scenarios, rich, educated white people started to follow evolution and the likes. She wiped her tears, almost smiling. "Granny makes Eph and I pray with her. But my dad doesn't notice that, because he's too busy starting sentences with, 'Well, you know, son. . .' when referring to Eph. I bet my dad wouldn't mind if I acted like Paris Hilton and Nicole Richie. Their antics are bragging rights for rich parents."

"Who?"

"Two girls who have a lot of money and a reality show. They don't matter." She shrugged.

"Let's schedule a session with your parents."

"No." Maliah shook her head. "My dad was breaking ground with his construction company before I was born. They've tasted money for too long to change their ways. Maybe I'm not a sex addict, but . . . this relationship we have is good enough. My father can brag about his daughter being in therapy—it's not taboo in the wealthy world right now. Just me attending is prestige points for him."

"Maybe I'm not a sex addict," she repeated to herself, scrolling through Gmail for the Hurt Room schedule.

ATSUN'S reluctance to connect gazes was starting to become a blaring red flag. At first, Maliah assumed the sub's cold shoulder had to do with her not being as freaky last week. But now, Maliah couldn't keep her eyes from traveling to a set of torture contraptions on the table. She shifted on her knees, unsure which was worse—heels that made her feel like she was walking sky-high or all the kneeling she had to do. In Maliah's opinion, getting on knees was a precursor to dick sucking, and she only sought one man's shaft.

"I'm sensing a bit of hesitation in you today, Pet."

Nori stroked her cheek. All the hesitation swirling in the pit of her stomach evaporated.

"It's nothing," she mumbled, chewing her lip, and then she stopped. The first hour she spent in his presence, Nori reprimanded her on stance and various quirks. No lip chewing. No finger fidgeting. Her hate for the rules was beginning to erect itself, until he crouched down.

Every time Nori came close to her, the center of the universe gravitated near. His lustrous dark hair touched his chiseled cheekbones as he moved.

Nori said, "Tell me your thoughts."

She licked her lips seductively, though pensive imaginary ants crawled across her skin. "Those look a bit more intimidating than the paddle Atsun and Master used last time."

"Your perceptive, beautiful mind gives me great pleasure. Shall we?" He took her hand in his, kissed the back of it, and led her to the table.

Maliah had never felt so small—in a good way—as Nori guided her. There were contraptions with handles and various long, leather multi-tailed whips. One had slits at the end of it. The other seemed more similar, except one was shorter.

"Which would you prefer?"

"Not that one." She snorted, then stopped. "I apologize, Sir."

His breath was dangerously close to her for a second. "I wouldn't hurt you," he said before standing tall. "What is your poison, Mal—Miss Honey?"

Maliah weighed her options and grabbed the handle of one of the items with a suede fray.

"Perfect for a novice. It's called a flogger, Miss Honey. They all are. And I'll let you in on a little secret: the one you chose is soft and gentle. It doesn't offer a sting. You picked the precise one I plan to use on you. We are going for a *soothing* experience, today."

Nori touched the handle of another flogger that was similar to the one in her hand. "Less tails, more sting."

She noticed that he stared at the canvas that dominated most of the wall. Maliah pretended to be oblivious but realized Ephraim had to be watching them. She also noted that Nori had just about kissed her a second ago. That egotistical ex of hers held all the cards. Despite her desire to feel any of these floggers on her body—by Ephraim—she came closer to Nori.

His intelligence was a sure sign to get into some woman's pants. Although not hers, Maliah decided to play Ephraim's game. Maliah pressed her lips against Nori's mouth. She hid a quick smile before moving away. "Thank you, Teacher."

"You are quite welcome." Nori licked his bottom lip and moved toward the last flogger. "This is the infamous cat o' nine tails. We won't be using it. Now this—" Nori held up a whip with a rectangular end. "Dragon Tail, created by yours truly."

She admired the elaborate dragon design on the handle. "Nice."

Nori's hand skimmed over hers, sending electricity flying. Maliah's cheeks burned when she realized he'd meant to take the suede flogger that she'd chosen from her hand. "I know your body, Miss Honey. This is all the *pain* you'll need today."

She grew quiet, and the awareness that Ephraim was watching them did her in. There was no denying his assertion that he knew her body. Maliah could hear the steam coming from Ephraim's ears, and the weasel was a room away from her. Instincts warned her to deny Nori's statement and leave, but liquid lust pooled at her sex. Besides, only Ephraim would benefit from it. Her spinster contract rules were going to come into play.

Nori placed her wrists into plush handcuffs at the front of her body, then commanded her to hold up her hands. Atsun had pulled the chain from the ceiling that descended to meet over her head. The maid then went to the wall and adjusted the chain, where Maliah was forced to stand in a wide-legged stance. She took a deep breath, her toes jamming down into the six-inch stilettos.

"Proper stance is important," Nori said, removing something from the pocket of his pants. He tossed up the small items, before applying them to her nipples.

She forced out a breath as the clamps bit down, but he didn't miss a beat while declaring, "You may have a Master, Miss Honey. Nonetheless, while I am giving instruction, *you are mine.*"

Her word was hardly audible. "Yes."

He twisted a clamp and pain sparked from that exact spot, radiating throughout her body. "I promised not to hurt you, but stance! Miss Honey, you have the worst stance I've ever seen in twenty years."

She extended her legs wider.

"Mouth," he growled, twisting the other clamp.

"Nori, please."

He rubbed a hand through his black, spun-silk hair. "Can't you see it in my eyes that I hate hurting you, Ma-Miss Honey!"

Her mouth untwisted, and she stopped focusing on the clamps. The thought dawned on her: *He's not supposed to touch me.* Nori had stroked her and kissed her downstairs in the guest room two weeks ago. After that, no more kisses. She recalled how Ephraim made her body milk for him when she wore the nipple clamps he had. Not that she wanted to say the teacher could do any better—he did not have the right to mend her hurt.

Only Ephraim.

That made all kinds of sense.

She'd hurt him so bad.

Now, he had all rights to her pain.

Maliah placed on a smile, took her thick legs wider, and pressed down her pelvis. As if she were on a stage before a million eyes, she presented the perfect stance.

A deep drawl of breath came from Nori, his restraint evident at the sight of the bulge in his pants. He groaned, picking up the dragon-tail flogger, which did not have any extra extensions. The tip of the tail was shaped like a flat-headed diamond. He rubbed it against her asshole. She perked up more for him, ass perfectly on display.

Maliah looked into dark, jaded eyes. In the depths of them, she saw a hurricane of desire. Her chocolate orbs fell. This was bad, very bad, the way he stared at her. Pressure radiated from him. And though Nori was a very attractive man, her rules would apply. No penetration. She loved Ephraim too much not to play *his* game the way he wanted her to play it.

Nori's Adam's apple lodged into his throat. It seemed like ages had passed, as if he were waging war in his mind, but it must've been mere seconds. The pain in her nipples was still too fresh.

He pressed the dragon tail down her spine, stroking softly.

Eph . . . I need you so bad right now. Part of her wanted to call out the farce. To get Ephraim in the room at this instance so he could take over. The other part of her mind had become tethered with the thought of being a true submissive. A submissive didn't call the shots, and so Ephraim would enter on his timing, not hers.

Nori came around to the front of her, slid the dragon tail across her clit. "Your breathing is perfect, Pet. Now, are you ready for a little pain, just a little for your teacher?"

"Please, Sir."

Nori picked up the flogger that she'd chosen, held it tight in his fist. Maliah braced herself for blinding pain. After all, those damn tit clamps had stolen the air from her lungs, after Nori had promised not to hurt her. Instead, she floated to the gates of sheer euphoria. The multiple tails seemed to stroke at her ass. It gave off a static of thuds that vibrated across her buttocks and straight to her pussy.

"Yesss!" she groaned.

Each succession of swats sent a zing to her second set of lips. Maliah stood tall, her passion crescendoing with each smack to her ass.

"This is what a Master does for his pet, Miss Honey." Nori put down the flog and returned to the dragon tail. The tip glided over the inside of her thigh. He went to his knees before her.

"Marvelous. You're dripping for *me*."

Her body shook as he caressed the tip against her clit. Nori gave her a few taps, before flicking his wrist. She did not feel an ounce of pain as the dragon tail assaulted her pussy, only delight. After a few pounds, a delightful moist sound filled the room.

"Fuck!" She squealed, orgasm triggered, without hardly building. That had never happened before. The flicks to her clit sent her throbbing walls pulsating and begging to be filled to the brim with cock.

"What a dirty pet." Nori clicked his tongue. "You're coming all over my dragon tail. Which of us should lick it off?"

"May I?" Atsun begged.

The door boomed open so hard that it bounced off the wall. Everyone's head flew in her Master's direction. His suit looked so hot on him that Maliah wanted to tear it off. A black leather executioner hood covered his gorgeous face. Ephraim looked about ready to slaughter her ass. Staring at him sent a river of cum flowing down the inside of her thighs.

One of Ephraim's hands clutched a black leather bag.

Within his other hand was another cat o' nine tails, the design even more intricate than Nori's, boasting twists at the end of each tail. The handle was gripped so tightly that the skin underneath his knuckles bled white.

"Leave us," Ephraim ordered. The eerie contraption that contorted his voice—the sound made her knees weaken and a delicious coat of wetness line her lips again. The tone gave off Keanu Reeves vibes, yet steelier.

Atsun's mouth trembled into a sneer. Her gaze still cast to the floor, she followed Nori. Maliah hadn't seen his reaction, though the predator walk of his warned that he wasn't happy about this intrusion.

———

ALL THE NERVE endings in Ephraim's body were shot. He'd stared at the video, not blinking the entire time. Watched the desire in Maliah's eyes. Noted Nori's control. Atsun was also at the brink of restraint. In fact, he'd bet a hundred grand that the bitch had eyes for Maliah too. While Nori passed him, he glared hard at the teacher. His pet had her arm on his shoulder, walking a few paces behind him.

Ephraim snarled, "Atsun, stay."

The tiny woman paused at the doorframe. Though he had no right to give her an order, Ephraim had seen the desire in her eyes earlier.

Nori nodded.

Atsun followed Ephraim, her entire demeanor void of any expression. *Well, you need to see this, front and center, bitch.* He smiled.

Ephraim returned his attention to the statue of a woman who consumed hours of his thoughts, years.

"I never get to see you, Master," she murmured.

He stood before her, head cocked slightly. "Did I permit you to speak?"

"No, Master."

"This is my bag of *hurt*, Miss Honey. When I'm done, you'll know the true definition of the word."

20

EPHRAIM'S TONGUE GLIDED OVER HIS TEETH. HE PULLED OUT the keys to handcuffs and handed them to Atsun. Her tiny, engine-red fingertips traced over the outside of Maliah's arm and up to her hands. Atsun untied the restraints over her head. When Maliah removed her wrists from above her head, she took a few uneasy steps. Atsun started to assist her, but she moved toward Ephraim. He guided her into his arms, helping her regain her balance.

"Thanks," she murmured.

He tipped her chin so that she could see into the darkness of the executioner hood to his bloodshot eyes. "I'm only preparing for the inevitable. Soon enough, you'll hurt so bad, Miss Honey, that you won't be able to stand."

Ephraim let Maliah go. She gulped, fear striking her gaze. Unable to look at her pain, Ephraim went to the table. With a scoff, his hand glided over all of Nori's silly toys. "Have you ever hurt someone, Miss Honey? Not physical, but emotional?"

"I . . ."

"Stop," he cut in, digging through the bag. "Your hesitation was enough answer. Let's see if that sticks-and-stones bullshit can measure up."

Ephraim paused, his jaw clenched. He wriggled it for a moment. "Atsun, the table."

She moved like a calm ocean to the far corner of the room. Without the lights in this area of the dungeon, the inversion table had been left in the dark against the wall. The damn thing was taller than her as she wheeled it over to the center of the room.

Ephraim took in the scent of fresh leather. The tabletop had a thin leather-padded board in the middle and jutted out into two to position a person's legs wider.

With the dungeon table in an upright position, Atsun assisted Maliah in moving onto the contraption. Fire shot across his skin as her tiny hands caressed his woman's wrists and ankles. Thick pads bound Maliah to the table.

He slammed his hand down onto the head of the board, and it went flying. Maliah gave a tiny shocked yelp. Atsun glared. He stopped the table when it was in a parallel position.

"Open her legs, slut," he ordered.

Atsun went to Maliah's left leg and pushed the board.

"Wider, slut."

She then went to Maliah's right leg, her eyes on Maliah's mound as she pushed the board.

Ephraim hooked an arm over Atsun's shoulder. "Pretty cunt—wide open, isn't it?"

The tiny woman gulped.

"If I offered you a chance to eat my pet's pussy, you'd reinvent head, wouldn't you?" He kept his eyes on Atsun's slanted, dark orbs, though he felt Maliah's boring through him. "Would you eat my pet's pussy, slut?"

"Please, yes." The sub moved forward in a trance. Ephraim took hold of her arm and pulled her back to him.

"Not yet. You might be the dirtiest little slut I've ever met," he growled into her ear. "Won't be the first bitch I had eat another one either. Though, that's because I don't eat pussy that I haven't met firsthand before. Hardly fucked the same bitch twice either, so there's that conclusion. What do you think of that, slut?"

A low, subtle growl roamed through Atsun's tonsils. "I think you missed out on a lot of good eats."

He sniggered. "We could've been friends, you and I. Now, look at that sweet cunt. Your Master got her wet. You got a little touch a second ago."

She flinched as his fingers dug into the back of her neck.

"Those little moves the two of you made will be your last. Fuck off, bitch."

One high heel in front of the other, Atsun left the room.

———

PUSSY SPLAYED AND EXPOSED, Maliah felt wider open than she ever had in her entire life. Fear had clutched her throat for a moment, then jealousy when Ephraim forced Atsun to stay. The only pain she'd consent to would be at her ex's hands. After the jealousy, curiosity consumed her at the sight of the table. Ebbs of emotion coursed through her body when they whispered with each other.

Atsun's narrow ass sashayed away, the door slamming. The greed at having his full attention now frightened her.

His suit and the leather mask covered every inch of his body, but she scented the anger radiating from him.

"Can you at least talk to me?"

He moved closer, gripped her mouth in his hands. Lips

forced into a pucker, Maliah expected a kiss. She received the fire of a hard bite on her bottom lip.

He went back to his bag of pain, pulled something out.

Heart pummeling in her chest, Maliah watched his every move. Something was covered in his fisted hand. He held it out, palm up.

Maliah gasped, "Wait—"

A red rubber ball gag was shoved into her mouth. Her jaw stretched to the limit. Fear prickled down her spine. *Ephraim, wait! Stop.* Tears welled in her eyes.

"Now you are prepared. It appears your teacher wasn't worth the cost of his training. Three whole weeks, what have you learned? Nothing." He kissed the tip of her nose. "We have three more weeks in the Hurt Room—maybe you'll come back for it. I'll still pay you either way."

The tears rushed down her cheeks. His "maybe" was tossed on all the ones she had for herself. Maybe an annulment wasn't a good idea. Just maybe they could make it work despite . . .

Or how about after a year had passed. Maybe she should get the fuck over him.

Then consider five years . . . maybe she should've met a man, fallen in love, married. Kids. Maybe!

The cat o' nine tails slammed down onto the skin at Maliah's hip. Instead of the delicious *thunk* of Nori's flogger, matches were being lit onto her skin.

Again. Again. Again. Relentless was the man she loved. All the emotional hurt she'd dished out was coming full circle.

He moved to the flesh at the inside of her leg, stopping the flog before the tails could pick up much speed.

With the sound of Ephraim's hard breathing, Maliah counted each hit. They consumed her skin in a rage of fire.

"Nori!" Atsun shouted at the tip of her lungs. She couldn't remove her eyes from the huge television screen. And she'd never shouted at her Master, save for climax.

He stopped at the door to the viewing room, the knob within his reach.

"Please, come to me," she begged, still observing the slaughter on the screen.

"I could kill him, Pet."

She'd done two things wrong in their relationship: shouted and questioned him. "You can't, Nori. But there are other ways."

He licked his lips. She could feel his eyes scouring her body, not in the way she was accustomed to, but with the willingness to listen. Though she never tore her gaze away from the television, Atsun suggested, "Have I not prepared every email to Maliah Porter per your request?"

"Yes, Atsun," he gritted out in impatience.

"You want her." Atsun's words strummed together in a seductive whisper.

Moments passed. He sniffed before speaking. "Yes. However, when I make a promise to my pets, I keep them."

"You are Noritaka Yamazaki. You chose your pets because we are all good-hearted. Yes, we are catty and manipulative. We are *pets*. I'm positive you can persuade the rest of us," she simpered. Though her tone was a perfect stroke for her owner, a living rage consumed her abdomen. Being in Ephraim's presence had been akin to placing a vice grip around her throat. Atsun Yamazaki did not shy away from pain—she coveted it. But that man was filled with too much pain to be a Master.

Masters nurtured their submissives. Masters were the

fathers that women never grew up with . . . or so she thought. They sought the best for their pets.

Her eyes pricked, and she held them wide for a moment to stave off tears. Atsun trained her voice to sound controlled. "We will construct an email for midweek. Meet her out of the confines of this place. Do what is in your blood and soul, Master. *Teach her.* Allow Maliah to have the same opportunities afforded to me and your pets." *Make her ours*, she pleaded.

"Prepare the email for my approval," he agreed. "Once this is complete, I'll expect a draft. I refuse to watch a single second more."

The door shut softly behind him. Atsun continued to torment herself. She watched the woman she coveted be dominated by someone so unworthy.

———

TINY WELTS BUBBLED along Maliah's inner thighs. Her wrists and ankles were hot. He could tell she desired to be free as he unlatched her from the table. She pushed up off the torture contraption and into a seated position. Ephraim pulled the gag from her mouth. With a whimper, she lunged herself into his arms.

"I'm not done, Miss Honey." He cuddled her to his body for a moment. "Hurt builds up and grows. That's what we're going for. The type you'll never forget."

He hardened himself to her silent whimpers and ordered, "You'll do anything for your Master."

She nodded.

"That was not a question." Ephraim placed her on the plush rug. "Now, hands and knees."

The tears had stopped dripping from her eyes. Her cheeks were a sea of them.

"Hands and knees. You have all that ass, and it didn't get an ounce of love."

Her movements were measured, tentative. Groaning met his ear. Ephraim ignored all of her feelings, because he was consumed by his own hurt.

The woman who was supposed to love him had transformed him into a cokehead and a manwhore. Ephraim never blamed a person for his subsequent actions no matter how dubious. But Maliah had been his friend first and foremost. He'd lost a lover and best friend, and she had to pay.

"Now," he said, rubbing the paddle over her luscious flesh. "We can play that fucking game of green, yellow, red. I'm not asking. We're both adults, here. So, you call out when you can't take the hurt." The hardness of his voice implied that he might not grant her requests . . .

THE AIR IN HER LUNGS HAD STALLED AS MALIAH SAT IN THE CAR. Though she was now of "drinking age," she preferred clutching her steering wheel. The act was more familiar than clutching a bottle while contemplating her choices. Then Ephraim had started out of the front door. The light in his eyes was enough to drive her to the end of a fifth of vodka. She gripped her small leather backpack and got out of the car.

"LeeLee, I know." He rubbed a hand across his handsome face, walking down the path. "It's a little party at . . ."

He mentioned the name of a historic mansion they'd attended a gala once, with his parents. A place that had captivated her from first sight. While he thought to downplay what should've been the second-best day of her life, white noise funneled through her ear. She clutched at the backpack. Before he could hug her, Maliah used it as a buffer between them.

Maliah licked her lips in apprehension. "Before the party, I have something I need you to sign."

"I'll sign whatever you need later. Right now, you look tired. How was the workout?"

"I didn't go." She mumbled the truth, not needing to add to the

list of lies poised at the tip of her tongue. Maliah opened the back-pack, pushed aside her wallet, and gripped the annulment papers. They burned like fire in her hands as she handed them over, with a pen.

"Okay. Where did you go? Was it a surprise?" *Ephraim asked, leaning the papers against the car. When his sparkling, mischievous eyes looked up from the paper, her gaze flew away from his. He glanced down. All the warm undertones of his tan skin flooded white.* "What the fuck am I signing, Maliah?"

"Ephraim." *Her tone became encouraging low.* "Just sign—"

"Annulment papers!" *Hands in fists, he started for the top of the paper, but she yanked it before he had a chance to rip them apart.*

"No," *she breathed.* "You can't do that. Sign them, Eph. I'm not asking you again. Sign them!"

He flicked at the papers that she held in her hands.

"Let's go inside, LeeLee." *He reached for her hand.* "Come here, baby, let's go talk."

The papers weighed heavy against her chest as she held them tightly. "Eph, I'm not going to ask you nicely, not again. Sign these papers. That's all we need to do."

"This is bullshit." *He stalked toward the front door with her behind him.* "Why would I sign them. We're happy. Aren't we?"

Ephraim had spun around at her. He was at his knees, arms flying around her waist, tears in his eyes, blindsided in the worst of ways by her actions. Since she wore a short-cropped shirt, his breath whispered against her skin. "We are happy, LeeLee. Someone got to you. Lied. Whatever they said, they lied."

Maliah pressed down on his arms, pushing him away from her.

He stood up as she started back on the heels of her Converses. "Maliah, whatever the fuck someone told you is a bald-faced lie. I've never cheated, never thought to. Never hit you. Never say* *anything to put you down. Have I mentioned all the reasons people divorce?"*

"We're not divorcing, Ephraim. We're erasing bad mistakes." *She stopped herself from cringing.*

He wasn't listening in his attempt to reassure her. "Money— we don't have money problems. You love my parents, your parents love me. Granny would be livid right now. What other problems do married people have?"

She numbed herself to his truths. While he made his case, Maliah spoke in a grave, low tone. "I hate you, Eph."

"You can't. I'm crazy, crazy about you, Maliah Ann Porter! I might not pray, but when I think of God, I pray to Him for you!"

While a ball of bile grew in the pit of her stomach, she spoke the lies again. "Hate you, Ephraim. I despise you. I'm dis-dis-disgusted by you. I don't want to see you again—ever."

His hand slammed into the cheery, yellow stucco on the side of the door. His thick shoulders heaved. Blood dribbled down his hand as he reached into his pocket for his phone. "C'mon, let's call Daniel. He's the mediator when we argue. We can have a chat, fuck it out later, LeeLee. This works."

"No, I don't want you to screw my brains out, Eph."

"What did I do?" *he began to say.* "What the fuck did I do?"

Nothing. *All he'd ever done was love her harder. She thrust the papers into his bloodied hand.* "All I want to do is never see your face again."

At one point on the table with her legs wide open, Maliah could've sworn she passed out. Now, with her ass in the air, she didn't have the luxury. What would he do if she fell out of position?

She wasn't wearing the gag. Stopping him may be an utterance away, if he listened. Though, she hadn't listened when he continued to ask her why. Ephraim had signed the papers, asking the same question. Then he'd tight-fisted them as she tried to take them back. She'd almost run over his feet to leave.

She took the pain.

She deserved it.

———

AFTER FIVE SMACKS that came in quick succession, Ephraim massaged the spot on her ass with the paddle. Then he gave the other voluptuous rump the same hurt.

Back and forth he went. Her tender brown skin sported a lovely red hue. Every so often he glanced straight forward where those two fuck-offs were, had they not grown tired of the show. Then he went back to the other ass cheek, alternating from one to the other, no remorse. Whimpers droned, followed by a subsequent scream as the paddle met the curve of her ass. Good times tormented his mind; they were even more relentless than the day she'd brought him those papers. Papers that he'd had examined six ways to hell over the years, splotches of his dried blood on them.

Ephraim pawed her ass. The hot rush of blood beneath her skin was warm inside of his palm. He hated himself for this. Not a moment of this made him feel better. She seemed to deflate beneath his touch. A second later, he fisted the paddle to continue his ruthless assault of her ass.

"I'm so sorry, Eph," she whispered.

He stopped, his wrist poised, paddle ready to strike.

"I'm sorry, Eph," she sobbed.

"Maliah?" He scooped her into his arms, falling back on his rear to sit wide-legged. He tormented himself for being pussy enough to ask. "How long?"

"Before we went away."

Her words *killed* him. Ephraim picked her up, and out of

the room he went. He rushed into the master suite, where no recorders had been installed. In the bathroom, he placed her into a gleaming porcelain tub with silver claw feet.

"Stay," he ordered. "Please stay."

MALIAH'S HEAD lolled against the tub, her muscles evaporating, body so heavy that it couldn't move. She was past the point of hurt. "Worthy" roamed around in her mind, in rapid sequence. Along with that torment, their last day together reminded Maliah of her parasitic ways. In one single afternoon, she'd suffocated all the good in their lives. She had torn his heart from his chest and kept it this entire time.

In the background, Maliah heard shouting and orders to leave. Then a door closed. Seconds later Ephraim towered into the bathroom doorframe.

He kneeled beside her, turned on the water. Steam rose, caressing his handsome features, soothing her skin.

She hadn't noticed the Epsom salt in his hands until he began to pour it into the tub. Water rose over her hips, mollifying the volcano of lines.

"I fucked up." He rubbed a hand over his face. "I never knew what I needed to be forgiven for, Maliah. But I understand that I won't . . . Why? Why did you come back? You knew who I was."

She stole his line, murmuring the words, her lips barely peeled. "I fucked up."

22

For the next couple of days, Maliah's mind toiled with the past. We Rise Learning Center had gone dark for August. This allowed families more time to prepare for the beginning of the school year. Every day, Ephraim stole more of her reality than he had in the past. Or had he? She couldn't remember the days following the crushing of his heart. She'd stayed away from their townhome and begged Tonya to get her clothing.

Maliah lay in bed, with the sunshine attempting to get into her bedroom. She'd nailed an old blanket over the wooden blinds, so tiny glimmers of sun permeated the frayed edges. Much of her room was blackout dark, sending her mind spiraling.

The man she'd encountered last was wounded in the worst possible way. He was a deplorable monster. She was worse. The worst kind of monster, who had hurt him without having fault. It took her an hour to flop over in bed and pick herself up from her sad existence.

She stared into the hallway to see the door to Tonya's was closed. Maliah stood in her pathetic living room. No television to offer mind control. She stared at the front door, then continued into the kitchen to put on a pot of coffee.

Every morning, a stack of pages snatched out from one of her favorite novels lay on the wicker chair in her front porch, the very chair Maliah vowed to burn after Ephraim came by the first time. In the last few days, he'd torn out pages from Toni Morrison's *Beloved*, Octavia Butler's *Kindred*, and Jane Austen's *Pride and Prejudice*.

Fresh grounds of coffee percolated as she thought about the first time she'd witnessed pages torn from her favorite stories. Maliah had thought it was an abomination, for all of two seconds . . .

Maliah had spent the night at Ephraim's home so many times. While her parents treated her like a free-range chicken— prior to the "free-range parenting" new age stuff—Ephraim's mother had rules. Rachel ensured the kids didn't sleep in the same room.

Ephraim and Maliah had to wait until the Levines were asleep before she'd sneak inside his room to be held tight. But tonight was different.

Sixteen-year-old Maliah rapped on the door. Her senses were on high alert that his parents could hear the soft knocking over a thousand feet away. She knocked again, chewed her lip, and whispered, "Eph."

Her slight fear of the dark usually took a back seat to the thought of them being together. She peered through the night and jiggled the handle, finding that it was open.

"Dammit, Eph," she whispered. Heart booming, Maliah stepped inside pitch-blackness and pulled the door flush behind her. She quickly felt for the lights and turned them on.

Her eyes brightened at the sight of a thousand pages. Paulo Coelho's The Alchemist *and* Brida *were center stage, along with pages shorn from Zora Neale Hurston and Terry McMillan. Each page was placed alongside the next. Most of the words were blacked out. Ephraim had to have taken ages to create their own love story.*

She picked up a page with tender care. Her eyes roamed over each blocked word that had been left specifically for her.

"I've wanted you for so long, Maliah," Ephraim said, leaning at the door to his balcony. "I didn't want your first time to be because I gave you a diamond necklace."

"I don't want a diamond necklace, Eph," she murmured, picking up another page. "This must've taken forever."

"Four months, fifteen days, seven hours. Twenty permanent markers."

"You forgot to add all the books you defaced for this." She hid a grin by plucking up another page to read how he'd made her beloved stories their own. She picked up more of the papers scattered across his vast bedroom that led all the way to him. When she picked up the last one, she looked up into his eyes and saw unbridled lust. They'd dry humped for the last two years. Her breath caught. The heady scent of his cologne, intelligence, and confidence embraced all her inhibitions.

Ephraim pressed a crinkled strand of hair behind her ear. "May I have you tonight?"

At the sound of the coffee beeping, Maliah backed away from the kitchen. She hadn't even taken a seat before their first time together consumed all her thoughts. It hurt like hell. Truth be told, that had been the first and last time Ephraim had caused her true pain until this past Saturday. She found herself outside, seated in the very chair he'd claimed. The pillow in her lap as she read a few choice words from the pages had started to tell a new story. It was ingenious.

She clutched the frayed pages of Charlotte Brontë's *Jane Eyre*. Ephraim had shocked her by reading it in high school while she'd taken creative writing and he'd taken a legal writing course. Since she hadn't given him attention, he stole her library book. The very next day, he understood her adulation for the story.

Tears blurred her eyes as she read, "Your worth," on one page. The next page had massive lines of permanent marker, with one soul word left unscathed: "Far." She skipped to the next page to read, "Transcends," and continued to read the entire message. *Your worth far transcends any fortune I'm capable of offering. But . . .*

She shoveled a hand into her hair and thought about calling him. But that wouldn't work. Seeing him would be best.

A LINE of white dust was on the center of the coffee table. Ephraim unbuttoned his cufflinks, jammed his impeccable linen shirt up to his elbows. He dipped his pinkie into the only thing in the world that stayed constant.

There was a knock at the door. He slid a shiny, odd-shaped figurine over the start of a good time, if he could call it that. Then he arose, his Italian loafers moving along the marble flooring to the front door of the suite.

Ephraim opened up without so much as looking into the peephole. He was met by dark brown eyes glossed with desire. A white blazer snatched her waist, her creamy breasts about to topple from the top. She wore white pants that flared all the way to the bottom and the same red lipstick Maliah had on the last time he saw her.

"You look surprised to see me, Ephraim. After all these years." Katina Gilmore cocked an eyebrow as she walked into the room. She popped the button of her blazer. Double D's as perfect as a mortal could create fell from their confines. The big melons sat perky and proud. "I thought we'd meet in the Maldives? These past few months there have given me life."

He rubbed a hand over his face. The daughter of one of the higher-up associates at Levine & Levine had an agreement with him. After they'd crossed paths in Spain, and then again in Amsterdam, they hatched a plan to meet once a month for sex. The same day every month. Their cell phones shared locations. Katina was his only tie to the past when he left the country.

"This isn't a good time."

"Your cock still work?" She sat on the couch, scooted over the fire glass figurine. "Does your dick work, Eph?"

"Don't ask idiotic questions, Katina."

"Well, if it's still in commission, you owe me a fuck. One will do fine, Ephraim. Although, make it hurt."

Katina bent down and snorted his blow in one long inhale.

"Damn." She pinched the bridge of her nose. "This is good shit. Almost as good as what's in your pants. Eph, I have a very attractive actor in France already if I crave hot and cold emotions. I came all the way to Greenwich when I checked my phone yesterday! I come here, the family expects me to say 'hola.' Make it worth it for me to have come all this way to see you, baby."

Had any other woman arrived at his door, Ephraim would've sent her packing already. As a matter of fact, they wouldn't have gotten past the threshold. But Katina did wild things with her throat. She had no limits. No limits meant no thoughts of Maliah for a few hours. With a wide mouth, Katina could erase Maliah for now.

He didn't want to erase her. Not for a moment. Not like he'd done in the past. The torment helped him survive now.

"Katina, I'll pay for your plane ride back to wherever you were vacationing." He went to squat down before her and pawed her face. "I'm not in the mood to fuck."

She whimpered. "You know, sorry would be nice."

He shrugged a little. "I'll have my private jet take you anywhere you'd like."

"Wow, it's the girl. Who'd have seen this coming? You rarely work, Eph. You're here for the girl, wow," she groaned. "Here I thought we'd attend one of my parents' shindigs. Screw in his office. We've done all the daring things, Eph. Let's sc—"

"Tell me where you'd like to go, let me make that happen." He rubbed her thigh.

"Sheesh, you're treating me like this is a breakup. Eph, you've forgotten our arrangement a few times and kicked out two, three, more women. *For me.*" She pressed her hand against her chest. "Is this the end? No more sex?"

There was another knock at the door.

His hands were very close to her erect nipples as he hooked the large button. Ephraim held his hand out for her, and Katina took it. She stood up in her stilettos and was as tall as him. Her mouth came close, and he took a step back.

"You're an asshole, Eph."

"Thanks. I've perfected the art, but trust me, you haven't met him."

At the door, he glanced through the peephole. "It's my mom."

A flurry of silent cusses came from Katina's mouth as she shook her fists at her side.

He opened the door.

"Son." His mother started into the room. "*Ms.* Gilmore."

"Rachel, I'm on my way to say hi to the parents. Should I tell them hello for you?" Katina asked. The lackluster in her tone would've made Ephraim laugh. Well, not with his mother offering a pensive smile.

"Sure." Rachel nodded.

When Katina left, he closed the door and hugged his mother. She had the same long nose but a large mane to match. His gorgeous mother held him tight. The top of her corky black hair tickled his nose. "My son, you are a brilliant, brilliant man. What would possess you to entertain the likes of that?"

"Mom, you're a good person. You don't judge, remember?"

"No?" She clutched his cheeks. "Katina doesn't have a single aspiration. No attempts. Not even a spin at a two-year college education, no endeavors, no life. You're too smart for her."

"We're almost on the same track. Her dad works sixty hours a week at our firm. My dad does too; at the same time she and I host yacht parties."

"Yes. However, when you take a case, once in a blue moon, your brain, your beautiful brain . . ." She continued to paw at his cheeks. He reached down so she could kiss his forehead. "What were we talking about, Ephraim?"

"My beautiful brain." He hooked an arm around her waist and escorted her to the couch.

Rachel's dark blue eyes searched the rumples of his bed.

"We didn't do anything."

"Good. Thank you for stopping the heart attack building in my soul."

"Mom, you're healthy. Marathons for various causes. You drink eight glasses of water a day. I prefer scotch."

"Thanks for the reminder." Rachel slipped a purified

boxed water from her purse and handed it to him. "Well, it's the heart attack or pulling your ear while we walk through the parking lot of the synagogue so that Rabbi Singer can pray with us."

"Appreciate the water, though the ear thing sounds bad. The temple has expanded since I've last been. Will my ear still be attached by the time we find her?" Ephraim asked as he sat her in the same spot Katina had used, taking a quick look at the table. A few dust particles were left.

Rachel chuckled softly. "We can pray for your ear too. You've been home for two weeks. How are things with Maliah?"

He slouched on the chair kitty-corner to her.

"Sit up, Ephraim."

Ephraim sat up.

"How will you facilitate a positive reunion with our LeeLee if you continue with the company that you keep?"

He rubbed a hand over his face, deciding not to mention his lifestyle. Ephraim's antics had been the topic of discussion on too many occasions. Not on one occasion had he responded. While Maliah didn't present a better alternative, he had to remind her of a few things. He opened the boxed water, saying, "Sorry, Mom. She's not our LeeLee anymore. Not yours, Dad's, mine. We lost rights to Maliah."

Rachel tossed her hands into the air. "Your first words had an entire sanctuary laughing, you know?"

"Yes," he mumbled. "You've said so before."

"I've also said that aside from your charm, you have a beautiful brain." She gestured, clinching her hands for a moment.

The water felt cool to his lips as he took a drink. He mused aloud, "Said that a few times in a few minutes already."

Rachel shot back, "Then use it."

"Tell Dad I'll be in the office bright and early tomorrow; I'll take a case." Ephraim glanced at the dusting on the table again. Blow made an awful distraction. He needed something impossible to deliberate, to defend a person worse than himself.

"No."

"I might return for good. Not a defense briefing here or there. I may set up shop, stick around."

"No."

"This is what you've wanted for ages? Me to come back." He cocked a thick brow. "Where is my mother?"

Rachel stood up and went to him. Her hand skimmed through his thick hair. "We've all made mistakes, Eph. You've spent ages watching Maliah from afar. Get in there. Use your *beautiful brain* and put in real effort."

Ephraim huffed. Little did his mother know, he'd tossed effort and bricks of money to fix their problems. Maybe the Hurt Room wasn't supposed to offer full-blown restitution for their past.

"I know Mom. I'm working on it. But I messed up."

———

"I MESSED UP," Tonya said, wrenching her fingers together. With a huff, she leaned against Maliah's doorframe.

You and me both, Maliah thought. She hadn't left the house this morning, except to read the note from Ephraim. Her eyes rose from the grant documents on her computer. She needed to email them back to her good friend and attorney, Landon Davenport, as soon as possible. Landon reviewed her paperwork every year and made necessary tweaks. So, she didn't want to abuse his friendship by sending them back too late. On Friday, he and the family were heading to Maui for a much-needed vacation. She set the laptop down. Sadness pierced her eyes. She hadn't been there for Tonya, not since Miami.

"Dust yourself off, Tonya. You can do so much better." Just hearing the sound of her own voice, she felt like a hypocrite.

Unworthy hypocrite. The Hurt Room hadn't helped. It only added one more thing for Ephraim to be baffled about. Why hadn't she said something? Why had she manipulated his emotions by returning without saying something?

So much beauty could have come from her return.

"Thanks, LeeLee. I am gonna do better. Ephraim's got a car on the way. I've got a boarding ticket to Buttfuck Egypt."

"Oh really?" A smile pulled at the edges of her lips. A big, genuine one. She hadn't gotten jealous at the mention of Ephraim doing something for another woman, though Maliah was shocked to know that he still had a hand in Tonya's recovery. "Where are you going?"

"Okay, not that far. Arizona is far enough. I ain't never been nowhere that my . . . that my ex didn't force me to."

"I'm glad that Ephraim could help," she murmured. At the mention of his name, she reminisced on another time. A time when they'd been unbreakable.

MALIAH HAD HELPED Tonya pack her bags. She'd found out that Ephraim had given the life coach a Target gift card for Tonya. The kid had enough clothes to get her through a few weeks. The little things she had neglected to consider when Ephraim had appeared, he had worked them out.

While waving at the SUV pulling away from the curb,

Maliah's phone rang. Ephraim's number blared across the screen. She didn't have the heart to answer. One day she'd see him face-to-face. One day.

ON WEDNESDAY, Maliah drove toward the Hurt Room. At the bottom of the windy hill, a community of homes had ample space for children to play outside. She felt herself almost smile again when slowing to a snail's pace for a group of kids in the middle of a makeshift baseball game.

Then she started up the incline, her heart shoving up into her throat. The homes became a lot more spacy. At the stop sign, the BMW veered left. Two more streets and she'd be at the place where Ephraim proffered ecstasy and stole it back again.

The brick home had foliage weaving down on each side. Flowers, which had lasted a Connecticut winter, bloomed like her heart had at the thought of meeting Ephraim at the Hurt Room.

The walls of her BMW were such a therapeutic haven that Maliah jumped when her mom swept out of a luxury vehicle. She hadn't noticed her earlier, when parking next to the car.

She forced a deep breath into her lungs, still in need of a few more moments to prepare and got out.

"Mother, you look beautiful." Maliah honed in on her fakery. She kissed each of Annaleigh's cheeks, then offered the customary feeble embrace. But the scent of her mom reminded her of her dad's grandparents. Granny once wore the same perfume. Maliah's arms wrapped tight around her mother. Encouraging words and memories flooded through her mind. Granny had been the reason she loved refrigerator magnets. Granny had polarized her from transforming into her own mom. Maya Angelou's "Still I Rise" had been the first poem Maliah had ever submitted to memory because of Granny. Her grandparents' pictures were on a plaque at the center next to the daring poet and civil rights activist.

"Maliah." Annaleigh's voice was a cool breeze, though she brushed her silk dress in shock by such a display. "You were holding on to me so tight. Why don't you come with me to the spa? I prefer to hold bags from Tiffany's, not *under my eyes.*"

On instinct, her hand went to her puffy eyes. She didn't know whether to apologize for the bear hug or her lack of sleep. "I'm sorry, Mother."

"Well, let's go, then?" Annaleigh held up her keys. "My treat, obviously."

"How is that so obvious?" The question exploded from her. Not so loud and demeaning as to shout at her mother—Granny would reach through the grave. But Maliah's tone was flanked by enough boldness to send her oblivious mom back a few steps.

"You're still the head of a nonprofit, Maliah. Therein lies why I said obvious, sheesh. Your business could otherwise make some money, but you have too many standards."

Not in bed . . . "Standards and morals that I refuse to let go," she chortled. Lots of educational nonprofits utilized college interns who needed the hours. With mostly voluntary positions, it eased the process of misappropriating funds. She played into her mother's hand for a moment. "What if I say Eph and I are seeing each other again. Then we can all go on him."

Annaleigh touched her cheek in thought. "I am getting a

few wrinkles—we can book a few more things. Are you joshing, Maliah? Is it true?"

Joshing? We are such a fake bunch. Maliah mumbled that she'd been "joshing" and started toward the double doors.

"Sweets," her mother called. How ironic. Her parents had refused to call her LeeLee, the nickname Granny had given her. But they stole the fuck name Ephraim gave her. "Sweets, you should reach out to him. I'll have your dad reach out to his parents."

The muscles in Maliah's body twisted. *I'll have your dad reach out to his parents.* She stopped herself from swiveling around on her shoes to tell her mother the absolute truth. But her mom called after her. Maliah closed her eyes and prayed that Granny was too busy enjoying heaven to look down on her now. She continued toward the door.

"You know, Maliah, if you were the type to follow through, we'd be set for life right now."

Maliah's hand grazed the wrought iron doorknob. Tears burned her eyes at the thought of what her mother was implying.

"You were so interested in education. Why didn't you utilize those brains where it counted and stop with the birth control!"

Maliah spun around with the firm belief that her father's mother couldn't possibly be mad at her now. "You're admonishing me for following through with college and not becoming pregnant?"

Annaleigh shoved a hand through her hair. "Sweets, the two of you lived together. Pregnancies were expected. Oh . . . did you honestly follow through with what I told you and stop taking your pills? Are you unable to have children?"

"Thanks for the concern, Mom." Maliah felt smaller than ever as she glanced down the lane at her mother. What if Ephraim's soldiers weren't marching? Everything was always Maliah's fault.

"We can see a specialist, Maliah. I'll clear my schedule to go with you. Once we're sure you have the ability to bear children, then you can call Ephraim."

"Clear your schedule," she murmured. The memory of her mother riffling through her panty drawers when Maliah was sixteen came back to her. Annaleigh had encouraged her to toss the pills then. In her mother's mind, a lady wasn't a statistic when cultivating a lifelong connection to a wealthy family.

"Maliah!" Annaleigh snipped. "Should we look into fertility treatments?"

In a daze, Maliah ignored her mother. Scheming and conniving flew over her head. Heart beating rapidly, Maliah glanced toward the door again. Suddenly the two-story door seemed to shoot into the sky. Her senses were moving into overdrive. She was beginning to lose herself in the notion that her connection to Ephraim meant that she was trying to entrap him. That she was no better than her mother.

This is why you're here, Maliah, she told herself. Maliah clutched at her throat and focused on the truth. She'd never use Ephraim. Never consider it. She was here to speak with Rick. She fixated on returning from Las Vegas, the happiest she'd been in her life. Then she'd had a meeting with the Levines. Ephraim had never known about the meeting, and she had to rectify that.

23

HAVING HIS ASSISTANT IN THE SAME ROOM WAS RARE. ROSA did all the time-consuming things. She'd visited Miss Anna Mae's for Yolanda's peach cobbler. She'd raised hell about having to venture into a sex store to buy the execution hood. It was last-minute when Maliah switched up the program on him last Saturday morning. She consulted with the construction company, who had added all the kinky quirks to his home. Now, the fifty-three-year-old with pocked skin and a bright smile set the box of magnets onto the table in his suite.

"You could've called me down," Ephraim said, coming from the bathroom. A towel was wrapped around his waist after a fresh shower, his thick, dark hair plastered to his head.

"Seven years of magnets, not so heavy." She shrugged. "I need something to do. You've never settled in one place too long except for the Maldives after Rebecca went after Daniel."

He snorted. "Eight years. Maliah's dad allowed her to start vacationing with my family when she was thirteen."

Rosa placed a hand into the box, where she'd bubble wrapped each one. "We've lugged this thing from continent to continent, and here I was off an entire year."

He went to the silver room service cart and grabbed at a tiny glass dome. Underneath was a cup of coffee. Without adding anything to it, Ephraim took a sip. "Put the PI on Maliah on notice."

Her eyebrow arched. She never questioned him, though, over the years, they'd become close. It was likely the only female conversation he had that didn't lead to sex.

"All right, fire the man who's watched your precious LeeLee for almost ten years, check."

Ephraim gestured for Rosa to sit down. He picked up another dome, this one larger and silver, then placed it in front of her. "Figure out how to get into my email system for the Hurt Room. I have something in mind."

"Like what?" She seemed wary of his plans. Had Ephraim followed his assistant's facial expressions, there'd have been no loss of control on his part.

"Eat." He gestured for her. "It's your favorite."

"*Digame*, Eph?" Rosa snipped in Spanish for him to tell her.

"You sure are asking a lot of questions today, Rosa. After you eat those pancakes—I pulled a few teeth to get cinnamon on them. Next, I'm going to insist that you go for the bar exam."

She rolled her eyes and began to cut her pancakes. "So, what will we be saying in this email? '*Please* meet me as scheduled on Saturday? I'll grovel and bemoan, my sweet LeeLee, and you can play Dom'?"

"Doubt that's what I'm going for, Rosa. Revoke Nori's access. And I'm not sure yet. Maybe I'll ask to meet her before? After? I don't know."

Rosa stuffed her mouth with pancakes. "What happened to flowers? I was kidding about the meeting. Might be better if you start with flowers."

"Maliah isn't a big flower person." He took another sip of the coffee. "Whatever I do has to be big."

She stood up, notepad and pen in her hand. Ephraim had hired her straight out of college; she'd been old-school then, and he appreciated it.

"One more thing," he sighed. "I have to find out who wrote the annulment documents that Maliah sent me. Yes, that shit makes me sound like a sociopath. The thought of never knowing might be the cause of some of the crazy things I do."

She chewed her lip thoughtfully. "Ephraim, we have hired computer scientists, anthropologists. There is no telling where it came from. We're missing something vital, here."

Ephraim pulled up yet another silver dome. This one had avocado smeared on toast and reminded him that he hadn't had a stiff drink in a while. Nobody at Levine & Levine would create the document. His parents loved Maliah. She'd been the first one at the office, reminding Dad to set aside a case because the flight was leaving for vacation. She'd been the reason he put down a disposition to go.

"Landon initiated the Hurt Room contract," he mentioned. Ephraim chewed in thought.

A subtle narrowing of his eyes made Rosa chortle as she often did. "Yes, sure, Landon initiated the contract. Your friend promised the utmost confidentiality."

"Landon was a year ahead of us, Rosa. He went to the same university that Maliah and I did. Call for my driver and get my email updated. Fuck that, disable the email address. My next move is going to piss her off too."

There was no going back to the Hurt Room. No turning back time. If she hated him for no reason, now she had an entire list of reasons to stay away. At least he had a scapegoat's face to bash in. Because it had to have been Landon who helped Maliah create such a vast mistake.

———————

ATSUN NEEDED the relief of not having her own submissive. With the most giving Dom in the stratosphere, she had a taste for Maliah Porter. They both did. Nori lay sideways on the bed, his head dangling over the edge. It always presented a rush when she got head, with her own brain tingling from the glorious work and gravity.

Her eloquent lips whispered just how good Nori tasted before she kissed a trail up his milky shaft. "Imagine Maliah is blowing at your cock," she said, giving the perineum a subtle bit of air. "She'd service and please you."

"Deeper, Maliah," he ordered.

Atsun swept his cock into her mouth, until the base of him slammed against the back of her throat. His dick head embedded against her throat with each thrust. They'd gone four entire days without confirmation that she'd see *her* again. Each day, she'd beseeched her Master.

Nori scrambled up and twisted Atsun's body down onto the bed. Her thighs opened wide, and her pussy blossomed. The head of his cock slid along her clit.

Her head rolled side to side on the pillow. "Master, please," she begged.

From the pocket of his button-up, he removed a clit clamp. Her nerves were on end as he applied pressure.

"Harder, baby, fuck me harder." Her voice was seductive, raw.

He threw one of her legs over his shoulder. Atsun took Nori deep, hard. He folded her into a pretzel position, tweaked the clamp until she howled like a wolf cub.

Each thrust was deeper, wetter, and with more force than the last. With her twisted body, he reached around kinks of arms and legs to find her throat and braced tight. Then his cock slid from her pussy and dove back in.

Atsun awoke in a daze, her body felt like it was hovering over the mattress for a few moments. A pool of sticky sex seeped into her skin. The world hadn't righted itself before her eyes yet, when she heard, "You may create the email, Pet."

24

MALIAH ENTERED THE HOUSE, CLINGING TO A HOPE THAT HER strained relationship with her dad didn't match the tension she experienced when she fled from her mom. Her flats were soundless against the black-and-white checkered floor. She lived less than half an hour away, though didn't make time to come home. They had church together and a token holiday

Maliah followed the sconces along the wall to her dad's study. Inside the room were all the makings of a staged home. The heavy, oak wooden desk. A thoughtful globe. A pendulum. For all of its magazine perfection, Maliah didn't find her dad inside. He rarely went into the study.

She continued along past it and toward the sitting area. Four french doors spanned the entire room, giving off a heavenly illumination. Her dad sat with a book in hand. Maliah arched an eyebrow. He removed a pair of prescription glasses that she hadn't known he ever wore.

"My baby." Her dad stood up.

"Hi, Dad."

Rick hugged her tight enough for Maliah to wonder if

he'd been given bad news by his doctor. He'd always been a tad more affectionate than her mom, but this was more than she could imagine.

"I haven't seen you at church in seven weeks."

She gulped, measuring her words to stop herself from an excuse or lie. "Yeah, it has been that long."

He rubbed a hand through his trimmed yet thick goatee, with flecks of silver. Then he sat, patting the seat next to him. "Maliah, you are almost two months behind on your mortgage . . ."

She opened her mouth to speak.

"Let me say my piece, Sweets." Again Maliah cringed at his choice of words. "I have a friend at the bank, so I know these things. Why wouldn't you come to me?"

She chewed her bottom lip. "I'm on a repayment plan."

Rick shook his head, thick lips pursed. "What if my friends knew of this? The Levines?"

"You're not friends with the Levines. And so what? Someone knowing is not going to make or break me. Thanks for the concern."

"Don't get smart. I *am* concerned."

"Me too!" she lashed out. All the good makings of the past had enveloped her body since Ephraim's actions. Now, the bad shit wanted to rear its head too.

"What do you have to be concerned about, aside from keeping your home?" He folded his arms.

"I'm sorry," she started, in no mood to go there.

"Had you come to me, there'd be no reason to discuss this!" He spat the words, each one applying pressure to her heart, making her angry. "You let me spend money out of the nose for that education *you have not put much use to!*"

"I change lives, Dad," she retorted. "Are you done

scheming and doing wrong?" Maliah bit back the tears in her eyes, closing them for a moment.

"Who do you think you're talkin' to?" he shot back. Rick had forgotten for a moment that he no longer used that tone of voice, that he'd distanced himself from the other side of his family. That "well, you see, my boy . . ." and other upbeat phrases were his go-to.

And that his being a clown around rich folk until he got a taste of that life had been her downfall with Ephraim.

She never cared too much for flowers. So Ephraim made those paper ones where you place your fingers inside, turn them. Those paper ones had the most endearing words. Even with his "could have been a doctor" handwriting, she never stopped loving those paper flowers.

That was how he'd proposed in Vegas. They were on the good side of tipsy, full bellies from a buffet. They'd been to a coed strip club, because Maliah couldn't shake her need to fuck. She'd turned twenty-one, and her therapist's denial of her being a sex addict still hadn't ended. Luckily for them, they hadn't argued. They'd half screwed in front of strippers on a pole, eyes for each other only.

So once she made out the proposal via Ephraim's words on a paper flower, she flew into his arms. He didn't have a ring, yet. She didn't need a marble-like diamond on her hand.

She needed Ephraim. Craved him so bad. Maliah determined that while some people went to Vegas and made a mistake, her heart had dominated all. They'd done what lovers did. They had the perfect story for their children—nix the strip club stint.

And then they came home from Vegas. He left another paper flower, explaining for her to do nothing. What a young alpha. He'd do everything. Have a grand party. Invite Yolanda, Daniel, his family, her family . . .

A smile controlled the muscles in her cheeks as she sat in the sitting room of the Levine mansion. They would soon know why she had such a glow. She'd been on her way to the gym, when Ephraim's mother, Rachel, had called her over. Mind in the clouds, Maliah went.

Rachel calling her over happened every so often. She'd call, needing help with some facet of a fund-raiser. Maliah would help. She'd call Rachel for lunch. This was the norm.

Rachel had brought Maliah's first mensuration pad during a vacation. Mrs. Levine knew the type of wedding dress Maliah wanted—had she and Ephraim thought to wait.

But as Maliah sat in the living room of the Levine home, Rachel stared at the plume of smoke coming from a teapot.

"Have some," Rachel had said, her smile not reaching her eyes, per usual. She pushed over the tray of sugar cookies.

Maliah grinned, bit back her tongue, hoping that her elation wasn't a tell. She and Ephraim had to witness the shock on his mother's face. The surprise, the jubilation.

Maliah picked up one of the fresh-baked cookies. "Oh my god, I'm supposed to be at the gym, Rach. You know these are my addiction."

"Abner will join us in a few." She'd said that five times already. Maliah needed to get back to Ephraim. He'd plan a wedding in an hour. While he had his quirks, he had assistants on the payroll already. She only needed a handful of people—their parents, Daniel, Yolanda. Maybe their friend Landon, who was studying for the bar.

Abner entered.

Maliah rose to hug him. He was tense. She'd felt the same tension in his frame while hugging him in the past. "Hard case?" she asked.

They sat for a while. The conversation stalled while Maliah groaned over another sugar cookie. "What's going on, Rach, Mr. Levine?"

"If I hadn't seen loopholes in your father's case, I wouldn't have taken it, Maliah," Mr. Levine had said. All those words spilled forth as Maliah was pouring herself jasmine tea into a pink floral cup. Maliah put down the teapot.

Rachel exhaled heavily. She said his name as she often did when he'd gotten cranky, though it usually accompanied a smile.

It dawned on Maliah that Rachel hadn't looked into her eyes today, not really. Not like usual.

"Eph and I are having a gathering tonight." Her tone was low. Instincts alerted her that there was something still left unsaid. The family who had welcomed her from the start and offered the best advice had "more ideas" she had yet to know. "Will you all be able to make it?"

"Maliah, we are talking about your parents," Rachel reminded her.

"If you and Ephraim are to stay married, we will all need to have a chat with them," Abner added.

"Eph told you that we're married already?" Again, instincts transformed her inquiry into a whisper, though the newlywed smile she knew would stay on her face for years stood frozen.

"Your father's activities will need to align with the Levine credo," Abner continued. No personal affect in his tone, he said, "There won't be any compensation for our services in the future. However, your father's actions should not warrant the need for us saving him. Do you think we can get that across to your father, keep the two of you lovebirds happy?"

"What are saying, Abner?" she asked. "What do my father's actions have to do with me and Eph?"

Rachel met Maliah's gaze for a fraction. "The two of you are lovely together. We have to assist your parents to mesh into that. With teamwork, everything will be lovely."

"Maliah, I'm not sure if you're aware we kept Rick from being indicted. He misclassified workers as lesser-skilled, underpaying

them. There were other potential charges such as falsifying information about payroll and employees."

"I wasn't aware," she murmured, feeling small beneath her
father-in-law's gaze.

"I hate being forced in this position to tell you, LeeLee." His
voice softened for half a second. "A worker was killed at one of the
construction job sites. The kid had hardly gotten a chance at life."

Tears formed in Maliah's eyes.

"Abner, you did not have to divulge such things." Rachel
pursed her lips. Then her mouth moved into a small smile. "Lee-
Lee, are you able to help us help your parents?"

Though Rachel had used such a caring voice, Maliah sat in
shock.

Since she didn't speak, Abner called out more of Rick's sins.
"He still underpays workers and falsifies payroll, Maliah."

Were they comparing her parents to the Beverly Hillbillies?
All the therapy sessions where her shrink had validated her
beliefs that her parents could have used a parenting class or two
came flooding back. My father let someone die on his watch
and got off, she considered.

"LeeLee, we—"

"No! What do Ephraim and I have to do with my father?" she
gasped. "They took one parenting class but didn't complete the
session. We had family therapy . . . But they stopped having time
to go! My dad's still up to his old schemes?"

"He's never stopped, Maliah," Abner snipped.

Rachel reached over and patted her knee. "Maliah, I've known
you for ages."

"Yes," Abner agreed. "Since you were a beautiful, little girl
with pigtails in your hair."

"What if my father keeps doing what he does? If I can't
convince him," she squeaked, a thousand thoughts zipping
through her mind.

"*I have faith that you can.*" *Rachel said.* "*We have faith.*"

While she played good cop, Abner asked, "*Do you want to ruin over a hundred-year legacy? Every Levine son has become a litigator. The media would eat us alive if our family had to defend your father, sweetheart.*"

"*No, of course not.*" *She knew the pride the Levines had for their history. It was set on a foundation of blessings. Ephraim's great-great-grandfather had fled Poland as Germany began to invade their hometown. The attorney was determined to build a new life for his family.*

"*Let's stop for a moment,*" *Abner said, picking up the teapot.* "*I see that I'm bringing you to tears. This hurts me as much as it hurts you.*"

Maliah knew he wasn't attempting to be sarcastic, but her body was racked with tears. He continued to speak; she hadn't heard a single word.

"*Leave us!*" *Rachel said.*

Maliah realized that the smile she expected to cling to for years had vanished as Rachel handed her a tissue.

"*Excuse me.*" *Abner placed his hands on his knees and arose.*

Rachel watched his departure. A feeling of being lost wrapped itself around Maliah. The discussion wasn't over. The "*hard*" *part, she felt had yet to come.*

Rachel sat beside her, placed an arm around her. Maliah burrowed her face into Rachel's neck and continued to cry. All she could think of was how changing her parents would be past impossible, and how much she loved Ephraim. He deserved better. The image her parents had gotten their talons into by any means was what the Levines epitomized. God, why did I pursue Eph? *She thought long and hard about the red signs of Rick's over eagerness to play into the role.* "Well, you know, son" *became a soundtrack in her ears.*

"*I love you, Maliah,*" *Rachel declared while rubbing her back.*

"You became my daughter years ago. Then, when your grandparents died, our connection strengthened all the more."

At Rachel's encouragement, years of happiness shuffled through Maliah's mind. Her grandparents' train had derailed a few years ago. The same happened to Rachel's grandma in Poland, so long ago. They'd been close; that connection had brought them closer. And Maliah valued any advice Rachel offered.

"But your father's current antics at his construction company is very disconcerting."

"I can't change him," she sniffled. Maliah felt so disgusted for her dad's misconduct. The death of an employee and skirting by hadn't stopped his conniving ways.

"I'll be honest with you, since Abner chose full honesty," she grumbled. "My husband was not going to take your father's case at all, after their first chat. Ephraim came home, and he told me he simply had no idea how to talk to you. I had to see that. My son, the trickster, the kid who is so attuned that he can make a person smile after a tragedy. I had to meet you."

"Rach, I love him." Her mind was tormented with how little of her parents she knew. If Rick was the cause of a young man's death, her mother had to be aware.

Abner returned to the room with stacks of legal paper clipped together. "You two, do this the right way. Have it annulled." He placed the papers onto the table. "For the time being."

"How dare you?" Maliah jumped away from Rachel's attempts to console her. She placed her fingertips on the papers and flicked them back over to him. The pages flew onto the ground; the clip had pinged off. Some pages landed on the floor or on the top of his loafers.

Instead of gathering them together, Abner held up a hand. "Maliah, once your parents are in line, then let's have a multimillion-dollar wedding."

"We're married—happily married," she screeched.

He reached down to stack them all in order. "And you will do it over. Diamonds, flowers— "

"We won't." She grabbed the stack from his hands and made the worst mistake of her life.

"WHAT HAS GOTTEN INTO YOU?" her dad asked. His question pulled Maliah from the past. Or it could've been how he'd taken an abrupt stand from the couch while asking it.

Maliah rubbed her hand over her face and then apologized. "Dad," she said, coming to a stand too. "I love you the way you are."

His body was stiff as she wrapped an arm around him. She embraced Rick, his arms at his sides. For a few seconds, they dawdled there like fish out of water. Then he hugged her back, the best one he'd ever given.

The Levines had never been anything but good to her. She knew they weren't lying.

Maliah could feel the tears rushing to her eyes, blurring them. "I need to go, Dad."

She'd signed the annulment papers because she wasn't able to see her parents change. These days, at We Rise Learning Center, Maliah welcomed the notion of a youth exceeding her expectations.

She started back down the hall, wondering why she couldn't give her parents the benefit of the doubt.

Dad called after her. "Is this about some boy? You should call Ephraim."

"Maybe." She was out the door. The sun cast a golden shadow across the sky. The moon prepared to dominate. These last few days had been awful. Now, Tonya was gone.

Maliah slid into the driver's seat of her car, the place

where her mind went rampant. She didn't want to think. She'd prefer the Hurt Room to lonely. The pain was more welcoming than any sort of thought, such as why hadn't she gone to her parents asked them to change. Chances were, they'd do it for a Levine's approval.

"Yeah, but you wanted them to change for you," Maliah murmured to herself. Her parents hadn't put much effort into her activities. One sixty-minute parenting class had left them livid. Three family therapy sessions, and then the excuses came. But their actions didn't matter. Just maybe her response to the Levines had been the perfect cop-out.

She'd never been worthy of a Levine anyway.

Pulling out her phone, she started for Ephraim's contact but noticed a Gmail notification on her screen. There were a few. An educational blogger that she stalked for arts and crafts. A shoe warehouse discount.

The Hurt Room.

The fancy emblem for the place that took control of her mind tempted her. What dark delights was Ephraim offering now . . .

25

TREES SURROUNDED THE LOG CABIN. THE PLACE WAS different than she'd expected to meet her ex. She didn't expect a single shiny knickknack.

Maliah sat in the car, her senses on high alert. The slope of a mountain and a cluster of trees made her reluctant to go inside. Not another home was in sight for over a mile. Not a single neighbor to hear her cries if he chose not to acknowledge "red."

She breathed in a rich, fragrant scent from the seductive French perfume her mother had bought for her one year. Bath and Body Works wouldn't do in this situation. Even if it hurt, she wanted to smell so good for him.

Maliah concentrated on the tender care that he gave her body when bathing her. Ephraim's brown orbs were enriched with disappointment in himself. He was a changed man. The one who she hadn't ruined in that moment. No matter how much therapy hadn't helped, Maliah knew she didn't want the bad Ephraim. She had to peel back the layers of the monster and claim back her love.

She got out of the car in a trench coat. Though it was a

warm summer night, she'd dressed in her best lingerie. It may have been assuming, but Google Maps had dropped off the face of the earth when she looked online. No Zillow to confirm what type of place they were meeting at. And she was unsure about a possible change of clothes.

Of course, dressing provocatively after their last encounter might have been too much. But his email promised that the Hurt Room was closed for business. That he planned to show her how a true Dom nurtured his sub. She craved this.

At the front door, there was a yellow sticky note. Not as ingenious as the pages plucked from her favorite stories, but she read it aloud. "Let yourself in."

Maliah glanced around before pressing her hand on the iron knob. There had to be blackout windows. The entire space was covered in votive electric candles—perfect for a cabin in the woods.

The open floor plan boasted new appliances in the kitchen. Maliah smirked. She didn't care how custom this place was now. Her high heel punctured something soft as she started to walk. She glanced down to see a note on the floor.

Maliah reached down and clasped the stick note. "There's wine in the fridge. The best."

A geek-squeal roared through her. She had all her thoughts collected. They'd drink and *talk*. She'd clear the air for both their sakes, and *please, oh please let it lead to sex.*

They were a dysfunctional breed. She'd brought that on them from the start with her desire to screw Ephraim at the spite of her father. *If* Rick did care. Either way, she needed her ex's cock like yesterday.

Her body raged, split on craving sweet or rough. But one

thing she coveted with her whole heart was for them to go back to the start.

Maliah went to the fridge. Inside was a bottle of red wine, white wine, and a sparkling rosé. She pulled out the chilled rosé and noticed another note on the glass beneath the bottles.

Her eyes skimmed over the tantalizing words: "There's a slip on the bed. Wear it. Nothing else."

Maliah uncorked the wine, giggled as the fizz leaked onto her fingers. She took a drag straight from the bottle.

She then went to the bed. A single red silk slip was on it. She undressed and placed it on. Her nipples rubbed ever so softly against the swoon-worthy material. She paused. Now what?

A radio came on, the music soft, low. Nothing about it screamed pain, hurt.

"Get on the bed."

She did as told, looking around. He was using the weird voice scrambler again, though it didn't sound as steely. Less Keanu Reeves the Pussy Slaughter, and more . . . something else Maliah couldn't quite put her finger on.

Maliah was unable to see him as the candles didn't illuminate the recesses of the vast room. She glanced at a darkened entryway that had to lead to a bathroom, though she couldn't make out Ephraim.

"Don't find me, Pet. Tonight is about you."

"Thank you." Her breathing slowed. Those words of his had sounded like heaven. What woman didn't want to have all the attention? Greed was hypnotic.

"There's a covering under the pillow. Wear it."

What kind of covering? Maliah stopped herself from saying. They could have their much-needed chat later. Also, a submissive took great pleasure in believing in her Dom.

She reached her hand beneath the pillow to find a black silk hood that would cover every inch of her face and drape down to her shoulders was under it. She held it, eyebrows pushing together.

"Please trust me."

She hesitated. The computerized voice was still on her mind. He sounded good, too good. But different . . .

With one last exhale, total darkness dawned on Maliah as she slipped it over her face. She found it easy to breathe, a lot more than anticipated. The only issue she had was sight.

"You have been perfect, Pet. Can I show you your worth tonight?"

"Sure." A half-smile teased her lips. She contemplated on Nori for the moment. Every time he had a question, she had a response that conflicted with the BDSM credo.

"With the mask on your face, Miss Honey, the rest of your senses will be heightened. May I tie you up?"

"Ye-yes." She didn't know why her voice was so shaky. Anticipation swirled in her abdomen.

His hand massaged one foot after the other as he placed each one into something soft.

"These are fur cuffs, by the way," he assured her.

Her senses were already heightened that it tickled a little. Maliah stopped the need to chuckle when coming to terms with how wide apart her legs were. The dress hardly covered her hips.

"Lay your arms on the pillows above your head, please," he ordered.

Another set of fur handcuffs were applied to each of her wrists. Maliah's heart started to race. No matter how tenderly bound her wrists and ankles, he had ultimate power.

"Our first instrument for pleasure," he began. His soothing voice stopped the stutter of her heart, darkness surrounding her. Maliah cackled at the feel of something soft against her calf leg.

"A feather." She settled down. The tingling trace that it left while ascending to the softest place of her thigh set her heart racing. Ephraim had never kissed the back of her knee. No one had. Her body shuddered at the thought of their first encounter. Ephraim had used the feather. The damn thing was so vanilla it put her at ease. Well, until he traced the lips of her pussy, getting the feather all wet.

This time, he alternated between the feather to his lips. His mouth pressed against every single spot that tickled. His lips were delicate while ascending to the inside of her thigh.

The feather inched toward her pussy. Then his mouth. With every caress, warmth coiled in the depth of Maliah's body. Again, and again, her Master worked his way higher. The anticipation tasted almost as good as his seed sliding down her throat.

"Breathe," he coaxed, his warmth so near her throbbing pussy lips. "A climax can be heightened further when you're breathing."

"I just . . ." She groaned as the feather splayed across her mound. "You're going to kiss me, right? Please say you'll kiss me."

She felt his abdomen compress before he broke into laughter.

HE HADN'T EXPECTED to laugh today. Not after the tail assigned to watch Maliah was rerouted to Landon. After the guy won a pro bono case, the investigator lost him only to find his *old friend* at Landon at home later. Who would Ephraim be to cut the man down at his house, in front of the wife and kids? Landon had cost him. But laughter was good for his bones right now.

"You're greedy, beautiful." Ephraim shook his head, glad that he'd paused his obsession enough to have Rosa shoot out a quick email. "But of course, I'll kiss your pussy."

He was close to her sex. Crazy close. "The sight of your cunt is so scrumptious, I have to kiss it."

But he didn't kiss it just yet. While the dubious man had switched focus from revenge to love, Ephraim promised to do it right now. Do all the stupid shit Nori suggested. Call her Miss. Honey. Use the feather, the idiotic ice. All the training he'd rushed the instructor through became his vice. For Maliah's sake, he'd do it right tonight. *Like you should've done in the first place, you impatient bastard*, Ephraim told himself.

<hr />

"THE SIGHT of your cunt is so scrumptious . . ." Maliah let those words spin around in her consciousness until her brain turned into mush. As if her treasure had a mind of its own, her clit jumped, her lips swelled. When the feather stroked against her pearl, all the air shot from her lungs.

She pulled at her restraints, saying, "This isn't fair."

"That's the furthest thing from the truth, Miss Honey. Your pleasure is my delight."

He felt near—too near to be tasting between her thighs. Maliah jumped as the feather stroked across the curves of her breast. A laugh raked through her. A good, hearty laugh. The kind nutcases had on the way to an insane asylum. So raw and innocent to the fact that torture and no control were about to meet up with them.

"You think this is funny?"

"I think this is torture," she shot back, grinning so hard that it hurt. She was thankful in this moment her face was covered.

He gripped at the seam of her slip, tearing it straight down the middle.

"Well, that made things easy," she commented.

The feather tickled at her nipple, hardening it. Like a dog who had learned a routine, she waited for his lips, felt his warm breath and her body burst into a million tiny fractions as he pulled her tit in his mouth. His teeth skimming against the taut skin added another . . .

"Oh God," she moaned. "Please tell me you're going to kiss me there. I beg of you, kiss me there."

"Miss Honey, I promised to eat your pussy tonight. Patience."

Every time he mentioned her pussy, her walls contracted. She could almost hear her sex growling at her. He placed the feather around her other nipple. Nerve endings were brought to attention.

After all the hurt she'd dished out and he'd returned, this delicate touch brought tears to her eyes. The lack of sight fucked with her mind. She chewed down on her tongue, begging herself to be as obedient as a sub. *LeeLee, you have it in you! Follow the damn rules*, she mentally chastised herself.

When the feather splayed across her mound, Maliah's legs shook. His lips were inches away—she could feel it, his warm breath the only thing that touched her body. Maliah licked her lips in blinding anticipation. Yet he moved away.

"Where are you . . ."

"Silence, please. No moving." He was already back.

A hitch sliced through her throat.

"No moving, no moaning. Not a peep."

It was at the tip of her tongue to question him about "moaning." Moaning loud and sex talk were an encouragement and incentive to continue a certain action.

When something as frigid as ice touched the tip of her nipple, Maliah sucked in a gulp full of air. No moaning made sense.

"Not a single sound, Miss Honey," he ordered. The ice glided across her nipple. Then her Dom's breath was a fraction away from her skin, warming the freezing area. His tongue dragging over the melted ice.

"Ohhhh." She squirmed, unable to help herself. The ice was gone, and his mouth descended on her nipple. Then the ice trailed along her skin, and try as she might, keeping still wasn't possible. All thoughts fled her mind except for one: she craved his touch. She craved her master's touch more than anything on this earth, yet he kept stealing it away.

He suddenly pulled away, but she could still feel him near. He had to be watching her, because she felt his gaze raking all the way down to her soul.

Her stomach trembled as the ice floated over her navel. His tongue entered. Her pussy cried tears of wetness, seeping down the inside of her thighs. Her inner folds wanted the same love and attention of her navel.

"Please, Eph . . ." she begged.

"Stop moving. And I did say not a sound, which means I can't taste you yet."

Maliah lost track of time as he used the ice on different places on her body. The cold trailed along her tantalizing brown curve. One time, followed by a subtle bite to her hip that left her groaning. Each caress left her brain delirious with desire. She hadn't expected something so minuscule as an ice cube to entice nerve endings all over her. Her nerves were ready to detonate, and her sex was ground zero.

His palm pressed over her lower abdomen, and the ice coasted across her labia. The torture lasted all of a second. When the ice moved away, Maliah whimpered again.

He pressed his lips to her chilled second set, his teeth grazing softly over her clit. Maliah's hands crumpled into tiny fists. An explosion had built up inside of her body so swiftly.

"Breathe," he ordered, the whisper coating across her sex.

Maliah wiggled her hips, achy with the thought of being filled. "Fuck." She gritted her teeth as the chill slid across her soaking wet core.

His cock slapped at the top of her pussy. Then the sudden flush of ice sent tendrils of shock waves through her body.

"I'm not going to make it!" she screamed, her arousal ready to topple over. All the resolve that a good bitch would have when waiting for her Master had flown out the window.

His body tensed a little. Then again, it tensed and contracted. *He's laughing at me, silently enjoying my torment,* Maliah thought. Though curses were at the tip of her tongue, she stopped herself from being noncompliant. She'd become an animal, a trained animal who relied on her Master. For longer than she thought she'd be able to survive, ice slithered over her sex.

"I'm dying," she groaned, finding it hard to speak. She could see herself now, all tied up and at his mercy. *And delighting in it.* His fingertips traced the inside of her legs.

She panted, like a dog who was ready to bark on cue. The waiting killed her. Her head swam in lust as his cock swam in the juices of her outer folds, yet he did not penetrate her.

"Oh yes," she moaned. This was the greatest feeling on earth, even if he hadn't fully caved to her needs. Maybe her Dom knew her body more than she did.

Greedy hands gripped at Maliah's ass cheeks. The sensation of a succulent breath against her lips, sent her into a spiral of cries. She screamed, "You are killing me!"

Her lower back arched as his mouth sucked at her pussy. Every sense was heightened: The decadent patter of her heart. The muscles in her stomach tightening as his mouth took a journey of her treasure. His tongue glided across her copious wetness, drinking the arousal unleashed for him. Her limbs shook as he pressed his lips against her button. He sucked her tiny clit through his teeth, soft, gentle, without a single ounce of pain, and she swore she was about to pass out.

"Please fuck me," she groaned.

"All right, my cock is disappearing into you now," he said. "Oh, your beautiful folds contrast so perfectly with my dick. You should see this."

ATSUN'S entire body shook with rage. Of course, Ephraim would lock her out of the Hurt Room server. In her long life, she'd met a hacker for the Triads. She'd been young then, and her sex couldn't keep him. But she'd inherited a few invaluable lessons from the hacker. Now, the only thing Ephraim had done right was to push his email out before Atsun had a chance to finish constructing her own. Hers was written with tenderness and affection for the woman she had fallen madly for. She'd been revising it when a message popped up on Nori's computer that *it was sent*. With the tricks at her disposal, retracting his letter would've been a cinch. But she worked a bit of code and saw that it was read less than a minute later.

She crouched against the window, her eyes on Ephraim. People said he was attractive, but she'd only ever been attracted to Nori. He was the father she never had. Her fingers gripped the frame of the windowsill as she attempted to make out the wrong man's words.

"He's trying to make amends," she whispered to herself. Reaching into her back pocket, she grabbed her switchblade. With the silver handle covering the sharp edge, she slid it across the inside of her wrist. Back and forth it went, while she concentrated on warm, soothing blood. Nori would be livid that she'd snuck out tonight. He'd be even more enraged about her owning a knife, so cutting herself was out.

The chill of night bore into her bones. Atsun chewed down on her tongue, watched her lover be forced into sex, and gulped down copper. She had to leave soon, before Nori left the room of one of his pets. Was she abandoning her pet by allowing Ephraim to stay here? Could she pick the lock, go inside, slit his throat, get her possession back?

"I'm so sorry, Maliah. I failed you tonight. But I promise you, on my entire life, I'll be back for us." Her words warmed against the glass, fogging it. Atsun's palm slid across the haze. She didn't need to see evidence of what she knew. One day, men wouldn't make the world go around. That'd be the day she saved her pet. She ran back into the night, heading to the main road to call a Lyft with Nori's phone.

MALIAH WAS HAVING the night of her life. Her walls snug and pliant, and glossed around his cock, sucking him down. His cock was buried inside of her heaven, growing thicker and diving deeper.

"What a pretty pussy. You feel exquisite." He had to be talking to her sex. Talking to her pussy, and damn, her walls rained down on his cock. "You are such a wet pussy, thank you."

"Mmmm," she agreed, overwhelmed by sexual stimulation. He staked claim to her hips, passionate in his fucking. With every few strokes, his cockhead came out, sailed over her clit, and dove deep again. His hard cock only exited her for a few seconds, but her body screamed for each one. Then those sweet strokes grew stronger, his dick dwelling deep inside of her. He pumped her pussy, so hard that with each thrust, she screamed.

The only hurt she felt was the rawness of her throat and the fucking of her mind as he came out like clockwork. Master stroked at her pearl and back in again. There was no way for her to time it, now. He'd switched up the rotation and given her what she needed all the same. Stark raving mad, she clenched her walls around his cock. It was the only protest that she had, the only way to beg his dick not to leave her sex. Master dwelled deep into her slit, pulled out, then slithered his hard, soaking cock around her clit. Slithered and slithered until she bit down on her coppery-tasting tongue. *You're doing well, LeeLee*, she encouraged herself, as his thick cock stroked her pearl. She continued to bite down on her tongue, not denying her master his pleasure. Their pleasure.

When it seemed the air in her lungs had died, her master slammed back into her. The force sent her breasts slapping her skin.

"Yes, yes, yes," she screamed, needing him to leave her bare so that his monster cock could slam back into her. His balls teased her asshole with each hard pounding. She thought to claim her love, say the words she hadn't spoken to him in years. But she settled for "yessss." Her voice was too raw and her brain too muddled to conjure the extra words.

"You want me to pound this pussy till it hurts, Miss Honey?"

Maliah tried to speak, her throat too sore to say so.

"Miss Honey, this is the last time I will offer you pain." He stroked deep, his strong body wrapping around hers. "Do you want me to pound your pussy till it hurts?" he growled in her ear.

"Hell, yessss," she panted.

"Tell me, Pet, that you want *my* sweet little pussy to ache, tell me!" His fingernails sunk into the flesh of her ass, and his cockhead collided with the brim of her cervix.

"Hurt my pussy," she whimpered.

He pulled out, did a deathly slow swirl of his cock along her clit. All the sticky juices tantalized and sent her into a tizzy. Then his cock took a slow dive into her. "Tell me you want me to beat my little, heavenly cunt."

Maliah gripped at her wrist restraints. "It's yours, I'm yours!"

In response, his cock stabbed ferociously at her insides, long, quick thrusts that sent her lower back into an arch. Each stab deep in Maliah was felt in her gut. The hurt sent her eyes rolling back in her head, her toes curling. She was too weak to hold her body up. Too many orgasms left her body on empty. She had to look like a rag doll, with him breaking down every inch of her good, good sex. Her screeches became nonexistent. No "yeses," no nothing. All she gave her Master were whimpers and mewing. Hell, if she could snatch one hand from her constraints, she'd suck her thumb, have a good cry too.

"All right, you're so tight, Pet. Squeezing my cock for all your worth."

She breathed her response, unable to keep up with his appetite. By some miracle, Maliah felt another explosion gathering in her core, limbs so tired she knew she'd have to let the eruption lead.

"Miss Honey, you can milk me now." Her spasming sheath captured his entire cock as she climaxed around him. His orgasm funneled straight through her in response. With his arms holding her tiny frame, they came together. Master fell into her. Muscles, limbs, his entire body crushed down on her, and it felt divine. The claiming of his arms wrapped around her, with their heartbeats pounding against each other.

Euphoria surrounded her, beckoned her to stay forever. But he climbed from her broken body.

"Ephraim?" she called out. Darkness captured her inhibitions. "Eph?"

She told herself not to panic, the yearning for him so strong. Maliah forced a deep breath into her lungs and focused on the sound of footsteps. She was in too much of a state of bliss to have a real conversation, though she needed his arms around her. They'd spent so many years on the wrong side of a good love story. She needed him near.

"Eph . . ." Maliah lifted her head as if she had the ability to search past the pitch-black.

Something warm and slick touched her foot. Lavender and mint floated toward her as he began to massage her feet. With her achy pussy satiated, Maliah groaned. "I could die right now."

"You're under strict orders not to" were the last words Master said to her.

———————

MALIAH AWOKE IN DARKNESS. Birds chirped outside, warning that it was no longer night. She pressed a hand over her face and met the silk mask. She pulled it off, the side of her head on the pillow. Upon turning over, she found the rest of the area empty, except for the furry handcuffs.

26

RETRIBUTION WOKE EPHRAIM AT THE CRACK OF DAWN. THAT and the private investigator who advised him Landon Davenport had left his house. He'd thought to awaken Maliah but wanted to separate their lives from the world he'd created for them. Also, she looked too beautiful asleep to awaken, and he'd been too focused to leave a note.

The sun beamed down. Landon Davenport dashed across the busy street, a pink box of donuts in his hands.

"That him, boss?" Yesiv mumbled from the front seat of Ephraim's SUV. Little did his driver know, he'd leaned against the window, watching the water-stained doors of the donut shop. He'd waited for this moment to corner Landon away from his dear wife and children. A family was all the important things that his *friend* helped cost him.

Ephraim slammed the car door, coasting on his Italian loafers. He pushed up the sleeves of his tailored suit and stopped at the parallel parked Tesla he presumed was Landon's. Had to be this one, or the one down the block.

His so-called friend was riding cloud nine as he meandered down the street. He planned to punch the whistle back into Landon's mouth, along with a few teeth. But Landon fell from his oblivion and waved.

"Ephraim, Eph! I haven't seen you since Abner's sixty-fifth. Three, four years ago, eh?"

"Yeah, that had to be the last time," Ephraim replied, chill as ice.

"I bought a couple donuts for the kids."

"The kids." Ephraim's mouth shoved into a smile.

"Being summer, they don't wake up until noon. But we have a 10:00 a.m. flight. Can I rain check you for the cigar lounge if you're still in town next week?"

Ephraim matched him question for question. "When's the last time you saw Maliah?"

His head tilted, eyebrows knitted. "We still attend the same Baptist church. Although, I haven't seen her in a month or two."

Ephraim decided to keep him talking. See what he could get out of him. Which was something he didn't do with certain clients. Some things needed to stay in the dark such as the extent of their guilt. And here he'd been in the dark for years.

"How about other correspondence? Phone, text, chat." Ephraim placed his hands into the pockets of his blazer, stopping himself from reacting. He'd let Landon dig his own grave.

The man hesitated for a moment. "Ephraim, I'm married, you know that."

"I do." Ephraim leaned against the driver's door of the Tesla.

"So, you two back together?"

"We're working on it."

Landon shuffled into the pocket of his khaki shorts for his keys. "Good. Great. I'll say that if Maliah has half the love I saw in her for you back in the day, then there are no reasons to worry."

The car chirped, doors unlocking as Landon's subtle signal that they were done.

Ephraim didn't move. He chewed his bottom lip, contemplated for a moment. The men had interacted on very few occasions in the past. His *friend* was a really good liar.

"So the cigar lounge . . . If you're still in town?" Landon's eyebrow rose.

"Landon, what the fuck would I look like wanting to have a powwow, with you? All I need to know is, why did you draft annulment documents for Maliah?"

He shuffled in his sandals. "What? The documents . . . well, yes. She asked—"

Ephraim's fist slammed into his nose. The pink box dropped. Chocolate, sprinkles, jelly, all sorts of donuts tumbled out. He brought his fist back for another blow, designated for Landon's mouth, when his arm was held back.

Yesiv bit out, "*Nyet*, boss."

Landon placed the side of his hand to the crimson stream coming from his nose. "What did you do that for?"

"She was my wife! You took her from me." Ephraim tossed a fist at his own chest. "*She was mine!*"

At this point, he'd fallen off the handle way too far. Ephraim didn't even lose his chill this hard after a good, long snort of coke. But Maliah was the best drug he'd ever tasted. She was his.

"*Uspokoysya*, boss." Yesiv ordered him to "take it easy."

Though Landon's eyes were brightened in confusion, he nodded.

Ephraim snatched his arm away from the driver. "She was my wife," he said again. For years, he was denied the declaration. All the energy he put into the celebration, he never got a chance to tell anyone that Maliah had been his wife.

"Maliah was your wife?" Landon pinched at his nose.

Yesiv remover his linen shirt, pulled his white undershirt over his head, and handed it to Landon. "Please," Yesiv said to him in a thick Russian accent, "did you create the annulment document or know who did?"

"I'm . . . my bad. I thought you helped her . . ." Ephraim's voice fizzled out. He pulled out a roll of cash, but Landon shook his head, even in a state of shock.

Yesiv started across the street, then paused. It was as if the driver thought Ephraim needed to be guided.

"I got it," Ephraim gritted out, opening the back door for himself.

"Boss, I've been driving for you for almost five years. Whenever you're in the States, I got you. But this is not you."

He laid his head back against the seat. Maliah had fucked with his head way too much. All these years, he'd never gotten over those papers.

"I'm not signing this shit, LeeLee. You're mine," he remembered telling her.

Before Ephraim invented the Hurt Room, there wasn't a single stain on his conscience as it pertained to Maliah. Loving her too hard, had that done him in? He needed a chalkboard and an entire outline of possible ways to get her back.

"Where to?"

"LeeLee's," he replied. She had to be home now.

Yesiv sighed, pushing the gear into drive, and pulled away from the curb.

Ephraim grimaced while glancing through the window at Landon. The attorney was reaching down with his face tipped up. While pinching his nose, he picked up the donuts.

Ephraim shook his head at the sight. Then he pulled his phone out to give Maliah a call. No more time was passing by without them clearing the air. Of course, the log cabin would've been the best place for them to set things right, but those annulment papers controlled his mind.

She answered at the last possible minute. He could hear faint pop music in the background and a peppy voice saying to "Kick harder!"

"Maliah, are you home?"

"Why ask? What happened to 'I saw that ass last night, sweetheart.'" She spouted off the statement he'd said from her front porch weeks ago. "You're my creepy stalker, right? You know where I am, don't you?"

Ephraim ignored her. Of course, he didn't, now that the investigator had led him into this ridiculous scenario. He snapped back, "Okay, so, I'm on my way to your house, then. You'll be there, or I'll figure out how to let myself in."

———

WHAT SORT of drugs was he on to declare he'd come to her house? Last night had been one of the most wonderful nights of her life, but Ephraim had left before they'd had a chance to talk.

"No, breaking and entering for you, Ephraim," Maliah chortled. "What do you want?"

"You," he replied. "Always has been you."

"Eph, are you on drugs?" She took it there.

"Why would you ask me that?"

"I can practically hear the wheels on your brain. They're rotating faster than I can go from zero to 100 in the Lykan Hyper, and that's quick. *Eph, I had a long night.*" She extended each word, offering him a hint. Seconds passed and he hadn't apologized for leaving her this morning.

She glanced into the dance/kickboxing combination class that she'd forced Yolanda to this morning. The gym had been on her way—the cabin was so far that a mini-vacation could've been on her way home.

Still, he didn't apologize. She dawdled. "Very Long night. Long and . . . and I'm tired. And I'm out!"

"Then we'll see which one of us makes it to your place first, won't we."

The phone hung up before she could have the last word. Maliah gritted her teeth and shoved it away.

Ephraim had given her the greatest love last night. Utter perfection. The bitter Maliah that didn't want anything to do with Ephraim and saw him as something so unattainable craved the thought of still seeing him. The Hurt Room offered them the grand opportunity to screw, no strings attached. No shedding the light. But not today. Not when her emotions were wrought with last night!

Maliah started for the glass sliding doors of the training room. The doors opened with a gust of air and fast-tempo music. Suddenly, there were too many people getting their "turbo power" on. The sweat had dried against her skin. The old sports bra and tights that she kept in a gym bag in the car started to itch her flesh. Her senses were on hyper-alert.

Everything irritated her.

Maliah headed past the weight section and slipped into the ladies' room. Restrooms were to her right, a steam room dead ahead. She turned to the left and glanced over an abundance of lockers. Which one? With the iPhone clutched in her hand, she lost herself in the thought of Ephraim.

A few seconds after staring at the lockers, Yolanda bumped her hip and brought her back to reality.

"When I said your ass was jiggling, I didn't mean for you to hide in the locker room. I said it as a means for you to work out harder." Yolanda grabbed her phone and punched in the code. "Oh, Eph. So, how did that conversation go?"

"He's on his way to my house."

"Well, by all means. Wake me up on my day off. Neglect me."

Maliah eyed the lockers, finding hers at the bottom. Instincts warned that talking about her ex today might not go in her favor. She gave a nonchalant response over her shoulder while unlocking the keypad. "I'm not playing by his rules."

"Humph."

"Well, forgive me for ruining your morning." Maliah yanked out her purse and exercise bag, too annoyed to change.

"My morning will get better, Maliah." Yolanda touched her arm and gestured for them to sit on the bench in front of the lockers.

"Awesome," Maliah murmured.

"What would be extremely awesome—your morning transitioning into something better. You send me '. . . Baby One More Time' by Britney Spears GIFS on Valentine's Day. V-Day, Maliah. I'm married."

Maliah gasped. "It's funny! Don't tell me that song doesn't have you singing at the top of your lungs in the car.

Can you stop telling me that you're married, Yolanda? Eph and I *introduced* you."

"For an ex, I've never heard so much 'so and so' and I. Sounds like you two are together. I wish I had gotten the MFT credential instead of Pupil Personnel in educational counseling. Clearly, you need a therapist."

"No!" She shot up from the bench. "Therapy and other people, that's what got me into this mess."

"Are you sure? You broke up with Ephraim, why?" Yolanda blinked rapidly, waiting for her to respond.

Maliah chewed her bottom lip.

"You have to know—some-damn-body must know! Eph has asked me a million times. I don't have an answer. Grant sure as hell doesn't have an answer. Daniel is oblivious. The list of our mutual friends who had to cut ties, pick and choose like the two of you were married. We should've divorced the two of you!"

"You're being mean to me, Yolanda," she sniffled, wrestling her purse onto her shoulder.

"You're an asshole, LeeLee." Her tone softened. "Not to me. Nobody else but Ephraim."

Maliah started for the door. She almost bumped into a teen, while shooting over her shoulder, "Well, tell me how you really feel."

"I did. I'm not the person who points fingers. We human beings aren't mannequins where someone is forcing to change us, but you screwed him over."

Maliah stopped in her tracks. She was seconds away from the exit. Yolanda continued to sit on the bench, spine erect.

"We've known each other long enough, LeeLee. I have to tell you the truth, now. I'm sorry I kept my mouth shut so long."

She tuned out her friend for a moment, who seemed to be content letting it all out. Not that anything Yolanda had said went against her beliefs. But she needed to get home and talk to Ephraim. The dynamic of a discussion scared her more than the Hurt Room ever could. Doing things that grown folks do took precedence in Ephraim and Maliah's life when they were way too young. His parents had played a vital part in her life. If it weren't for her grandparents, who saw her as her and not a means into a rich family, then the Levines had sculpted many of her happiest memories.

"You're right," she said to Yolanda. "Eph and I are going to talk about it now. Later, I'll tell you."

"All right, you tell him first. Me and my nosy self can live with that."

———

SHE SLID INTO HER CAR. All the while, the front of the gym beckoned her to return, to waste time and not break Ephraim's heart further. Because she knew, out of all the scenarios playing in her head, Ephraim Levine, Esquire, latched onto certain ideas. He was relentless in his love. He must've executed ways to figure out what went wrong, and each one originated at the fruition of the annulment. She told herself if he hadn't succeeded, then he did not need to know.

"You are an asshole," Maliah mumbled to herself.

The words must've gone into one ear and out the other because she drove around until the gas light blared. She filled up at nightfall and headed home.

———

IN THE CAR, she cast a glance toward the porch. A trickle of disappointment pulsed at her chest. *After all those threats, he's not here.* There was no picking Ephraim's brain these days. In the past he literally had a gold mind—pun intended. She could pick his brain, pull at the strands of intelligence, and be in awe that she had him. Now, he had lost it. Fingers numb, Maliah found herself clutching the steering wheel, thoughts of last night warming her mind. Their moment played on repeat.

Back in the day, she had trouble calculating his moves. The spontaneity placed breath into her lungs, gave her the best exhales. She had to practically threaten him to leave the guest bedroom at his parents' home on a few moments. *So, last night meant nothing—*

"LeeLee, if you don't stop condemning him!" In her need to push Ephraim away so he could marry someone that wouldn't ruin his legacy, she'd made him an enemy. Lord knew, no other man compared in that regard.

Maliah cut those drowning thoughts, grabbed her bag, and got out, the BMW somehow suffocating her. Took her down to "woe is me." To think, she'd been chickenshit and hadn't come home earlier.

The warm summer's night licked at her flesh. Maliah pulled her purse across her body, letting it flop on her hip. She wrapped her arms around her bare midriff, wishing she had changed from the sports bra and tights.

Maliah's Nikes crunched over the gravel. She swung the picket fence open, praying that last night not control her mind tonight. *Or all the rest of the nights until my old age.*

Up the front steps, Maliah let herself in. She swung the door open, flipped the lights, and her breath stalled. *American Horror Story* had entered her life. Not the jumpy bits, but the parts that made the hair on a person's neck stand up.

The little furniture she hadn't pawned over the summer to save her house was nowhere in sight. Furthermore, in its stead stood a mocha leather couch.

Gnawing on her bottom lip, Maliah went to the side of the couch. Tiny bumps rode the skin of her forearms as she touched the spot.

A flashback stole her for a moment, along with all the feel-good moments of Ephraim hitting it from the back. She'd been gripping the side of the couch, when her fingernails claw and pierced into the armrest.

"This is . . ." Mind blown, she stopped speaking.

It had to be the mocha leather coach their friends refused to sit on after one of Ephraim and Maliah's sexcapades. Their college friends had learned not to sit on either one's dorm bed, and then their couch at their townhome. They could buy new furniture, but what was the point? Ephraim once read her favorite books to her while they lay after their lovemaking. *On this couch.*

The walls of her pussy contracted, not giving a damn about her confused state. Maliah moved away from the couch.

"That's an illusion. This is all an illusion," she mumbled to herself.

The old end table . . . Maliah grazed a hand over one of her favorite theorist textbooks. Next to it was the last issue of *Cosmopolitan* magazine that was in their college townhome. Sanaa Lathan graced the cover. Not a single flaw, then and now.

The old, big standing mirror was near the door to her kitchen—it reminded her to slow down on food. An icky blanket was placed over it. She could almost hear Ephraim persuading her that food was her ass's best friend. Maliah pressed a hand to her chest, forcing herself to breathe.

Every inch of the room conjured another memory. She started toward the hallway but stopped as the kitchen caught her eye. Maliah entered, placing a shaky hand against her mouth. The cheap, used refrigerator she'd never get used to had been replaced by their old two-door one. Her Honey Nut Cheerios sat on top of it. But what blew her mind were all the magnets. Those little tidbits of memory were in precise placement. Except for Niagara Falls, which dominated the center.

"Well, he's definitely been here," she thought out loud.

She sauntered down the hall, flicking on the light. The bathroom was cluttered in black hair care and facial products, all of which were there when she was younger. *Eph has lost it.*

Maliah gripped the handle to her bedroom and pushed it forward. She pressed on the light switch. The room illuminated, offering another blast to the past.

"You are crazy." She enunciated every syllable. Ephraim sat in an oval-shaped chair she'd hated until finding how comforting it felt while riding his cock in it.

"Do I have your attention?"

"Leave, Eph." The hard edge she'd grown accustomed to wedged its way back into her life. She forgot all about making amends because Ephraim had gone too far. "Come back when you're ready to be civilized."

"Fuck that. You're telling me about the annulment. Right here, Sweets. We can fuck first, let off steam, but you're not leaving my sight until I know everything."

Measuring her every movement, Maliah gulped. "No sex. We—" She paused, wanting to say they should've cleared the air last night. A chat and then sex. It dawned on her that last night was perfect in every way. "We can talk." She shrugged, rooted to the threshold.

"Somewhere along the line, we got the lines messed up. You get your control when you get your kinks, Sweets. Not out of the bed."

"Okay." Her shoulders flopped. Maliah couldn't deny that her need to be behind the steering wheel helped her flee from him for so long.

"Sit."

"No orders, Eph."

"Sit there or sit here." He cocked a grin, pointing at his pants. His wide-legged stance made it so easy to halt the truth. Maliah knew he'd be livid about his parents.

She settled at the edge of their old bed, a plethora of hot, sexy memories eager to swallow her whole. Maliah jumped back to her feet, pressed her hands toward where her pants pockets should be, needing to fidget. But she realized she was still in tights.

"How dare you walk around like that all day? All that ass for every man to see." He wagged a finger at her like a reprimanding daddy.

"Why are you here, Eph? To chat it out or fuck? We *can* go on forever like this . . ." *Because the truth hurts. I prefer to dysfunctional sex to the truth.* Maliah detested the cold sound of her tone. Then she gasped, seeing his fist clutch the edge of the chair.

"There was me and there was you." He pointed a stiff finger at her. "We loved each other, Maliah. What the fuck is wrong with you." Ephraim's hard voice ended in a seedy growl.

"Stop digging for answers. You could be—" She paused, throat constricted. "Married right now. Happy, in love. You're tormenting me, Eph."

"Good." He sat forward in the chair.

"You feel like hurting me like you did in your room of horrors?"

He sat back, the muscles splaying beneath the prickled skin at his jaw. He needed a shave. Sleep too.

"What if someone else led to the end of us?" She shrugged. A desperate part of her wanted to keep Rachel out of the picture. To let the past stay there. He was so mad for so long about them. How would he react to his parents?

"Yeah, someone did. Someone—" Ephraim cleared his throat. "—helped you draft an annulment. An untraceable annulment."

Maliah started back and forth in front of him. His eyes bore through her as she paced. She chortled. "I meant, like unfaithful. Like I cheated."

Ephraim stopped her pacing as he stood up. He placed his hands on her forearms and dragged his palms up to her shoulders to knead the tensed area. He shook his head. " I've never believed that. The world would've stopped going around. You were mine. We were happy."

His warm breath tickled Maliah's mouth. Before he could descend, she tilted her head away. The bristles of his jaw scratched at her cheek.

"Eph, stop saying beautiful things and leaving me beautiful words on my porch. You don't get to sit and ponder me for hours."

Ephraim grabbed her cheeks, pressed his mouth to her forehead, very rough in the way he kissed. The man did things like that. They were in a tense moment, and he rode that wave and added to it.

"It's the closest I get with you Maliah," Ephraim replied.

She backed away, and he retreated to the chair. Once again he dominated it, had all the confidence while sitting there. She moved along the length of her bed. Needed to get her head in the game.

Maliah cast a glance in his direction, ready to divulge the truth. She stopped moving. "What happened to your hand?"

"Bullshit! You're not giving me a fucking Dr. Jekyll, Miss Hyde. Cut that shit out, LeeLee."

With a huff, she stressed again, "What happened?"

Maliah started toward Ephraim, but he was up in a flash. The space between them disappeared. He towered over her, her ass flush against the wall, the chill of it against her back.

All the feel-good tingles took over for a mere moment. She was ready to assimilate to any command he had. Yet awareness dawned. Determination glinted in his unwavering gaze. Ephraim Levine had one request from her, which ceased either of their pleasure.

"Who prepared that annulment, Maliah?" His mouth peppered her face with kisses. His hand had slipped into her pants, covered her hot pulsing mound. "You love me—you want to know if I'm hurt."

Ephraim's fingers pinched at her clit, sending a river rushing between her thighs. "My hand isn't in pain, Sweets. I've only ever been hurt by you."

"You don't need to know, Eph," she breathed against his jaw.

"I do, Maliah." His two fingers punctured her sweets, and then his thumb clamped over her clit. The pain brought tears into her eyes, until he stroked it all away. "Your body reacts to me. Let's go back to us. You tell me, we fuck everything else, go back to us."

Maliah pressed back against the wall, her breathing becoming erratic. An orgasm started to drench down on his fingers. Listening to Ephraim was playing with fire. Craving more than the fuck fests at the Hurt Room was like swimming in lava.

"Eph," she moaned. "You don't—you don't want to— fuck-fuck!"

While his fingers continued their pursuit, his other hand swooped around, holding her steady as he got her off. "Tell me," he growled, fingers moving in rapid succession. "You want this dick deep inside you. All that juice running down my fingers, Maliah. Tell me and I'll give you what *you really want*."

Waves of tiny orgasms blossomed through her, yet tears stung her eyes. All she'd ever done was hurt him, push him away because he had the type of parents that invested in their seed.

"Keep coming on my fingers, Maliah." He pressed his lips against hers. "Could be my cock. All you have to do is . . ."

"No, no, Ephraim." She slapped his face. The painstaking disappointment in Ephraim's eyes clutched at her heart. He stepped back a few paces. Maliah glared at the bedroom door. There was no way in hell she'd get past him, not with the anger radiating from his body, the tension in his jaw.

Maliah straightened her tights, then placed a hand around her waist.

"You were twelve." Ephraim held up a finger, eyed the juice rolling down it, and licked. "You were twelve and you stole every inhibition inside of me, all the thoughts, all the musing. I didn't have a single joke to tell. Not a word to explain my feelings."

"Stop living in the past." The worst of them all called the kettle black.

"You were thirteen, begging me to screw you! Fucking

screw you, Maliah," he growled. "You're worth more than that."

Shame clung to her chest. It hurt that he'd been so perceptive. Like a real submissive, catty and with no cards left, she tossed out the only claim she had. "Am I worth more than what you did to me at the Hurt Room?"

Regret flashed before his gaze, but Maliah saw him going to that place where lovers go to break each other. Just like at the Hurt Room when he picked up the flog, then the paddle, he was bringing her down with him.

"I was a horny fucking teen, Maliah." Ephraim's eyes narrowed, dragging over her frame. "I wanted to fuck you before you even said something. You wouldn't stop, wouldn't. I had to be the —"

"Oh poor, horny pubescent boy, you should've fucked me!" Maliah screeched. *Wow, I'm painting myself in a bad light.*

"No! I waited for the perfect time. Made it worthy of you."

She plucked a pillow from the bed, needing a stronger barrier against his verbal assault, his dead-on assessments.

"All our lives together, I made our love perfect. I gave you good memories. Making memories with you was—*is* my favorite thing to do, Maliah. *Let your pile of good things grow*," he said, evidently recalling what her Granny had said. "When your grandmother told me that, I knew that all my good days, hours, seconds, all that good shit led to you, Maliah!"

"We were good together," she murmured, aware just how detached she sounded. Ephraim Levine had a legacy much bigger than the man—though the man was attractive, confident, everything. The Levines didn't need to be sullied by any headlines her family had tied to them. Maybe Maliah wasn't a part of a drug dynasty, but she couldn't have it. Couldn't have Rick's greed ruin the people who nurtured and advised her for years.

Imaginary steam bellowed from Ephraim's ears. The wheels of his brain worked overtime. Maliah stopped herself from being the messenger. He bit at his knuckles. "What the fuck did I do?"

Quicksand took root of her feet, dragging her down to her knees. Maliah's gaze lowered, rather than watch the hurt and pain on his face. "All I made for you were bad memories. Bad ones, Eph."

"No!" His hand slammed down onto the side of the dresser. A block of mocha wood tore from the edge.

"Eph," she murmured, noticing a gash on the side of his hand. She came near, but he moved away. Damn, how the roles were changing, and it hurt.

Hurt worse than his house of horrors.

Ephraim rubbed the side of his hand against the comforter, cussing beneath his breath. The gash didn't continue to leak.

"We need a moment, Eph. Let's talk tomorrow, when the sun is out, shining." She cringed at herself; she sounded like an idiot.

"You are my sun!" Ephraim shouted at her. "Why the fuck don't you get that, Maliah?"

She'd edged her way to the door now but stopped. One thought went through her mind. *Him.* She'd contemplated this before. Years did nothing to deter him. Her harsh presence, her willingness to push him away, still had no effect.

"I'm not leaving tonight, Maliah. Fuck sunshine, you are my sun! Your smile was enough reason to shove the sun aside, move the world." He stopped, scratched at his jaw in contemplation. "I was a baby, crawling around and could make a person laugh. To this day, my mom reminds me of my knack for it."

She stood stock-still, unrelenting to his emotion. He'd mentioned his mom.

"Maliah, no laughter caught me until you, and there was no reason in the world to make a person laugh after. You were perfect, until the annulment."

"Ouch," she replied. She chewed on her lip, pensive at the thought of telling him. Maliah's father wasn't changing anytime soon. For a second, she thought to put herself first. Before her family's covetousness. Before her not profit. Before everything, like Ephraim did. "Let's try us, and start new—"

"And you tell me who helped you. Who screwed with that little head of yours, Maliah?"

She started for the door. This conversation would be either black or white, no gray. No past. "I'm not going into the past with you, Eph. Why can't we push forward and be happy?"

"I. Have. To. Know."

Maliah started for the bedroom door, now, with the confidence that Ephraim had no idea what he'd asked of her.

He didn't have to know.

Over her shoulder, she tossed, "I offered to start something new, better, but—"

ALL THAT ASS was constantly sauntering away from him. Ephraim had gotten the best news of his life. They could start over. Shit, he had a contract for her to sign. A dotted line for her signature that required her to *try*. To try and give him a chance to rectify things he hadn't known he'd screwed up. His arm scooped around her waist, pulling her back to him.

"That's not how this works, Miss Porter." His breath tickled her neck. She smelled of salt and sweat, all delectable. "You said, let's start new. We have to tweak this arrangement, sweetheart. I never stopped claiming you. What made you do it!"

She murmured, "You're being stubborn."

"No, I'm preparing for all the good shit that follows these hard times we've had. I will not repeat history, will not let you from my sight if I think you're preparing to flee." His breath licked at her neck with each steely word. "Now that you've been debriefed on where I stand, verse me on what *I'm not aware of.* Let's not fall into the same snare, shall we?"

His muscles wrought, jaw clenched tight, he waited. She had one choice available to her. And he'd caved to her too many times in the past before.

"Ephraim, you're smarter than this, baby." Maliah's fingers skimmed over his forearms. Ephraim continued to hold her close as she turned around in his arms. Little did she know, her silky, soft palms against his face might as well have been a kitten pawing at a bear.

"Eph, you are a dream," she murmured against his mouth.

Ephraim understood this wasn't the time to fall into the snare of physical attraction. All he needed was enlightenment, and they weren't fucking, eating, or sleeping until he had it.

"I bet you have hired the best private investigators in the world." Her voice was lush, apologetic. "Because I was so cruel and shut you out, Eph, you let the thought of not knowing guide you. Can you take my apologies please?" Her mouth pressed over his.

Hers pleasing.

His taut.

Hers whispering how long she'd dedicate to his pleasure.

His glued into a tensed frown. "I'll let you make it up to me, LeeLee. We've always enjoyed the makeup."

Maliah grabbed a shock full of kinky hair. "You're so relentless. That's why!"

"Why what?" He grabbed her shoulders. "Most women want a man to love them unconditionally. Maliah, what the fuck is wrong with you?"

"And you won't stop. I bet you've thought about it every day—"

"Yes! You and that paper."

"Ephraim, there isn't a single moment that I haven't regretted—"

"Maliah!"

"You know." She clung to him now, her mouth muffled against his chest. "You spent so much money in an attempt to figure out what you know. So much money because it's disposable, Eph. And you *didn't want to know what you already do.*"

"Hell yes, and I'd throw more money at the problem but now you're here and you'll . . ." Ephraim stopped ranting. Her face was clutched in his hands. *I know?* His abdominals braced for the impact of what he *knew.* Always knew.

Letting her face go, Ephraim's hands flopped to his sides. His head tilted. Almost ten years of contemplation derailed in his psyche.

Maliah held on to him. He felt like his limbs would give out, but his woman was strong enough for them both.

He pressed his face into the top of her heart and silently vowed that they had forever. Then he breathed into her coconut strands. "They wouldn't. They love you."

"They do," she replied, smiling encouragingly.

They couldn't! Ephraim guided her hips to his side and started for the door. His parents had lots to answer for. And here he thought he could bash in the face of the culprit. Hurt that person more than Landon.

Well, Ephraim Levine could hurt his parents more than he had Landon Davenport. To be honest, when Maliah left, he drifted. Mom had begged him to come home on so many holidays. His dad had mentioned retiring a few years ago.

But this wasn't enough.

This wasn't enough hurt.

Maliah pulled back on the soles of her feet as he grabbed her hand. "What are you doing?"

"I'm going to talk to my dad . . ." *It will be my last chat with him for the same duration of time I've missed you.*

"You don't believe me?" Her tone was so small behind him, he almost didn't stop to reassure her.

"No, Dad and I are going to have the same chat that—" Ephraim stopped to clasped her face. "We need answers. Then that's it. Maliah, I—"

"What do you mean that's it?" she screeched. "They wanted better for us."

"Better for me!" he exploded. His parents had ruined his life.

Ephraim calculated a thousand ways they could pay in half a second:

He'd open his own law firm. Then he'd stick around to take some cases. Hire the best attorneys and curate a list for partners. If that snubbed his parents enough, he'd stick it to what was most important to them.

He'd send his parents cards. All major holidays. Mother's Day and Father's Day, with pictures of his kids.

Four kids.

Oh, and poach his father's clients. Every single one of the old man's clients.

Ephraim was a man who contemplated. And he needed more time to figure out how his parents could pay.

27

MALIAH FLEW TO HER KNEES, TUGGING AT EPHRAIM'S BELT. The way he made her jump a second ago had to be a taste of how angry he truly was. His shout still echoed in her ear. *"Better for me!"*

They were a pair who argued until either one's mouth was filled with the other's sex. Yet, the silence always killed her. He had shouted, and then he'd grown quiet.

Quiet with devious thoughts, the Good Guy, the Comedian, had a vein pulsating in his neck, jaw stiff. She unhooked his belt and pulled.

"Please, let me suck your dick, Sir," she begged.

A little animosity evaporated. She begged him again. He helped guide his cock to her lips. He growled, pushing into the resistance of her mouth, the head punching her tonsils. She sucked with fervor, though the tension in his body hadn't faded.

"Deep, Maliah," he growled.

She moaned in desire as his fingers knotted into her hair. He controlled the thrusts, fucking her mouth with vigor.

With her mouth sloppy wet, Maliah sucked at his cock. Her hands held his muscular thighs in an attempt to feel his body loosen. Ephraim Levine's entire being was a brick, like his cock.

The girth of him pained her jaw, but she stroked his cock with her tongue like her life depended on it.

C'mon, Eph. Calm down. She hoped her head game was enlightening to conjure a spell. But she might as well have been kneeling before a tree at Pachaug State Forest.

He came into her mouth without warning. All the good, thick seed was more than she could gulp down at once.

Excess ejaculation dribbled out of the side of her mouth, trickled down her jaw and neck.

She held even more cream in her mouth and held it open a little so he could get a peek. The first time she did it, Ephraim laughed and called her crazy. It was a funny, erotic joke every once in a while.

Not today.

"What the fuck did they do to you, Maliah?" Ephraim pulled his pants up, buckling his belt. He held a hand out for her.

"You kept everything?" Maliah stood up. She glanced around again, half her mouth tipped up. *Well, does kill 'em with kindness work in this instance?* "I walked into the twilight zone. Eph, nice spin on the little things. I love it."

Maliah's effort to change the subject backfired. Ephraim growled, "What did they do? How did they convince you with lies?"

"Eph, I need you to take a moment to digest the information." She gestured, taking a seat on the edge of the bed. When he didn't claim the seat beside her, Maliah breathed deeply while arising. "You've had resentment for an extensive period of time. So, your first line of defense—"

"Did they alter photos?"

"What?"

"Indiscretion? Manipulate you into believing I cheated? You seem so bent on us not going over there, *right now.*" The situation had reversed. Now, Ephraim stalked, back and forth. He punched a hand out before him, the air offering a *swoosh* as he stalked across the room. "What the fuck did they do, Maliah?"

"No, idiotic stripper photos or the likes." Maliah shook her head. "You sound like an attorney, Eph."

"I am one!"

"You're scaring me."

"You need to talk!" He stopped before her, ran a hand over his short-cropped, wavy hair. "LeeLee, I've waited for ages to have you, baby. To think my parents were the cause of the dissolution of us fucking hurts. Okay, so let's talk."

He'd slowed down enough for both of them to sit at the edge of the bed. Shock waves of intensity came flying to Maliah on repeat. Pulling her lips into an o, Maliah exhaled.

Ephraim groaned, hands over his face. His voice was stifled while saying, "I didn't do anything wrong."

"You were perfect," she replied, gulping in more air. "So good to me that I refused to cause you resentment later on."

"Resentment?"

Maliah turned on the edge of the bed so that her hip was parallel to it. She took Ephraim's hands in hers. "Ephraim, your parents weren't fully at fault. They simply had an idea and . . ." her words faltered. Cheeks burning, Maliah dropped her head.

All the animosity had drained from Ephraim's body. All that was left was a man who deserved the truth. The truth in its entirety.

"Rach always was so close to me," Maliah murmured.

She shoved a kinky tress behind her ear. "She cared that you and I . . . weren't having sex until we were ready. And you were right earlier—I would've let you have me anytime you want. All the years we spent dry humping . . ." Again, her attempt to lighten the moment, even if it were a minuscule attempt at that, didn't penetrate. "My parents probably would've high-fived me for coming home pregnant as a teen." Her throat became strangled.

"I don't care what anyone thinks, Maliah." Ephraim took her hand in his.

"That's some serious perfection, Eph. I remember when we were twelve and you wouldn't speak to me."

He chuckled for the faintest moments. "You were fucking beautiful. Those puffy pigtails kept bouncing across your skin, your lips. LeeLee, you're tied directly to the hardest moments of my life. All those times we crept around as teens. Those good times. Then the breakup blindsided me."

Maliah's eyes closed, and she concentrated on his groan. The sound of it was the pure definition of sex. The way Ephraim contemplated their past—such a good past they had.

Her thumb roamed around his callused hand as he held her in his lap. "Your parents aren't all at fault."

"You said that."

She groaned. "I know. Shit, this is hard. My dad embarrassed you every time you came to dinner or we went out. It made me cringe when he said . . ."

"*Well, you know, son?*" Ephraim mumbled, not an ounce of annoyance or care.

"My dad and mom didn't come to my back to school nights. If you or Daniel weren't graduating with me, I doubt they'd have made those."

"Maliah." He squeezed her hand a little.

"Okay, well, my dad. Maybe he would've attended, but the two of you sweetened the pot. He hardly tried though, when it came to other things. For example," she began, dread filling her abdomen. "I had a poetry recital once; on another occasion, I had a mock reading. You didn't get to go for one reason or another. My dad used that as his excuse too."

"Damn," he said, wrapping an arm around her.

"Then there were the times when I went to therapy. Dr. Hart created a plan where my parents were supposed to come every other week. Just an hour. They failed." She paused. So far, he was attentive to her rambling, not stopping her to inquire what his parents had to do with this. Maliah chewed her lip for a moment. "Do you know why Abner was defending my father in the first place?"

Ephraim looked away and then met her gaze. "Yes."

"God, that's . . . okay, that was obvious, huh?" She started to stand, but he was holding her.

"Rick isn't the worst person my dad has ever defended. We have a diverse clientele. I have to, Maliah."

Her hands shook as she gestured. "But why not change? My dad got friggin' immunity—is how I see it."

Ephraim pawed her face, then kissed her forehead. "I'm marrying you, not your dad."

She didn't correct him. *Married.* Just made herself comfortable in his arms. "My father had blood on his hands and had no intention of changing his ways, Ephraim. That's what Rachel and Abner brought to my attention."

"Okay?"

She bounded off the bed to stare at him. "Not okay! I wouldn't have made it years with all the love you give and then it fades."

He blinked. A few beats passed.

"Ephraim Levine, I went three entire months tormented with you ignoring me." She pressed a hand against her heart. "Do you think I'd survive going half a lifetime with your love *as your wife* and then . . ."

"Then what, Maliah?" He got up, caressed the back of his knuckles across her cheek. Then he kissed the lone tear that started to fall down her face. "You are so beautiful, Maliah. All I ever saw was giving my love to you, for the rest of your life. My little LeeLee."

"And then my dad does something unforgivable again? Your family has a legacy, Ephraim. One that I had firsthand knowledge of as a child. I came to respect your parents, your grandfather, Ian, you . . ."

He laughed for a second. "Fuck a legacy, LeeLee. We aren't dumbass twenty-year-olds anymore."

A flood of tears fell down her face. Maliah tried her best to explain, but her words became jumbled. "There was one other reason."

"What?" he asked. Ephraim pondered her over, but her gaze was cast downward.

Maliah chewed her lip before saying, "Also, I never thought I deserved you in the first place."

28

THE ENTIRE TRUTH LEFT MALIAH LAID BARE BEFORE HIM. HE saw it in her stance, when she'd said those foolish words. Yes, his parents still had to pay. Ephraim never assumed her dad thought so highly of him. And now, he'd use that as his motivation to make the Porters put their daughter first.

But before Ephraim would construct a plan for all of these things, he had only one notion on his mind. "You never thought you deserved me, woman?"

Her head lowered.

He tipped her chin, kissed more tears. Then his words skimmed across her salted cheeks. "Then we will have to rectify that."

Ephraim Levine, Esquire, had his job cut out for him, and he'd fulfill it to the fullest extent.

ON FRIDAY MORNING, Maliah had almost told him that the sex they had trumped the devotion he'd given in the cabin. But her voice was raw from moaning and screaming. Sex peppered her skin. And her Tempur-Pedic mattress—the only item in the room he hadn't swapped—sagged comfortably between them. The bedpost was just about ready to cave. With her cheek against Ephraim's chest and his hair tickling her nose, she spoke. "My bed-frame better be somewhere safe."

He gripped a fist full of hair, pulled a little. She moaned at the teasing massage. "Be glad I didn't keep our mattress. All those lumps had you swerving on my cock."

"Ohhhh, hydraulics," she reminded him, moving an imaginary stick shift. "We had some good sex."

Ephraim's hard abdominals moved beneath her as he laughed. "We have to make up for it."

"I thought Canada . . ." She paused as he removed her from him.

Ephraim moved down the bed, gripped her hip, and pulled her pussy flush to his nose. The growl rumbling through him vibrated at her clit. It sent a symphony of spasms at her thick inner and outer folds.

"Not fair," she murmured. all the sex they'd had between her thighs. "I'm dirty."

Ephraim's hand skimmed the flesh at the inside of her thighs. His fingers went in pursuit of her treasure. He breathed against her pearl. The warmth against her tiny bud took something out of her. Maliah clutched at his shoulders, stopping herself not to beg for his mouth. The words fled her mind as she waited for his mouth to claim her pussy.

"You taste so good dirty," he said, his breath glided over her swollen lips.

"Kiss me, Eph." She ended the beg by piercing her lip with her teeth. Then Maliah pressed her pelvis down, offering him all access to her.

Not submitting to her request, Ephraim's palm

continued its delicate roaming up and over the apex of her sex. She stopped breathing, waited for him to enter her again with his fingers. Desperation made her crave even a small offering. He did not enter her.

Ephraim's fingers teased her coils, coaxing without inserting. Maliah's legs started to shake, her pussy screaming to be filled up. Ephraim kneeled before her and placed a hand on her ass, steadying her trembling body. His face burrowed into her belly. His muffled words sunk into her skin. "After all the lip you give, Maliah, that cunt is all wet for me."

"I stay wet for you," she groaned. Widening her legs, the harmony of Maliah's moans implored him to enter her.

"Drip down my fingers," he growled as his fingers dove into her core. "The faster you drip for me, the faster I get a taste."

Her entire body was on fire for him. Hips arching, she offered his fingers free rein of her soaking treasure. The sounds her pussy was making for him became the pure definition of erotica. Breaths heavy, they listened to the nasty, wet noises.

"You're wet, but I'm thirsty as fuck. Quench my thirst, Maliah."

Legs planted wide, Maliah's toes curled under as Ephraim got her off. Stars blurred her eyes, when the lips of her pussy convulsed around his fingers.

EPHRAIM REMOVED his wet fingers and stood up, his dick at attention. Her eyes had swept across his broad chest, down his abdomen. Then her smile widened, glued to his cock. The left side of Ephraim's mouth tipped in response. Sticky juice rolled down his fingers into his palm. He planted his two fingers under his nose with one hand, gripped Maliah's ass with the other.

His chest swelled with pride as he drunk in the sight of what was once his beautiful wife. Though they'd seized the title for a choice few weeks, his obsession with Maliah continued to run deep. His hands rubbed along the side of her brown curves, hypnotizing him to enter her body.

"You're supposed to be giving me head, Eph."

With a cocky smile on his face, he took a lick of his finger before twirling it around in the air, signaling for her ass.

"Mmmm, I love that type of head." She spun around.

"Damn, look at those chocolate mounds," he groaned. Her ass was plastered on his face. "All that's missing is a jewel for your little pucker."

Maliah glared back at him as if to tell him what to do.

His eyebrow rose in response. "Is there something you'd like to say?"

"I do too much asking, and you're bound to do the opposite."

A slight smile flashed on her face while she turned back toward the headboard. When he bit down on the left cheek while slamming a hand down on the right, Maliah gasped. "Ephhhhhh!"

His breath tickled across her ass. He pressed his tongue against her hole, attempting to push past the resistance.

She shook. "Oh, Ephraim, fuck, shit . . ."

"That's right, keep calling Daddy's name." Ephraim licked, stroked, and prodded her asshole with his tongue until her pussy came slamming back against his chin. She was begging for more penetration, but her tiny hole wasn't ready. Gradual and meticulous, his tongue glided her honey well that begged for entry. His nose knocked against her anus while he licked and tasted like a ravenous wolf. A wave of satisfaction settled in Ephraim's massive chest as her legs began to shake.

Maybe he couldn't breathe, but he continued to let his nose probe her ass, while his tongue assaulted her slit. But he wouldn't abandon such a gorgeous, little hole.

"Wait here, Sweets." He bit at her ass again.

As Ephraim climbed off the bed, Maliah reached around to finger herself.

"I said wait." He went over to her body, skimmed his hand over her back and down toward her breast. "Unless you'd like me to bite something else?"

Maliah simpered and snatched her hand away from her glossy cunt.

With a smile, Ephraim went to her top drawer.

"You seriously went through my things?" she growled.

"Should I bite your sweet nips, Pet?" He pulled out a bejeweled ass plug to the sweet sound of silence. With lube in the other hand, Ephraim made quick work of glossing the tip. Then he returned to his black beauty. Maliah stayed in impeccable position, her fat ass calling out to him. He licked his lips and pressed his palm against her lower back. Ephraim didn't have to use words to perfect her arch. Maliah complied, tutting those voluptuous meaty cheeks. Like a dog, he salivated at the meal before him. Cunt lips puckered between her thighs—check. Sweet, little asshole that only ever belonged to him—check. Ass for days— check. He had all the time in the world.

The small of her back formed the perfect arc. He caressed at it, letting her juice all into his mouth. As she exploded, Ephraim slid the bejeweled persuasion into her asshole.

"Oh shit, Ephraim . . ." she hollered, orgasm extending. She grunted his name with every other obscenity. He ate ferociously, his nose nudging against the anal plug, knocking it deeper, while her body rocked, swaying side to side.

Cock heavy against his thigh, Ephraim growled. His manhood had gotten so damn hard. But he allowed her to continue to convulse into his mouth. The anal plug, now perfectly inserted inside of her luscious ass. As the flare of liquid lust faded, Ephraim gripped at Maliah's hips, since she might lose balance. Her body became weak, but he wasn't done with her yet.

"Get in position, Sweets," he ordered.

A deep moan came from her glistening skin. He reached around to tweak her clit. "You wanted to rub this sweet, little cunt earlier?"

"Oh yes," she groaned.

Ephraim entered her tight cunt, and her walls embraced his cock. He submitted to memory how snug she was with the anal plug in her ass. Pressing his mouth against the small of Maliah's back, he stroked deep into her.

"Fuck, you keep coming for me, Sweets," he growled. If he'd thought her pussy was tight before, it was on a quest to milk him for all his worth. Ephraim created a rhythm. He'd cum in her mouth sometime earlier and her pussy a while ago, which kept him from erupting so soon.

Her voice had gotten raspy, and she fell into the bed.

"I can't stop fucking you," he groaned, as she came again.

Ephraim pulled at her hair until she turned her face to the side. He pressed his mouth against hers in a hard kiss. "You are the best part of me, Maliah."

She smiled against his lips, breath ragged. "I love you so much, Eph."

He'd been ready to cum, but her declaration made him want to continue fucking her. To love her until she couldn't speak the words, until they were ingrained in her mind for eternity.

Ephraim flipped down onto the bed, pulling her on top of him. Her tits toppled down. He rubbed at her back.

"Fuck me, baby," he told her.

"Eph." She rode his cock, with a groan.

"Do it for me."

All the courageous love Ephraim reminisced about Maliah came to fruition in that moment. She came back alive. Warm brown skin coated in sweat. Beautiful mane in disarray. All her beauty was his to behold, and he had a plan to fuck her until the morning light. Ephraim was relentless enough to do just that.

29

MALIAH SLEPT BETTER THAN SHE HAD IN HER THIRTY YEARS OF life. She groaned, purring deep into her throat to confirm if she could speak. Only because, well, she wasn't ready to speak at all. Sleep continued to claim her. Ephraim held her close, with one arm around her waist. That was another thing. Besides sleep, she hadn't felt so safe since their marriage.

She opened her eyes to see a mug of chamomile on her nightstand. Steam rose from it. She pulled up onto her elbow and took a sip.

"You're woke."

"Ouch, fuck," Maliah screeched, spilling a smidgen of the hot, steeped water. She turned around in the bed and sat against the trusty headboard. Ephraim sat on their old favorite chair, cleanly shaved and in a fresh suit. Her dreams of him still holding her close had transitioned till morning. She hadn't noticed him get up.

Maliah smiled at his black blazer. "You have things here, don't you?"

"Things?"

Rubbing a hand over her face, she gestured, still needing to gather her bearings. "Clothing, Eph. Sheesh, you are a nut."

"You like the tea?"

They both knew Ephraim had her pegged. She smiled a little. "My favorite type and brand. You're all nice and dapper-looking. When did you sleep? And/or go to the specialty grocery store that has this brand of tea?"

"I don't shop, Maliah. I remember shit and delegate. All the rest, I have an assistant for that." He stood up.

She climbed onto her knees with the linen around her. Maliah grinned, watching his gaze almost rip through the sheets. A few beats passed. All she craved was his claiming, but her sex throbbed. And she wasn't sure she'd be able to walk today, anyway. "So, does this assistant shave your jaw and wash *you* and make sure you look good? Damn, you smell good too."

He leaned against the edge of the bed, kissed her forehead. "I can't afford all of that."

"Oh shit, is the filthy-rich Ephraim unable to pay for a good washing?"

Ephraim ruffled her puffy hair. "My assistant is almost as old as my mom. And if she's not telling me about myself, as you often do, then she's mumbling something in Spanish."

"You speak Spanish."

"Yeah, she thinks I've got the bare bones, which works for me. Rosa's her name. She's got morals like you."

Maliah's head tilted for a moment. *She's got morals like you* ... "What does—"

"You want me to draw you a bath or turn on the shower?" He was already turning around and hadn't heard her.

"Why?" Maliah lay back with a cringe, aware of where his head was headed. She'd polished his cock last night for this very reason. To slow him down. To give him a chance to simmer and let the truth marinate before acting ruthlessly.

But she'd been angry with the Levines too. Rachel had volunteered during the We Rise Learning Center opening day. There'd been a call to action throughout the community—might as well have been light-years away from hers. But she came and she interacted with kids.

That was Rachel's first time attempting to tell Maliah she regretted her husband's notions and her own. Ephraim's mom had volunteered for an entire month before they had a real conversation. Now, they had mended their relationship. Rachel still came to read to the younger kids for the holidays, Rachel still mentioning how Ephraim *needed* LeeLee every so often.

"Can't we go away somewhere? I have a few weeks before I open up shop."

"Maliah, you know good and well we're going to see my parents today. Whatever we do after that is your call."

She rolled over onto her stomach and pretended to suffocate herself.

———

AGAIN, the Hurt Room was less than a mile away. This time, Maliah was much closer as the Levine estate was one block up. Well, the tippy-top of the hill, captivating and stifling at the same time. The structure was large enough for a private school. It had lofty windows that begged a person to look inside.

The wrought iron gates trickled open and Yesiv zipped through. Ephraim had offered Maliah to drive any one of his sports cars, but she wasn't in the mood. She sat stiffly on her side of the SUV. He had his side.

"Maliah, this is inevitable. Better now than later. So, start thinking about where you'd like to go after—if it makes you feel better."

"I'd feel so much better knowing your plan of attack, Ephraim," she retorted.

"Just verbal." He smiled at her; it was cool and overshadowed her flippant remark.

"Humph. They're your parents, Eph. Don't forget that."

"You're more invested in my legacy than I am, Maliah. You should be elated to know I plan on utilizing all those litigation arguments my father taught me."

"Put yourself in their shoes," she said as the SUV came to a stop. "No sides need to be taken, Eph. Just be empathetic to . . ."

"I am being empathetic to all the years I haven't had you. Justice will be swift and according to—"

The passenger door opened, and Maliah hurried out before he could continue. "Thanks," she mumbled to Yesiv.

Ephraim was around the car in seconds. He gestured between the two of them. "As much as I love fighting with you, LeeLee, you're on my side in this. May not know it, but you are."

The double doors opened. Rachel came outside, fidgeting with her pearls. She wore a collared top and tapered pants. She stopped at the top step, white pillars on either side of her. Placing a hand over her mouth, she eyed the two of them in sheer elation.

"Eph and LeeLee!" She started down the stairs.

"Act accordingly," Maliah mumbled before moving along a lengthy row of prized roses. She met Rachel halfway, matching the energy of her embrace.

"I had no idea Ephraim was bringing you to lunch," she said. "I'm going to pull his ear all the way to the veranda."

"I'll pass," Ephraim responded in a brisk tone.

Rachel froze. She had to snatch her son's ear on so many occasions in the past. Never did he talk back, at least not without a joke attached.

"He knows," Maliah warned.

"All right." Rachel wrung her fingers together. "Then we have lots to talk about. Can I hug you, son?"

Maliah chortled, narrowing her eyes at Ephraim while addressing Rachel with a stiff smile. "As far as I recall, he's never had to be asked for a hug."

Her remark went unanswered as Ephraim started up the steps.

"Eph!" she snapped.

"I'm not in the hugging mood, right now, *Sweets*. We're here for lunch and only lunch."

Rachel's mouth tensed a little. Maliah looped an arm through hers.

"Thanks," his mother murmured. "I knew the day of reckoning would come. This entire time, I prefer it over the guilt."

THE FOOD SMELLED DIVINE, but Atsun wrinkled her nose. In her attempt not to inhale too much of her all-time favorite meal, she stiffened in her seat.

Bright floor-to-ceiling windows were at her left. Nori had made the requirement that they needed natural light while assisting Ephraim. All of the catty subs she'd grown to envy had a room in their rented house, which was a few blocks from the Hurt Room. A place she wished she was at. She wanted to be in one of those rooms, closer to where Maliah Porter had once been. To delve in her sub's pain—nobody knew it yet, but Maliah would be her sub. She clung to that connection. But they had three more weeks at the Hurt Room. Tomorrow would mark an entire month. *My one-month anniversary with Maliah . . .*

Though, it didn't appear Ephraim would honor their contract, the lease on the house they were staying in would end in a few weeks. Didn't matter—Atsun wouldn't leave Connecticut without her pet. But she played her part, eyes downcast. Humble.

I fucking hate humble, she thought to herself. As a child, living on the streets of Kawaguchi, Japan, it took ages for Atsun to learn how to play her hand. The city offered so much opportunity for unwanted girls—long as they gave up their souls. She'd learned not to be hungry.

Until Nori.

Four seats away, at the opposite head of the table, her Dom chewed thoughtfully. Piano music droned, and he lifted the jade chopstick, wrist moving to the tune, before taking a big bite. Aside from his mouth being set in a straight line, there were no other indications that he was livid.

Well, there was a shoddy, old leather collar at her neck, restricting most of her breath. And the loud growl of her stomach.

"Please feed *our* pet," Nori gritted out.

The bejeweled collar that was passed around once a week was on another sub's neck. The sub slinked over to Atsun and dropped a cat bowl filled with her favorite meal inside. She stood back, rubbed a graceful hand over the bejeweled collar.

That's my collar, bitch. Atsun smiled. Darkness charged in her eyes, but humble reigned.

The other sub pursed her lips, not in agreement with Atsun heaping coals of sunshine on her attempt to be petty.

"This pad thai is pleasing to my palate," Nori said. "But I believe our pet is hungry too."

Our pet. Atsun gulped down a bit of bile, which was restricted by her tight collar.

". . . Our pet may prefer more seasoning. Season it for her, Thandie."

The cunt leaned over Atsun's cat bowl, moved her shock of black hair to the other side of her neck. This offered Atsun an impeccable view of the most coveted collar Nori had. Then Thandie spat in the food.

"Thank you. You may feed our pet as we converse." Nori flicked his wrist.

Atsun's claws dug into the palm of her hands as she watched Thandie spoon a bit of food. The glob of spit slid off the side of the fork. The sub offered another round of seasoning straight onto the spoon. Atsun presumed she used a spoon for the sole purpose of heaping food down her throat.

"Open wide, slut," Thandie ordered.

Atsun had been Nori's favorite for so many years. Besides, Thandie was a small pup, having joined them for a token ten months now. Other pets had been humiliated this way for their misbehavior.

Not Atsun. She always wore a crown and the collar!

She held open her mouth.

"Wider, slut," Thandie spat.

And she did. Wide enough to take a beast of a cock. The slimy food slid down her throat. Every second reminded her that she'd be Domme soon.

"We are leaving this weekend, Atsun."

Mouth held open, she stopped herself as opposed to

telling Nori the truth. Thandie added more seasoning with each bite.

"The only reason we've stayed this far is because you, as well as all of my pets, agreed to return home next Sunday. It doesn't appear that Ephraim will include us in tomorrow's session or any follow-ups, Atsun."

Thandie's eyes narrowed at her, and Atsun smiled. Thus far, he called them all his pets. His belongings. Only *our pet* during humiliation, when allowing another sub to help with punishment. Never did he use their names.

"Do your worst, bitch," Atsun said under her breath, while Thandie's face was so close.

The girl hawked deep down in her throat and tossed phlegm onto Atsun's spoon. Then she shoved it down Atsun's throat.

"And do not mistake us having this conversation to mean you have the right to question me, Atsun."

Thandie forked up more food.

"Leave us, Pet!" he ordered.

The clip-clop of Thandie's eight-inch stilettos competed with the jazz music.

Now, Atsun used her wiles. Tears burned her eyes, and she gasped before the dam broke. And damn, it was a perfect scene, made all the more melancholic while she wore the shoddy collar.

Nori looked away from her, reminding Atsun of how nurturing a Dom he was. She'd endured worse humiliation when in trouble, ate worse things because physical punishment wasn't a punishment at all.

"She is not ours, Atsun." He slammed his chopstick onto the table. "Not ours. We don't have rights to Maliah."

"I know," Atsun sniffled.

"You're regressing, Atsun. Returning to the kid I met

years back, who needed to be spanked more than fucked."
Nori shoved his stiff fingers through his hair. "Atsun, if I
release you, what life would you have?"

A good one, with my bitch, thank you very much, she
thought. While Atsun's heart sung, considering her contemplations, more tears fell. She clung to the façade to buy
herself time. Or, to buy Nori time, rather. Her Dom needed
to see the light, or he'd lose his best submissive. Noritaka
Yamazaki hadn't come to terms with the gift she was offering
him. Atsun was Nori's gift until she took siege of her own
faith. And dropped him.

30

ONE OF THE REASONS EPHRAIM FELL FOR MALIAH, AT FIRST sight, was her smile. Spunk radiated from her as she talked to the two girls manning the double Dutch. He couldn't for the life of him see through her tarnished lenses, that she wasn't worthy enough for him. She'd tried so hard to be bad when they were growing up. It took prayer and the realization that she was worth heaven not to screw her at the age of thirteen.

She wasn't bad—she was good. And right now, he preferred the callousness that he hadn't understood for almost a decade. The animosity was to be redirected to their parents. Only seemed fitting. Why wasn't she furious with them?

He watched her like a hawk as she marched over to Abner, arms wide. His father had come out of the house a few seconds after Ephraim denied his mother a hug. That shit hurt. She'd birthed him, but this wouldn't be the extent to their recompense.

"I have missed you, young lady," Abner said with more emotion than usual.

Ephraim's eyes narrowed somewhat as he watched their interaction. *LeeLee is still angry with him*, he gauged. *Well, why isn't she showing it?*

"And you, you rascal." His father turned to him. "You brought our beautiful Maliah home, no warning. I'll have to check the wine cellar myself."

Ephraim flinched as his father went in for a hug. He stepped back. "We're here for a discussion. Mom offered lunch. Grab all the wine you'd like, Dad, but I can assure you it won't be enough to get me happy and tipsy."

Abner scoffed. "Then less talk."

"Food first." Rachel tried on a smile.

Twenty minutes later, they were out on the veranda that overlooked much of Greenwich. Below them were the tennis courts and the calming rush of water from the infinity pool. Before them was a feast of food, reminding Ephraim of all the Thanksgivings that were denied him.

"I thought we might've prepared too much." Rachel gestured toward the chef, who stood at attention at the end of the table. "It's rare that I see my son. Now, I wish I'd made Granny's famous peach cobbler."

Maliah's smile brightened at the mention of her grandmother's name. Ephraim frowned harder. He didn't want the manipulation of his parents mentioning her grandparents. He didn't want Maliah to soften her heart any more to them.

"Well, I see ham with pineapples and cherry juice, so I am elated anyway," Maliah mentioned. Her grandmother had also taught his mom a prized honey baked ham recipe.

"I can still remember our first holiday at your parents'," Rachel said.

"Oh goodness, I remember as if it were yesterday." Abner walked out of the french doors that led to the kitchen, two bottles in hand. A rosé for Maliah and a red for himself and his son. "Rachel didn't have the chance to cook and brought that restaurant-bought ham."

Maliah chuckled. "I already knew that you could throw down in the kitchen, Rach. Though I was a little worried when Granny gave you the look. Then I was a whole lot more worried when you two had an apple pie cook-off."

"Those were the days. Well, I won fair and square." Rachel brightened for the first time since being snubbed by her son. "And I was content that nobody took a single bite of my ham since I scored a recipe."

"Best investment you've ever made, honey," Abner assured her.

"So this is where we're at?" Ephraim snorted, sitting back in the overly cushioned chair.

"Eph," Maliah groaned. "You're hungry. Let's eat, then talk."

"Who would like to pray?" Rachel asked.

After a bout of silence, Abner sniffed. "I'm the man of the house, I'll do the honors."

While he prayed with closed eyes, Maliah peeked at Ephraim, who glared at his father. Her fingernails embedded into the expensive material of his pants. He still didn't close his eyes.

"You are too stubborn," Maliah whispered, while reaching over to pick up the mashed potatoes.

"I am what I am, and you are mine."

Arms folded, Ephraim watched as Maliah piled food on both their plates. She'd remembered not to give him yams. He took small comfort in her tender care, although he didn't plan to eat.

Across from him, his father placed down his fork after a single bite. "A man can build bridges and his legacy will be that of the man who built bridges. But a single one, out of a wealth of success, can fall. Then that man's entire legacy falls. He's now known as the man whose bridge fell."

Ephraim clapped his hands. "We are Levines. Shit doesn't fall. Everything's in order, right?"

Again Maliah's fingernails found their way to his thigh. The pricks she offered were nonexistent to him as his eyes bored through his dad's.

"Your grandpa's health was beginning to decline. I had to choose between a future blowup—no disrespect to you, Maliah. If I could go back, I would. But I had my own pressure to deal with, Ephraim."

"First it's the analogy of a bridge, next it's Grandpa Ian?" Ephraim slammed the side of his fist onto the table. Maliah's hand darted to the stem of her wine to stop it from falling. His red seeped like blood into the linen.

"Yes, let's bring Ian into this." Ephraim sounded as if he were preparing to badger a witness. "Do you recall the relationship he had with Wentworth? They were best friends. The best of fucking friends until Wentworth got his little heartbroken."

"Don't bring up, Nolan," Abner scoffed. "Our circumstances are vastly different. This is nothing like him."

Maliah's eyebrows knitted together "Daniel's grandpa Wentworth? What—"

"Yes, LeeLee. Wentworth or Nolan, depending on how close you were to the greedy bastard," Ephraim began. "Old Money Bags was Nolan to my grandpa Ian. There's another legacy or tradition that ended because the ass was full of himself."

"Son, you are crossing the line!"

"No. This is crossing the line: *'We will be like Nazis.'* Is that what Nolan told Ian, when Gramps tried to help him out?"

"It was much bigger than that, Eph."

"Daniel's inheritance was tied up in the fact that he had to marry someone like him. Blue eyes. Blond-haired. That clause made Crackhead Becky show her ass and try to take his company."

Maliah stopped digging her fingers into his thighs. Daniel's cousin, Rebecca, was an awful person. There was no doubt about it.

"We all know that Nolan wasn't racist, Eph," Abner spoke after a few seconds.

"I had no idea . . ." she murmured.

"Nolan was heartbroken over a young lady, much like yourself, Maliah," Rachel shared. "Ian cut ties, socially with the Rutledges after Nolan lashed out. His words were uncalled for. However, I'm glad that my son and Daniel were able to cultivate a relationship."

"Why did he mention the Nazis." Maliah murmured. "He's in textbooks shaking hands with MLK and helping desegregate schools."

"The short story is, Nolan fell in love with their family chef's daughter, Tamar. She was a teacher, who I would've loved to meet." Rachel smiled. "She didn't shut her mouth when it came to accommodations at schools. Nolan had a means, and he was right there with Tamar when marching at schools. It was while the state was at odds with the Supreme Court, he did everything for her. Then he went to the army, came home with amnesia."

"But why create such a clause in his will?" Maliah asked. "He forgot Tamar? What happened to her?"

"Yes, he forgot that he loved her. Nolan forgot everyone. Tamar and Ian were at his side. His father, Fredrick, had the best neurologists in the world there as well. Let's say that Fredrick wasn't all that nice to Tamar and preferred this change. However, she was in a car accident around the time

Nolan's mind righted itself. Tamar died. So he decided that his parents were right—" Rachel gulped. "—that a marriage to someone of their choosing would have to do."

"That's the most tragic story I've ever heard," Maliah sniffled.

"There you have it." Ephraim gestured. It almost seemed that the misfortune persuaded him to soften his heart. But his eyes narrowed, and his voice grew grave with anger. "So, Dad, what if something happened? What if something happened to either one of us"—he took Maliah's hand —"and *my wife* and I never got to make amends?"

Everything stilled in that moment. Not a single bird chirped. Had this been his closing remarks, an imaginary jury of twelve would be putty in his hands.

He dug his case home with the only option they had.

"Now, Maliah and I are back together after so many years. We will marry and have children."

"That's great, son," Abner agreed.

"We've waited for this day." Rachel stood from her seat and started around the table. Before she could console him with a hug, Ephraim offered their only choice.

"The two of you will have pictures of our children growing up. Holiday cards." His teeth clenched in contemplation. "Maybe I'll forgive you in nine years, maybe sooner."

Rachel's hand was almost at Ephraim's cheek before she snatched it back, clutched her chest. "Eph, you wouldn't do that to us."

"I would. I am."

Maliah stiffened at his side. "I don't like this, Ephraim. You've never treated your parents like this."

Abner hung his head. "Honestly, the day you two parted, things were not the same. Son, think about . . ."

Tears stung Maliah's eyes. Tamar and Nolan's past sounded like the wrong side of a love story. Maliah started to turn toward Ephraim. She wanted to kiss him. Just a single taste of his lips would do in the presence of his parents, but her stomach shot into her throat. In the same instance, the man she loved had become a tyrant. Blood boiled in her veins as she listened to him mention holiday cards as his parents' only ties to their grandchildren.

Abner sounded wrought with emotion as he said, "Honestly, the day you two parted things were not the same. Son, think about what you're saying!"

"I've thought about it long and hard," he growled. "For years, I was obsessed with who helped her with the annulment."

"What about forgiveness?" Abner tried.

Ephraim gritted his teeth. "You made me out for a fool. If we weren't blood, what I've declared would be the least of your worries. As a matter of fact, I was not done."

"Ephraim!" Rachel stared down at him.

"Mom, the photos are for your benefit. Dad, you may want to stay your retirement because there is no more Levine & Levine. Prepare to have all your clients . . ."

"Ephraim, you're an ass!" Maliah finally found her voice.

"This is for us—"

"I'm so sorry." She pushed out of the chair.

Ephraim started to stand.

"No, I . . . I've got this," she shot over her shoulder while heading toward the french doors.

With her entire body knotted in pain, she scurried through a huge kitchen and out into the foyer. Maliah clutched at her stomach, going upstairs to her old bedroom.

She went inside and into the adjoining bathroom. Falling to her knees, she clutched the basin of the porcelain toilet and spewed the little bit of lunch she had.

She felt his presence before he entered the room.

"Don't touch me!" The order escaped Maliah's lips, and she heaved more water than anything else.

Ephraim gripped her kinky hair, drawing the tresses away from her face as he kneeled beside her.

"What if you hadn't made it all the way up here?" he asked with a half-smile after a few more moments of her gagging in the toilet.

"You don't get to—" She wiped slobber from her lips. "You don't get to make jokes right now."

He held out a hand, reminding her, "I made a pallet on the floor for us that one night . . ."

She took his hand and stood up with a grunt. "Yeah, right, you folded all those comforters for me. My first hangover. You were dumb enough to hold me while I slept. Or did I sleep?"

She glanced into the mirror at him. Ephraim leaned against the doorframe. Were he someone else, Maliah might've been embarrassed. They'd known each other too long. Besides, the last time, he wiped the bile from her mouth.

"You slept a little. I didn't at all." He hooked a thumb over his shoulder. "You think they'll let me get you a bottle of water? Your timing was all wrong. I hardly got to see the expression on Abner's face."

Ignoring him, she pressed on the water spout and pooled lukewarm water on her hands. As she reached forward to splash her face, Ephraim kneaded her back with his knuckles. It felt so good that she forgot to stop herself from sighing.

"LeeLee, I should've given you a heads-up about our plans," he apologized.

Some part of Maliah wondered if his anger had given her an upset stomach or something else . . .

Something that worked into his plans of allowing the Levines to watch their future children grow, from afar. *LeeLee, you sure as hell can't be pregnant*, she reprimanded herself. As if the admonishment would unimpregnate her. Maliah had to confirm, but not now. Not with Ephraim being so vindictive.

He pressed his forehead to her, and she pulled away before he could hold her.

"Damn, you can't be mad at me."

"Well, I am." She started to open drawers, recalling that Rachel had stocked the bathroom after her first menstruation with all the items she needed. *I need a monthly right now*, Maliah told herself, snatching out a packaged toothbrush and paste.

"Go talk to your parents, Eph. Tell them you're angry—they're understanding people. Then tell them you need some time. But not years. That's between you and God."

She started to brush, and he pressed his pelvis against her ass, planting his palms on either side of the counter.

"Okay, Maliah, so we're playing the religious factor. On those grounds alone, you forgive me."

Through the reflection, Maliah saw his eyebrow arch as he took on a cocky grin. She growled low, then continued to brush her teeth.

"You're my LeeLee. My good girl."

She finished brushing her teeth. Then she turned around and pressed her hands against his chest, wanting space.

There were too many thoughts swarming through her

head. Such as how she'd seen a gynecologist before her first stint at the Hurt Room. You couldn't catch a sexually transmitted infection by yourself, at least she thought. But she'd just gotten back on birth control.

Fuck, fuck, fuck! Maliah gathered that she hadn't finished the first pack of birth control before having sex. And she sure as hell didn't recall them using a condom at the cabin!

"Eph, move." She pushed at him.

"You're a Christian, Maliah. You have to forgive me."

"You're Jewish, but somehow I doubt you follow the rules."

He pressed his thumb against the side of her mouth, wiped it. Then his mouth went to the same spot. Part of his lips were on her, but not enough. In an attempt to fight the attraction, Maliah pressed against his brick-like chest again.

"We kind of need to have a talk. A serious talk."

"I've had all the serious I'm going to do today, Sweets." Ephraim's large hands scoured over her ass, and he placed her on the edge of the table. "So, I've pissed you off. That's rectifiable." His mouth descended on hers, tongue darting into her mouth.

Maliah's arms flew around his neck, her pelvis pressed against him.

"That's right, even if you have an attitude, I am hard as fuck for you!" He massaged his groin between them.

"Eph," she groaned. "We vowed no more dry humping. Don't do this shit to me!"

He chuckled softly, placing his hand between them to pull down his zipper. He took her hand and guided it over his swollen cock.

"Depends. You still mad?"

She licked her lips, shook her head no.

Ephraim fisted his cock and got to his knees. He hiked

up her slip dress, the silk of her thong offering the only confliction.

"I can't hear you from down here," Ephraim said while nudging his nose against her clit. Her panties were drenched for him. She started to tug them down when he held her wrists. "Maliah, I didn't hear you."

"I'm not angry," she gritted out. Silly Maliah—she attempted to rock her hips and press her pussy against his mouth. But her ass started to slip off the counter. She yelped with a start.

Ephraim gripped her thighs and slid her farther back.

"You love me, don't you?"

"Yes!" Her fingers roved through his thick, short waves. "Please, Eph," she begged.

"I thought so," he replied, pressing his hand behind her neck and helping her scoot back on the countertop. He pressed her legs wide, then let his hands drag titillatingly slow over her hips to her inner thighs.

Ephraim pushed his pants down, took a wide-legged stance, and plunged his cock into her. Her body would've slammed back had he not still had a firm grip on her thick thighs. Ephraim plowed to the hilt of her cunt. Her throbbing walls pulsated around him, all ready to milk him for his worth. The orgasm came blindingly swift for Maliah. She screeched his name at the top of her lungs.

She grabbed ahold of his shoulders, but he'd pulled out. His erection stopped right between her thighs. "Look how glossed you got my cock," Ephraim groaned.

"Fuck meeeee," she begged, attempting to reach around the grab his ass, but he was just out of her realm.

Ephraim's forehead pressed against hers. "We are a team, Maliah. Say it."

Her mouth was chock-full of saliva, and she hadn't

noticed till this moment. She was hungry for him. Mad like an animal. She gulped down her desire. "We're a team."

In response, he filled her pussy up again to capacity and then some. Maliah's legs flew wide as she hollered, "Ephraim," again.

"That's right, Sweets," he murmured against her lips. "You want me to cum all over this cunt. Keep gripping my cock, beautiful. Not yet, baby. You keep coming all over me. Keep coming."

He ground into her. White blinding light went off before Maliah's gaze as his manhood slammed deep.

"Oh, oh, oh," she began, having forgotten the spoken language. "Oh, fu, fu, fuck!"

Ephraim slid out, his heavy cock popping down on her clit, the sensations further magnetizing her to him. Her legs shook so bad that she could hardly hold them around his hips.

"We're a team, right?" Ephraim planted a kiss on Maliah's lips while the crown of his cock massaged her sensitive pearl. "You're mine."

"I'm yours," she stuttered out. Like a fiend, she attempted to reach around and grab his butt.

His dick slithered around her thick folds, toyed with her nub, and sent spasms shuddering through Maliah.

"And when I have a belief," he said, grabbing the back of her neck, "you agree. No matter what."

She whimpered. His hold was strong and further reminded her that the man she loved had changed. But she needed this.

"We're a team, Eph." Maliah's breath brushed against his lips.

His tongue zipped into her mouth, and they sealed it with a kiss. Ephraim's cock slammed through her treasure.

This time, he screwed her until his eruption surpassed hers. Maliah's eyes rolled back as his seed filled up her pussy. His sex was the pure definition of a drug.

EPHRAIM FLUFFED the left side of Maliah's kinky hair as she sauntered down the steps of his parents' home. She stopped at the bottom of the stairs, her eyes bright with paranoia. She asked, "How bad do I look?"

"Beautifully fucked." He pulled an arm around her. "Sweets, you look beautiful, okay?"

She sighed, and then she glanced around them as if she'd forgotten where they'd been. "Can you be . . ."

Ephraim continued down the steps with his hand in hers, pulling her along. He expected a complaint, but she seemed to be holding her tongue.

As they walked through the house, he noticed his parents had moved the party indoors. His father had a fresh glass of wine; his mother didn't drink, but looked like she could use one. They sat on stools at the lengthy island.

"Let's not be too hopeful, Mom and Dad. Every word I said, I meant. However, who am I to predict the future. Maybe I won't snatch all the clients at the firm. Maybe I'll send videos instead of photos."

Maliah jabbed him in the ribs, and he continued. "But the two of you raised me to make decisions. You snatched said decision away from me. Let it be known, you're not the only ones on my shit list. LeeLee's parents are at fault too."

Abner took a long sip of his wine, all the way down until the glass was washed in a red residue. "Ephraim, we need you to be more reasonable. Your mother is hurt."

"Yes. When a stack of dominos is on the move, all

involved are affected." Ephraim chortled. "There, I matched you shitty analogy for shitty analogy."

"All I wanted for us to do is wait. Give Mr. Porter time to get his house in order!"

"Mom, you get butthurt when dad takes a certain case, don't you?" He pushed a few strands of her hair behind her head, but otherwise, he felt nothing for his mom.

"I'm not in agreement with all his cases, Eph. I've always been vocal about that." She tried to touch him.

"Still no excuse."

"All right," Abner gritted out. "Yes, I've defended a select clientele. A senator's kid who did ungodly acts, a billionaire who had certain requirements. But Maliah was entering our family—"

"She's entering my family, Dad." He'd gone far enough and was done with this conversation.

Maliah stood forlorn, chewing her thumb and the other hand around her waist. He took her by the waist and whispered, "Where should we go first?"

"We will see you later," Maliah addressed the Levines as Ephraim tightened his hold around her tiny frame.

He caught his mother mouthing, "Thank you," to Maliah while he ushered her toward the door.

Outside, they stopped at the top of the steps. He cinched her waist again. "LeeLee, I asked you a question."

"I already regret signing those documents. Don't make me further regret the man you've become because of my mistake."

Ouch.

He wrapped his arms around her, pressed his forehead to hers. "Maliah, I don't plan on ever letting go of you. I'll work on being the man you loved from day one . . ." *But I make no promises.* He smiled down at her. "Pick a place, Sweets."

The tension in her body fizzled, and she melted into his arms. With her mouth pressed against his neck, she murmured, "You've surprised me all day. Might as well continue."

31

WHAT EPHRAIM HAD IN PLAN FOR MALIAH SURPASSED THE definition for being surprised. A profusion of emotions wrapped around her. And instead of being reminiscent of the old Ephraim Levine she fell for so many years ago, he was all that and more. A few days ago, the private jet touched down after she'd had a good night's sleep in the bed.

This was the best Saturday morning of her life. Maliah learned that Ephraim had taken them to the Holy Land. Cocky as ever, he'd mentioned something about being in Israel. That alone should be an ample enough reminder to her that she couldn't be mad about his choices. While Ephraim still had his hand in vengeance, she had to play Saint Mary. She'd burst into laughter but couldn't help the love blossoming in her stomach for him.

They spent the day like the innocents they'd once been, wandering around Jerusalem. The rich, beautiful land and intellectual conversation about faith warmed her soul. It also allowed them to cultivate their old connection, which was on a higher level than just sex.

———————

On Tuesday morning, Maliah pressed back on her stilettos as Ephraim guided the small of her back. They had spent so many wonderful days in Jerusalem.

"Let's stay here a while longer, Eph," she groaned as he led her up the stairs of the jet.

He pressed against her and whispered into her ear, "No, I've gone twenty-four hours without having you. We have a magnet for our fridge. This is all the memory I need."

"You do realize that God can hear you whisper perfectly fine." She stopped moving to chuckle. Arching an eyebrow, she asked, "So, you've gone seventy-two hours without what?"

Ephraim plucked her up by the waist and carried her the few more steps inside. He set her down on the first seat, kissing her forehead. Then he replied to her question, "*Certain situations* that I plan to make up for."

"Yummm," she murmured.

The door to the cockpit was open. Needless to say, the pilot, who'd witnessed her attitude firsthand while on the flight to Miami a month ago, had gotten used to the thought of them.

"Where are we going, now?" Maliah asked the pilot.

"Well, Ms. Porter, I would love to tell you." His light gray eyes went from her to Ephraim's. "Mr. Levine, this one is a firecracker. Can I please tell her?"

"Not one word," Ephraim said.

The pilot shook his head, laughing a little while closing the door to the cockpit.

"We've got a perfectly good bed." Ephraim nudged his head to the sleeping quarters at the rear of his jet. "And we have an hour until our next destination."

"That's not much time." Maliah tried to jolt out of the chair, but he caught her again. This time, Ephraim lifted her until her thighs slammed around his waist.

"Damn," he groaned, walking toward the back. "I'll get started on you soon as we're in the air."

"Oh, so you're growing a conscience?" An aura of giddiness surrounded Maliah as he moved into the tiny room and laid her on the bed. "After all the sex we've had, you still refuse to do me in Israel."

He stood up, staring down at her. She moved up onto the bed, pressed her legs wide.

"No panties," Ephraim said in a throaty, deep voice as the jet jerked to a start. "Who am I to make you wait, Sweets …"

MALIAH EXPECTED the Sistine Chapel or the Roman Colosseum when they arrived in Rome. She breathed in the earth as they walked down a street, which was simply ruined and divine all in the same instant. Ephraim donned a dark blue suit. Maliah wore a stark white slip dress that caressed the afterglow of sex on her brown skin. New stores were entwined with ancient ones. They passed by a window of what she assumed was a general store, due to the display of medications toward the back of the building. Maliah's pace stalled. She contemplated about her sick spell at the Levine home. Overcome by being the center of Ephraim's world, she had forgotten all about her pregnancy concern.

Ephraim took her face into his hand, glanced over at the store and back at her. "You need something, Maliah? Rosa can get it."

A shaky smile forced its way onto her face, but she

shook her head to stop herself from sharing her concerns. "I haven't even met your assistant yet. She's here?"

"Rosa's a bit antisocial. She rides in the cockpit. I'll introduce you to her later. You need anything?"

"No." She shook her head again. His dark, captivating eyes scoured over her in an inspection. Maliah forced her smile to solidify on her face. "Maybe some vitamins—I'm not twenty anymore."

He almost smiled at her. She feigned disinterest in the conversation while glancing across the way. A restaurant that appeared to be hundreds of years old had hordes of people walking in and out. But she watched him from her peripheral. *Damn, he's too smart to trick*, Maliah told herself. She wanted to grab a pregnancy test, get over the dirty details. Not alert him unless it was necessary. Not with Ephraim having scheduled Sunday dinner at her parents' house. She had four days until another insanity starring Ephraim and her family. Maliah wasn't in the least bit ready.

Maliah spoke again. "Maybe we should cross the street." So far, she'd glanced everywhere but at him.

"Why?"

She nudged her jaw a few buildings down. There were two men in black, who put the movie to shame. Coiled wires hung from each of their ears, no doubt to have secret, techy conversations to other men in black. They looked suspicious, or rather like they would kill to keep some royalty safe.

Finally, Ephraim chuckled. He slid his hand around her waist and guided her in his strong arm. A few minutes later, they stopped right in front of the men. Maliah glanced up to see a golden plaque. Giati's Jeweler had been around since the late 1900s, and he or she sure as hell wasn't allowing people to window-shop. Instead of windows, there were tiger head moldings on each side of the double doors.

"Mr. Levine," one of the men said with a curt nod, before they both went to the silver-plated doors and started to open them.

"They should check my credit score, Eph," she quietly cackled. "I don't belong here."

Ephraim's arm tightened around her in response. "You *belong* to me, and I only do the best."

A deep exhale flew past Maliah's lips as she took in the sight of the floor-to-ceiling marble. In lieu of glass partitions, black velvet columns were placed around the room. On the top of each pillar, one sole jewel, whether it be a necklace, ring, or bracelet, was held in a thick glass encasing. There was minimal jewelry. Maliah considered hawking the tiniest piece to ensure her grandbabies' grandbabies had a good life. And placed around the room were also comfy, sheer white leather love seats. In the center of the room, a woman dressed in white with bloodred pumps sat with her lengthy legs crossed.

Shit, Maliah thought, *I look like the idiot at a wedding who tried to show up the bride!* Jewelry stores hired beautiful women to increase sales, but the woman with jet-black hair had to be a model.

The model's lips matched her stilettos and were tugged into a pouty smile as she stared at Ephraim. "It has been a few months," she began, accentuating her hips as she rose. "I have the perfect watch for . . ."

The model stopped speaking. "Who is this beauty?" She all but spat the words.

"The future Mrs." Ephraim continued to clutch Maliah, claiming her like a prized possession. "Alex, I spoke with Ms. Giati yesterday. Please send her my regards for closing the store while you give her a call. I need you to see if she has something new for me."

Great, they clearly know each other, Maliah contemplated.

Alex, who Maliah swore was not named Alex at birth, but something sexier like Alexandra sputtered. "Like a watch . . ."

"Like a custom engagement ring," he gestured, irritation rising over his face.

Alex reached down to where she'd been sitting and plucked up a cell phone. Maliah continued to watch her reaction while she strutted over to a pillar that stopped at her waist. Every single movement the woman made was fruit for the reading. It was another reminder that Maliah did not need to be pregnant. Not yet. On top of wanting Ephraim and his family to fully mend their relationship, and then her own, Maliah couldn't be.

Bile crept up into Maliah's throat, pausing all of her excessive preponderances. "I need the restroom. I need to use it," she blurted. Ice churned in her veins at the thought of how odd she sounded. Maybe she sounded like she had irritable bowel syndrome. But Maliah started to speak again when Alex handed Ephraim the phone and beckoned her over.

Ephraim stopped placing the phone to his ear. "Sweets, do you—"

"No, she can help me!" Maliah growled.

Alex strutted quickly toward the back of the store and down a hallway. Maliah matched her stride for stride.

The model, who had to twilight as a jeweler, flicked her wrist at the sign to the restroom. "Please do not dirty it!"

Maliah stepped into yet another grand room. The scent of lavender was infused in the air. She reached over the gleaming toilet and tried to hurl, but nothing came up. After a few seconds of dry hacking, she straightened up. At the triangle-shaped mirror, with a jewellike frame, she popped her fingertips to her cheeks a few times. Then she sprinkled a bit of water on her face to give her skin a fresh-dew look. Because, well, her mom did such things, and Maliah had never been big on makeup.

She opened the door to the bathroom, and her eyes narrowed. Where the hell was Alex? No, Maliah did not need an escort. However, she did not need a jaded woman who knew what Ephraim's sex looked like to have any seconds alone with him. They had their dysfunction, and he was *hers*. With a switch in her step, she moved back down the hallway.

In the main room, Maliah glanced around. Her heart stopped constricting. Ephraim was in the far corner, still on the company phone. Her brown orbs did a sweep of the room to watch for Alex.

The woman spoke in a lush, Italian tone, "Are you done letting it all out?"

The bitch had the nerve to sound sexy while being rude.

"Oh, yeah." Maliah grinned, letting her almost-flat belly pudge out some. "We came from a buffet. So much food. You know how that goes, right?"

Alex's claws clenched as Maliah sauntered past, hiding a smile on her face. The second she reached Ephraim, he said a few more words in Italian before pressing the Off button on the phone.

"They know I'm not a patient man, Maliah." He pinched the bridge of his nose, then started toward one of the podiums. "But the designs aren't ready. That means we will get a better deal."

"On what?"

"Your engagement ring." He hooked his arm around her

waist again. "You don't want any of these. Other people have viewed them."

"Actually, I don't want anything from this store." She was surprised at her own bluntness.

EPHRAIM WATCHED all that ass he'd grown to love as Maliah started toward the doors. She pressed and pressed at them, but they didn't budge.

"We can't leave, LeeLee," he said. "Alex, can you please?"

"Why are you asking her!" Maliah snipped, pressing again at the handle. "It's stuck. It's st—"

Alex pressed a lever on the inside of her bracelet, and the deadbolts of the jewelry store clicked. Ephraim groaned, noticing the flair of embarrassment on Maliah's face as she stalked outside. The two security guards didn't move an inch from either side of the door as she paused, glancing which way to go.

"Where did we come from!" Maliah growled.

"I miss jealous LeeLee." He pawed at her ass cheek.

She slapped his hand away, but he held tight. There was too much meat for him to let go without a fight.

"I was not jealous, for the record. I don't like diamonds, flashy, gaudy, huge diamonds."

"We weren't there for flashy, gaudy, huge diamonds," he replied, leading them down the street. "I had intentions on something custom. Ms. Giati's grandfather was working on a design all night, preparing for our arrival. Then he got sick. Listen, I'm sorry, I had no idea Alex would be here today."

"Am I going to meet someone you fucked on every continent?"

"Wait, wait, wait." Ephraim stopped walking, and he yanked her flush against his chest. "I can't ask you that so—"

"Hello, you're the reason why, Eph! I can't even screw a brick wall in Greenwich without you knowing."

Damn, for the life of him, he'd missed the arguing. They'd have great sex later, but for now, Ephraim laughed at her joke. It topped whatever she'd been attempting to say before their arrival at Giati's Jewelers.

"I'm being serious, Eph."

"All right, then. I am who the fuck I am, Sweets."

"A whore?"

"No, well, I was." He paused, chewed his bottom lip for a moment. "What I'm saying is, I'm unapologetic about the time that we weren't together, Maliah. While you're running around forgiving Tom, Dick, and Harry—"

"AKA, Rach and Abner, your parents!"

"Them too." He shrugged. "Then you can forgive me for things that I've done while we weren't together. God knows, I'd die before cheating on you, Maliah."

All the animosity clutching at her throat seemed to drain. She licked her lips, then groaned. "What did you do with her? The two of you—what was it? I have to know?"

"Just—"

"Don't tell me." She ran a hand through her thick hair. "Did you sleep together, like overnight? Wake up to pancakes."

He stole a kiss against her forehead, murmuring, "You're tormenting yourself, LeeLee."

"Shit, sounds like I have a hundred regrets, then." She pressed her face into his chest. Though her tone was soft, urgency radiated through her body. "Or more? How many regrets do I have, Eph . . .? Don't tell me. I'm so sorry, baby."

His arms moved around her body, pulling her into a

tight embrace. Her erratic questions had jumped around enough to save him from responding to the "overnight" inquiry. There was only one other woman that Ephraim Levine had slept with. Katina Gilmore. A few times one of them were too tired to leave the other's hotel room. For now, with Maliah harboring guilt for their breakup, she didn't need to know. One day, they'd share everything, even deep dark secrets, like they used to.

32

ON FRIDAY AFTERNOON, MALIAH DOWNED TWO SUPPLEMENTAL pills. She placed the glass onto the counter as if she'd taken a few shots of whiskey to the head. Her mind had become a clash of thoughts during her first encounter with Ephraim's assistant. Rosa had dropped off the multivitamins about an hour ago. Now, all she had were regrets:

Signing those damn annulments.

Not believing her parents were willing to change. Who could doubt it, after Abner had shared that Rick still used his same antics.

All those times she spent ruminating over Ephraim. Every single day was a moment they couldn't get back.

And the pain she put him through. The Hurt Room could never compare to how she'd treated him.

While seated in the bedroom of a luxurious hotel in Italy, she let an entire cycle of grief roam through her. Yesterday, her outburst had been uncalled for.

"LeeLee," she groaned, rubbing her hands over her face while sinking farther into the chair. "You have to get back to those good times."

She pulled out her cell phone and thought to call her father. She had this sudden need to prepare him for Sunday. To remind him that they were family and regardless of their estrangement, things were going to change. Maliah's thumb hovered over Rick's contact, when a text message popped up.

"Congrats. You are my beautiful daughter!—Mom," she murmured. Something about that curdled her stomach. For one, her mom texted her as much as leprechauns sighted unicorns. Second, there'd been cricket sounds in the place of calls and texts during her grand opening of We Rise Learning Center. Dad had come, and he'd made his apologies for her mother, such as "tea with the ladies." Or maybe he'd mentioned a spa.

"Hey, Mom, love you," she started to text. They weren't big on "I love yous." Her grandparents more than made up for it, but they weren't here to make up for her mom's response.

Maliah read her mother's response out loud with a chuckle. "I wish I had more time to prepare. I'm auditioning chefs for Sunday dinner (wink emoji)."

What blasphemy. Maliah often rolled her eyes at her mother. This was where Annaleigh's biracial upraising seemed so stilted. Who auditioned chefs for Sunday dinner? Out of all the days in the week, that should be the day food was made in love. She tried to stop herself from analyzing her mother's statement. Annaleigh had the right to "audition" chefs to ensure dinner was "perfect." *But when will you reach out to me, for me, Mom*, she thought.

Another text pinged in her hand. As Maliah read the words, her stomach churned. "I'm so happy you have a second chance. I'll make us an appointment, just this case."

Why couldn't her mother stop with the first sentence

and be happy for her and Ephraim? No, Annaleigh's concern was her ability to bear children. Maliah started to fling her phone across the room when a Gmail notification came through.

The Hurt Room brand had conditioned her pussy to twitch like crazy. At the sight of it, Maliah gulped down desire and opened the email.

"For your fifth visit . . ." she began. Tomorrow, she had an outing. Well, somewhat of an outing. She had to be in Amsterdam by midnight. The email boasted information on a pop-up sex club. "Well, I suppose no more Saturday mornings. Might as well switch up the program."

She moved out of the chair, paused from stepping to the wet bar, and headed for the door. In the living room of the suite, Rosa sat with a tiny notebook in hand. She didn't have the feel of an assistant in old-school Nike Cortezes, jeans, and a shirt. Her demeanor didn't scream tourist or anything else. Just plain, old efficient.

Ephraim leaned against the wall, chatting with her. She snorted every few seconds, while jotting down his words.

"Rosa needs a raise," Maliah said with a pep in her tone. "I like your style."

"Why thank you," the woman responded, offering a faint smile. "I keep telling 'em that."

"You get paid ridiculously well, Rosa." Ephraim folded his arms. "Besides, once you've made all these calls, you can enjoy the sights before I need you again."

"Eh, I don't like crowds." Rosa rolled her eyes. "He gave me tickets to Disney World one time, to be an ass."

Maliah asked, "So, what are you two working on?"

"Very bad, bad things," Rosa mumbled.

"If I tell you, no lip?" Ephraim asked as Maliah sat across from Rosa.

Arching an eyebrow, she replied, "I'll try."

"Rosa's scheduling meetings for attorneys that I'm going to poach."

"That's not the bad part, Eph," his assistant interjected.

"Oh god," Maliah murmured. "You're still planning on starting your own firm."

"Aye, so you know." Rosa shook her head.

Ephraim moved toward Maliah. He caressed her cheek while standing before her. "I'm setting roots in Greenwich, for us."

Maliah placed her hand over his, but there was no stopping him as he stroked her skin. "You already have roots," she reminded him.

"You go get some sleep."

"It's not even 7:00 p.m. yet, Eph."

"But you're not a night owl, and I need you prepared for tomorrow." He winked, taking her hand to help her up. "Go rest, put on the television. Call room service for a massage. I'll tuck you in shortly."

Her mouth perched to the side. Now, that she did not mind.

———

IN THE MORNING, Maliah clutched at the scent of him. With a groan, she peeled one eye open to see that she'd commandeered Ephraim's pillow. He was nowhere to be found. He'd sexed her to sleep last night, though she was beginning to crave their Saturday-morning routine. A fist full of Saturdays at the Hurt Room sounded nice. She lay on her back, staring at the chandeliered ceiling, and gave a tantrum of movements.

"He's up, he's plotting evil things." She hashed it out. "I'm going home . . . LeeLee, you are not going home."

"Would you like a cup of coffee?" Rosa's voice from the door sent Maliah zipping up into a seated position. Ephraim's assistant had on another pair of unflattering jeans. A button-up swallowed even more of her chubby body. She smiled. "Eh, I've seen a lot worse than a personal debate."

"Does Eph have meetings this morning?"

"Yes, and no, *Mija*." Rosa came into the room and sat on a chair. "Not the type of meetings that worry you. One of his clients, a pop star, whose habits are as *platinum* to fund as his record is in jail. He's had to postpone his first video conference with his so-called A-team."

Maliah detected a note of sarcasm in Rosa's voice. She sat back against the headboard and asked, "You've worked for Eph for a while now?"

The woman winked. "You're asking me how assimilated I've become to his ruthlessness?"

She dropped her head back with a sigh. "Yes."

"I'll tell you, that man of yours is cunning and intelligent unless it involves you. Then he lashes out."

Sitting up again, Maliah placed an arm before her belly. Ephraim's assistant had to be in her late forties, early fifties. Wisdom brimmed from her, but she was after all Ephraim's assistant. Could Maliah ask her a few questions swarming in her head?

"I know you weren't around when we parted ways," Maliah said, kneading the back of her neck. "But has he changed a lot?"

She stared at Rosa, clinging to her body language, her every move. She had to know if things went south and she was pregnant . . . How would they handle their growing seed? There were options, but Maliah Porter was on the other side of thirty. Was Ephraim so accustomed to the life of a bachelor?

"My sixth anniversary as Ephraim's employee is coming up soon. Aside from crude jokes, I believe the only problem you'd have with him is if he were defending someone else. That's not an option for Eph. Maliah, you haven't a thing to worry about." Rosa slapped her hands against her knees and got up with a grunt. "Coffee before your flight. It's a short flight, but I've been told to remind you to rest all day. After your trip to Amsterdam, we head back to the States before dawn."

"No, thank you. Coffee would do worse to my mind than I already do to it." She sat back in bed again. They'd to sleep on the flight back to Greenwich. Meaning, they'd probably return in time to squeeze into her Baptist church while the preacher was gathering his second or third wind. *Damn, you, Eph*, she thought. This short vacation hadn't been long enough. Ephraim's inexorable ways had shortened it even further.

33

"My pet, my pet, my pet . . ."

The hissing came from either side of Atsun. She crouched down between two employee vehicles. Heart thumping in her ears, she waited for the snarls to drown out. She'd ran off the second their Lyft XL arrived at the loading and unloading area of the airport. With five of her Master's best on her tail, Atsun had zipped across the street. She'd sprinted through the airport parking structure. Since their departure was from a small airport, it had been easy for Atsun to run through the guest parking structure. She'd jumped the partition to the employee parking section.

Those bitches stopped following.

"My pet, come here . . . we love you" faded into cackling as the others stalked back the way they came.

For all intents, she was having a sorry Saturday evening. This morning, her heart had been shattered into a million tiny pieces. This was her second weekend without her possession. Nori thought he was so fair, allowing them to wait these two weeks before he told them all to pack up.

Her chest heaved, and she cried. Last night, she'd

slipped past the online security parameters for the Hurt Room and saw that the beast had taken Maliah to Amsterdam. Nori had to have known all along. He'd changed the passcode on his laptop. Who did he think she was, some old lady who'd never used a computer?

"Ma'am, are you all right?"

So focused on how the only thing she coveted was always outside of her grasp, Atsun looked down at herself. She was crouching in a dried oil puddle. Then she glanced up, offering the appearance of sudden confusion as she stared at a man. His big belly almost blocked his name tag. "Matt" was from technical support. She looked into Matt's soft blue eyes and tentatively touched the old, leather collar around her neck. With her short skirt, she opened her knees a little wider. Then her hand fell from the collar to the draped opening at her chest. His eyes went there and simmered a little before softening again.

"Can you help me?" she murmured, playing up her accent.

His eyes didn't move, but his fat jaws shook as he reached into his pocket.

"No cops, please." Atsun's chest heaved a little. "I-I-I'm what you call bride—sex bride. They mail me here, to you . . ."

In her attempts to manipulate, she'd forgotten to take a glance at his wedding finger. Atsun's teary gaze flitted from his for a second to his hand, and she held in her sigh of relief.

"You're a sex bride. I am so sorry." He still clutched his cell phone. "Who mailed you here, sweetheart?"

"Please." She popped up, clinging to him. "Please keep me. Keep me safe while I get away from them."

He didn't let her go but took a few paces back to glance

between the two cars. "Ma'am, I don't know if we're being watched."

"You save me." Atsun's mouth was inches away from his thick ones. "Can I thank you before you call *cop*?"

His tongue darted out over his lips. "Thank me . . ."

"Yes, please." Atsun's lips surged against his, pushed her tongue into his mouth, and sucked on his. A small erection pierced at her thigh. Matt the Technician had to take her home. He was her savior, and he just didn't know it yet. She'd stay with him until the bastard brought her sub back. Though, she did not have any plans besides meeting Maliah again via the Hurt Room email, she knew that pressing forward, her days would be so much kinder. Both of their days would be.

GRACHTENGORDEL, Amsterdam

HEADING ACROSS THE TARMAC, Maliah started for her cell phone. The pilot had left her without a single order. Rosa had stayed in Rome, and Maliah hadn't the slightest idea what to do in a foreign country. With a cool breeze fighting the warmth of the rescinding sun, she glanced around. She noticed an SUV toward the end of the asphalt. Leaning against the passenger door was Yesiv. The Russian had scared her during their first encounter. His presence and the recent cultural climate with the States and Russia. But he had this good aura.

He was holding an iPhone and used his other hand to offer one of those innocent waves.

"I thought you were only to hound me in the States when I refused to go to the tyrant?"

Yesiv turned the phone around, and she got a good view of Ephraim's face on the FaceTime application. She couldn't make out the background, but he appeared to be in business mode. His thick eyebrows were untensed at the sight of her.

Ephraim said, "Yesiv is the only driver I trust for you, LeeLee. You tell me if he does anything wrong?"

"Sure. Can I tell Yesiv when you do wrong?"

"*Nyet*, boss. I'm rooting for you twos like eh . . . Mariah Carey's 'Emotions.'"

Maliah burst into a laugh.

"No more '90s music for you, Yesiv." Ephraim started to glance away. "Maliah, follow my instructions to a T. Love you, see you later."

"Wait . . ." she began as the call disconnected.

"I'd have parked closer, but the boss wanted to see the look on your face. He says you"—Yesiv pointed his head —"you're in your mind too much—or something."

His massive hand went toward the back door, and he opened it. Yesiv helped her in, checked to make sure she wasn't obstructing the door, then closed it. When he got into the SUV and pressed the push to start, the radio popped on.

A sports commentator came alive with debate. "Killer Karo is a beast in the cage, and I can tell you what I expect during this next—"

"Sorry," Yesiv killed the station.

"Killer Karo?" Maliah asked.

He turned in his seat. "Okay, I'm not supposed to listen to '90s music, but I'll tell you about the greatest MMA fighter in the motherfu—ahem, sorry. I'll tell you about him, if you'd like. At first, I thought Vassili Resnov was weak sauce. Like what you say when someone pays money to win?"

She smiled. "I guess rigging the game? Who's Vassili?"

"Vassili is Killer Karo or people shout Kill 'em Karo, when he's ready to make someone his . . . uh, a submission," Yesiv said, and Maliah could tell he was trying not to cuss in her presence. "First, I thought he was rigging the game when I heard about him in Venice—California, but he's from my home."

Since Yesiv hadn't started driving, Maliah asked, "Why did you think he was cheating to come out the victor?"

"His family is bratva. His old man is—I can't say it. I have no way to say it to you—you're a girl. So you have to know they are bad. Not Karo. He is good. And when I first saw him, I . . ." He paused to touch his eye duct. "It was beautiful sight. Blood. Gore. Almost death, eh."

"Yesiv, can you do me a favor?"

"Sure. I can tell you about his—"

"I like pop music too."

Maliah sat back in the seat as Yesiv got the hint. The poor fluffy teddy bear turned back in his seat and flipped the radio back on. The sports commentator mentioned some sort of chokehold before Aerosmith's "'I Don't Want to Miss a Thing" blared.

Yesiv crooned so loud that she pulled out her phone, curiosity piqued. A simple Google search made Maliah's eyes bug out. *Damn, Karo could kill the—*

IT WAS HALF an hour till midnight. Her skin felt refreshed. Usually, naps during the day made Maliah wake up more lethargic than before. She'd followed the letter Ephraim left for her and dressed in a rose-shade bra with matching thong. A camel-colored trench coat covered all of her curves. Now, she was back in the SUV, this time for a short ride around the canals. The moon reflected off dark water. Every alleyway of the ancient structures made her think dark, paranormal thoughts. She wrapped herself further in the coat, glad that her long kinks of hair blocked much of her side profile.

She clutched the letter in her hand.

Dear Pet,

You will need every second of rest that you can get. Tonight, I will test your wills, and you will love it.

—Master

A million tiny goosebumps rose across her skin. Before she'd ventured to the Hurt Room, Maliah would've fought someone off, if they desired the title of "Master." One month ago, she fled Nori's first instruction, when he mentioned that her "Master" would meet her soon. Now, she had a broader understanding of the term. Ephraim was her Master during this sort of sex, and she'd surpassed "accepting" the term for money. She craved this.

The SUV lurched to a stop. To their left was an old, abandoned warehouse. There had to be light-out curtains, because the moon reflected against a few of the windows. Those windows had broken glass. Gaze glued to the crumbling structure, Maliah's shoulders tensed when Yesiv opened the door. The driver mumbled an apology.

"Where are the rest of the cars?" Maliah gulped, taking his hand to get out. This had to be the most unpopular sex club.

"Everyone has drivers, Miss Porter." Yesiv held out a piece of paper and nudged his head toward the building. "I'll watch and make sure you enter."

She glanced through the haze of the night. A steel door was barely made out within all the grim and graffiti.

Yesiv touched her shoulder. "Boss waits for you."

Damn you, Eph. Her legs shook while her high heels clicked onto the cement. She started toward the door, stopped, and squinted at the words. While she mentally cursed him for withholding this last bit of information, Maliah began to read.

Pet,

Knock three times. Wait two seconds. Knock twice. Wait one second. One knock. When the door opens, say . . . "Through me forbidden voices, Voices of sexes and lusts . . ."

"Wow, this is a Walt Whitman poem," she told herself.

At the door, Maliah stood there for a moment. Her mind had been a war zone of thoughts yesterday. Those contemplations were beginning to fade, all because of Ephraim. She focused on the letter, then placed it in the pocket of her jacket. Fist poised at the door, Maliah breathed deep before completing the knock sequence.

The door opened and a man in black gazed across her. With vigor, she started to recite the poem.

"Levine owns you, just go." He cocked his head.

But I actually learned this poem in high school! Maliah wanted to argue and stall. Past the man, a hallway was cloaked in darkness. One dim light at the end kept clicking, and a few bugs fizzled off it. By the time Maliah reached it, the little bit of illumination had faltered again. Her heart lurched in her throat.

34

THE SECOND DOOR MOVED WITH SLOW PRECISION, THE STEEL of it as massive as Fort Knox. Music played, not so loud that it jarred, but enough to send a pleasant vibration through Maliah's chest. The place had a trendy nightclub feel. Neon lights, slick glossy black bars in various areas for drinks she probably couldn't afford. Dark floors offered more action than dancing. Men wore the finest suits or those black leather cutout pants. Then her eyes focused in on a few thongs eaten up by muscular asses. The women looked straight out of Vicky's Secret, and that was on a gradient from a shade of "sweet" to "fuck me."

In the center of the floor, a woman gave a man head. There were sheer curtains for various alcoves. The sound of murmuring and sex mellowed with the music. Maliah's eyes glued onto a Domme who held the chain to her submissive. His thick neck strained, the collar around it strapped too tight.

Maliah started to ask, "Can you bre—"

"You are Eph's sweetheart." A woman with thick lips, butterscotch skin, and a sistah-girl frame, wrapped in a red teddy, glanced at her up and down. She blocked the path where the Domme had taken what Maliah would call a choking victim. The mixed chick's mouth curved at the edges. "You are so sweet."

Maliah's mouth was open for a moment.

"Nice teeth. Consider closing your mouth. Men will take that wide open mouth as a challenge. Some women too."

Her mouth zipped shut.

The mixed chick laughed and then held out a hand. "I'm the Black Dalilah."

Her claim made Maliah all the more uncomfortable.

"Okay, sorry. You're easy prey. I'm Heaven. Please stop with those wild, big, gorgeous eyes. They're mighty tempting, but I only devour male subs, and your Master is a good friend of mine." She rubbed a hand over Maliah's shoulder in a quick soothing movement. Something told Maliah that Heaven carried the conversation on for her benefit. Heaven added, "Friend like Lawyer, I know subs can be catty when they're not fully aware. But you aren't a true sub, and I do not allow fake subs in my establishment."

"Oh . . ."

"Kidding. Everyone's fully vetted. But please do not address a Dom or Domme about their submissive. Each person has disclosed their contract with my establishment. No contract between a Dom and a sub is a disgrace, sweetheart. And *I do not fuck with* fake Doms. Posers aren't aware of the areas of the body to inflict pain; even vanilla posers make me vomit. Their misinformation disgusts me, and they are all handled."

"Oh." Maliah nodded, unsure of how to respond.

Heaven licked her lips. "Subs are a different situation. Their pleasure, pain, *life*, is in the hand of their Dom. Trust is so beautiful, sweetheart. This establishment ensures that all Doms follow the rules."

"Um, okay," Maliah murmured. Heaven's outlook reminded her of Nori's statement, though her stance was much more intense. A Dom should keep his or her submissive safe and follow a contract.

"Shall we?" Heaven held out her hand. "Listen, if I don't escort you, your blood in a shark tank. I'll give you the grand tour."

It was on the tip of Maliah's tongue to decline the grand tour as she watched a woman on her knees, her ass full of cock, and every time she gasped her mouth became full of cock too.

"Hypnotizing, isn't it?" Heaven said, taking hold of her hand.

They passed by even more displays, and then Heaven stopped as a man with Nubian black skin moved toward her. He wore cutoff jeans like he'd been shipwrecked on fantasy island for a few years. He removed a thick blunt from his mouth, pressed his lips to hers, and her eyes rolled back.

Heaven breathed out fragrant, high-class ganja. Maliah eyed them both, tempted to be a fly on the wall in their bedroom or wherever these two got down.

"Domme, please tell me what I can do for you," he said in a dreamy islander accent.

Heaven skimmed her hand along his thick neck, then gripped. His white teeth contrasted against his pleasant mouth as he tried to breathe.

"Bring me the closest server." Her tone stayed sexy while she choked him out. Only her hazel eyes warned that she was angry—aside from constricting his throat. "You need to leave, now!"

Heaven flitted him away and addressed Maliah. "My

bitch has yet to learn. Greet our newest guest by falling to his knees and saying hello. *Then serve me.* Some subs are untrainable. I'd hate to tell him it's not working out. I'd loathe every second of it, sweetheart. He agrees to every form of punishment and humiliation—and he succeeds! Why can't he greet people with respect! This is my place. I have a brand to upkeep."

Maliah blinked a few times, not sure how to respond to Heaven's venting. Clearly, her pet had eyes for only her. Seconds later, a server came by with a tray of drinks.

"Please, sweetheart." Heaven gestured toward the drinks.

Maliah came to terms that her name was now "sweetheart." Heaven was a weird one but had good Southern hospitality to new people. Maliah grabbed a double shot of tequila and tossed it back.

"Another, sweetheart," Heaven implored with a sultry voice. "Just to clear the air."

She took another. "Thanks."

They continued to walk around, Heaven alight with vigor about her establishment. The lips between Maliah's legs made delicious quivers at every sight that she saw. Standing with the owner was like foreplay as Heaven moved closer to people. She showed her a cock slithering into juices. Maliah wrapped her arms around herself, wishing Ephraim were nearby.

"You are wet now?" Heaven asked.

Maliah figured that the woman wasn't hitting on her like Atsun. Almost like their conversation could be conducted over a cup of coffee in this world. Her cheeks burned.

"You are. I can finish the tour, but Ephraim wanted you a little crazy before I took you to him. I'm sorry, sweetheart— all of us Doms have our preferences. And I can read you already. You crave a good fucking. Let's get you to Eph."

They walked past more partitions. Some were open. Others were closed with black curtains, others with rice paper, where a glimpse of an outline was enough to get off. Either way, closed ones intrigued Maliah the most. Screams of joy triumphed and screwed with her mind, made her want to view such delights. When she felt her pussy might implode with the desire to be filled, Maliah exhaled.

Heaven moved aside a rice-paper wall to reveal a room. Ephraim sat, top buttons undone to display his chiseled chest and a peppering of dark hair. There was a flogger in his lap. He had his arm lazily over the back of the chair, and damn did this place look like his throne room. She gulped at the sight of the flogger but was still magnetized to him.

"You requested an audience. Please confirm that you'd still both like that opportunity," Heaven inquired.

"I would." Ephraim's voice became heavy as he looked at Maliah. There was a faint smile of approval on his face, and she craved more of it. "Pet, would you agree to an audience?"

"She's simply beautiful. The entire house will stop fucking for you, I'm sure," Heaven said. "I had a previous arrangement, I'll cancel it."

Maliah licked her lips. "Will it hurt?"

"It has to hurt," Heaven blurted. Then she smiled. "My apologies."

"Yes, it will, Pet. You know it has to hurt," Ephraim growled.

No. No. Fucking no! "Yes." Maliah's own words echoed in her ear.

"If he doesn't make up all the pain," Heaven began, giving a cocky grin.

"I'm your fucking attorney, Heaven. Don't finish that statement." Ephraim replied.

"What? I intended to offer her my sub. He only loves me anyway."

The banter between the two did nothing for Maliah, but she moved toward him, fear vibrating through her body. She hadn't noticed that she was clutching the knot of her trench until Ephraim's hands went over hers. And like Heaven predicted, a crowd was already descending on them, and Heaven hadn't said a thing.

Men and women watched as Ephraim's callused fingers soothed across the back of Maliah's hand. He went to his knees, kissed her flesh.

"You have to open up for me, Pet," he whispered.

Her fist shook as she held on to the knotted trench coat. More people came to attention. Heaven called for seats. Maliah stared at them. The notion that she shouldn't stare at them watching her was far from her mind. She watched Heaven; the woman seemed like #DommeGoals for colored women. The mixed chick was seated, two men kneeled beside her. Then more Doms sat, with their pets before them. Nobody made a hassle about her not letting go. Their eyes were the only things beckoning her, with comfort and nurture.

Ephraim's head moved beneath her trench coat at the sound of gasps. They craved this though showed a delectable courtesy as his tongue slithered across her sopping wet thong. She eyed them as his tongue thumped through her thin material against her clit. They were thoughtful, artistically so.

Maliah's legs planted wider, though she didn't let go of the knot keeping her clothed. Ephraim's tongue continued to scour over the silk, and her pussy cried for him.

"Pet." His head popped back from beneath her coat as she stood there. "Will you let me hurt you?"

Worry flashed in her gaze. Yet, her mouth was about to become traitor to her apprehension. Ephraim went back beneath the covering of her trench coat. This time his fingers tugged down her panties, and he removed them.

He addressed the audience. "They're soaking."

Her body wavered as he spoke. Ephraim made like he would throw the thong at the people; some of the Doms' hands were poised for the token. But he chuckled. The crowd applauded.

Ephraim slipped the thong into the back pocket of his pants. This time he looked at the crowd as his hand skimmed up her thigh. Their eyes moved titillating slow, glued to his hand as he ascended to her treasure. His fingers pressed between her lips.

"Throbbing cunt. Imagine a mouth, it's so wet," Ephraim told them.

There were moans and groans of lust. Heavy breathing.

"Get off for me, Maliah, right now."

Her knees started to buckle as his fingers pumped up and down.

"Don't tense, sweetheart," a pet said from the crowd. Maliah's scream of desire matched the sound of said pet's face being slapped for speaking.

"That's right, Pet, give Daddy something to drink." Ephraim continued to pump. His other hand gripped around her waist, holding her steady. Maliah's rising orgasm became a melody across the entire area as more people arrived.

Ephraim stood up, showed the crowd his fingers and how juice was beginning to drench down his hand. He licked it all up to a round of heavier breathing.

"Now, may I remove your coat, Pet?"

"Yes," she gasped, no hesitation. Maliah found that her

hand was no longer in a fist, holding the knot siege. Her body was loose, no tension.

Ephraim undid her knot. Then he pressed his lips to her ears. "They can't see this beautiful cunt of yours. I'm too jealous for that shit," he whispered with a sexy grin. He removed the thong from his pocket. There were a few "awwws" from newbie subs, who were swiftly reprimanded for making a noise.

Ephraim helped her into the thong and then removed the cloak. His eyes darkened with hunger. Though her bra and panties covered her, Maliah felt deliciously exposed.

He moved back to her ear, made like he was giving her another kiss. "May I use the dungeon table? I want you to see that it doesn't have to be all pain."

A flash from two weeks ago came to mind. Worst session of her life. He'd hurt her so bad.

"Please, Pet," he whispered again.

Eyes closing a bit, Maliah gulped.

"Thank you," he replied.

Ephraim made a gesture, and one of Heaven's submissives jumped from the ground. He moved away from the stage.

Heaven stood up. "We haven't implemented the rules for you all, and some of you do not seem to be aware of the general rules." She eyed the pet who had been slapped the first time. "The golden rule is do not ever address someone else's sub, without prompt!"

The Dom who'd slapped the girl issued an apology for his pet.

"I understand. For now, our guests have allowed us a treat. This pet has not been flogged with an audience. Therefore, any of Master Levine's requirements that are disregarded from now on will be cause for removal." Heaven stalked back and forth in front of the crowd, all stilettos, ass, and hips. How quickly she'd become the star. "Our Dom has consented to 'getting yourself off,' if you must. This has been such a beautiful preview I'd almost understand the need for masturbation. A few of you are seasoned in that you comprehend the true *delight of waiting*."

She paused, pointed a talon-like fingernail across the room. "Some newer Doms, you have to know that I'm a teacher, first and foremost. I'd be remiss if I did not take the opportunity to advise this is a teachable moment for each of your pets. Gratification is best served after you've been privy of all the spoils presented to you."

She mentioned a few things about an extended climax. The passion in her voice made Heaven as captivating an instructor as Nori.

"Now"—Heaven's sultry voice boomed across the area—"you will thank the Dom of the hour. Then aside from moaning and motherfucking groaning, we will not hear a word. Am I understood?"

Pets across the room murmured their consent to her rule. Doms nodded their appreciation.

On key, Heaven completed her speech as her sub carted a dungeon table into the room. The spotlight returned to Maliah. With the dungeon table in an upright position, Maliah backed toward it, the thick flesh of her ass against the leather padding. She took on a wide-legged stance in position to the planks. Her hands above her head moved wide as well to accommodate those planks. Ephraim tied her onto the table. This time, he moved the table into a parallel position without giving her whiplash

He placed her body parallel to the audience. Nori's training came to her mind. Short, thin bristles were . . . fuck, she did not remember. Thicker bristles meant . . . Her heart boomed in her ear. With her legs jutted wide, she had so much stimuli to consider. The people. The wetness against her thong. Heaven's orders.

Her very first experience with a flog.

Hurt so bad.

She wasn't ready.

Ephraim pressed the flog against her the flesh inside of her thigh, and it tickled. But it wasn't enough to stop the rage of worry consuming her mind.

He'd hurt her.

Almost irreparable.

Though his eyes darkened with lust, Maliah looked into the depths of them. She saw the rich goodness that had always been there.

"Pet," Ephraim began, "I must present the rules to you for everyone to hear. Green is . . ."

"Good," she groaned.

"Yellow?"

"You'll—" She stopped hyperventilating. "You'll soften or go back."

"Red?"

"You'll stop."

"Now what do I want to hear, Pet."

"Th-thank you for this pain, Master," she murmured. She groaned again, entire body restless with fear. The flog tickled again at her inner thigh before rising. The air parted ways as it went up and came down a lightning bolt. A thump radiated across her skin. Pleasure pulsated through Maliah's body, her pussy orgasming on the spot to the light feel of the flog.

Wow, he's doing this for me. The thought hit Maliah like a whirlwind. Ephraim knew she'd be too afraid to use a flog in the future after the Hurt Room became the horror room.

And so he'd brought her out of her element, included so many variables that her mind went mad. But the first stroke of the flog against her flesh dissipated every thought.

The last few days of worry obliterated from her mind. Babies. Pregnancy. Forgiveness. Family estrangement.

None of it existed.

All that was left was the beautiful pain he offered.

"Color?"

"Green, Master, green all day," she moaned.

A few charming laughs crossed the room. Ephraim's tongue flitted across her breast. He then stroked his hand over the hardened nipple. Maliah prepared herself for the flogging in that tingly spot. The whip went down over her heavy breast, making it bounce off the other one. Tiny bits of pain radiated from her nipple. Other than that, electric shock waves jolted through her body. Her pussy responded in desire.

"Color?"

"Green, Master."

"We are warming up," he said. She searched his eyes for a definitive of how painful this would get; so far, Maliah craved more. Maliah took every strike with pride and desire. Each flogging came with a stroke here and a stroke there.

"Now, you have such a beautiful ass, Pet. You can endure more pain there. Embrace it," Ephraim said, his thumb roving over the soft patch at the inside of her wrist as he removed her from the table.

Heaven's pet appeared to move the dungeon table. Maliah's eyes widened a little, and she did a little two-step in her stilettos to get out of his way. She had forgotten all about the people watching her. She dared take a glance. Only a select few were pleasuring themselves. Others looked to be on the verge. The rest radiated lust but had the skill to stave it off.

Ephraim brushed the curve of her neck with his fingers, stealing all of Maliah's attention. "Hands and knees, Pet."

Maliah moved down into formation on the ground, surprised at the thick material layered over the floor. She hadn't noticed it, with her shoes. It was soft enough for her knees. She placed her palms on the cool material. Ephraim's hand rubbed across her ass. She expected him to address the crowd before, like he'd done with finger-fucking her. But when she looked back at him, he was too enamored with her flesh to speak. His mouth was set into a prideful grin. He stood before her, kneeled down, and tied her wrists together with a piece of silk.

Then Ephraim moved behind her. He started to work at twining her ankles together but stopped to bite the flesh of her ass. Hard, lusty breathing broke through the crowd. He made quick work of tying her ankles together.

"Embrace this sensation, Pet." He worked the sides of her thong. Maliah moaned as the material pressed against her throbbing clit. She eyed the new flogger in his hand. It wasn't a cat o' nine tails, but now she recalled that the thinner tails brought more pain. Concentrating on how her thong had sopped up more juices, Maliah waited.

EPHRAIM HAD to get this right. This colleague and good friend, Heaven, would toss him out on his head if he treated his pet the way he had in the Hurt Room. And he had to get this right so that Maliah didn't fear a flog in the future. Not that they had to use one. But because she was his woman, and he did not want her to fear a thing.

Ephraim moved behind Maliah so that his mouth was against the material covering her ass. Between those juicy cheeks of hers, he bit the silk of her thong, moving it out of the way of his mouth. There was no way in hell he'd let people he didn't know see a prize that belonged to only him. His tongue darted past the soaking silk and against her tiny sphincter. He screwed her ass with his mouth, and then his tongue soared into her cunt. He had to get her off before using this new flog. It had to hurt. There was no way around the pain. She needed to feel it. But unlike before, she needed to love it. Maliah's pussy lips squeezed at his tongue, offering more sustenance for him to drink. And he had his fill of her orgasm.

When complete, Ephraim sat back on his haunches and wiped the juice from his mouth. Men whacked their cocks and women fucked themselves. Jealousy wanted to consume him. Yet, this was a small price to pay for Maliah's mind to clear.

She did not stop thinking for shit.

And all the different things he'd allowed were for her full cooperation.

As her legs shook, he gave a small chuckle. He pressed the small of her back, forcing her legs to strengthen and her to arch more. "You don't have the right to give up on me, Pet. We haven't started yet. But if you need, you concentrate on how I ate that sweet ass and pussy. Let's show them how much you can take."

"Yes, Master."

A seed of worry zipped through her eyes as she glanced back at him. Ephraim knew had he not pulled all the moves to get her here, Maliah wouldn't have agreed to another flogging. He prepped her ass with a stroke of the tip of his finger. Then he flicked his wrist, and the flog bristled across her ass.

Hitching a breath, Maliah screamed.

"Color."

"R—Green."

She was red. *Damn it.* Ephraim stopped. The flog he was using had an intensity between what must now be her favorite and one that would make her cry. He had to have chosen the right one. He'd spent so much time deliberating on the extent to which he could go without turning back. He let his tongue hide beneath her thong again. When her legs tremored, he slapped at the side of her ass, and she moved back into perfect formation. He assaulted her clit a few times, saw her warm brown skin tingle, ready for another orgasm.

Then he moved his mouth and used the flog. The sound of the flog slapping against her flesh was the only sound in the room. People had stopped breathing, waiting for a prompt he had denied her just last week.

"Color, Sweets?" Ephraim asked, using their shared nickname for her as encouragement for her to take this pain.

"Green," she moaned, glancing back at him.

"You ready for more?" His chest tightened. If she said no, he'd carry her out right now. Not allow her to endure another moment. The look in his gaze told her so.

She smiled. "Please, Master."

"Fuck, I like to hear you call me that."

Each time Ephraim flogged Maliah, his tongue slithered over her darkened flesh. Or his mouth pressed softly against every inch of the pain, pulling her back toward him. He asked her after each swat, and not only that, he watched her for any signs that she was being too good to him. He heard the movement of the air before the impact shattered across her skin. It all made his cock stiffen with need.

After a while, Ephraim noticed a glaze over Maliah's eyes. She'd entered subspace. No fear was to be found across her curvaceous body, and the crowd knew it too. A slight hush of groaning came from them. His blows came in succession, leaving her bulbous ass to turn a lovely shade of red.

———

WAS THIS SUBSPACE? She felt tears in her eyes and a giddy smile tasting the edges of her mouth. She glanced up to notice Ephraim's chest swelled with pride. He'd gotten her here to this point of glory where every hit brought her to the heights of heaven. The erotic feel of him spanking against her ass made her mouth pool in saliva.

"Can you take more, Pet?"

He was asking her something, but she felt like Heaven's sub who'd gotten in trouble. Beautifully high, and willing to do any of her Dom's bidding.

"Can you take more, Pet," he asked again.

"More." She bit her bottom lip.

"Fuck, you are beautiful, Pet," he replied, the flogger slamming down on her skin. His eyes were on her ass, and he'd started to unbuckle his belt. "Can I have you now, Pet?"

With her mouth so constricted in desire, she couldn't speak. She nodded vigorously.

"Leave. Everyone, leave!" Ephraim growled.

Before she could eye his magnificent cock, the rice-paper partitions were placed before the entrance to the room. Maliah arched her back, ready for him to take her. His finger moved aside her thong. His erection swept inside of her pussy in one hard jolt. Her ass was warm as he pumped his cock inside her, but she'd stopped feeling the pain of his flogging a long time ago. Ephraim conquered the ache that grew like a volcano deep inside of her. His hand went to the back of her neck, pressing her down until her ass was the only thing in the air. He continued to grip at her hair, while thrusting his cock past her quivering pussy lips.

"Ephraim," she screamed. Her gaze flashed toward the shadows of people watching through the thin walls. It made her feel wild. She called his name at the top of her lungs until her voice was raw. Maliah couldn't stop coming all over his cock.

"That's right, Maliah," Ephraim said. "I'm breaking you, Sweets."

"Fuck, fuck, break me," she begged.

His dick moved through her like a bull, all stamina, no breaks.

Maliah realized that the enticing moans belonged to her. She'd stopped screaming. Had no power to. Her throat was so raw right now. All she had left were her whimpers as he slammed through her. His hot, hard erection stretched the walls of her pussy. Maliah turned her head while he continued to force her face down. She watched the shadows of people on the opposite side of the rice-paper walls.

They were still there.

Hordes of them.

She smiled as Ephraim slapped at her ass and punched her cervix with his cock. This was the kind of sex that finds had while high on drugs. Nothing stopped them. Throat fresh with the only pain she knew how to feel right now, she growled as another wave crashed through her. In the end, Ephraim gripped her hips, holding her ass up until his seed went pumping inside her. He let go, and Maliah's entire body fell flush against the ground. Her heart boomed against the soft material of the floor as Ephraim lay beside her.

They lay there for a while, the crowd dwindling some.

Maliah started to pull out of her thong, but Ephraim's hands went over hers.

"You're not wearing the trench coat until we exit the first set of doors, Maliah," he said, moving the thong back into place. "Everyone will see how sweet that little thong got, and they'll know I got it so wet."

Her throat whizzed for a second as she gave a soft chuckle. "I'd have never met you here before the Hurt Room."

"I know." Ephraim's finger played across her belly button, the innocent touch he'd done so many times in the past that the sex club faded, and they were teens again. Teens that were new to this shit but had loved each other for a longer time than they'd known how to fuck. Like before, his mouth stopped a fraction above her belly button. His words whispered across her skin, "I love you, LeeLee."

For a minute second, babies and pregnancy scared her. But Maliah pressed her hands into his thick hair and pulled him up. "I love you so very much, Eph."

His mouth was all over hers. Their tongues danced, bodies magnetized. Maliah wrapped her legs around him as he moved on top of her. Then he groaned against her lips.

"We have to go, Maliah."

"No," she murmured. That brilliant mind of his had returned to torturous thoughts. They were supposed to make her parents pay now. She clung to him thinking, *Ephraim, you have to be good.*

"I promise to give you a hot shower and wash you good on the jet, but that's the only sleep we will get. We'll arrive on time for the beginning of church."

"Wow." She rolled her eyes with a grin. "You couldn't screw me anywhere in the entire Israel, but you can mention church . . . in a sex club."

He got up, holding out a hand. "Married people are here, so we won't burst into spontaneous combustion."

She chortled louder. "I have to know, Eph, why the hell wasn't Heaven my trainer? She's got some black in her. You know black people try new things when other black people try them. Also, she's not a lesbian, so you could trust her." *That friggin' Atsun creeped me out at the end!*

"Believe it or not, she would've saved you from me." He rubbed a hand across her face.

Maliah moved into his arms, holding him tight. "I'm not mad at you, Eph. Unlike some people I know, I've learned to forgive those that have done me wrong. Done us wrong."

She prayed that her words reached his spirit. But Ephraim said nothing as he walked her through the night-club to a round of applause and cheers.

35

As promised, they relished a steaming hot shower. Ephraim loved her body to sleep during the long ride from Amsterdam to Greenwich, CT. Ephraim drove them to the Baptist church her family attended. While walking through the parking lot, a few "welcome backs" were tossed his way, and a few for her too. There was something about doing bad that made her steer clear of God as if He didn't see all. She hadn't attended since signing the contract for the Hurt Room. They meandered, hand in hand, with other attendees. Maliah glanced at the tiny building before her. It looked like a one-story house from outside, with a sloped roof and a huge cross out front. The place packed out though, with good music and a good sermon.

"Eph, it's Landon." She squeezed his hand, nudging her chin to the family a few paces ahead. "Landon, Sherri," she called out.

Her attorney friend and his family were moving rather quickly. Maliah's eyebrows pinched together. But then she noticed their youngest leading the way. She shrugged. "I guess we can tell them we're back together later."

"Sure."

Her eyebrow darted up, but Maliah's mother called out to them. Unlike Landon, Maliah didn't have a valid excuse to continue. Maliah turned around to see her mom moving past a row of cars. Rick was still pressing the alarm button for his luxury car.

"Mrs. Porter, you look as lovely as ever." Ephraim hugged Annaleigh.

"The two of you are a sight yourself," Mrs. Porter replied. She gave her daughter the customary kisses and a less passionate hug. "I secured one of the best chefs on the East Coast, you'll love him!"

Maliah bristled. Her mother's willingness to fixate on the most rudimentary notions irritated her. *Jesus, You might not be taking favors from me right now, but please be a fence.*

A FEW HOURS LATER, Ephraim, Maliah, and Annaleigh sat at a table fit for a magazine catered to lavish homes. From the ceiling, globe-like crystals shimmered down where the chandelier once dominated. The only variable missing was silver domes of food. At this point, Maliah would've come alive at the aroma of food, but there wasn't one. It reminded her of being a toddler and going to her grandpa for food. He'd joke and offer her air pudding. Maliah hadn't learned until she was over fourteen that air pudding was real. When she brought her grandpa and granny some, they threatened to send her home.

"When are we eating?" Ephraim pressed up against Maliah's side.

"Shhhh, we will eat soon." She laughed a little. She didn't have the heart to tell him why her mother kept checking her phone. The "best chef" in all of America wasn't all that considerate of people's time. He'd arrived at about the time they got out of church. Granted they'd been out for a while, but Maliah smelled nothing.

She'd grown up with Granny starting the ham hocks late the night before. Then first thing Sunday morning, Granny's old voice cracking while she sang gospel. Lord knew how Maliah pulled herself from bed to help wash greens before a lengthy church service.

Ephraim wanted soul food.

Her oblivious mother was about to deny him of these delights. And Maliah's stomach cramped at the thought of how his angry belly would be later on. Should she stop this charade? No good things could come out of a vengeful man who was still hungry.

She started to catch her mother's eye, to ask her to check on the chef and his crew, when Ephraim caressed her cheek.

"I forgot how long the pastor could be," he joked. "At least I caught up on my church."

Maliah's usual snarky retort would've been "then I hope you're done with your vendetta." With a smile, she folded her arms. "*You caught up on your church attendance*? Really? When's the last time you've been? Since me?"

"I'll have you know, Daniel made me go last year."

"You attended, from start to finish?" She enjoyed their argument; it took her mind from the hunger pains.

Ephraim rubbed a hand over his sexy, square jaw. She kissed him on his lips. "Don't lie to me on a Sunday, Eph."

"All right, I may or may not have entered said church. Daniel and I met outside to chat business."

"Oh the Crackhead Becky stuff, huh? I should've been around. We could've double-teamed that hoe."

"We'd have handled her, right then and there." Ephraim

smiled and made a gesture as if he was about the grab a drink. But there wasn't even a glass of whiskey to be had.

"What are the two of you chatting about." Annaleigh cleared her throat, setting her phone down again.

On the drive from church, Ephraim promised not to talk "vengeance" until they'd eaten. Little did her mother know, Maliah was trying to tame the bear. She patted Ephraim's shoulder. "Nothing much. This one needs alcohol. Something, anything. Or food."

Her mother held up her perfectly manicured fingers. "I told you two, ten more minutes. Your father disappeared for another work call. The chef is working miracles. We'll eat soon."

I can't smell these miracles! Maliah forced a smile.

FIVE MINUTES LATER, Mr. Porter appeared in the doorway with a chunky crystal bottle filled with amber liquid. "All right, you two."

"Rick." Ephraim stood. "You know me well."

"Well, you know, son, nothing but the best for you. How many times have I told you that?"

"Don't drink too much, hon," Annaleigh interjected as her husband pulled a few old-fashioned whiskey glasses from a display.

"What do we have here?" Ephraim asked as her dad set the glasses in front of them.

"No thanks, Dad."

His eyebrows pulled together. "I spent a fortune on therapy for you after you stole your way into my good stuff, Maliah. Now you're old enough to—"

"She said no thanks," Annaleigh snipped, taking another glance at her phone. Probably more embarrassed about the wait to feed them than a need to play mama bear.

"Are the two of you—" her dad began, but someone had cleared their throat.

They all glanced over.

"Thank God," Annaleigh sighed.

The chef had four servers dressed in slacks. Each one held a silver dome plate. They sat the food down before everyone, and the chef explained the first course.

The domes were removed from silver chargers and china plates at the same time. Maliah hid a desire to chuckle.

"You said duck—where the . . . Where is it?" Ephraim gritted out.

On the center of each plate was the tiniest bite of food, topped with foam and drizzle. The garnish had more sustenance.

"How dare you!" the chef began.

"We are pretty hungry," Maliah hardly got out.

Ephraim shoved the food away. "I'm not eating this shit. I'm fucking hungry!"

"Shit—shit, sir?"

"Look at me, I'm 207 pounds. I need real food." Ephraim started for his wallet. "You cook something else for me and—"

"Ephraim," Annaleigh gasped.

"Yes, ma'am?" he barked.

"Hon, the boy is right," Rick began. "This . . ."

Maliah sat back. "Mom, whose side are you on?"

She'd witnessed more wrath from her mother at a tea social by picking up the wrong fork. Part of her wanted her mother to follow through with her anger toward Ephraim.

"What do you all like to eat?" Ephraim was oblivious to it all. He pulled out his phone as the chef retreated, arguing up a storm about keeping his retainer. "I'll call. Get us something, then we can chat. Or shit, should we forgo the food, Maliah?"

She closed her eyes for a moment. Team Eph was a good plan. It meant clearing the air and having him on her side during the entire ordeal. But her stomach churned, and not from hunger.

"What business do you need to talk, son?" Rick used the fork to topple the foam on the tiniest slither of meat.

"I can't do this." Maliah popped up.

Ephraim stood too.

"I'm not doing this!" She pressed a hand against her chest, needing air.

"Sweets," Rick began.

"*Maliah*, sit down," her mother ordered. "Last time you dined with us for dinner was ages ago."

Their daughter chortled. "Well, my apologies. Because it's not happening today."

Ephraim glared at her.

WHAT WAS SHE DOING? They were a team. Despite hunger pains, she'd been on his side. They'd laughed a little while waiting for those plates of clouds. Now, Maliah wanted to let her parents win again.

Rick stopped playing with the dog vomit to appeal to his daughter. "C'mon, Maliah. We'll call for pizza—"

"Pizza?" Annaleigh snorted.

Ephraim's shoulders stiffened. He hadn't noticed how unnecessary Annaleigh was. Who argued about food at a time like this?

All right, he had. But he also craved revenge for all the

time lost with Maliah. As far as he knew, Annaleigh didn't have rights to an argument. Again, not until she endeavored to feed them food from Earth.

"Maliah, let's have this chat now." He wrapped an arm around her.

"No." She pressed away from him.

"What's going on with the two of you!" Rick asked.

Ephraim found himself appreciating that Rick wasn't calling him son. That the man cared. Though, he wasn't giving Rick a pass.

Ephraim began, "We have—"

"To go," Maliah cut in. She whispered against his jaw, "Eph, I'm not playing with you. Either you go to my home, or I go to wherever you plan on staying tonight. Those options are contingent on you stopping. *Now*, Eph."

The finality of her tone worked for him. "Now" was the sole word that a lawyer like him could manipulate at a later date.

Of course, Ephraim would set aside his plans.

For now.

36

THEY'D STAYED AT HER HOUSE, WHICH ASSURED MALIAH WITH easing into her next move. The sex had been gritty last night. The tone set by her attitude and her knowledge. Ephraim had the ability to lie to any given honorable judge.

Why not her?

Now her eyes were wide-open as she took a seat. The white paper beneath her bottom scrunched and tried to move out of the way as she sat on the examination table.

She'd left early and thanked God when her new gynecologist had availability today. Maliah chewed on her lip and waited. The nurse had squeezed the life from her arm for a blood pressure test and warned her of the evident. Maliah almost mentioned the theory she learned from reading another scientific journal, that doctor offices have this sort of effect on patients. But her blood pressure was high, with thoughts of the piss stick she'd handed the nurse.

Picking at her fingernail, she considered how she'd proceed. While she didn't want a pregnancy to steer her course of action, Maliah knew her options. Pregnant or not, she'd have her parents and the Levines together during a meeting on her terms. They'd all make changes. If they didn't, it would be the hardest thing she had to do in her life.

But I can't keep Eph from our baby, regardless of his mindset, she considered. *No. I can. He has to come to terms that it won't be about us anymore. Our baby shouldn't be involved in a family feud!*

After all her mulling, she murmured to herself, "Please don't let me be pregnant."

There was a knock at the door. Dr. Oruga, who Maliah had learned was from the Philippines and enjoyed her job, came inside, a bright smile on her face. "The educator, right?"

"Yes." Maliah cringed. Her first and only appointment had occurred less than two months ago. With a six-month supply of birth control pills, deducting her reason to be here was simple. "I started the first pack—I know you said not to have unprotected sex before completing a cycle. I did almost get through week three, then . . ."

"You're not the first to make a return trip so soon, Ms. Porter. The one-pack rule can be challenging." Her doctor patted her shoulder. "I have the results of your pregnancy test."

———

MALIAH WALKED out of Dr. Oruga's private practice. As she paced along the parking lot to her car, she slipped out her phone and searched for her old therapist, Dr. Hart.

The prestige website boasted affluence and esteem.

"Sheesh, I couldn't afford this when I worked at a private school." Maliah opened the car door and slipped inside. She pressed the radio, connecting it to a call with Ephraim's assistant, Rosa. After a few formalities, she said, "I need your help."

"What can I do for you, Maliah?"

"Please schedule a meeting for Ephraim's family and my parents for a sort of Dr. Phil intervention."

"Should I reach out to his producers and see . . ."

"That sounds very helpful." Maliah knew she liked Rosa. "I have another therapist in mind. One with history."

After their quick chat, Maliah merged onto the freeway. She dialed the center where Tonya was staying.

A few beeps came through the speakers, and Maliah turned down the volume. A receptionist answered, and after a few beats, a familiar, raw voice came through the line.

"LeeLee, ya miss me?"

"Oh, I expected you to hate me by now. I'm so sorry. These past few weeks, my level of support had been none existent . . ."

"Girl, I have kept you right here with me. In my head, complaining."

"Complaining?"

Tonya chuckled. "Complaining and reminding me of how to put me first. I failed as a super senior, before finding a good teacher—which is you, LeeLee."

"Awe . . ."

"Now, I'm following through."

They got off the phone with a plan for Maliah to come by in a few weeks. Daniel and his wife's baby shower was the week after next. If Rosa pulled through by securing her old therapist, this Saturday she'd be telling everyone about her doctor's visit.

37

WEDNESDAY

So far, Ephraim had three stellar attorneys sitting tight, ready to put in notices at work. He'd stopped another shit-storm from blowing up for the pop star. Now, he needed to switch his focus back toward the greatest love of this life.

His Bluetooth was glued to his ear as he stood on a platform at the tailor's store. The walls were old-school wood paneling. Nothing about the place screamed riches, but the Italian who owned it made his suits perfectly. Ephraim held his arms out. The prototype suit fit against his shoulders and arms.

"Rosa, what's taken you so long to get Quintin on my calendar?" he spoke into the receiver.

"Be patient. You want this, that, everything. *Aye Dios!* Give me time."

"All right, is my home on the market," he said, referring to the Hurt Room. Ephraim had considered another night there with Maliah. The place left him with mixed thoughts. They had good times there. Bad times, definitely. And he'd been stupid enough to let Nori and Atsun into the fold—though that was the only option.

"*Si*, the Realtor is happy."

Ephraim's phone pinged. "Rosa, I have to go. Get me a meeting with Quintin. After we've fortified that angle, we can launch my new legacy."

"And if we cannot get Quintin?"

"You know me, Rosa." He pressed the button on his ear to switch over.

"Son?"

Oh, fuck. Screening his parents' calls had come easy. The tailor offered him privacy while Ephraim stepped off the podium. "What?"

Abner sighed through the speaker. "I've analyzed every second of my mistakes, son. What I did—"

"You're the man who built all the bridges but had one single catastrophe, Dad. You made that analogy, right? Or was it something shared throughout your legacy?"

"Our legacy!" Abner's voice was strangled. "I preyed on Maliah's confidence in our family. That's how it looks; however, I still stand by my actions. The two of you were supposed to—"

"To what?"

"Wait a little while. Get a little older."

"Abner, your story is changing," Ephraim stressed. "First, it was Rick's indiscretions. Now, the variable was our ages?"

He pulled the Bluetooth from his ear. The tiny device skidded across the wood floors. Ephraim sat wide-legged on a stiff, leather chair. Maliah's gorgeous face roamed through his mind. Their family squabble had done a number on her stomach during encounters with each of their parents. Or was she anxious about something else?

THAT EVENING, Ephraim moved around the kitchen in Maliah's home. An apron was draped over his V-neck and slacks. A whole chicken that Granny taught him how to prepare was roasting in the oven. He had a box of instant mashed potatoes on the counter. He'd have to hide them and pray Maliah's grandmother didn't come from the grave to strangle him for making. When the front door opened, he slid the taboo box behind her Honey Nut Cheerios, on top of their old fridge.

"Mmmm..." Maliah groaned.

"How was your drive from New Haven?" He moved through the living room to help her. She'd stopped inside the door to kick off her stilettos.

"Long as hell," she retorted as he scooped her into his arms. "Two more weeks until I have to complete that mission every day."

"Should we find a place closer?" Ephraim carried her into the bathroom, the tub steaming with suds for the bathing he'd perfectly timed. He glanced down at her since she hadn't answered. Pressing his mouth against hers, he said, "What would you like to do, Maliah?"

"Sorry," she replied after tasting his lips. "I had no idea you'd offer to do such a thing."

"What thing?" He stood her up, pulled her shirt over her head. His hand skimmed along her neck, up her jaw and cheekbone. "You must be really tired after that drive."

"No, it's not that." Maliah began to strip from her skirt and then her bra.

He forced himself to look away, craving that connection where sex wasn't necessary. A heavenly bonus, but not a driving force in their relationship.

"Shocked, Eph. That you'd live anywhere out of Greenwich, that's all."

"I'd go anywhere for you, LeeLee." He started for the door. "I'm going to finish cooking. We should talk about our plans. The dinner with your parents needs to be rescheduled. I'll try to be more cordial when I—"

"When you offer them heinous ultimatums?"

"When I learn more about why you were afraid to talk to your dad, Maliah," he gritted out. Ephraim chewed his lip and softened himself. "You say don't focus all my feelings onto my parents. That you had a part in signing the annulment."

"Yes," she sighed.

He grabbed a tuft of his thick, wavy hair. *Fuck, Eph. You're doing it wrong . . .* "This is for us, LeeLee. I'm evaluating all the angles. My parents are paying retribution. We fucking paid it. You and I spent so much time apart." He pulled her into his arms, hugging her tight. "Your parents are the only ones oblivious to everything. So, take a bath. Let's have a good night. We can hash it out in the morning."

Ephraim left her in the bathroom. He returned to the kitchen and leaned against the countertop. He thought about his actions, and how Maliah had reacted at her parents' house.

About ten minutes later, Maliah's lush tone came from the hallway. "Sit down, Eph."

He glanced across the living room to see a puddle of water forming at her feet. He did as told, keeping his eyes on every inch of Maliah's curves. Ephraim pulled the chair away from the table and sat down, wide-legged.

"Can you do me a favor, Eph?"

His gaze fell to the soft curls between her thighs as her knee slid beside his hip and the suede chair. "Anything." He gulped.

Maliah straddled him. "Love me, tonight. Feed me and love me, okay, Eph? That's all you have to do."

Her voice was soft and innocent like it had been their very first time. Ephraim burrowed his face into her breasts, breathing heavy. His hand clasped the meat of her tit, thumb rubbing harsh over the bulb before he sucked it into his mouth. There were no words necessary to avow how he'd love her tonight.

MALIAH LOVED EVERYTHING ABOUT EPHRAIM. He'd always been the good in them, no matter how it seemed. Loving too hard might have been a fault of his, but she clung to him. Her hands roamed through his hair as he suckled on her nipple. Two fingers filled her up, forcing her lower back to arch against him.

"I love you, love you, Eph," she moaned into the top of his head.

His teeth continued to grate over her areola. Ephraim grabbed her about the waist, hoisted her up, while he used his other hand to unbuckle his pants. The instant she was back on his lap, his cock slammed straight through her slit. She bit down on her lip, staving off the pain of taking his thick erection without warning. But her pussy was slick and ready to accommodate all his massive meat.

As he brought her to the hilt of his cock, Ephraim groaned into her boobs. "You are mine, and I love you."

Maliah readjusted her hips, swirling down on his manhood. She twirled up and twisted down, bringing every inch of his cock into her valley, titillatingly slow. With her slippery walls squeezing down on him, Maliah concentrated on when his thighs would tighten beneath her body. Loving him like this would make him cum fast, but she craved his seed.

"Maliah ... Sweets ..." Sparks danced in his dark gaze.

The look in his eyes made tears pierce hers. This was the look of a man who had lost himself in love with her. He was crazy in love with her. Maliah forced all the guilt from her mouth, allowing her sopping pussy to mend *them*.

Ephraim growled in her hair. "Not so fast, Sweets."

He'd been almost to his brink when he lifted her. His hand swiped across the table, and the plates and forks he'd sat out went crashing. The tapered candles clanked onto the floor as Ephraim placed his treasure on the table.

He wasn't ready to bathe her pussy with his cum, and she could tell. The animal in him had unleashed. She pressed her achy breast against his hard chest. Their heartbeats were more in sync than ever. Maliah laid her head back on the table, watching his abdominals work as he rocketed in and out of her body. His fingers clutched into the skin at her hips. Her breasts smacked her in the face with each press.

"Ephhhhh," Maliah screeched. Fireworks blinded her. A static of vibrations from her labia worked at his cock. Ephraim came hard, his explosion was so rough that Maliah orgasmed on his dick many times as his seed unleashed into her. Her body went into a shock of violent, mini orgasms, calling his cum deep inside of her pussy.

"I love it when you cum all over me." Ephraim stood back up. He reached down, pressed his lips against her stomach, and planted a kiss there. "Can I be your Master tonight? I have one thing for you to do?"

"Anything."

His mouth cocked to the left as he sat back down in the

chair. "Clean me so that I can feed you, Pet. Then go wash yourself off so I can eat you for dessert."

Maliah got to her knees in front of his cock. The damn thing never went flaccid. She was about to press her lips to his thick, glossed meat, when Ephraim gripped her hair and pulled her up.

"What should you do first, Pet?"

"Thank you, Master." Her cheeks warmed.

Ephraim kissed the top of her head. Maliah pulled his cock into her mouth. She licked every inch of their love-making off him.

"My balls, Pet."

Her mouth glided across his sac. She took care in cleaning him off. Ephraim felt his cock doing the happy dance, ready for another round. But he'd promised her dinner. Then they'd have round two.

Then maybe, he'd sound like a fool in front of Rosa. Only with Maliah had Ephraim been so indecisive. The Hurt Room email had been disabled. Did it have to be?

38

FRIDAY

THE DEPLORABLE CONDITIONS THAT ATSUN LIVED IN WHILE growing up didn't compare to Matt. The front of Matt's chest and all the way down his bloated belly to his nuts was covered in sweat. He had the habit of clinging to Atsun in sleep. The sticky fur of him would infuse into her skin overnight. No matter how she washed the next day, his grimy scent followed. She lay on the crumply bed, waiting for him to leave.

"Atsun . . . Atsun . . ." Matt rubbed at her shoulder.

She allowed her body to be moved by him and pretended to snore harder.

"Babe, I need you to remember . . . don't go out."

Sure, not until I can catch up with my sub, you fucking bear!

She forced out a fart. Matt backed away, gagging and stumbling over cans of beer on the ground. The bedroom door closed.

"Yeah, like you're Mr. Hygiene," she murmured. Across the room were pictures of women that Matt never had a chance with. And not because he'd brought her to his mother's home last week. He had computer games at his desk.

Every gaming console, with even more games, were scattered on the matted carpet.

She listened to the conversations of Matt and his mother. The woman smacked a kiss—somewhere on his body—Atsun presumed. They talked about his irritable bowel syndrome. Atsun suspected Mommy Dearest handed him a brown paper bag of approved lunch items.

After another twenty minutes, she went to the table, swallowed in one of Matt's white tees. The MacBook powered up. Cracking her knuckles, Atsun worked her magic. She channeled all the lessons the hacker from the Triads had taught her. He'd been a deviant in bed but made up for his dark delights with code.

In seconds she bypassed Nori's new password for his email. The bastard still had access to the Hurt Room's cache server, all because of her. She thought to reroute it to Matt but decided that he could view this.

He needed to view this.

Her reaching out to Maliah.

And Nori would know because she'd add a little phrase that meant something to the two of them.

"I'm trading up, Nori." She almost grimaced. "Master" had been his name. "Well, you're Nori now. Just Nori, *baka*."

After a few minutes of searching, fire seared across her veins. Ephraim used the server five days ago; they'd met at a pop-up club in Amsterdam. Mistress Heaven had been a sight to behold, yet she had a harem of male subs.

"You didn't want me, I don't want you either," she said, clicking out of the email. Atsun logged on to social media and found Maliah in seconds. A smile crossed her lips. Her lover owned a learning center and helped children. She wished she'd known Maliah as a child. Maliah could've saved her then.

Didn't matter. She'd save Maliah now.

Her fingers typed successions of code until she found out Ephraim's current whereabouts.

"All right, are you two expecting to be together tonight?" She cocked an eyebrow. "Doesn't matter, Maliah's mine . . ."

39

MALIAH TOLD HERSELF NOT TO COME INTO THE OFFICE TODAY. But her team had started brainstorming a "back to school" night for We Rise Learning Center. Events that brought out families never ceased to amaze her. They'd propositioned the schools in the neighborhood and provided them with flyers. Yet, every so often, a parent entered the center at the end of their wit, who hadn't known about the free services available.

"Okay, Takis chips." She shook her head. "What happened to old-fashioned sugar. Like cotton candy? Isn't that enough brain rot?"

"We're getting them in the door." Rina winked. "Takis on day one only. That work, boss?"

"All right, I'm done chatting food. We have Ms. Brown willing to bring her cricket machine. And . . ." She paused as the Hurt Room emblem came up on the front of her phone. "I should take this."

Maliah excused herself from the table. She and Ephraim's sex life had taken a turn back into greener pastures since Wednesday. She stalked down the hallway toward her office, weighing her options. She'd be blind-siding him again with the meeting with their parents tomorrow morning. *Please don't be for tomorrow morning, Eph!* Maliah closed her office door and hurried to her seat. Ephraim's MO was to change her mind about things. And another Saturday morning at the Hurt Room was tempting.

She clicked on the link and breathed easy. Tonight. They'd meet tonight.

THE SETTING SUN cast an orange glow as Maliah's BMW pulled up to a house about an hour away from Greenwich. In fact, it was intermediate from her center and the lives they knew. She eyed the roses and smiled, deciding that the area was charming. Ephraim's inquiry about her wanting to move closer to New Haven came to the forefront of her mind. It was hard to imagine Ephraim living in a small home, but it was similar in size and style to hers.

"Well, I can live without a concierge." She pressed open the white picket fence, which was another similarity to her home. At the front door, she stopped and noticed a piece of paper duck taped to it. The words read, "Let yourself in. Come to the last door on the right. Do not enter any other rooms." Her eyebrows pulled together. *Oh, this is like the cabin?*

Maliah placed her hand on the knob. It didn't offer an ounce of slack. She let herself in, then paused. The house had outdated features, each room broken up by a wall. That would have to be changed. She stepped into the kitchen, picked up a cookie, and popped it into her mouth. Her teeth crunched down on flaxseed and other good-for-you oats.

"Yuck!" she grumbled. Beside the plate of cookies were

brown paper bags for individual lunches. On one of them was the name "Matt."

"You need to start listening to your Master, Pet." A familiar voice gritted into her ears. Then Maliah felt a prick against her neck before she fell into open arms.

Atsun! And the bitch was strong enough to hold Maliah while she fell into a dreamless sleep.

NORI'S NUMBER popped up on Ephraim's iPhone. He pressed the Away button. The idiot had received all compensation owed to him as far as Ephraim was concerned. Nori had gotten all but his last payment, flights, and house rental. The works.

He sat in the stuffy leather chair at the cigar lounge. Ephraim waited for the final piece of his new legacy to walk through the doors. He glanced at the gold Carrera marble walls, astonished about not visiting here in the past. With a cherrywood box on the side table, he was ready to offer Quintin the best cigar, along with the deal of a lifetime.

Ephraim stood as the black man walked in, his mouth set in a line, his entire face unreadable. Quintin didn't have to smile; he'd do it for him. Ephraim shook his hand.

"You know." Quintin gestured. "I begged for a spot at Levine & Levine for years. Sent my resume. Hell, I sent all the news clippings for the front-page cases I won."

"Abner disrespected you," Ephraim agreed with him, staring him directly in the eye.

"Don't bullshit me, Mr. Levine. You're at war with your father. I'll let you finesse me. What can you offer that I don't already have at my current firm? I'm almost—"

"Almost," Ephraim chuckled, sitting back down. "Seven

years, Quintin. The honeymoon is over. You are not a partner—you'll never be."

"On you?" Quintin glowered through him while gesturing toward the box.

"Of course."

"Then I'll take the best they've got," Quintin replied, opening the box. "Shit . . . these are all the best they've got. I've never seen this box."

"How many times have you been here?"

The flash in his gaze meant that he didn't want to answer. The dick-measuring had commenced.

"How many?"

"Couple of times, over the last few years." Quintin rubbed a hand through his short twists. "Don't fucking tell me this is your first rodeo."

Ephraim crossed his heart. "Fuck yeah it is. But that is of no matter to you, Quintin, because you are on your way to the best of the best. Do you have yourself an old lady? Someone you've been making promises to?"

Quintin dragged his hand over his face. "All the time."

"Stop making promises, show her what you mean."

He wagged his index finger at Ephraim. "You know, you are a slimy—"

"Slimy motherfucker that knows his shit. That's why we aren't debriefing each other, Quintin. You have capabilities. I have opportunities." Ephraim glanced at his buzzing phone. Nori's international number flashed again.

"Take that," Quintin assured.

"Take that and give you a chance to doubt what my firm will do? Nah, I'll have to pass." Ephraim pressed the ignore button. "This was a done deal when you stepped into this fine establishment, wasn't it?"

A few beats passed before Quintin nodded his head slowly. They shook hands. "My assistant, Rosa—"

"The assistant who's been hounding me so hard? My lady chucked my phone from my loft because of her calls."

"The one and only. She'll present the contract to you. There is no room for negotiation. I can be a slimy asshole, but I'm fair in certain instances. Best and final."

Ephraim left Quintin to his cigar and started out of the door. His thumb was poised to dial Rosa to tell her to commence the second phase when he accidentally answered Nori.

"Mr. Levine, you must listen to me!"

"That's where you're wrong."

"Atsun tapped into the Hurt Room server. She's meeting Maliah as we speak!"

"What—where?"

"I'll forward a screenshot of the email. There's another thing."

"What?" he growled.

Nori's voice was hardly audible. "She's bipolar. I have her medication."

He hung up the phone. An email indicating that *they* were to meet in an area about an hour away flashed on the screen. Ephraim dialed Maliah. She didn't answer.

Then he called his father . . .

MATT HAD COME BACK to the house about an hour into his shift, claiming fatigue. He wanted to screw. Atsun had offered him head. Her actions removed the threat from her evening plans. The instant Atsun bit the tip of his member, his mother came into the room, and she'd had to use a few lamps across her head. Now, they were tied in the hall closet. She'd given Maliah a shot of something. Matt's mother had left a full syringe when checking in on him earlier. Atsun used it as a pure impulse.

With her panties and bra clean from the laundry, she went into the last bedroom on the left, a guest bedroom that had a sewing kit on the side of the bed. Maliah's arms and legs were tied with strips of linen, against the copper post.

"Please, Pet." She straddled her, giving her face a few slaps. "Mistress is sorry for hurting you. I don't even know what you're on, but you've gotta wake up for me."

Maliah's face was glued to her chin. Her head hadn't even lolled. Atsun swatted her face harder. "Please! My love, wake up for me, *please!*"

She placed her hand into the inside of the ties to touch Maliah's wrist. A rapid heartbeat banged against her fingertips and then it stopped.

40

ABNER'S GOLFING BUDDY WAS CHIEF OF POLICE IN THE TOWN where Atsun was to meet Maliah. The entire squad was lined up along the street. Ephraim jumped out of his sports car half a block away and sprinted down the street. He wrestled his tie from his throat, jumped over a tricycle, and headed straight for the yellow tape surrounding the place.

"Sir, you can't—"

"Ephraim Levine, Lawyer. *I'm the lawyer!*" His mind churned with thoughts as he eyed a coroner across the street. The doors were shutting. "*Where is Maliah?*"

"Ephraim," a commanding voice called him from the top steps.

"Who's dead?" His heart deflated. "Who's dead?"

Chief Ramsey strolled down the steps. "Don't you worry about that, Ephraim. Maliah is not here."

He watched as Nori's pet was escorted out of the house. He felt himself ready to lunge at her but had to put his rage aside. Years of anger pursued him, and he'd finally let it go. He asked Ramsey, "Where's Maliah?"

"This little filly let her boyfriend bleed to death. She

gave Maliah a shot of some medicine some time ago. Your father is the reason why we all got here before Maliah's anaphylactic shock became deadly. We've found the prescription and have sent the information to the community hospital. Do you need an escort?"

"No," he sighed.

HE HAD ALL the money in the world—enough to prepare their broken relationship, and more than enough to screw their love right back on down to hell. Ephraim fisted his hair as he sat in the waiting room at the hospital. He thought to have her moved—somewhere better, somewhere with the best. So many thoughts wrapped around his mind. But every move seemed to be the wrong one with Maliah Porter. All the other chips in his life were stacked just right. He was at phase two of a long-forgotten pact for revenge. But nothing mattered as he sat in the waiting room.

"Eph." His mother's voice reached out to him before he could look up.

He stood, legs stiff, moving into her arms. "Mom."

While Rachel clung to him, his father rubbed his back.

Voice strangled, he said, "Thanks, Dad."

"I'd do anything for you, son," Abner replied. "Maybe I've done too much in the past, but anything. Rick and Annaleigh are on their way too."

A doctor in ER scrubs stood back with a somber expression on her face.

"Please tell me she's okay," Ephraim replied. For the first time, he wasn't a lawyer. He didn't have to spew out about how good of an attorney he was. How he could sue them for every last brick laid in the hospital. "Please."

"Ms. Porter is doing well, Mr. Levine. She woke up from surgery about an hour ago." Her smile wasn't quite there yet. "However, I'd like you to be there when we tell her that there was too much trauma for the baby. We lost the baby, Mr. Levine."

He was floored.

THE NIGHT REACHED out to Maliah. With it came a heart-wrenching reminder. Maliah knew the instant she felt alone in this world. She hadn't tethered to such memories since pressing wet ink onto the annulment papers and signing her name. Losing Ephraim had once been the worst mistake of her life. Now she missed a part of her that she never had a chance to say hello to, hug, cuddle, love.

A fury of tears blurred her eyes. This was all her fault. She'd lost her baby. Maybe she was conniving like her mother. Maybe she'd subconsciously gotten herself pregnant. *I did this to myself*, she cried silently.

One day, if she hadn't been strong enough to sign those forsaken papers, Ephraim would've been able to read her. He'd learn her mother's plans, and he'd accuse Maliah of entrapment. Dr. Hart had explained that her brain's need to feel guilt was false, but Maliah never believed it.

Now, consequences were laid out. She'd prayed for her tiny, growing seed. Had so many prayers for him or her since Dr. Oruga had broken the news to her. She tried to wrap her arms around her stomach, but the IV drip stopped her. She wrestled with it until Ephraim's voice came from the darkness.

"Stop, LeeLee, stop." His command was backed with force and love.

"No." She continued to wrestle with the pole. The tape on the inside of her elbow snatching away. The hurt reminded her that she was alive. And the plans Annaleigh had for her as a teen had done this to her.

Ephraim leaned over the hospital railing and held her. Slowly he moved his body over the contraption until he was cuddling her, his breath against her ear, calming her.

"I'm okay."

"You're not, and that's okay, Maliah."

She had the urge to bite his forearm as his strong arms held her close. He hadn't been there earlier. That wasn't his fault. Ephraim had always been the good guy. The funny guy. He had no fault in him—*until her.*

"I am okay, because, because . . ." She paused, gave a hard gulp to smooth her tight throat. "Might not have been your baby."

"Maliah, I don't care if you were pregnant when we first started meeting. I love you and I would've loved the baby too." His voice seemed strangled. He was saying the things she needed to hear.

She bristled. "I was only three weeks, Eph."

"Then what do you mean it wasn't mine, Maliah?" He stopped speaking to sigh. "I'm sorry. We don't have to talk about this right now. All that matters is you're in my arms."

A wry chuckle broke free from her. "Stop saying such sweet things. Atsun had this all planned out. Three weeks ago, I met—I met someone in a cabin. I thought it was you. Was it you? No, don't tell me. I'd rather believe that it was Nori's, and this was divine intervention."

"Was it one of the best nights of your life?"

She laughed until tears started down her cheeks. "I hate you, Eph. Under any other circumstance that would've been funny. You're too confident while asking."

"Well, was it?"

"Hmmm, he is a world-renowned Dom," she cried. The hot water burned her eye ducts. "We've had so many best nights of my life. Amsterdam was one of them—daring and sexy. The day you stole my virginity—thoughtful. I could go senile and never forget how you tore those books out. But yes, the cabin was the best night of my life. Please tell me it wasn't you, Eph. Tell me that my unfortunate circumstance killed . . ." She paused to wipe away the tears she drowned in. "Killed Nori's baby."

"Maliah, it was me."

41

THE TRUTH TORE HER HEART OUT, STOLE IT FROM HER.
Maliah wasn't sure how long it would be gone, but Ephraim
had enough love for them both, in the meantime. The sun
shone through the window, offering a cloudless day. With
the hospital bed up in a reclining position, she sat with her
parents to her left and Ephraim and his parents to the right.
Her old therapist stood at the end of the bed. Before
Ephraim called them inside, Dr. Hart assured her that they
could reschedule. She was also encouraged to consider grief
counseling.

Grief counseling.

"I brought you all here today," Maliah began. With a sip
of water, she paused. Her throat raw from so many tubes
being stuffed down it. "We have to all be on one accord. Or,
when Ephraim and I have children—" Her mouth pulled
into a line. "—we cannot allow you in their lives."

"What are you talking about!" Annaleigh snipped.

"Shhh." Ephraim cut a hand across his neck.

"Mom, you first. You've been manipulative and vile to me
in the past," Maliah said.

Annaleigh's light brown eyes seared through her. The conversation they'd had a week back about her not securing the golden ticket in the past was written all over Annaleigh's face. Embarrassment mottled the tip of her ears.

Maliah paused for a beat, before referencing the level Annaleigh stooped to while burning her hair to prove that it needed to be relaxed. Relief swallowed up the redness on her mother's face. Maliah gulped down a need to correct her. Maybe she wouldn't share how Annaleigh begged her to entrap Ephraim, but this story hit home. "Mom, I identify as a black woman. If Ephraim and I have children, I'll praise their beauty and uniqueness. That's regardless of them having nappy hair—blue-eyes and blond-hair—whatever!"

"I had an Afro when I was a kid." Abner winked.

"Me too, Dad." Ephraim shook his head, holding in a smile. She could see the sadness in him. The loss of their child had to come second for him because he had to be there for her.

"I don't recall any of this," Annaleigh said.

"Then you won't see our children." Maliah shrugged. Lies weren't flying today. Complete with addressing her mother, she spoke to Rick. "Dad, our family is divided. We have an array of members who have done what they had to survive, especially after Granny died." She licked her lips, remembering how a few cousins of hers fought over her grandparents' home. "But have you stopped fighting to survive? Are you content with your business? Can you treat your employees like Granny is looking down at you from heaven?"

Rick cleared his throat. "We all know I've made mistakes in the past. Maliah, you tried to come to me about this a long time ago?"

Rivers streamed down her cheeks. She hadn't been able

to open up to her dad the day after returning the annulment to the Levines. Her father was her last ounce of hope, and he'd let her down.

"I had no intention of talking to you about it then, Maliah, and I pushed you away. Told you to be happy I was your father and not one of my brothers." He lowered his head in guilt. "I'm ashamed to say, I didn't change my ways. But I will."

Annaleigh rolled her eyes.

"I can't speak for your mother," he added, "but those brothers I looked down on now have better relationships with their children. Can we strive for the same, Maliah?"

She nodded.

"Mr. and Mrs. Levine." Maliah addressed the family that had once been thick as blood to her. "You gave me a test. I failed it."

"No, LeeLee." Rachel came to her side, rubbing her arm.

"I should've been stronger. Should've known how much I mean to Ephraim and fought for us. And I should've given you all this ultimatum back then. I won't have the two of you in our new family, if your antics are comparable to high school squabbles. No going to one person to say something about the other person. I'm not having it." She started to hold her hands across her belly, an instinct that she'd learned instantly and needed to break. She glanced at Ephraim, noticing the flit of sorrow in his eyes. "Eph, is there anything we should add?"

"You covered it, Maliah." He nodded.

"Then I'm on to you, now."

"Me?" He arched a brow.

"Yes, you. Eph, your intelligence is a strength. Lots of times it hinders you. No more simmering in thought after someone has jaded you. Got that?"

He came to the opposite side of the bed and reached over. "Yes. However, I must remind you, Sweets. What are the rules when you're in bed?" he whispered in her ear. "I'm your Dom when you're in bed. True?"

Maliah skimmed the back of her knuckles along his strong jaw. She pressed her mouth to his earlobe, cheeks burning at the thought of anyone hearing. She hadn't expected a smile to broaden her face for a while now, but she mustered one and tossed back the banter. "I've been trained well. I'm topping."

EPILOGUE

South Bahamas

BALLOONS LARGE ENOUGH TO CARRY COTTAGES AWAY BILLOWED in the turquoise sky. All of them were yellow. While Ephraim had never attended a baby shower, he didn't know what to make of the color. Despite that, it offered a cheery backdrop as he sat in the driver's side of a rental. Maliah's fingers wove through his.

"It's too soon for shit like this," he mumbled. Although no animosity was found in his voice, they'd attended a few sessions with her therapist. They also had more appointments to continue. Her dad even asked to sit in when she was ready. Maliah didn't know what to make of her mom, but life wasn't a toy model.

"Daniel FaceTimed us, Eph. His wife is hormonal; he needs us."

Ephraim dragged a hand across his face. Cars were parked around them. Family and friends and other familiar faces had arrived to celebrate the baby. There was supposed to be some sort of firework display to share the sex of their kid. Daniel had used that line in prompting them to come at the last minute. He wasn't aware of their reluctance, and they weren't ready to share.

"C'mon, Eph. You grew up around Daniel. He was a guarded little bitty thing. Let's go celebrate his happiness."

Ephraim turned in his seat to look at her. His hand skimmed across her cheek. "We're team Eph and LeeLee. We need a plan for . . ."

They were like the ocean now, emotions coming in waves. Luckily, with a good man like Ephraim, she could cling to sadness later. Although, they endeavored to keep the low points for therapy. "A plan for boredom? We can sneak out for sex." Her eyes glittered.

"Heh, yeah, that too. If it's too much or we decide to duck out early, then let's stick to our tried-and-true game plan."

She bumped fists with him. Ephraim got out of the car, came around, and opened her door. He held out his hand, and Maliah took it and rose from the passenger seat. The long dress she wore reminded him of something you'd find in Greece, but doused in many colors began to blow. A gust of air shocked Maliah, and her hands went around her stomach. Ephraim reached down, removed her hands, pulling her into a tight embrace.

"I love you, LeeLee," he said into her ear. Her body beamed with happiness. His mouth pressed along her shoulder and trailed up her neck. When he reached her lips, his large hands covered her empty womb. She placed her palms over the back of his hands.

His forehead kissing hers, Ephraim looked down

between them as they cradled her belly, which stayed taut and tiny. "Are you sure you want to do this, Maliah?"

She grabbed his hands and held them between their bodies. Atsun now sat in jail for attempted kidnapping and second-degree murder charges. Since her treachery, their hands were forever touching each other.

Maliah stepped a pace back from him, gave his hands a tiny squeeze, and spoke. "One day, Eph, we'll have children. Maybe before, or maybe after we can take another trip to the Hurt Room. The only difference is, we love each other so much now that we will never invite anyone else into this love. Okay?"

"You're right."

"Things happen for a reason. Our baby was . . ." She paused, and Ephraim stopped himself from scooping her into his arms. Maliah sighed. "Our baby never had a chance. Our baby was so, so little, Eph. I thank God that I hadn't grown any closer to him or her before that woman manipulated us."

"Are the two of you done creating your game plan?" a familiar, jovial voice called from behind.

They turned around to see Yolanda hip-pump her husband. "Grant," she chided.

Maliah wasn't ready to tell everyone about the ordeal. Ephraim tugged an arm around her waist and pulled her close. "We are the two greatest at ditching parties."

Grant chuckled.

Yolanda searched them over before mirroring Maliah's smile.

"Hey." Maliah winked. "At least we come up with grand schemes to leave our friends' boring parties."

"That's true," Grant said, hugging her first, then shaking Ephraim's hand. "I distinctively remember the two of you offering the worst lie ever to Landon at his learning society event. But for our housewarming, we got a reality TV argument before the two of you ditched us."

"Impeccable performance by the way." Yolanda hugged Maliah so tight that they shifted side to side.

Ephraim watched the two women start toward Daniel's tropical home. The men hung back for a second.

"I assume those crazy tactics of yours worked, bro." Grant gripped his shoulder. "I have to give you kudos. I thought you'd fail royally."

An image of him driving mad, crazy, to the home Atsun held Maliah at flashed before his mind. The total, utter loss of control swept over Ephraim like never before. "I almost failed her."

"Good." Grant hadn't caught on to the severity of his statement as they stared at the balloons again. "Baby showers aren't for men. I'd rather be fishing."

"You and me both."

"How about we get into a fight. Punches, kicks, all the works. Then we can find some cold beers."

Ephraim laughed. "You're supposed to be my down-to-earth, sane friend."

"All those romance books I edit have skewed my ethic bone."

They stood in the lot, Grant interested in talking more than entering. Ephraim had to go check on Maliah and see how she fared in comparison to whatever baby showers had to offer. He made an excuse, already starting toward the door, "Let's make sure Daniel's safe."

"That's actually a good reason not to check on him. Yolanda hated my guts while pregnant," Grant replied, heading after him.

Palm trees lined the walkway up to the front door. At the

entrance, Ephraim's eyebrows came together. There was a craps table in the center of the grand foyer. A "high roller" sign, like he'd seen in many of the casinos he frequented, was at the end of the table. A dealer sat on a stool with a stack of chips. Then he noticed that the chips were pink or blue.

The dealer said, "Care to make a guess? All proceeds go to Daniel and Desire's prince ... or princess ..."

With a smile, he pulled out a stack of cash and handed it over. "Boy."

She hocked over a blue chip.

"Girl," Grant predicted. "At least one of us has a 50/50 chance of being right."

Aside from the blue or pink chips, the rest of the party was overwhelming yellow. Ephraim greeted old friends, dodged others, and made his way across the open space to seek out Maliah.

"Eph," Daniel shouted. He had on a muted yellow linen suit.

"The fuck are you wearing, bro?" Ephraim patted his shoulder, handing over an envelope. "This is from the old man. Bonds for the baby. But if you need to use it to up your wardrobe game, I won't say shit."

Daniel chuckled, taking the money. "I'll call Abner myself and thank him. You're bound to forget."

"Not with the way you're dressed, Danny Boy." He rubbed a hand over the lapel of his suit.

"Whatever, bro. You can look like a million bucks for both of us today. I'm good with it."

Juliet came over, hooking an arm around her brother Daniel's shoulder. "Ephraim, you sly bastard. Maliah's back on your arm—I take it you're not sniffing pussy tonight?"

"Juliet, the language," Daniel gritted out.

"Just one, Jules. Best pussy I've ever had the pleasure of sniffing, tasting, all that good shit."

Daniel glowered at him. Ephraim shrugged. He and Juliet always clashed. A little never hurt anyone.

"Get over yourself, Daniel." Juliet chortled. "Y'all think I might've been too young to remember? Eph and LeeLee, sitting in the tree . . . K-I-S-S-S-S . . ."

Ephraim pawed her cheeks. "What have you been drinking, kid?"

"Anything I can get my hands on. Wine. Jack. Weed." Her youthful cheeks vibrated in his palms as she giggle snorted. "Baby showers suck."

"Baby showers *what*?" a hard, feminine tone came from the left of them.

Ephraim gave her cheeks another pat before letting her go.

Desire clutched at her chest, her beautiful face marred by a frown. Ephraim understood now why his friend donned an awful yellow suit. The married couple was matching. Ephraim did a double-take at her stomach. It'd be a miracle if their baby didn't drop and reveal as a boy or girl before the fireworks tonight. As Desire began to sniffle, Ephraim looked around the room. The place had hushed. Apparently, the wife had had some meltdowns before his arrival. He caught sight of Maliah. Her hand moved in a rainbow arch as she mouthed, "Hey."

He started to say "hey" back.

"They need you," Maliah mouthed.

Ephraim took that as a sign. "*Desirenda*, you little freak." His hands touched the sides of her swollen stomach. It hurt, the thought of Maliah's belly not growing with love. But he channeled his funny bone. "Damn, girl, let me tell you how pretty these toes still are . . ."

MALIAH PLACED her hand over her lips, hiding a smile. Desire chewed out Daniel for not mentioning her toes. This was a bittersweet moment for Maliah. One day, she'd get to slam Ephraim for anything due to pregnancy hormones. To think, she had years in the making, with regard to practice. Ephraim would love every moment of her hormonal, argumentative ways. Ephraim became the comedian. He lit the fire between two lovers, and tears clouded her gaze.

"You're crying, LeeLee," Yolanda gasped.

"I'm so happy." *Sad and happy.* Her mouth trembled into a smile.

Yolanda placed down the virgin piña colada and hugged her. "Girl, when you feel like it, tell me everything. Everything that happened between you and Eph, from day one. *Because I'm your day one,* okay?"

Rubbing a hand over her flushed face, Maliah nodded. Yolanda was the closest thing she had to a sister. She'd noticed a slight rift between them when her friend couldn't fathom her need to break away from Ephraim. Maliah decided that she'd tell her. After a few sessions with her old therapist, she craved transparency. Life ran a lot smoother when people who cared about each other were unapologetic about their feelings. Sincerity and honesty meant everything. She glanced over to the scene that the barely-legal-to-drink Juliet had caused. Daniel held Desire with tender care.

A true smile curved the corners of her lips. She and Ephraim would have that one day. But for now, she planned to play a few baby shower games. Then she planned to pick a fight with her man to save them from the rest of said games.

AFTER A GAME of guess the poopy diaper, Maliah grabbed a handful of Reese's Cups. Those had been the only melted diaper contents that she'd been able to guess. She found Ephraim, Daniel, Grant, and a few other men near the unlit fireplace.

She almost smiled, recalling all the times they started arguments. It was all a ploy so that they could leave and screw. It had been a juvenile antic that began when they were sixteen. They'd learned how good sex was, and nobody was keeping them from it—not even some girl from their private school's sweet-sixteen birthday party. The girl kept mentioning that everyone had to stay until they went outside to see her gift. Obviously, she was getting a convertible—which she didn't allow Maliah to ride in to school the next day. Who cared? Maliah *had* Ephraim in the birthday girl's bed, while she squealed about her gift.

Maliah set her mouth to start arguing

Daniel tipped his beer. "Oh shit, LeeLee, you and Eph are ducking out now, huh?"

"After the fight," Grant chimed in, with a smile.

"I've pretty much got all the money in the world," Daniel said, with a shake of his head. "Why didn't I predict this? Why didn't we have popcorn?"

"Popcorn, theater candy, the works," Grant added.

Her cheeks burned.

Ephraim cleared his throat. "Maliah is in trouble. We'll be back . . ."

He took her hand and pulled her along toward the many sliding glass doors.

"We were horrible, you know," Maliah groaned as they headed out on to the shore. "We're too old for this shit."

"There are always starving actors that we could hire, LeeLee."

"Or," she began, "we can learn how to navigate the party world again."

"Nah," they said together with a laugh. They'd never been big party people. She'd have her books out on a Saturday night, reading them until Ephraim took over. His voice made the perfect narration. Depending on the book, the love of her life also enacted the sex scenes even better. And they enjoyed a strip club or porno on occasion. But Ephraim and Maliah were self-centered, in that they only craved each other.

Various hearths dotted Daniel's vast backyard, the ocean coming close to the edge of them. Firelight flickered across their smiling faces. Maliah said, "Besides, I'm not drunk enough to fake argue."

"I wasn't in the mood either. But now that we are outside, might as well find somewhere private for sweets," he said, holding out his hand.

"While we scope out a good place," Maliah replied, kicking off her shoes. Her feet trudged through the cool sand. "Mind sharing what happened between you and our friend, Landon? Because—" She paused to nudge her head back toward the house. "Landon is right inside celebrating with everyone. He and Sherri hardly said hello to me."

"Well, if it's the Landon I know, I got him in the divorce."

Maliah pushed him.

Ephraim fell purposefully in the sand. "How about here?"

She climbed on top of him, her hands popping softly at him before he held her down.

"Hello, Eph, you have very few friends. Mean as you are. Landon was my friend and a free attorney at that!"

"I'm a free attorney."

"No," she groaned. "You're expensive as fuck! I have to suck your dick, hands behind my back, while standing on top of my head for your help." She chortled.

"And you should," he breathed as if the logic were written in stone.

"Don't be an ass, Eph. My friend ghosted me. Hello!"

"So what?" He pawed her face.

"Landon ghosted me *and 160 youth at my learning center.* What do you know about that?"

"I don't recall anything about 160 kids." Ephraim arched an eyebrow, pressing himself on top of her. He started to unbuckle his pants. "Really? 160? Do I want to continue with this . . ."

"You do," she growled. "But first, what happened?"

Ephraim ground his erection into her pelvis, pressing her legs around him. "Landon smelled my scent on you. All this claiming. No more Landon."

"You are not a wolf! Too much sand—I need to be on top." Heat flushed over her body, despite it being a chilly night.

Ephraim rolled her back over and popped his hips. She landed straight on his erection. All she had to do was move her dress out the way and push her thong to the side.

"On the contrary, Maliah Ann Porter, I have X-ray vision to this ass." He smacked it while she mumbled about his obsession with it.

Maliah glanced down at him, her kinks of hair framing her face like a mane. Ephraim pawed her breast from the top of her dress and began to suck on it. She could hardly speak. "This isn't that type of love story, Mr. Levine."

NEWSLETTER

Join Amarie Avant's newsletter at amarieavant.com and receive an exclusive free read or follow Amarie Avant on BookBub for the most up-to-date releases and deep discounts.

ABOUT THE AUTHOR

Thank you so much for reading "Ephraim's Hurt Room." Please leave your review on Amazon and or Audible. If you haven't met the brilliant, stubborn attorney before, Ephraim can also be found in "An Alpha's Desire." That story actually revolves around his best friend, Daniel, and his pursuit for love. Also, the devilishly sexy Ephraim is featured in the series "The Good Mistress" which is also on Audible.

Speaking of Audible, FEARLESS will launch exclusively on Kindle and Audible this Holiday Season. Prepare to meet the MMA fighter, Vassili Karo Resnov, as he fights in the cage, fights for the heart of a gorgeous woman, and ultimately fights to keep her safe from the king of the Bratva . . . his father.

Amarie can be found on Facebook, Instagram, Twitter, and Goodreads. Don't forget to join her group 'Amarie Avant's Aroused' on Facebook to interact with her, read sexy exclusive snippets, and join the fun!

9 781697 880243